W9-CFC-526

MOLLY TAKES THE CAKE

MOLLY TAKES THE CAKE

BOOK 1 *of the* RIVER OAKS SERIES

The Taylor Sisters

MOLLY TAKES THE CAKE
BOOK 1 OF THE RIVER OAKS SERIES

iUniverse books may be ordered through booksellers or by contacting:

iUniverse
1663 Liberty Drive
Bloomington, IN 47403
www.iuniverse.com
1-800-Authors (1-800-288-4677)

ISBN: 978-1-4917-7247-8 (sc)
ISBN: 978-1-4917-7249-2 (hc)
ISBN: 978-1-4917-7248-5 (e)

Library of Congress Control Number: 2015913340

Print information available on the last page.

iUniverse rev. date: 9/4/2015

To our parents, Chuck and Bette Taylor.

Mom, you taught us the joy of reading and the importance of kindness. You will always be our inspiration and our rock. We love you. Your recent passing is still a fresh wound, but in the twinkling of an eye, we will see you again.

Dad, you've gone before us but left us with your gift of storytelling. Here's to the hours of tales about wounded butterflies, gelatin-filled swimming pools, and gasoline-guzzling gas bugs. We miss you every day.

With love to all our guys: Gary, Bill, Billy, Brian, and Andy. Without you, our lives would be empty.

And to the great Creator, Author of all stories, Giver of the Word: thank You for using our humble pens.

Contents

Acknowledgments

A million thanks to those whose comments and encouragement have made our job as writers even more rewarding.

Special thanks to Natasha Anicich for her insightful editing and humorous commentary. We wish your dimples were contagious. May you find a Phil of your own someday soon.

Thank you to Christie Syftestad, word painter extraordinaire. Your brushstrokes brightened our pages.

Thanks also to Irene LaVigne for the extremely helpful editorial input and ever cheerful encouragement.

We owe a huge debt of gratitude to Denise Blanton, our lifelong friend and comma connoisseur.

A big hug to Bill Jornlin for giving us the "guy perspective" on our writing.

We'd like to express our utmost gratitude to Nancy Cavanaugh, who took the time to listen—always.

Our logo was designed by the very talented Rhian Awni. Her designs can be found on Etsy at ReaniDesigns.

The authors' image was created by Raggedy Annie Photography, ©2015. Find more of her work at Raggedyanniephotography.com.

Cover image by Osuleo from thinkstock.com.

Special thanks to Andy Jornlin for being our own personal techno go-to guy. You kept our computers running smooth as silk and solved all of our nerdly problems. We couldn't have done it without you.

We'd also like to thank our real Pastor Joe (Gildone), who kept us on the straight and narrow and who, like his River Oaks counterpart, has always had such a good listening ear. You helped us understand the importance of stories.

CHAPTER 1

The Trouble with Corduroy Couches

The bell jingled over the doorway of the old bakery as Molly Tauber pulled the door closed behind her and locked up after another long day. It had been a satisfying one with a new contract for yet another of her wedding cakes. She sighed and looked with longing at the faded Help Wanted sign in the window. It had been months since Mrs. McCreary had retired after working for Molly's family for more than thirty years. Now that both of Molly's parents were gone, the bakery was solely in her hands. When her father died, she left her job in the city to help her mother run the bakery. In spite of Molly's help and encouragement, her mother pined away and left this world to join her beloved husband.

Fine cake flour flowed through Molly's veins—always had. Her fondest memories as a child revolved around the bakery and learning and laughing at her parents' sides. Despite the pressure and long hours, Molly couldn't dream of being anything other than a baker … unless, truth be told, it was being a wife and mother, but her long-distance fiancé, Jared DeLucca, made it clear that marriage wasn't happening anytime soon.

"Another wedding cake order," she said out loud with a wistful sigh. She had been engaged for years now and couldn't help but wonder if she would ever be icing her own cake.

She walked past the lake and waved to Bob Peterson, who had just caught his limit of fish and would soon be frying bass for his wife, Betsy, and their granddaughter, Violet. Ancient oak trees, rolling hills of summer gold, and a lazy river that fed into the lake lined with cottonwoods and willows formed the backdrop of River Oaks. Willow Lake served as the centerpiece of the town and divided River Oaks from her upscale sister community, Canterbury Heights. Molly couldn't picture herself raising a family anywhere but her small Northern California town.

She stepped off the curb to make way for two small girls who were playing hopscotch on the sidewalk. A robin chortled from the adjacent lawn as it plucked a worm from the lush grass. The air was filled with birdsongs and music. And there was that piano again, its haunting tones gliding from a nearby open window like so many bird wings.

A quartet of dragonflies lent their color and grace to accompany the solo pianist. She often wondered where the music came from but was too exhausted after a day's work to investigate. With practiced step, she avoided the poplar-tree roots that emerged from cracks in the sidewalk. She remembered when the tree was not much taller than she was. Two more blocks to her doorstep on Periwinkle Way, and she would be home.

As she reached the door, she caught sight of her reflection in the glass panel. Her nutmeg-colored eyes had lost their sparkle, and even her normally sassy curls seemed to have given up their bounce. She tucked a few strands behind her ear as she fidgeted with the keys. She was a striking brunette with natural highlights, but today the lights seemed to have gone out. "Ah, home." She flopped onto the corduroy sofa, too tired to think about eating dinner. Later, she would head over to Clyde's

Grill for a bite. She propped her feet up on a pillow and took a well-deserved nap.

Molly zipped up the blinds and let the morning in. She turned the hanging door placard to Open and straightened the Help Wanted sign. It was seven o'clock, and she'd been up since three thirty. Happy to be a morning person, she still needed that first cup of coffee. With french roast brewed, doughnuts glazed, and the smell of marzipan on her fingertips, she poured a cup and sat down, listening to her favorite smooth jazz, which accompanied her baking each morning. She paused to look the place over. In spite of its age, it was remarkably modern in a retro sort of way. The black-and-white checkerboard floor tiles showed little wear, and courtesy of Handyman Jim, the walls shone with a cheerful coat of butter-yellow paint. *I need to think about reupholstering the seats of these wrought-iron chairs*, she noted. *Oh, good grief—I forgot to shine the curved glass display cases this morning. Look at those kids' nose and handprints from yesterday.* She sighed. *So much to do.*

She sat with her hands around her coffee mug and prayed aloud. "I can't keep doing this by myself. God, please send me a helper." It was a bustling business, one her great-grandparents had started and named after her great-grandmother. It was the center, and arguably the heart, of River Oaks. She gave a yawn. Business had been good—too good. Last night she had fallen asleep with her clothes on and woke that morning with corduroy lines on her face from the cushions of her sofa.

At 7:10 a.m., like clockwork, the bell above the door sounded. "Morning, Molly. I'll have the usual." Though she was engaged, she couldn't help but appreciate her best customer's honest good looks, especially those dimples, not to mention that cleft in his chin—not that she noticed. His mischievous blue eyes gave him away the first time they met, and his uplifted left eyebrow, expressing itself independent of its twin, only served to confirm that laughter lay in wait. Here was a man who was unable to mask his playful nature, someone she could call a friend. Someone who could lift her spirits.

"Sure, Phil. A fritter and a cup of joe coming right up. Speaking of Joe, have you seen him yet today?"

"Yeah, he's out there, fishing on the lake. I'm sure he'll be in later with his usual fish tales."

The bell rang again, and a tall, heavy-set girl with an over-crowded backpack entered cautiously.

"Good morning," Molly said, noting the girl's uneasiness. "What can I get for you?"

"Umm … have any cream puffs?"

"Sure do. Anything to drink?"

"Got milk?"

"Always." She poured a glass, smiling. "Are you new in town?"

"Uh, yeah. I'm … uh, looking for a job. I saw the Help Wanted sign. Are you still hiring?"

"Sure am. Any experience in a bakery?"

"No, ma'am, but I learn fast."

Put off by the word "ma'am," Molly said, "Just call me Molly." She handed her the cream puff and a brimming glass of milk with frothy bubbles on top. "So, what brings you to River Oaks?"

"I just got out of high school, and I'm out on my own. I'm willing to work hard."

"That's an admirable quality these days," Phil observed.

"This is Phil McGuire," Molly said. "He's a computer programmer and a frequent flier around here. And what's your name?"

"Lyra—Lyra Reinhardt."

"What a nice name," Phil commented. "Sounds, well, musical."

"I guess so. I hadn't thought of that." She managed a smile. "I do love to sing." After a pause, during which she contemplated her cream puff, she asked timidly, "Do you know if there are any good churches in town? I need to, you know, get back into it." Looking down, she slowly, even daintily, consumed the rich, cream-filled pastry.

"There are plenty of churches in River Oaks. Phil and I go to Fishers of Men Community Church. I'll go get you the phone book. If you find anything interesting, you can use my phone to get the details."

"Thanks, Molly," Lyra said, relaxing a little. She was a large girl, big-boned and dressed in jeans and a T-shirt that were clearly too small. Her dark brown hair lay flat and lifeless across her forehead and at her shoulders. She didn't look like an ideal candidate for a bakery job, but Molly saw something below the surface.

"Now, about that job," Molly said. "How'd you like to start tomorrow morning? Say, 4:00 a.m.? We bakers keep early hours, you know. We can discuss the particulars then." Molly was happy to see a smile replace the tension on Lyra's face. "I think we'll get along just fine."

Later that week as Molly was rearranging her display case, Phil slouched into the bakery. "What's going on, Phil?" Molly asked. "You look like you lost your best friend."

Phil unfolded a card from its oversized pink envelope. "In a way, I have. It's a wedding invitation from Ronnie." He continued to stare at it with vacant eyes. "She grew up next door to me. I've loved her my whole life. We've always been there for each other." He put it back in the envelope. "Now that's all going to change. It had to happen sooner or later, I guess …"

"Are you going to the wedding?" Molly asked casually as she followed him to his usual table with a cup of coffee and a warm apple fritter, its glaze dripping.

Phil plopped the invitation down on the table. "I don't know." He stirred his coffee, fixing his eyes on the half-and-half as it swirled into the dark beverage. "It's up in Seattle. She left California years ago for college and stayed there. I guess that's where they're going to live."

Molly sat, unbidden, next to him. "I think you should go, Phil. It'll give you closure and let her know that you've moved on. It'll give you more self-respect." She shook her head. "Heck, I'm a fine one to talk about respecting yourself. I've been engaged for years, and I don't even have a ring."

Phil's eyebrows rocketed skyward. "Engaged? You never said anything about being engaged."

"Well, I am … sort of."

"Seems to me you're either engaged or not."

"It's complicated."

"Try me."

"Well, Jared's a resident at a hospital in Washington, DC. We met in college …"

It was hard for Phil to imagine Molly at any job other than the bakery. "So what did you study?"

"I was an audiologist—you know, testing hearing, fitting hearing aids."

"What?" he asked with an exaggerated hand to his ear.

Molly rolled her eyes. "If you only knew how many times I've fallen for that."

"I'm sorry," he said, his eyes unrepentant. "Go on."

"I was head over heels for him right from the start. I'd finally decided he'd never notice me, then we wound up sharing a table in the cafeteria on a really crowded day. Not the most romantic setting, but we'd meet there for lunch all the time. He's really brilliant and has such a kind heart. He's a doctor, and it really touched him when he rotated through the ward specializing in facial deformities in children. That seems to be where his heart is."

"You mean, like harelips?"

Molly winced. "It's called a cleft palate, Phil. No one wants to be called a rabbit mouth. Anyway, yes, I'm talking about that kind of thing—and worse. Jared couldn't shake the sight of those broken faces, and he decided to become a specialist in facial reconstruction, which means more years of schooling. We were going to be married when he got out of med school, then his internship, then his residency, and now his specialization." She took a deep breath.

"Long-distance romance?" he asked.

"I'm not convinced it's so romantic, but it's definitely long distance. And a sure thing," she added. "It's good knowing he's there, working faithfully toward our future. We share a lot of dreams—a house full of kids, living right here in River Oaks, and all that good stuff. How 'bout you, Phil? Are you dating anyone?" She got up and distractedly rearranged the half pie in the display case to show its boysenberry filling to advantage. Looking back at Phil, she watched him push what should have been an irresistible fritter aside and stir his already-blended coffee. Molly held her ground, releasing a questioning eyebrow as she leaned, arms crossed, on the glass counter.

"There's only been one girl for me." His eyes searched the past, clearly finding her there, and smiling. "Ronnie." He stared down at the elegant pink envelope. "We've been friends for as long as I can remember. As we grew up, we grew closer, confided in one another, and were so close we could finish each other's sentences. You know, that sort of thing. She's always been open about dating other guys, and she's picked some losers, but I've always been there for her. I thought that sooner or later she'd see that we were supposed to be together."

"Well, that's a situation that even fresh fritters can't fix. Here, have a cannoli. No, have two."

CHAPTER 2

Of Nerds and Nose Mittens

Phil had been in a funk ever since he'd received Ronnie's wedding invitation two weeks earlier.

When Molly could stand it no longer, she marched up to the table where he was aimlessly folding and tearing the paper straw wrapper from his Mountain Dew into smaller and smaller pieces. "Uh, hi, Molly," he said, sweeping the impromptu confetti into his hand. "There—there's something I've been meaning to ask you." He looked up with shadowed eyes. Her smile gave him the courage to continue. "It's about the wedding—Ronnie's wedding. I know I should go like you said, but I can't go alone. I don't want her to know I don't … you know, have somebody. I mean … of course I'd pay for your flight, your room, and everything."

"As your date?" Molly asked. "Sure, count me in. I'd like to meet this Ronnie you've been talking about. I have to admit I think she's the ultimate fool. Let's show her what's she's missing," Molly said with a wicked gleam in her eyes. No one hurt *her* friends and got away with it, not if she could help it. Molly grinned. She already had plans for Ronnie's enlightenment.

"Let me help you with the sweeping," Lyra offered late that afternoon.

"No, you go home and relax," Molly said. "I'll take care of this."

"You sure?"

"Yep, I've got it. See you tomorrow." As Molly swept up bits of sprinkles and crumbs from under the tables, her thoughts began bubbling to the surface. *Why did I tell Phil he should go to that wedding in the first place? What made me jump at going? I just haven't had any fun in a really long time. When do I ever get the chance to dress up?* Her broom grew still. *What would Jared think? Should I tell him? Would he even care? I wonder if he'd be jealous? I doubt it. Am I trying to get back at him? Maybe I'm more angry at him than I care to admit. And what about Phil? Could he be interested in me as more than a friend? Nah, I'm just thinking too much.* She swept her questions into the dust pan along with the crumbs and tossed them in the trash.

Her plans took shape the following afternoon when she left the bakery in Lyra's care for a couple of hours, and headed out to find the perfect little black dress along with bold red leather, high-heeled shoes and a small red moire taffeta evening bag to match. It had been a long time since she'd bought a new dress, and she approached the task with so much enthusiasm, she felt like a little girl playing dress-up. As a girl she had preferred flouncy dresses that she could twirl in, but this time she found the figure-hugging dress more suited to the task. Shimmy prevailed over swirl.

Back at home, while looking into her full-length mirror in full battle regalia, Molly realized that the last time she'd felt pretty was a very long while ago. Jared always made her feel beautiful, even in her conservative slacks and lab coat. In fact, that was just about the only attire he'd seen her in. His long hours at work and an intern's salary were not conducive to many nights on the town.

Often she'd questioned his decision not to marry until he was a fully trained specialist. In Molly's opinion, if they were married and living under the same roof, at least they would see each other in passing, but Jared was adamant. He didn't want to get married until he could support her and the children they hoped to have. And so she waited.

Molly sent the prickles of longing, hurt, and anger to the back of her mind, safe behind the crumbling facade where she'd hidden them. Jared loved her—that was what mattered. She had been his fiancée for so long that waiting had become a part of her, how she envisioned herself: the lonely lady in waiting … and waiting.

Until Phil, she'd told no one in River Oaks about her far-off wedding plans except Pastor Joe. She'd learned her lesson early on. The last thing she wanted was advice—or worse yet, warnings. But she knew Phil. He'd keep his qualms to himself, as indeed he had.

The frown in the mirror told her she'd best tend to the matter at hand. She shifted her shoulders, turned, and viewed herself from the side. Not a bad figure for a twenty-nine-year-old. Now for the hair. Her naturally curly locks were in their usual perky spirals. She'd scheduled a styling at Pearl's Salon and a mani-pedi for a day before the wedding. It wouldn't do for her fingernails to be caked with flour as they so often were. She looked down at her low-vamped red stilettos, which accentuated her tiny ankles, and she gathered the red silk stole on her shoulders, enjoying its drape and shine. She'd go out and have a good time with her friend, and then she'd come back home to wait some more.

Molly glanced at Phil as they sat together in the plane, and studied him. He stared straight ahead, his jaw clenched and

Adam's apple bobbing above his classic Star Trek T-shirt. She patted his fisted hand.

He turned and offered a half smile. "Thanks, Molly," he said over the sound of the engines. "I couldn't do this without you."

"I wouldn't miss it for the world," she said with a deceptively sweet smile.

"I hope he treats her nice," he mumbled.

"She's a big girl," Molly assured him.

"When it comes to men, she's still a little girl, looking for someone to take care of her, and that little girl has lint for brains sometimes. I can't tell you how many nights I've spent on the phone with her after some new muscle brain broke her heart." He heaved a sigh. "Well, I hope she got it right this time." His shoulders sank. "Now that she's actually getting married, I don't feel right about looking after her the way I've done all these years. It's not my place anymore. I'm not even sure I'll play a part in her life at all." His blue eyes pleaded against the obvious.

"You're doing the right thing, backing off," Molly said.

"It's hard." His hand clenched.

"I know." Her hand again found his. She decided to direct his attention to more immediate matters. "Okay, Phil, if we're going to convince Ronnie I'm your girlfriend, I need to know a whole lot more about you. What's your favorite color?"

"Blue."

"What kind of blue?"

"You know. Blue."

She breathed a slow, heavy sigh. This was going to be more difficult than she thought.

"Okay. Let's make it cerulean," he said. "Now, I'll bet your favorite color is yellow."

"Yellow and red, but I look awful in yellow. How'd you know that?"

"Molly's Sunshine Bakery? How could it be anything but yellow?"

She smiled. "Enough about me. What's your favorite food? Your favorite restaurant?"

"Pizza. Roma's Pizzeria is about the best there is. Sausage, mushrooms, and garlic with cold tomatoes. Now *that's* a pizza! How about you?"

"Chinese. Favorite music? Favorite musician?"

"Jazz. Love that jazz. Any type of piano music, really. It's my favorite instrument. David Benoit, Dash Fortran, Jim Brickman, Josh Groban, and then there's Jim Chappell when I need to think."

"Oh, I *love* Dash Fortran," she gushed.

"Who else do you like?" Phil inquired.

"Andrea Bocelli and Earl Klugh."

"Klugh … jazz guitar, right?"

"Right, Phil. Now back to you. Favorite hobby?"

"Well …" He looked this way and that. "I collect Marvel comics," he whispered in a conspirator's tone.

"No way. I took you for a DC comics man."

"No, it's Marvel all the way. My brother Matt is the DC man. And I'm slightly addicted to online video games, especially Death Legion. Love killing those zombies. I could stop any time I want to—I just don't want to."

They laughed. "Back to business," Molly said. "Tell me about your family."

"What do you want to know?"

"What a girlfriend would know after a few months."

"Let's see … My folks have been married for forty-six years. Happily, for the most part. I have a much older brother, Tim—that's Dorian's dad—and a younger brother, Matt, who's my best bud. And ever since Dorian moved in with me, he's been like another little brother. My folks always stood behind us and encouraged us. Put us through college. I wish they lived closer; they're in the Bay Area. Anything else you need to know?"

"I'm just getting started. Pets?"

"Tuffy, a Heinz 57 terrier mix. Lived up to his name, picking fights with the neighbor's German shepherd. He had to be stitched up so many times, maybe we should've named him Quilt. Poor Mom. She did all the home care for Tuffy, knowing it was just a matter of time before he snuck out again. People didn't keep their dogs in their yards back then, and Tuffy kept paying the price."

"Favorite TV show as a kid?"

"*Star Trek: The Next Generation*. And yours?"

Molly was pleasantly taken by surprise. No one had asked her such a silly but meaningful question in years. It was refreshing: Phil actually wanted to know about her. "Don't laugh. I had a crush on MacGyver. Speaking of crushes, who was your high school sweetheart?"

"Ronnie. Only Ronnie." His smile withered. "Tell me about yours."

"A kid in my youth group at church, Rob. He was so cute and sweet and hilarious. His dimples went in one side of his face and out the other. I was crazy about him." She chuckled. "He spilled popcorn all over me on our first date. My best friend, Denise, was supposed to double date with Rob's best friend, but at the last minute her father told her she couldn't go when he found out we were going to a drive-in. So I ended up going out with two guys on my first date, with his friend playing the saxophone in the backseat of the car. Then after Rob and I had dated for a while, one of the girls in the youth group told me that he denied ever going out with me. I was absolutely crushed. I never had the courage to confront him, and he never asked me out again. I still haven't quite gotten over it. But he sure did have nice dimples. Sorry, I got sidetracked. Who were your friends growing up?"

"I had this friend Mitchell who was a bigger nerd than I was—if that's even possible. We played a lot of video games together. We used to joke about starting a club for nerds only: as an initiation rite, they'd have to recite the periodic table of elements backward."

"You're not a nerd."

"What's wrong with being nerdy? Without us, our technological world would grind to a screeching halt. Besides, who else gets to set his own hours and work from home? To work is human; to nerd is sublime. And you? Who'd you hang out with?"

"My best friend Denise lived across the street. We'd spend every free moment playing with our Barbie dolls and watching TV together, playing in my wading pool—even after we'd outgrown it—having ping pong and checkers tournaments with her sisters at her house, and making sugar cookies that floated on all the oil we'd poured onto the cookie sheets to keep them from sticking. We were always arguing. Once, she got really mad at me and told me to go home. I yelled back, 'We're at *my* house. *You* go home!' I've never really been much of an arguer, but I have to say, I miss our quarrels. They were all so superficial and unimportant that they were funny, at least in retrospect.

"One of my best college friends was Vicki, a gal whose folks were from the Philippines. She was the president of the College Life Christian Group. She came up with the craziest activities for us. We always went to the same Denny's after our meetings and had the same waitress every Saturday night. We were such a pain to wait on. One person would order french fries, one would order a Coke, and then there was the onion rings. We were all too broke to leave a tip. We got a little … let's say, loud at times. In fact, eventually they got wise and started seating us in a separate room in the back, and pulled the folding doors closed. But they were always nice to us. As college kids, we always left a mess. Vicki thought we should give our waitress a good laugh, so she and I knitted thirty-two nose mittens. When the waitress came with our order, all thirty-one of us were wearing the nose mittens. We even made one for her. After that, she didn't mind waiting on us so much. Enough about me. Now, for the really important question: Are you ticklish, and where?"

Before they knew it, their very informative flight had landed, and they found themselves at the posh hotel where the wedding would be held. They checked in and wheeled their suitcases into the elevator on the way to their adjacent rooms. "Good thing the wedding's going to be here," Molly said. "That cab ride was something I'd rather not repeat."

"Yeah, that driver was insane."

"I think he has to be, to drive those streets. I've never seen such horrible traffic."

The elevator opened, and they found their rooms. For the first time there was an awkwardness between them. Though they'd seen each other nearly every day since they'd first met two years ago, they'd never visited each other's homes. In fact, she didn't even know where he lived. Now they fidgeted at the doors that hid little more than bedrooms, and neither was comfortable inviting the other inside.

"Why don't we get some coffee?" Molly broke the impasse. "It won't be as good as mine, of course, but it'll have to do."

"As long as we don't have to set foot in that cab again."

Their comfort restored, they dropped off their baggage and met in the hallway. Fortunately, the hotel housed a café. Unfortunately, as predicted, the Up All Night Café served tragically stale coffee. At least, that was Molly's assessment. To make matters worse, it was very pricey.

"That Lyra certainly is a good kid," Phil said, making conversation as he waited for the scalding coffee to cool.

"I consider her a major blessing," Molly agreed.

"What's her story?"

"I'm guessing it's a sad one. I suppose we'll have to wait until she's ready to talk about it."

"A couple of times she's been about to tell me, and then she chickens out," Phil said.

"Me too, but give her time. You're a really good listener. She'll figure that out sooner or later."

"A good listener. Ronnie used to say that. A lot." Misery had set in again, prompting Molly to give him the lecture she'd been putting off for an opportune moment.

"Ever been fishing, Phil?"

"Yeah, a bunch of times with my dad and uncle, until they realized I was rooting for the poor fish. Why? Is this another crucial bit of information like you were getting out of me on the plane?"

"You know how to play a fish to keep it on the hook?"

"Yeah."

"Well, Ronnie's playing you just like a fish. She lures you, reels you in, and throws you back. And you just keep taking that bait."

"Ronnie would never do that. Not to me."

"You need to see what's going on, Phil. She's been using you all these years."

"How could you say that? You don't even know her."

"Watch and learn, Phillip," she said.

"Well, what about you?" he challenged. "What's it like being engaged for—how many years? Don't you feel a little taken for granted?"

"That's different. He's pursuing a calling."

"Shouldn't he be pursuing you?"

"He knows I'll be there when the time comes. We have an understanding."

"Seems to me that 'understanding' has been going on for an awfully long time, Molly. Just an observation."

"I think we should concentrate on the matter at hand. Let's let Ronnie see what she's missing. You're no longer at her beck and call. I'll lead, you play along." She punched his arm. "This'll be fun. I promise."

CHAPTER 3

Flambé and Fish Bait

Phil and Molly had drunk enough coffee to keep themselves awake for half a week—a foolish move since both felt the need to unwind. They were just getting into the elevator to head back up to their rooms when a commotion sounded from behind them.

"I distinctively told you to order the pink calla lilies to match the ones on the cake, Mother, not the white ones. White callas are so common."

"I'm sorry, dear. It was a simple mistake. There was just so much to do."

"I knew I should've had the wedding planner take care of the flowers. At least she listens." Ronnie rolled her eyes. The bride-to-be continued her tirade as Molly glanced at Phil and found him wide-eyed, listening to the exchange escalating as bride and mother entered the elevator.

Molly mouthed the name, "Ronnie?" and wasn't surprised to see him nod. Molly grabbed his hand.

"Why, Phillip!" Ronnie's petulant scowl faded to reveal a lovely face, smooth and creamy of complexion, with dramatic brown eyes and thick, black hair tumbling down her shoulders. Molly surmised it was probably a recent dye job, judging from its perfectly uniform color.

Molly stepped in front of Phil and, without relinquishing her hold on him, extended her hand. "You must be Ronnie. I've heard so much about you. I'm Molly, Phil's girlfriend. Isn't he just the nicest guy ever? He's so cute and smart and strong and funny and thoughtful, and isn't he the best listener you've ever met?" Molly was enjoying the look of dismay on Ronnie's face as the bride-to-be considered and began to regret what she was casting aside. All the while, Phil stood there red-faced.

For once, Ronnie was speechless, a welcome state for which her mother was most grateful, as this had been her only reprieve in three days.

Ronnie recovered. "Oh, you didn't tell me you were bringing … was it Milly?" Ronnie was dressed to travel rather than impress. Suddenly, her pricey Jennifer Savage ensemble felt almost shabby. Ronnie was uncomfortable seeing her bright-eyed rival with the lush head full of sienna curls.

"It's Molly. She's my girlfriend."

"Phil and I met at my bakery. It wasn't long before he became my best customer. We fell in love over napoleons and tiramisu," Molly said as she lightly tapped his nose.

Ronnie sneered. "I hope you don't gain too much weight, eating all those fattening foods."

"Oh, no chance of that. We burn it off on all those long walks by the lake every night. Don't we, Sweetie Pie?"

"We sure do … Muffin." Phil hoped Molly didn't notice how clammy his hands had become. He feared sweat would be dripping from their fingertips before long.

"I certainly understand the need to pay penance for all that unhealthy junk food. I met my husband-to-be, Michael, at his gym. Actually, he owns a chain of them. He became my personal trainer, and, well, how could he resist?"

"Mrs. Willmington, how are you doing?" Phil changed the subject. "You look great. Not a day older."

"Oh, Phillip, you always were my favorite of Ronnie's … friends."

"Aw, thanks, Mrs. Willmington."

"Please, call me Sophie. We're all adults now, you know."

"How nice you're here with your … friend. I never pictured you with a baker. But it takes all kinds," Ronnie said, poking Phil in the chest. "Oh, Phillip, I can't wait for you to meet Michael. He's nothing like the wimpy guys I've dated. He's a *real* man, and is he ripped!"

Indignant that the harpy had toyed with Phil for so long, Molly said, "Sounds like a big catch. How'd you land that one? I bet he put up quite a struggle." She made no attempt to hide the uncharacteristic cattiness rising to the surface.

A chime announced their arrival at Ronnie's floor. She and Molly glared at each other as Ronnie and her mother exited. As the door slid shut, they could hear Ronnie sputter, "Can you believe that little bi …"

"Ronnie!" her mother cut her off mid word. "You know I don't like to hear you talk like that."

"Who does she think she is, coming here to my wedding with my Phillip?"

"He's not your Phillip anymore."

"What are you talking about, Mother? He'll always be my Phillip."

"You've chosen Michael. It's time to let your relationships with other men go."

"You're so old fashioned, Mother."

"I'm happy he found someone nice like Molly. Did you see how he was holding her hand? So sweet. I could tell they're crazy about each other. You should be happy for him."

"When will you join the twenty-first century, Mother?" Ronnie slipped her key card into the door of her bridal suite.

Molly and Phil were silent for the rest of the elevator ride. When she could stand it no longer, she blurted, "What did you ever see in that girl?"

"What do you mean? She was smiling and everything. Maybe she's just stressed out about the wedding."

"Did you hear how she slammed us? Made fun of my profession? And she called you a wimp."

"I didn't hear anything like that."

"I've got a lot to teach you, Sweetie Pie. You men just don't realize that in the realm of women, a smile on the face can easily mask a dagger to the back. Men just can't see the difference."

Phil laughed nervously.

"This is the last time she's getting away with it. I can't wait to watch her squirm." Molly's eyes took on a dangerous glint.

"Huh?"

"We'll see how she likes a dose of her own medicine."

Standing in front of their rooms, Phil announced, "Hey, we haven't eaten."

"Why don't we both change for dinner and go to the restaurant downstairs? Totally loaded for bear, of course, just in case Ronnie's rehearsal dinner is there. What do you say?" she asked with a playful grin.

"Yeah, why not?" He shifted uncomfortably, standing in front of their rooms. "You were pouring it on pretty thick for Ronnie, but thanks. I appreciate it. There's no way she'll see me as a loser with a gorgeous woman like you by my side."

She waited for him to look up from his shoes. "All those things I said were true, Phil." With an awkward hug, she left him in the hallway. *Did he just call me gorgeous?* She replayed their conversation in her mind.

Like her, he closed his door and pondered what had just transpired.

The maître d' led them past the finely carved marble pillars and fountain to their table with its exotic floral arrangement. Molly and Phil were about to be seated when Ronnie rose from among her rehearsal dinner entourage at a nearby table. "Oh, it's Phillip and Mandy," she said with a beauty pageant wave which Molly chose to ignore. "Michael, you simply must meet Phillip."

Phil called over his shoulder as he was seating Molly. "You're in the middle of your rehearsal dinner. We don't want to intrude."

Ronnie walked over and grabbed his arm, almost sending Molly sprawling. Phil caught her arm and pulled her upright as Ronnie dragged both of them to her table. "Come on, Phillip. You just have to meet Michael."

"I guess we can just say hi." He cast a glance over his shoulder at Molly. "We can see that you're busy."

"Never too busy for you, Phillip. Never too busy for you." She stopped at her fiancé's chair. "Michael, this is Phillip and Milly."

"I'm Molly," she interrupted.

"Oh, yes, Molly. Phillip's my oldest and dearest friend." She jerked Phil's arm toward her.

Michael looked puzzled. "Funny, I haven't heard a thing about you. What'd you say your name was, dude?"

"His name is Phillip. He's the one who always helps me with computer stuff all the time."

"Oh, the computer geek you talked about. Once," Michael said as he scouted the table for his glass.

"I prefer the term *nerd*," Phil said, tongue-in-cheek. He could feel the heat from Molly seething beside him.

Ronnie's father, Douglas, got up to warmly shake Phil's hand. "Phillip, how are you doing? Haven't seen you since you moved to that little town. How's life treating you there?"

"Mr. Willmington, nice to see you. I'm still working with computers, programming up a storm and loving what I do. And this is my girlfriend, Molly."

"Nice to meet you, Molly. The name's Douglas."

"Nice to meet you too, sir."

Sophie stood. "Why don't you two join us?"

"No, we have our own table over there. We'll see you tomorrow, though," Phil said with a wave as they returned to their table.

"Geek," Michael said under his breath.

"Michael," Ronnie reproved, laughing.

Back at their table, Molly and Phil decided on lobster and fillet mignon. Ronnie furtively looked sideways and watched Phil crack open the lobster shell for Molly. She smoldered as Phil and Molly passed forkfuls of food back and forth to each other, laughing playfully. Ronnie craned her neck to see Phil's hand atop Molly's slender fingers. She made a mental note that at least there was no ring on her rival's left hand.

Then there was dessert. "We're going in for the kill," Molly said. "I've been watching her from the corner of my eye. We've got her simmering. Let's see if we can get her to boil over. We need a plate of chocolate-covered strawberries."

"Oh, I love strawberries!"

"No, Phil, they're not just for our enjoyment. They're for Ronnie. But not for her pleasure."

"What?" Phil responded, confused.

"When she sees you feeding me a chocolate-covered strawberry, she'll blow a gasket."

The strawberries arrived, clad in dark chocolate glory. "Now, how exactly is this going to work?" Phil asked.

"Let me show you. Feed me a strawberry as if I am the love of your life."

"Uh, okay …"

"Make sure you get some chocolate on my lips, 'cause you're going to have to kiss it off."

"What?"

"That's right. Trust me," Molly assured him. "This is going to be fun. Just wait until you see her face."

"Okay. Here goes." He plucked up the nearest strawberry and raised it uncertainly to her lips.

She breathlessly accepted his offering with a flirtatious fluttering of her eyelids. She giggled as chocolate spilled down the corner of her mouth. Warming to his part, he leaned forward and kissed the well-placed chocolate.

Across the room, Ronnie put her hand to her chest and gasped, inhaling a spoonful of banana flambé.

Michael, who had just finished his recertification in CPR, began to perform the Heimlich maneuver on his uncooperative bride-to-be, unaware that she was having no real difficulty breathing.

Ronnie elbowed him in the gut. "Stop it, you idiot!" she hissed through clenched teeth. "I'm fine." But it was too late. The room had gone silent with every eye trained on her—Phil's in particular.

"I can't believe that worked," Phil said, incredulous.

Now it was time for Molly to return the favor. She delicately chose the largest strawberry, held it to his lips, and advised him to eat it slowly, very slowly.

At this, Ronnie slammed her fist on the table.

"Babe," cried Michael, "are you still mad at me?"

Back in his room, Phil was just settling into bed when his cell phone played his Star Trek transporter ring tone. Hoping it was Molly, he pushed the "on" button.

"I can't stand to see you with Milly. She's—"

"That's Molly." His patience was waning.

"Whatever. Seeing you two together made me realize that I have feelings for you, Phillip."

"Really? Well, it's a little late for that now."

"But I don't want to lose you! I have strong feelings for you, Phillip. I always have. I just didn't recognize them."

"Look, Ronnie, I've been on your hook since we were kids; you reel me in, you let out the line, you reel me in again. All my life I've been a fish in your pond, at your beck and call. You can't bait me anymore. I've moved on."

"What? But, Phillip, I think … I think I love you."

Confronted with the words he'd waited his whole life to hear, he said firmly, "Those words should be for Michael. I'm off your hook." And with that, he cut the fishing line and hung up the phone.

"Phillip?" she called beseechingly into her cell phone. "Phillip?" She heard Michael stumbling up from the bar downstairs.

"Babe," he slurred, through the closed door, "I can't find my key card. This is our room, isn't it?"

The night before Molly had left to go to Washington with Phil for the wedding, Jared had called her and mentioned he was now planning to do medical missionary work in Brazil. He had met a small group of doctors that were setting up a clinic there, and they had asked him to join them when he finished his specialty training. He had jumped at the opportunity to help change children's lives. Unfortunately, in his enthusiasm he had failed to consult Molly and instead informed her of "their" new plans.

Molly gave Jared an ultimatum. Would he choose her, and they would marry within the year? Or would it be his plans for more schooling and a missionary doctor's life in South America—without her?

Jared called her with his answer after Molly had tucked herself into bed in her hotel room. "Molly, I really believe I've got to follow God's leading. Those kids need me. They need you too. You know how many of them have hearing problems. How could you deny them? How could you deny me?"

"Those kids need you, but I need you too. This relationship has always been on your terms. I've let you treat me this way because I love you so much, but I can't keep waiting the rest of my life, Jared. And I can't see myself living in South America, not even for a month. I don't even speak Spanish."

"It's Portuguese. And it's only another three years to finish my specialty. Then I'm sure we could find a great place to live in Brazil. Think of it as a great adventure. This is my dream, what I was created for, to help kids. I can change their lives. I'm called to this, I'm certain."

"And I'm called to run my bakery. I'm called to start a family. I need for us to be together, not thousands of miles apart."

"You could sell that old bakery when we get married. We'll be together forever. Come on, Moll. It'll be the experience of a lifetime."

"Jared, I don't want to raise our kids where there are pythons and cholera and malaria. I want them to grow up where I grew up, to have the opportunities I've had. I'm not 'called' to live in South America. Besides, you'd be leaving me constantly to do work in remote villages. I'm tired of being alone all the time. When is it my turn? Everything always revolves around you and your plans!" She paused. "You know, I've taught you how to treat me. This is my own fault. I've always been the one to defer my dreams so you can pursue yours. All that is about to change. You can no longer treat me like I don't matter. You can no longer string me along and keep taking on another year here, another three there. This missionary thing, that's a whole lifetime. Look, I want to get married, settle down, and start living our lives together. I want kids. When's that ever going to happen?"

"We could do that in South America. It's not all that bad. Our children could grow up bilingual, seeing the world, seeing God at work."

"That's not the life I want. I never signed up for the missionary life. That wasn't part of the med school/internship/fifteen thousand years of residency package."

"Yeah, well, things change."

"And so have I. Look, Jared, it's Brazil or me!" She hung up.

"Molly? Molly? Molly!" He redialed, but she didn't answer. With resignation she pushed and held the off button on her cell phone.

Phil was concerned when he couldn't rouse Molly's cell phone at ten the next morning. When he could stand it no longer, he knocked at her door. The Molly who opened the door was not the spunky one he had seen the night before. Her eyes and nose were red. Even her curls drooped.

"Uh, are you ready for breakfast?" he asked, knowing she wasn't. "Did I interrupt something? Are you okay? Did I do something?" He fired off his questions, feeling more insecure as he went.

"It was just a long night."

"I didn't sleep very well either," he commiserated.

"Come on in."

He walked into the room and was quick to notice her Bible open on the bed and lots of tissues overflowing the waste basket by the bedside. "What? You coming down with a cold? Should I get something for you?"

She shook her head.

"Come on, Molly. I've poured my heart out to you. A friendship goes two ways."

"I'm fine, I'm fine," she said unconvincingly.

"You're not fine. Tell me what's going on? What did I do?"

"It has nothing to do with you. Jared called last night." She drew a deep breath. "He says he wants to be a surgeon for kids in South America. I told him how I felt before you and I left for Seattle, and this is what I get." She plopped down on the bed.

"South America? You don't seem the type to go for that kind of life."

"I'm not." She grabbed the tissue box and blew her nose loudly.

He sat down next to her and placed his arm around her. "Cry, Molly, cry. Go ahead, let it out."

"He needs even more training, and I've already waited for so long," she sobbed. "It's been eleven years! I just can't wait any longer. But I feel so selfish. A lot of kids with facial deformities have hearing problems too. What if God really wants me to go there and help them? I love Jared, I admire him—really, I do. But I don't want to be left alone in some God-forsaken jungle. I don't even speak Spanish—or is it Portuguese? And how about what I want? He never even discussed the idea of being a medical missionary with me. He *told* me he was going. To live. Not just a missionary trip. To live! And what about our kids? I want them to have a childhood like mine. Is that so wrong?" She looked over at Phil expectantly with puffy, dark-rimmed eyes as she blew her nose again. "I just can't believe that after all this time, he's made such serious decisions about our future without considering what I want, and it's a far cry from what we both said we wanted when we first got engaged. I guess he was so sure that I'd just go along with the program no matter what, because I always had … until now."

"Have you prayed about it?" Phil asked.

"It's what I did all night."

"Any answers?"

"No." Her lip quivered.

"If God wants you to go to South America, He'll change your heart, and you'll know."

"What if I'm not listening because I don't want to?"

"He can change that too. He'll get your attention. Just tell Him you're willing to have him change your heart if that's what He wants. Give yourself some time. It'll all come clear to you."

She wiped her nose and said in a tiny voice, "I think I'm hungry."

"Come on, Muffin. I'll buy you breakfast." He managed to coax a smile from her.

"Can we eat somewhere else? I don't want to run into Ronnie with my face all puffy like this. My eyes are so red and swollen." She blew her nose one last time.

"Come on. There's a Mr. Pancakehead restaurant down the street that I saw yesterday, on our way here. She would never go there."

"Let me go wash my face first and get myself together. I'll be ready in a couple of minutes." She headed off to the bathroom.

Poor Molly, Phil thought as he stared out the window at a small flock of pigeons promenading on a nearby rooftop. *How could he treat her like that? I'd give up my career in an instant to have someone like her.*

At Mr. Pancakehead's, Phil and Molly were being seated. "Marianne?" Phil exclaimed. "Marianne Hanson! What are you doing here in Seattle?"

"Phil? Is that you? Is Molly your …?" she asked.

"Yes, she is … we're together. How do you two know each other?"

Molly explained, "Marianne and I have worked a few weddings together. She's the best photographer around. Just about every bride on the West Coast has heard of her."

"Thanks, Molly, but you exaggerate. I do love my work, though." She handed him one of her business cards and patted her Canon camera, which never left her side. "Looks like you may be needing this in the future."

"That's right, you're a photographer. Of course! You used to take all of the pictures for the high school yearbook. Wait, are you here to do Ronnie's wedding? I didn't think you two got along. What would make you want to shoot her wedding?"

"A twenty-five-thousand-dollar contract. She used to call me Strawberry Face, Pimple Popper, and Zit Girl in front of everyone back in high school, when my acne was so bad. She made my life a living hell. Imagine, now I can *shoot* her and get paid for it too. I'm a firm believer in what goes around comes around. Who's got the upper hand now?"

Phil rose to Ronnie's defense. "She wasn't all that bad."

"She was to me, and she was to you too, Phil," Marianne asserted.

Marianne's assistant, Linda, walked up and said, "We'd better go back to the hotel and start shooting Her Majesty."

"With our Canons!" Marianne chuckled. They held up their matching cameras they dared not leave in the car.

Over his meal of fried eggs, country potatoes, and three pancakes, and her plateful of french toast—both with crisp bacon—Molly asked, "Hey, you said you didn't sleep very well either. What's the matter?"

Phil looked down at the rectangular pieces of pancake he had been driving through puddles of syrup on his plate. He took a bite of bacon, chewed it slowly, and summed it all up in one word. "Ronnie."

"You shouldn't lose any sleep over her."

"Well, I took your advice."

Molly sat up straighter and nibbled at her bacon. "What advice?"

"You know, my being the fish and her reeling me in and throwing me back. She called me on my cell last night. I told her I was done with that."

"What? Good for you!"

"Yeah, but then she said that she didn't want to lose me. That she … loves me."

"What? The night before her wedding, she tells you that? Great timing. What did you say?" she asked pointedly.

"I told her I'm off her hook. For good. I cut the fishing line when I hung up on her. She called a couple times after that, but I didn't pick up, and I dumped my voice mail without listening to it. I couldn't have done this without you. Our talk last night changed my whole perspective."

"You're going to make me cry again," she said in a high voice, fanning her face with her hands, her eyes tearing up.

"It's true," he said softly.

"What's wrong, babe?" Michael said as he woke to the sound of breaking glass.

Ronnie bellowed from the bathroom, "Stupid glass!"

"I'll call for someone to clean it up." He lifted the phone then put it back down. "Hey, are you okay?"

"I just hate that Milly girl that Phillip's … dating. The little tart. Did you hear how rude she was to me?"

"Rude? No, babe. What happened?"

"I ran into her in the elevator with Mom. It was, 'Phil this and Phil that.' Then she had that smug look on her face when we were eating dinner, like she was looking down on me. She's going to ruin my wedding day. I hate her! How could he fall for someone like her, without even consulting me?"

"What do you care about Phil anymore, anyway? He's just a geeky old friend. Not everyone can have someone as hot as me. And you, babe, are mine, all mine." He pulled her into an unwelcomed hug.

"But I hate her," she whined.

"She's not that bad."

"So now you're taking *her* side?"

"No, I'm saying don't let a couple of nobodies ruin your day. Do you want me to ask Phil not to bring her?"

"No, no, you're right. She's a nobody." *But I'll show her*, she told herself.

"You didn't buy a wedding present?" Molly asked, incredulous.

"Uh, no. Was I supposed to?"

"You don't get out much, do you?"

"No, I guess not."

"Let's go shopping and see what we can find for them. What kind of stuff does she like?"

"I dunno. She likes pink."

"Pink what? Platters, tablecloths, stemware, dishes, towels, toenail polish?"

"You know, pink," he said without enthusiasm.

"Okay then. Looks like my job's cut out for me. Hmm ... I know. Let's head down to Pike Place Market. They have all kinds of cool shops down there. We're bound to find something pink."

Fortunately, their cab driver was far more civilized than the previous one. Phil opened the door for Molly with a flourish. "After you, Muffin."

"Why, thank you, Sweetie Pie," she said, entering the cab.

"Sure thing, Muffin."

"Are you two on your honeymoon?" the cab driver ventured. "You're talking so ... nice to each other. Don't hear that very often in this profession."

"No," they said as they shook their heads in unison.

Molly got out her cell phone and took a selfie of them at the traffic light. They made faces with their heads together. "Maybe I should e-mail this to Jared and let him see the fun he's missing."

"Yeah, right after we e-mail one to Ronnie."

"Ever been to Pike Place Market?"

"Can't say that I have."

"Well, you have to experience the ambiance of the magnificent fish market."

Phil wrinkled his nose. "Fish market? What does that have to do with Ronnie?"

"Ever hear of a fishwife?"

"Yeah, she is kinda feisty, isn't she?" He smiled a sad smile as he paid the cabby and helped Molly out of the cab.

They passed a rack of T-shirts. "Oh, look," Molly said, "we can get them matching shirts. They can switch them back and forth. See, this one says, 'I'm stupid,' and the other one says, 'I'm with stupid.'" After a lengthy pause, she said, "Okay then, moving right along. Check out the fish." Molly gestured at the open-air market. "These fish actually swallowed the bait, hook, line, and sinker. Remind you of anyone?" she taunted.

They watched as a man took an enormous fish from the iced wheelbarrow and hefted it into the arms of the next worker, who tossed it to the next. The fish continued along the improvised salmon ladder to the last man, who slid it into a bed of finely crushed ice.

"I wish my uncle Ben could've seen this. Man, that guy loved to fish. When he'd come to visit, seems like that's all we ever did. We'd go out on one of those big fishing boats, and I'd spend part of my time with my head over the railing, but I'd go anyway. Uncle Ben was so funny that it was worth it. Other times we'd go stream fishing. I remember once I went to visit him, and he took me to this place called Taylor Creek. We took off our boots and waded into the freezing water to get to a better spot. We caught our limit, but when we came back for our shoes, we saw a group of Girl Scouts running off, giggling. We found our boots, all right. I didn't know that Girl Scouts learned how to tie knots, but there was no question as to what badge they were after. And there we were, swarmed by mosquitoes and trying to untie hundreds of knots. The mosquitoes finally got so thick that finally we just grabbed our boots and ran barefoot through the pine cones and rocks to the car."

"Sounds like tons of fun. Now, we've got to go find that present." She pulled him by the arm into an antique store peopled by an old man with an equally old beagle, which welcomed them with a slowly thumping tail.

"A pink floral chamber pot. A perfect gift for any occasion," Molly said sarcastically.

"That's pretty. Is it one of those soup servers?"

"Not exactly. This is what they used in the middle of the night in the absence of indoor plumbing."

"I guess that would give 'pea soup' a whole new meaning."

Molly shook her head with a groan. "Okay, so it's not the perfect gift. You find one."

They meandered across the street to a gallery of hand-crafted art pieces. "Ronnie would love this." He pointed to a stained glass lotus flower lamp edged with dragonflies. "I want to get her something nice." He looked at the price tag. "Oh," he said with a droop to his shoulders. "Not *that* nice."

"How about this?" Molly indicated a long, gold-framed painting of a branch filled with pink camellias.

"It's too wide. It must be at least five feet. I'm not sure she'll have the wall space, and we don't know if it'll fit."

They briefly stopped at a bookstore which displayed an ornate family Bible in the window. "Don't bother," Phil said. "She's not much of a reader. She'd probably use it for a doorstop."

"What about wind chimes?" Molly set an enormous chime to tolling its resonance.

"Too loud."

"Perfect. Let's find the loudest one."

They traipsed into a housewares store. "Salad bowls? I betcha she'd like these," Phil said hopefully. "She's always so concerned about gaining an ounce." He bent to examine the boxes below the display. "Shoot, they're out of the pink ones."

"How about this tea set?"

"Tea's not her thing. She's more of an espresso girl."

Molly dragged him to the cookware department. "Oh, Phil, look at this beautiful twelve by nine baking dish! And the nine-inch tart dish with the fluted edging ... and then there's the enameled cast iron roaster. Look! It's five and a half quarts in flame red." She sighed. "Which do you think she'd like?"

"She doesn't bake. Or cook. Or eat most of the time."

"What kind of woman is she? Never mind—I guess we've figured that out. So much for the kitchen."

"How about sheets? There might be some pink ones."

"Phil, do you really want to get into her sleeping habits? Let's try another store."

They passed a shop with silk flowers in a hand-blown vase. "Oh, flowers! She loves pink flowers. Let's see if we can find a pink flower holder."

She shook her head. "You mean vase?"

"Yeah, that's what it's called. A vase." He smiled as he picked up a beautiful sixteen-inch rose vase with a swirl of darker pink twisting through the crystalline tower. "It's perfect," he said with more than a little relief.

At the cash register, Molly said to the clerk, "We're going to a wedding this evening. We need to have this boxed and wrapped. Is there anywhere around here that does wrapping?"

"Oh, we'll take care of that for you," said the dreadlocked girl behind the counter. "You might want to pick a card too."

"Here's a good one." Molly handed Phil a card depicting a generic couple holding hands in front of a duck pond.

"I don't know what to put. You fill it out."

Her pen flashed. "May you be as happy as we are," she read her note aloud.

"'Happy as we are'?"

"Yeah—neither of us is all that happy right now."

"Brilliant sentiment, Muffin," Phil said with a grin.

She smiled, her eyebrows raised.

CHAPTER 4

Dearly Beloved

Molly was thinking about Jared as she slipped into her black Jennifer Savage dress. "We've been engaged for all these years, and he's never even given me a ring," she told her reflection. Zipping up the back of the dress, she turned to look in the full-length mirror. "If Jared could see me now," she said. "Too bad for him. His loss."

Molly applied more makeup than she normally wore; she had to feel confident to face her competition. And Molly *would* compete. Wholeheartedly. As she outlined her lips, the thought struck her that she could be giving birth to her first child under a mosquito net in a remote jungle in Brazil. She steadied her hand and drew the resolute curve of her lower lip. "I'm not giving birth in a jungle." She filled in the outline with Moi Toujours Moi "Ravishing Red," put on her red heels, and gave her hair a quick once-over. She turned sideways to the mirror and said, "Jared, eat your heart out. You won't be seeing this in any jungle."

Buttoning up his shirt, Phil thought about the swirly pink "flower holder" he'd bought for Ronnie. He knew she'd love it. He flipped up his collar and placed the tie around his neck. He couldn't help but think that he should be the one bringing her roses to fill the vase. Images of her kissing him as he handed her dark pink roses left him even sadder. He cleared his throat. "I waited too long," he said softly. Phil tied his tie, looked in the mirror, and forced the smile he'd be wearing the rest of the evening.

"Two words, girls: boob job. That's what it's all about. Dr. Sharps, he's the one responsible for this divine body." Ronnie extended her arms and slowly turned in her satin robe with the word "Bride" encrusted in rhinestones on the back. "He made me the woman I am today. Not that it isn't a lot of work to maintain my perfect figure, but I have my personal trainer, Michael, to help me with that."

The aesthetician swept in with the hairdressers. A flurry of activity ensued as hair and faces were attended to.

Marianne and her assistant busied themselves shooting detail shots of flowers, jewelry, dress, and veil. They got stunning shots of the bridesmaids, but Ronnie refused any pictures of herself until her makeup was just right.

Ronnie's mother, Sophie, was there, offering encouragement, grateful that at last her daughter was settling down, even if her husband-to-be wasn't exactly the sharpest knife in the drawer. She made her way over to Ronnie's cousin Michelle, whom Ronnie had allowed into her entourage only as a favor to her mother.

Her inclusion was anything but a favor to Michelle. Nearly nine months pregnant and looking monstrous in a hot-pink-fuchsia halter—thrice altered to accommodate her expanding waistline—she lay on the bed a hot mess, her feet propped up with pillows. "Oh, my ankles are so swollen. I don't know if I can wait another three weeks. And this *would* have to be on the hottest day of the year."

"Quit whining, Michelle. This isn't about you. Now, get your feet off my pillows," Ronnie snapped.

"Michelle, don't worry. She's just stressed out," Sophie soothed. She gathered throw pillows from the couch and put them under Michelle's feet.

Ronnie, clothed in ridiculously revealing panties and a robe, sipped at her pink passion fruit energy drink while she waited for her maid of honor, Jeana, to bring over the dress.

With a flourish, Renaldo, her gown designer, entered the bridal suite. "*Très manifique*," he crooned as Jeana held up the dress. Renaldo was the chief designer for the Willmingtons' clothing company, Animal Magnetism. The dazzling white gown was designed like a waterfall with a train that pooled in the back. It was extremely form-fitting with opalescent sequins top to bottom. A single strap in the front branched into three sequined strands in the back.

The bride-to-be shimmied into the gown while Marianne, perched on a ladder, shot down at the event. Ronnie whined, "Renaldo, I'm going to be positively raw. These sequins are rubbing my underarms and shoulder already."

"Well, if you had shown up for your last fitting … Sequins can be so tough on the skin. I tried to talk you into satin edging around the arms and neckline." He cocked his head to one side. "I tried to warn you, darling, but you said, 'Sequins, nothing but sequins,'" he said with pouty lips. "See you downstairs, Sweetie. Oh, and try to keep your arms away from your sides." He blew a kiss across the room and left hurriedly.

Marianne said, "Don't worry, *Sweetie*, we can Photoshop out all those red abrasions as well as the blemish in the middle of your forehead."

"Really hideous," her assistant, Linda, murmured none too softly.

"Don't worry," Marianne comforted, "We'll take care of it."

Ronnie shot them both a withering glare.

Jeana began zipping the dress while Ronnie pulled the fabric together. As luck would have it, the zipper tab caught under her acrylic nail as her maid of honor gave the final tug.

"Jeana, look what you've done!" Ronnie wailed. "It's my ring finger!"

"It wouldn't have happened if the dress hadn't been so tight."

"Form-fitting. It's *supposed* to be form-fitting. Now, somebody had better find that nail because I'm not leaving without it!" she bellowed.

Whitney and Courtney, twins, frantically scurried off to search floor and furniture while Marianne turned from the scene to roll her eyes at her assistant.

"What if we can't find that nail? I can't go out there looking like this. It's my ring finger!"

The aesthetician cried out, "Here it is on the counter. I have some glue that should hold it on." She busied herself with the nail, finishing with the final warning, "Try not to touch it till it's dry."

Marianne and Linda continued their usual prewedding routine until the wedding coordinator arrived to announce there were only fifteen minutes remaining. At that moment, Ronnie stood at the mirror to put on her shiny, dark pink "Tantalizing Tulips" lip gloss. Her wand slipped from her hand and fell, marking the length of her dress. She screamed and threw the tube across the counter, knocking over the cocktail glass of energy drink onto her veil. Ronnie started to swear.

Sophie said in an almost convincingly calm voice, "Veronica Leigh, get hold of yourself. We can fix this with some cold water."

"Shut up, Mother," Ronnie said, followed by more curses.

"Don't you talk to me that way! You know how I feel about that kind of language." Fed up, she drew a deep breath. "I'm leaving. You're on your own."

Ronnie's bridesmaids crowded around her like worker bees attending to their queen.

No fan of swearing and volatile brides, Marianne figured it was a good time for a break. She and Linda excused themselves. As they headed to the elevator, Marianne smiled and whispered, "Bridal karma. And this, my friend, is why we always get paid in advance. Never forget that multipage, armor-clad contract."

As the two photographers left the suite, Michael caught the door and poked in his head. "Hey, babe, did I leave my cell phone in here? You look great, babe. Really classy."

"Get out, Michael! Don't you know it's bad luck to see me before the wedding?"

"But I already saw you in bed this morning. What does it matter?"

"It matters. Get out!" She threw the cell phone at him.

"Good throw, babe." He caught the phone and retreated.

The coordinator walked in to announce that the ceremony would begin in five minutes. Amused, she stayed to watch two bridesmaids trying to dry the veil with a hair dryer.

Michelle stood in all her pregnant glory, tried unsuccessfully to see her feet, and said, "Could I get some help here?" She didn't know how she'd ever get those strappy sandals on her swollen feet—if she could even bend forward far enough to reach them.

"Deal with it. This is not about you. Can't you see I'm in a crisis here?"

"What happened?" the coordinator couldn't help but ask.

"You don't want to know," said Tiffany, one of the bridesmaids.

Ronnie turned. The coordinator tried to ignore the faint pink line down the front of her gown, but her curiosity got the best of her. "What's that pink line on her dress?" she asked Tiffany.

"You don't want to know," Tiffany repeated as a sequined, very strappy silver stiletto flew dangerously close to the coordinator's face, hit the door, and fell to the floor.

With one last warning, the coordinator left to wait outside the door, avoiding flying shoes. Her hand was to her mouth as she stifled her laughter. If ever there was a bride deserving of a disaster, it was Ms. Willmington.

Ronnie's maid of honor, Jeana, placed the veil with its accompanying tiara on Ronnie's head.

"There. You look gorgeous," Whitney said.

"Stunning," Courtney agreed.

"No one will even notice that stain on your dress," Tiffany added in an abortive attempt to be helpful. "We got most of it, anyway."

Reyna, the resident cynic, shot her a furious look. "That's all she needs to hear. Shut up, you idiot. Like she needs you at all!"

Ronnie slipped into her sparkling stilettos and checked herself out in front of the mirror, which covered an entire wall of the suite. Her bridesmaids paid homage to her shoes, which seemed to be the only item she was wearing that didn't have a stain at this point.

"What about *my* shoes!" came an anguished cry from the bed. "Somebody help me with my sandals!"

"Just because you're having a baby doesn't mean you have to be one," Reyna said.

"Then I guess I'll just have to go barefoot and pregnant."

Reyna shrugged as she shoved Michelle's feet into the pink strappy heels.

"Ow! They're too tight!"

"Stop whining!" the bridal party said in unison.

Michelle sat, looking down at the way her feet were ballooning out between the straps of her sandals. With a groan she waddled after the others and out the door.

Ronnie hit the button to the first floor. As she switched her bouquet to her other hand, a rhinestone stud on the bouquet stem caught on the newly repaired nail and, unbeknownst to her, popped the fingernail off.

There were a plethora of different thoughts and emotions running through the minds of the guests and attendants as Ronnie prepared to glide down the satin runner.

Phil and Molly were seated on the aisle near the back, lost in their own worlds. Molly wondered if she'd ever see her wedding day, and Phil was berating himself. *If only I'd let Ronnie know how I felt all those years.* He shifted in his seat. *How am I going to make it through the ceremony? Maybe it's not supposed to happen.* He couldn't help but hope. He pictured Ronnie facing her guests and shouting, "I can't go through with this! It's you, Phillip. It's you that I love!" The violin solo snapped him back to reality.

The spill on the dress and veil, Marianne mused. *I couldn't have planned it any better myself. Oh, how I love my job!*

Michelle was feeling sicker by the minute. She whined silently, *My feet look like waffles. I think Reyna fastened those shoes extra tight on purpose. I hope I don't fall. I'm feeling wobbly. I hope it's a short ceremony. I should've peed just one more time before I left the suite.*

Reyna was looking over the second groomsman. *He looks pretty hot,* she told herself. When he glanced her way, she thought, *That's right, check me out, baby.* She was walking a runway instead of a wedding aisle.

Courtney thought, *I know I look better than my sister.*

Whitney was convinced that her sister was jealous of her. They all were.

Tiffany wondered, *Where am I gonna get the money for a boob job?*

Ronnie stood on the threshold with her father, who said, "You ready, Princess? I remember when you were just a little—"

"Stop it, Daddy," she put a quick end to his sentiment. "You'll make my mascara run."

"The Wedding March" began with a rumble. Everyone rose as the bride began her very slow sashay toward her eager groom. She slowed even more when she reached the row where Molly and Phil stood. Ronnie turned her head, looked him in the eyes, emotionless, then turned back to her chosen path on the ivory satin runner.

"Who gives this woman?"

"Her mother and I do."

"Dearly beloved …"

Michelle emitted a series of gasps and looked down as fluid poured out from under her dress.

"What's going on?" Michael said, his voice unhushed. "Gross! Did she pee herself?"

"Her water broke, you nimrod," Reyna grumbled. "She's having the baby—now! Somebody call an ambulance, and let's get this over with."

Ronnie stepped aside, protecting her train from the puddle.

"Somebody boil some water!" Tiffany called out.

"More like get some towels," Reyna said acerbically.

"I can't believe you did this to me! You're only here because of my mother," Ronnie growled from a safe distance.

"I'm sorry, Ronnie. It's not like I can help it," she said in a strained voice through a rather hefty contraction.

Marianne and Linda were snapping fast and furious photos. "They'll never believe this at the next photographers' convention," Marianne whispered to her assistant.

Molly slapped a hand over her mouth, struggling to contain herself.

Within minutes an ambulance was on the scene. They loaded Michelle onto a gurney and whisked her from the chapel.

Ronnie stomped out.

A spark ignited in Phil's heart. *Maybe it's God's way of saying those two aren't supposed to get married,* he thought hopefully. He started to rise, about to go to her rescue, when an iron hand gripped his arm.

"Don't be her fish, Phil," Molly whispered. "That's Michael's job now."

Meanwhile, Michael rushed out to find Ronnie. She'd collapsed on a bench outside the chapel, sobbing.

"Come on, babe. We don't need her. Let's finish it and get this party started."

"She ruined my day," she pouted.

He coaxed her back to the chapel where the minister and crowd waited uneasily.

"Now, where were we?" Michael said.

"I believe we were at, 'Dearly beloved,'" intoned the minister.

When he reached the question posed to the guests as to whether there was any reason why the two should not be wed, Phil's heart lurched. *Should I say anything? She did say she loved me.* This was his last chance. He looked around, seeking an answer.

He got one in a bone-chilling glare from Molly that eloquently said, *Don't you dare.*

Ronnie extended her graceful hand to receive her ring and looked down in horror at the absence of her acrylic fingernail on her ring finger. She gasped and then screamed. "My fingernail is gone!" She stamped her foot. "This is just too much."

"It's just a fingernail, babe." Michael pushed the ring onto her reluctant finger." Go ahead, Rev, let's get 'er done."

Speaking quickly, the minister completed the ceremony, asking for the vows. She shoved the ring on Michael's finger, and he kissed his bride without further incident.

"I've never done much dancing," Molly confessed. "Jared has always been too busy or too broke for a night on the town."

"Me neither, but it doesn't matter. Most of the people here are already too blotto to notice." He tentatively put his arm around her slender waist and took her hand in his. After feeling his face heat up, he looked down at his dance partner, who was experiencing a similar change in complexion.

She looked up at him with a slow smile, then looked at their joined hands and back up at him.

"This isn't so bad," he whispered into her hair.

Molly chuckled. "Well, that's a real boost to my ego."

They normally chatted in their times together, but this was a unique situation—exciting, yet somehow comfortable.

"Uh-oh, here comes the Bridinator. Watch this," Molly said, planting a very deliberate kiss on Phil's lips.

He didn't have time to respond before Ronnie cut in, shoving Molly aside to dance with Phil. Dancing away with him, she demanded, "Who is this Milly?" Her dark chocolate eyes were smoking. Then in a velvety voice, she pleaded, "You're my very best friend. You've always been there for me. I don't know what I'd do without you."

"Well, I guess you'll be finding that out," he said earnestly, "because things can never be the same between us. Marriage is a sacred thing, Ronnie, and I wouldn't do anything to jeopardize yours. Let Michael be your best friend now. That's how it should be. You two go well together. I'm really happy for you. That's all I've ever wanted, for you to be happy. You know that, don't you?"

Ronnie broke free and raced to the restroom, presumably to tend to her makeup which had, for some reason, begun to make its way down her cheeks.

"That went well," Phil said glumly to Molly as they resumed their dance. "I feel like I just shot Bambi."

"I'm proud of you, Phil. Who needs that deer, anyway? It's hard to let go of someone you've loved all your life—but so right, given the circumstances."

"Yeah, I guess." He sighed and pulled her a little bit closer.

As they danced, Molly relived the kiss she'd bestowed on Phil, the roughness of his facial hair, and the unmistakable scent of hotel soap. It felt so spellbinding that she found herself wishing for an excuse to do it again, slower. Unfortunately, Ronnie kept her distance. *I'd better cool things down a bit,* she thought to herself. *Jared would be crazy jealous if he could see me here with Phil. But right now, I don't particularly care.* She snapped closed her conscience.

Phil's spirited attempt at disco dancing left Molly in stitches, and his rock and roll moves weren't half bad. But it was the slow dancing that was her favorite. She felt guilty enjoying herself when she was *supposed* to be engaged. But tonight was, after all, just an act … wasn't it?

While Molly visited the restroom, Sophie asked Phil for a dance. Phil made light conversation, "So, Mrs.—Sophie. What a lovely wedding in spite of Michelle's mishap. Any news on her and the baby?"

"No word yet. Phillip, I'm so glad you could come. I don't know how Ronnie could've made it to this day without you. I always thought you two would end up together."

"Yeah, we've been friends for many years, but I guess it wasn't meant to be."

"I don't know how she'll manage without you keeping her level-headed."

"I can't be that person anymore. But Michael seems to be a really mellow guy. He'll be good for her."

Sophie bowed out when Molly returned. His hands around Molly's waist felt strangely natural.

Chapter 5

Cut the Cake

Marianne had finally gotten Ronnie's attention. "You know, I can Photoshop in that missing fingernail, no problem—for an additional charge, of course. At the same time, I can soften those deep facial lines and remove the pimple on your forehead, as well as eliminate the stains on your dress and veil."

"Just do it." Ronnie turned in a huff and marched off.

The DJ announced over the PA, "Ladies and gentlemen, the Janakovskis now invite you to the cake table. It's time to cut the cake."

Phil and Molly made their way to the edge of the crowd and guessed at what kind of cake lay under the rippling, white fondant. Molly surmised devil's food, but Phil insisted it was something pink. "Do they make strawberry cakes?" he asked.

Molly couldn't believe he would ask such a question. "Of course, silly."

They overheard Ronnie say, "I love you, Michael," followed by a long, resounding kiss.

"Babe! What a kiss! We ought to get married more often."

The guests laughed with relief.

Molly assessed the cake while the wedding coordinator guided the Janakovskis through the cake cutting process. The cake was a work of art with extravagant detail. Its five tiers were topped with a custom porcelain rendering of Ronnie and Michael. Light pink calla and stargazer lilies spiraled down the pristine white cake with fondant that resembled pleated silk. Molly admired the way the airbrushing had been able to capture the texture of fabric.

Michael guided the knife to cut a rather large slice.

"Oh, Michael, that's such a big piece," Ronnie protested.

"You know I like cake, babe."

She delicately fed him a small bite of the pale pink cake. Everyone clapped in approval. "Your turn," Michael warned. He picked up a large wedge.

"Oh, not so big!"

"Open wide, babe." Gently but firmly, he forced the cake up her nose, strawberry and whipped cream filling dribbling down her chin and onto her dress.

She gasped, "What have you done?"

"Babe, it's only cake. Just wipe it off!" He chuckled.

Ronnie snatched up a pink linen napkin and blew the cake out her nostrils as the guests watched in amusement. "I've had enough!" She hitched up her slinky dress and took a step back. She stuck her hand into the base of the cake, at which point the crowd began to part. With an unladylike roar, Ronnie flung the handful of cake with all her might at Michael, who ducked just in time as the cake rocketed past him and into the face of a very unsuspecting Molly. Everyone watched as it then plopped down her little black dress.

Nonplussed, Molly brushed a finger full of cake off her cheek and sampled it. "Mmm, strawberry chiffon. Tasty."

"Molly, your dress!" Phil stared in disbelief.

"Nothing a little dry cleaning won't fix."

But Ronnie wasn't done. She reached for another hunk of cake for Michael to wear, and missed again as he ducked behind Jason, his best man.

Jason stared dumbfounded through a veil of cake. "Dude, can't you control your woman?" he spluttered. Jason lunged toward the cake, grabbed a handful, and hit Ronnie with a sizable wad, some of which flew over her shoulder and onto Reyna, who was taking refuge behind her.

Reyna gasped and looked down at her dress. "You picked the wrong person to mess with—even if you *are* hot." She snatched a fistful and hurled it at Jason, who successfully dodged the projectile. Fragments landed on members of the crowd as Ronnie went back for more ammo.

"Veronica, you stop that this instant!" her father demanded.

"Cake fight!" was proclaimed by eager participants while Sophie and Douglas took refuge under a convenient dining table. Many others abandoned the reception altogether. Douglas's head popped up from under the linen tablecloth. "Veronica Leigh, you stop this right now!" He ducked back down as a piece of cake skimmed the top of his head.

"Do you know how much we spent on that cake?" Sophie said to Douglas.

"How much was it?"

"You don't even want to know."

From under the table, Ronnie's parents could hear their friends leaving and commenting: "What lowlifes." "No class." "Can you believe it?"

Sophie moaned, "We're ruined! Ruined!"

From a nearby table, Michael's father fumed. "What has he married us into? Our reputation is demolished!"

Michael's sister assured them, "It'll never last. I give them six months, tops."

"Come on, you guys. Loosen up. It's not that bad," Michael's brother said.

His father warned, "Don't get any ideas, Barton. If you do this to us at your wedding, we'll disown you."

His mother said, "At least the wedding wasn't home in Boston. None of our friends are here to see this, just family. They won't want this news to leak out either. We're safe."

The wedding coordinator slipped in to rescue the top layer of the cake, wondering if the newlyweds would ever see their first anniversary.

Ronnie saw Molly out of the corner of her eye and unleashed a large culinary projectile in her direction, effectively crowning Molly with frosting. Ronnie was just snatching another slice to bombard her as yet unscathed target, Michael, when he grabbed both of her wrists in one hand and glopped cake down the neckline of her dress. Sensing her fury, he took off running.

Marianne was captive on her ladder, avoiding the occasional chunk of cake with its dripping strawberry filling, shooting as quickly as she could so as not to miss a single volley, and congratulating herself on her all-inclusive contract that afforded her the right to use these images as she saw fit. The Internet wickedly came to mind.

Phil, who had, like Michael, remained ungarnished, finally shrugged and said, "If you can't beat 'em, join 'em." He rushed into the frenzy surrounding the cake's remains just as Molly marched up to Ronnie, a frightful look in her eyes.

"Lovely wedding, nice cake," Molly said, smearing a dollop of filling onto Ronnie's tiara. "Did you know there's a spot on your dress?"

"I hate you! I hate you, Milly!"

"Oh look, you have a spot on your veil too. Right here." She plunked down another blob of cake and ground it into Ronnie's hair and veil.

"You little …! How dare you take my Phillip away from me!" Ronnie reached behind her and scooped up another clod as Phil approached, now dripping with strawberry filling.

"Oh, Molly, it looks like you missed a spot," he said, pointing at one of the only uncaked swatches on Ronnie's dress.

As Molly attended to the clean spot, Ronnie, wild-eyed, shoved a lump of cake into Phil's face, screeching, "Traitor! You, of all people! I never thought you'd turn on me."

"And I never knew it would be so satisfying." He turned to Molly. She scraped the cake off his lips and planted a big one on him.

The cake nearly spent, Marianne climbed down from her ladder and sidled up to Ronnie. "Are those … strawberries I see on your face?"

Ronnie narrowed her eyes and picked up some cake, taking aim.

Marianne warned, "Ah, ah, ah! Your wedding pictures are in my hands. I could make them *very* memorable, one way or the other."

Ronnie plopped her high-calorie weapon down on the table.

Relieved at the temporary disarmament, Phil asked Molly, "You wanna dance, Sweetie Pie?"

The DJ, who had safely hidden behind his equipment, switched from "La Bamba," which he had chosen to accompany the cake fight, to the classic slow-dance tune "At Last," in hopes of luring people to the dance floor and restoring some remote semblance of order.

As they danced, Molly sang softly, "I found a *Phil* to rest my cheek to, a *Phil* that I have never known."

Phil responded, "You smiled and then the spell was cast, and here we are in heaven."

Laughing harder, Molly joined in, "For you are mine at last."

Watching Molly and Phil, Michael said, "Come one, babe. It's our wedding. Let's dance. This'll all be just a funny story to tell our grandkids someday, a day we'll never forget. I love you, babe. Dance with me?"

Unaware of the cake she'd stashed behind her back, he bent to kiss her, and she smooshed the side of his face. Finally, she laughed.

"I guess you got me. I gotta go get me a beer," Michael said, smiling. "The guys are over there waiting for me, and I'm one thirsty dude."

Two by two, remaining couples made it to the dance floor, seemingly oblivious to the fact they were all wearing cake, leaving behind the last of the stargazer lilies and callas trampled underfoot.

After a few songs the DJ invited the guests to join the bride and groom for the bouquet and garter toss. "All you eligible ladies, please gather on the dance floor for the throwing of the bouquet."

Molly stood behind the milling throng of eager young women while she shadow-boxed behind them, checking over her shoulder to see Phil smile.

"One, two," called the DJ, "three!"

Ronnie hurled the bouquet, sending it rocketing over the crowd of desperate women. After reaching its apex on the beam over Molly's head, it rained down loose flowers, and the rest of the bouquet plopped straight into her arms. She raised her brows and blinked twice.

Before she could react, the photographer raced up to her. "Oh, wonderful," Marianne exclaimed, "Now we'll get a shot of you with the bride."

Ronnie walked away. Marianne snapped a few shots of Molly demurely holding the bouquet, and one with her grasping the bouquet in front of her with outstretched arms while making a kissy face.

"Single gentlemen, please join the groom on the dance floor for the garter toss," the DJ said with half a chuckle.

Ronnie sat on a cake-splattered chair while Michael stuck his head under her skin tight dress, almost suffocating in such tight quarters. He made a great production of tugging off the garter with his teeth as she feigned embarrassment.

Phil looked at Molly with an expression oozing with, "Eew!"

"On three," the DJ counted. "One, two, three!"

Michael secretly took one last chunk of cake from his pocket and threw it instead of the garter. The guys made quite a mess wrestling for it before they discovered its true identity. Then he turned around and tossed the actual garter to his best man, Jason. They high-fived each other. "Dude!" they cried, butting chests.

The DJ made his final announcement. "Our very pregnant bridesmaid, Michelle, has just given birth to a baby girl, seven pounds, eleven ounces. Her name is Tempest." A round of cheers and applause burst forth from the remaining crowd. Even Ronnie smiled.

Later, as the last of the guests departed, the wedding coordinator and her assistant stood by the door. Along with the small, framed pictures of the "happy" couple given as favors, they handed out black plastic garbage bags to save their guests' auto upholstery on their rides home.

Phil and Molly paused in front of their rooms. "Can you believe a cake fight at her wedding?" Phil said. "I still can't believe it. She was always so … prissy."

"That's the most fun I've ever had at a wedding reception," Molly remarked. "Did you like her new hairdo? Strawberry really is her color." Molly fished a business card out of her purse and held it up. I'm glad Marianne gave me her card. I hope she posts the pictures online. There's a few I'd like to purchase."

"I was dreading this day more than anything, and it turned out to be more fun than a root canal. Even better than level three of Sidewalk-Surfing Zombies. Thanks for coming, Muffin. You made all the difference."

"Sure thing, Sweetie Pie." She tapped his nose, and they both started laughing. "Thanks for the invite. It really helped me get my mind off of things."

Poor girl, Phil thought, *Jared's been stringing you along all these years.* Heedless of the sticky frosting and filling on their clothes, he gave her a sympathetic embrace, a bit longer than a friendly hug. For just a moment, she nestled her head against his chest. As they awkwardly said good night, Molly closed her door and leaned against it, whispering, "What just happened here?"

Phil leaned against his door and murmured, "That Molly is hot!"

While flying home from Seattle, Phil and Molly reminisced about the events of the previous day. When the conversation lulled a bit, she picked up her book and attempted to read, but she was really just thinking. *I'd give Jared back his ring if he'd ever given me one. Why am I wasting my life waiting to marry someone who doesn't care about what I want? Our life has always revolved around him, and it always will. I'm not cut out to be living in a jungle somewhere while he runs off to play the hero. I'll always be left behind, like I am now. Why am I doing this? Look at Phil over there. He cares about what I think. He actually listens to what I say—really listens. Why can't Jared be more like Phil? Hmm, I never really noticed what a great profile Phil has until now.* She leaned in a little closer. His eyes were closed, and so she felt comfortable studying him. *Such a gentle expression when he's asleep. Yeah, why can't Jared be like Phil*? She dropped her book into her lap, slid sideways a bit, and stared at Phil's relaxed expression. *Hmm …*

Phil had been relaxing in his seat when the chit chat stopped between them. Molly had pulled her book out of her purse and begun reading, a signal the conversation had ended. He'd reclined his seat and closed his eyes, not really sleeping but just thinking. What a temper that Ronnie had. He'd forgotten how she could be at times. The cake incident was something he didn't think she was capable of. It was, however, quite comical when he thought about it now. She was out of his life forever, and after Molly's fish bait lecture, he was almost glad.

It'd been wonderful dancing with Molly last night. How easy she was to be with. He admired her spunk and unflappable response to being pelted by Ronnie's cake. Here was a woman of uncommon character. After all the mornings he'd spent with her at the bakery, why hadn't he seen this before? Jared clearly didn't know what he was missing.

He felt Molly's weight shift toward him, and he sensed her eyes searching his face. He wasn't sure what to do. Finally, he opened his eyes and met her gaze with a slow, knowing smile, revealing his perfect set of dimples. The awkwardness melted away as Molly reclined her seat and rested her head on his shoulder.

Chapter 6

Double Mint Wedding

While walking home together after church, as was their custom, Phil and Molly passed by an enormous, colonial-style house with ornate iron gates shaded by a row of magnolia trees. "I wonder who lives there," Phil mused. "That's some mansion."

"That's the Waldorf's house," Molly answered.

"Have you ever been in there?"

"Heck no, but I'm about to. They called me recently to order wedding cakes and truffles for their identical twin daughters' weddings. It should be quite the affair, a double ceremony. And if I know those girls, it'll be sky's the limit. I think I'll just hang around after I deliver the cakes to watch the fairy tale unfold. The Waldorfs have been part of our community for generations. I've heard that they accumulated much of their wealth from gold mines way back when, and they used that money to invest in stocks and real estate—quite wisely, as you can see. They're often at the bakery. You've probably seen Joanne Waldorf; she always wears lavender and smells like it too. I have to air out the place every time she pays a visit. Anyhow, they knew my parents back in their school days. Nice people."

"I'm not sure I want to be that wealthy," Phil replied.

"Me neither, really, but it sure will be fun seeing the house all decked out for the weddings. I wonder how they'll do a double ceremony, anyway?"

Phil shrugged. "Beats me. Sounds too complicated. I wonder why the girls don't want their own, separate ceremonies on different days?"

"Curious, isn't it? Identical twins are an entity all to themselves. The girls told me that no one really understands the bond between twins unless they *are* twins. The quirky thing is that the grooms are twins too. Sadie and Kallie—that's the girls' names—said that they had always longed to find identical twin guys who would understand the unbreakable bond they share."

"Looks like God answered their prayers," observed Phil.

The two parted company as Molly turned left on Periwinkle Way, and Phil continued on, as usual, alone.

The twins' wedding day snuck up on Molly more rapidly than she had imagined. Lyra had become a huge help and was actually taking on some of the larger baking tasks. It was wonderful to have an extra pair of hands while making scores of chocolate mint truffles. Sadie's "Death by Overdose Chocolate Cake" was finished, with its scrumptious mocha and mousse fillings—a real emergency room of chocolate delights. One would not guess at the decadent surprises waiting inside this cake. The outside looked demure with delicate ruffles of eyelet skirting each layer and silk butterflies fluttering over the cake, but look out when you sliced into it!

Molly was just putting the finishing touches on Kallie's vanilla bean cake with whipped lemon-curd cream cheese filling. Kallie's cake had a more challenging decorative motif on the outside: a complex pattern resembling knitted lace circled each tier. Magnolia sugar blossoms and mint leaves danced down the side of the cake.

Although the girls' tastes in cake were polar opposites, there were some things they could agree upon. One was mint. They both adored it and had peppermint leaves artfully placed on the outside of each cake.

Each cake had a unique topper. Sadie's was a bride grabbing a groom by the collar, attempting to drag the reluctant participant to the altar, while Kallie's depicted the groom carrying the bride through a rose trellis. Each cake was to sit on a sterling silver, custom-made cake pedestal, with the bride's and groom's names engraved upon them.

"Exquisite, if I do say so myself," declared Molly with the last bit of sugared lace placed on the final tier.

"A work of art," Lyra agreed.

"Let's load 'em up and move 'em out," proclaimed Molly. "I'll bring the van around."

"How do we do this?" questioned Lyra.

"Very carefully," whispered Molly, not wanting the cakes to overhear their plans.

The cake board slid slowly and gently from the table onto the wheeled cake cart Molly's dad had designed and constructed for just such occasions. *Such a clever device*, Molly thought. Suddenly, she missed her father terribly.

After wheeling the cart out to the van, she pushed the hydraulic lever, and it slowly lowered the cake to just the right height to smoothly transfer it into the waiting refrigerated vehicle. That was her dad, always finding ways to make her life easier, even now when he was gone. "Thanks, Daddo," she murmured. One more cake to load, and they'd be on their way.

On the brief trip to the Waldorf Estate, Lyra spoke up. "Molly, thanks for giving me a chance to work at your bakery. I'm having a great time and learning so much. You've been very kind to me. I love the little cottage at the McCrearys' you helped me find. I've never had a place to call my own before. I don't know how to thank you."

"Oh, Lyra, you don't realize just how much you've helped *me*. I couldn't have kept up running that place all by myself much longer. What an answer to my prayers. You're doing a fabulous job. You seem to anticipate what I need before I even ask."

"My mom used to call me her little anticipator when we'd work in the kitchen and cook when I was a kid. I miss those days," admitted Lyra.

"Do you ever see your folks?" Molly inquired.

"Nope," was all she said, and looked out the window as she reviewed an unpleasant past.

Molly sensed Lyra didn't want to talk about it. Molly still didn't know her well enough to probe any further, but she made a mental note to follow up in the future when Lyra felt more comfortable with their friendship. "Here we are," squeaked Molly. "I'm so excited for the girls to see their cakes."

It was to be an outdoor ceremony. To the left of the house lay their vast pond. Water lilies graced the water's surface, and the grounds were the picture of perfection. An old willow tree dipped its supple branches into the pond's edge, and a large gazebo stood beside it, lending shade for the many guests' chairs set up for the occasion. Magnolia blossoms and tulle festooned the end of each aisle of ice-blue, taffeta-covered chairs. The twins had agreed on two different shades of blue for their bridesmaids, peacock blue for Sadie's and Cinderella blue for Kallie's. Each would be the other's maid of honor with Sadie's vows coming first, since she was the oldest by almost five minutes.

Their father, Robert, would walk the girls down the aisle simultaneously, one on each arm, after he escorted them out of the horse-drawn, white, pumpkin-shaped coach that was to come through the elaborate front gates of the estate.

What a lot of hoopla, thought Molly. *I'd be happy with a quick "I do" ceremony in Pastor Joe's office at this point. Just grab a couple witnesses off the street, and I'm good to go, she reflected.* But she had to admit that all this frou-frou was dreamy.

"Hey, Molly." Lyra had punctured Molly's dream bubble and brought her back to earth, at least temporarily. "Where are we putting these cakes?"

"Oh yes, the cakes. They will be set up in the ballroom. Come on. I'll show you."

Molly's cake trolley proved once again to be worth its weight in platinum. Wheeling those substantial cakes on a stable platform was ever so much easier than carrying such heavy creations by hand. Transferring them to the pedestals was the only real trick to it. With Molly's instruction, the cakes were moved without a hitch.

"Molly, you really take the cake," Lyra said with a playful wink.

"Yeah, good one." Molly rolled her eyes. She pulled her cell phone from her pocket to capture a few shots. She'd have to talk to Marianne about buying a few pictures of the cakes for her cake portfolio. Where was Marianne, anyway? She hadn't seen her yet today.

Molly and Lyra surveyed the room. Each guest table had a floor-sweeping silver tablecloth with sky-blue, sheer overlays. At the center of each table perched a floral arrangement of blue hydrangeas with stephanotis, asparagus fern, and bells of Ireland in what looked like an upside-down bell jar resting on a silver stand. A canopy of matching blue fabric created an artificial sky, draping gracefully from central ceiling to wall to floor. Hundreds of candles flickered an invitation from the numerous tables. With a sigh, Molly walked to the far end of the room, utterly impressed.

She joined Lyra at the window, gazing out at the gathering

crowd, when suddenly Lyra gasped and backed away. "What's wrong?" Molly asked.

"Uh, I'm sorry. I have to go."

"Lyra, what is it?" Molly frowned.

"Uh, I don't feel good. I really have to go."

"Well, let me take you home. There's plenty of time."

"No, it's okay, I'll walk. It would do me some good."

"Are you sure you'll be okay?"

"Yes. I have to go." She went out the back way. Molly watched her bolt through the open gate and run down the sidewalk.

Molly looked back out the window at the scene that had alarmed Lyra and wondered what had triggered her sudden flight. If she were sick, Lyra wouldn't be running. What was out there that could've rattled her that much? Puzzled, Molly shook her head and wandered off in search of Marianne.

As they waited for the twins to make their grand entrance, Molly was by the pond talking with Pastor Joe. "Well, it's five minutes till show time," Molly said. "Do you ever get nervous before a wedding?"

"No, not really. This one's a biggie though. I'll be glad when they all say, 'I do.' They're good kids, well suited for each other. So when are you and Jared going to tie the knot?"

"I've been meaning to come talk with you about that, Joe."

"What's going on?"

"Nothing, and that's the problem. I'm just so sick of waiting. We've been engaged for years, and he just keeps putting it off till he's done with med school, till he's done with internship, till he's done with residency specializing in facial reconstruction. Now he tells me his next stop is Brazil. To live. I don't want to live there."

"You've been patient long enough, Molly. If he really means

to marry you, he'd better get with the program. Do you want me to talk with him?"

"Really? Yeah, Joe, I do. We definitely need premarital counseling. But how are we going to do that when he's all the way in Washington, DC?"

"If he really loves you, he'll find a way. There's always conference calls. Does he ever get any vacation time?"

"A couple days off here and there, but then he's always studying or sleeping. He calls whenever he can, but it's just not enough."

"Do you really love him?"

"Yes, for so many years now."

"Does he really love you?"

"Yes, I'm sure of it."

"Then what are you waiting for? Get married and move to DC."

"And leave the bakery? I can't just leave. We have plans to marry and live here; we've talked about it from the beginning. I've suggested that we get married sooner, but he says he wants to wait until he's all done with his training so he can really concentrate on us without any distractions. We wouldn't have much time together anyway with his crazy schedule. I think he's already married—to his job. I wonder if I'll always feel like a second wife. Sometimes I just hate medicine. I'm always competing with it, and it always wins."

Joe gestured toward the approaching carriage. "Well, here they come. Stop by the office this week; it sounds like you need to talk this out some more."

"Thanks, Joe. I'll do that."

The mother of the grooms, wearing a periwinkle bugle-beaded dress, was seated first, the beads swaying gently side to side as she glided down the aisle. She was followed by Joanne Waldorf in a sheath dress in her signature lavender with an intricate, hand-knitted lace masterpiece wrapped around her delicate shoulders. Molly smiled, watching Joanne's careful steps in her lavender suede heels so as not to leave divots on the white runner.

Once both mothers were seated, the quartet began to make its presence felt. Led by a stately harp that dwarfed the other instruments, they launched into a lilting rendition of "Ode to Joy."

The grooms and their groomsmen entered from the side and took their places in front. The twins' resemblance to one another was remarkable. If it wasn't for the two different shades of blue that they wore, no one would be able to tell them apart—except for their twin brides.

Sadie's bridesmaids were first down the aisle in stunning peacock-blue halter gowns. Kallie's maids followed in strapless Cinderella-blue gowns.

The elaborate gates parted as the matched pair of white Lipizzaner horses trotted up in measured step, and, necks arched, came to a halt alongside the white satin runner. All guests rose as Sadie stepped out of the carriage, assisted by her father, Robert, who then gave his hand to Kallie and escorted the two girls down the aisle together.

Marianne quickly aimed her camera toward the grooms. Devin's eyes found their home in Kallie's. Sadie's groom, Kyle, looked as if his knees might give way at any moment. The camera turned to capture Mrs. Waldorf, who was on her second lace-trimmed handkerchief, soon to be on her third.

The quartet of violin, cello, flute, and harp welcomed them with the graceful tones of Pachelbel's *Canon*. Sadie was ravishing in her halter-style gown with its deep neckline and a mermaid silhouette. The organza overlay was resplendent with pearl beads and Swarovski crystals on the bold paisley pattern of white punctuated with dainty flowers. The back of the gown plummeted past her waistline in a daring *V*. The paisley pattern continued downward to the flaring hemline.

Kallie's gown was more demure with swirls of cornelli ribbon forming loose flower shapes with dewdrops of crystals sweeping from her left shoulder, across the neckline, and down the right half of the bodice to display a lovely shoulder. The swirls continued down her back, ending at the waistline. From a horizontal band of flowers, fitted pleats softly unfolded from the right side of her waist. In a similar fashion, pleats converged from her hips to a centered back flower. Her train gently followed her down the aisle, the soft swish of organza across the satin runner barely audible above the musical strains.

Molly looked on from under the willow tree, thinking how splendid it must be to be the one walking down the aisle for a change.

CHAPTER 7

To Dent a Bentley, or One Lobster to Go

Back in the bakery, Phil and Molly continued to relive the momentous events of Ronnie's wedding two weeks before, much to Lyra's amusement. Molly sat next to him, propped up on her elbows and leaning against him as she laughed.

The bell announced a customer's arrival.

Molly turned to greet the newcomer, and she gasped. "Jared! What are you doing here?"

Jared approached deliberately and got down on one knee. "Molly Marie Tauber, will you marry me?" He pulled a black velvet box out of his pocket and popped open the lid. Pillowed inside was the most fabulous diamond she'd ever seen, emerald-cut and glistening in the light of the bakery's picture window.

For a moment she couldn't catch her breath. Then Molly sank down to her knees. "Yes! Yes!" she cried.

"Mrs. Molly DeLucca. Do you like the sound of that?"

"Yes! I thought this was never going to happen!"

As he stood, Jared held her hands and drew her up to a standing position and into his waiting arms. As they kissed, Phil looked down at his half-eaten apple fritter and silently slipped out of his chair. He left unnoticed, without a word. Crestfallen, he trudged back to his old Victorian house a few blocks away.

"Jared, I can't believe you're here. You're supposed to be in Washington, DC. You can't just take time off like this," Molly exclaimed.

"I came today because I don't want to lose you. You mean too much to me, and I want us to be together. So why don't you get someone to take over the bakery today, and let's you and I go celebrate. How do you like your ring?"

"It's beautiful. Gorgeous! But Jared, you can't afford this, not on a resident's salary. We should take it back and get something smaller."

"Don't you like it, Moll? I hoped you would."

"No—no! I love it! It's just that it's so ... big. I'd be happy with something much less expensive. Really!"

"You deserve this, you really do. I've made you wait so long to get it, and you've been so patient, waiting for me all these years. You've earned it."

"Well, I love it, and I love you." She called over her shoulder. "Lyra, would you mind taking over for the rest of the day? Jared and I have some celebrating to do."

"Sure thing, Molly. I'd be happy to." Lyra walked forward and held out her hand. "By the way, I'm Lyra. I've heard so much about you, Jared," she said. They shook hands, and Lyra chortled. "Now, you two crazy kids run off and have fun. And, oh, congratulations."

"Thanks," they said in unison, and off they went, leaving the bell above the door ringing furiously with their enthusiasm.

Lyra thought to herself, *I'll bet Molly didn't even notice how poor Phil slunk out of here. He looked absolutely crushed. He must really have it bad for her. She doesn't even have a clue. That must've been some weekend they had together. Why can't she see him as more than a friend? He's so handsome ... and those dimples. If I were her, I'd never let him get away.* She sighed. *I wish he'd look my way. When he smiles, I just melt inside. He could never like me though. And what does Molly see in that Jared anyway? Sure, he's handsome, but he doesn't care what she wants. Well, at least not until now. Molly's too nice. I just hope she doesn't end up sleeping in the jungle somewhere.*

With that, Lyra picked up her dishcloth and continued cleaning the tables, tossing Phil's half-eaten apple fritter into the trash bin. "What a waste of a perfectly good fritter," she said as the brass bell over the door announced a customer.

Phil's nephew, Dorian, had come in for a late-afternoon snack.

"You just missed your uncle Phil," she said. "He headed out of here rather quickly when Molly's fiancé, Jared, came in and got down on one knee and gave her a big old honkin' diamond."

"Oh man. I guess I'd better stay away from the house for a while; he'll be wanting some space about now. I bet he's pounding on his piano this very minute. He and Molly have gotten pretty close lately, especially after Ronnie's wedding. I think he's really gone on her. That's too bad that she's taken now, with the ring and all. He was talking about her just last night, saying what a great woman she is. I was wondering if he was starting to have a thing for her. He has the worst luck with women … kind of runs in the family."

"Really? What's that supposed to mean?" Lyra questioned.

"Well, you know I'm divorced, right?"

"No." Lyra sat down at the table with Dorian. No one else was in the bakery, and she hadn't had a break for hours. "What happened?"

Dorian proceeded to tell Lyra his story.

How could this be happening? Phil wondered. How had he even dreamed that a girl like Molly could possibly be interested in him, plain old computer nerd him? It was, after all, just a charade they had played at Ronnie's wedding. *God, forgive me for wanting to make Ronnie feel jealous*, Phil prayed. F*orgive me for wanting to get even with her for not loving me. Molly was just being a good friend, but I want more than just friendship. Father, help me. I have these feelings for Molly, but now I've lost her too.* He slid onto the piano bench and dropped his hands onto the keys, making a discordant noise. Phil closed his eyes. *That's how my life feels right now*, he thought. He wanted to pound the keys as hard as he could. *Keys*, he pondered. *Keys—I always have my hands on keys, whether it's a piano or on my computer. If I'm so good with keys, why can't I ever find the key to someone's heart*? He let his fingertips loose on the old ivory-keyed baby grand; they seemed to know just what to do on their own. Releasing the tension of the heartbreaks he had encountered in the past few days, he played on. Starting softly with a lonely melody and working his way through a wide range of emotions, the music swelled and changed tempo as it wove its way through his heartstrings.

Walking hand in hand, almost on air, Molly and Jared heard a faint piano playing in the distance. "Whoever plays that piano plays with such feeling," Jared observed. "We should find out who it is and have them play at our wedding."

"Yes, isn't it lovely? I often hear them play when I walk home from work. I'll have to find out who it is."

They made it to Molly's front porch swing. She sat and patted the cushion. "Do you know how long I've waited for you to just sit here on this swing with me? Forever. I still can't believe you're actually here." She leaned against his strong chest as he wrapped his arm around her.

"Believe me, I'm here all right," he replied, taking her hand in his. "This is such a quaint little town. No wonder you love it so much. How's the bakery going anyway? Are you still stressed from too much work?"

"No, not at all with Lyra here. She's taken the extra load off of me, just like the doctor ordered." She elbowed him playfully.

"How about I take you somewhere nice for dinner? Where's good? There are some cool-looking restaurants on the other side of the lake."

"Nah, too hoity-toity. Let's just walk over to Clyde's for dinner. I love it there; it's so cozy."

"Cozy, hmm? Okay, go change. I'll take you anywhere you want to go."

Molly went into the house, leaving Jared out on the front porch to get acquainted with the swing. *I wish my little black dress was back from the cleaners*, she thought. *I guess I'll have to wear some old thing.* She pulled out a classic red dress from the back of the closet, one she hadn't worn since she moved back home. Wiping any last bits of residual cake from the red stiletto heels she had worn to Ronnie's wedding, she slipped into them like Cinderella. *Wow, twice in one month! I thought I'd never wear these shoes again.*" Her heart quivered as she zipped up the racy red dress and fussed with her curls. A little makeup would do the trick, and then she'd be ready to rock. She stopped to admire the one-carat diamond, alive with fire on her left ring finger. Beaming, Molly wondered just how she was going to keep dough off of it. What a wonderful thing to be concerned about for a change.

Jared caught a glimpse of her as she stepped out onto the porch. "Oh, man, look what I've been missing!"

"You likey?" Molly asked.

"Me likey, all right!" Jared exclaimed, truly impressed with his fiancée's perfect curves and rebellious curls. "I've never seen you look more gorgeous, Moll." He pulled her close and kissed her with the passion of a man who hadn't seen his true love in nearly a year.

After an hour or so, Phil went into the kitchen and found everything bland. He choked down a few bites of a turkey sandwich and thought how Molly and Jared were probably celebrating right now at some fancy restaurant on the other side of the lake. Phil sat and stared aimlessly at his blank laptop screen for a good long while, and then plodded back to the front room, where his piano patiently awaited his inevitable touch. He opened the front window to let in the soft evening air and caught a glimpse of the full moon perched in the branches of his neighbors' birch trees.

It was a long, slow walk to the restaurant. When they came in the door, all heads turned to see Molly on the arm of this handsome mystery man.

"Whoa, Molly, is that you?" Clyde said as he came up to the counter with his eyes wide open.

"Hi, Clyde. It's me, all right. I'd like to introduce you to my fiancé, Jared."

Everyone in the restaurant tried their best to eavesdrop and find out what was happening with *their* Molly. Quiet whispers began popping up around the room, speculating as to who this man was.

"We'd like your best table, please," said Jared.

"We're kind of simple around here," said Clyde. "One table's about as good as any other. How about here?" He pointed to a central table, knowing that everyone there would want to have an equal chance of hearing just what was going on.

"That's great," said Molly. "Thanks."

Jared came around the table and pulled out Molly's chair for her.

Mrs. McCreary slapped her husband, Sam, on the shoulder and murmured under her breath, "Why don't you do that for me anymore?"

Mr. McCreary looked heavenward and shook his head. "This guy is trouble already. He's making the rest of us men look bad. I don't think I'm going to like him much," he grumbled.

"Shh!" warned his wife. "They'll hear you."

The light from a small candle at the center of the table found its way to Molly's new diamond, sending sparks flying around the red tablecloth. She gazed at the miniature constellation admiringly. "Jared, I wish we could just freeze time right now and stay in this moment forever."

"Yeah, but then we'd never get to the wedding—or the honeymoon." He raised one eyebrow with a flourish and looked deep into her eyes.

She suddenly felt a bit warm and looked down at her menu. While fanning herself with it, she remarked that the fresh catch of the day, trout almondine, sounded like a good choice.

"Do I detect a hint of shyness, Miss Molly?" he teased.

"Yep," was all she could say.

Continuing down the same path of blushdom, Jared asked, "So where are we going on our honeymoon? Jamaica? Italy? Maui? Some exotic hideaway?"

Just then Clyde came up to take their orders.

Meanwhile, the other guests were visibly straining to hear, but they had a tough time of it because the young couple mostly spoke in hushed tones.

"Drat!" said Betsy Peterson to her husband, Bob. "They're talking too softly. All I can hear is something about Italy, or something. Who is this guy, anyway? I've never seen him before. I hope he doesn't take advantage of our sweet Molly. He looks like he means business, if you know what I mean. Just look at his eyebrows."

"Molly's a grown woman now. I'm sure she can handle his eyebrows," said Mr. Peterson as he took another twirl of pasta primavera. "She's too smart to put up with any shenanigans that she doesn't welcome. We shouldn't be eavesdropping anyway, Betsy."

"I'm just worried about her. He doesn't look like her kind of man. He barges right in here, asking for 'the best table in the house' like he owns the place. Look at him looking at her. I don't like this one bit. He's not her type at all."

"And just what is her type anyway?" Amusement crinkled the corners of his eyes.

"Not him!"

After placing their orders, Molly continued their conversation. "We don't need to go anywhere extravagant or anything. We could just go somewhere on the coast for a few days. We don't have to spend a fortune to go somewhere. As long as we can be together, I don't care where we are."

"Really? Well, how about South America?"

"What, like a cruise or something? That could be really fun."

"I'm so glad you think so, because I was thinking we could check out Brazil."

"Brazil? Why Brazil?" she said sharply.

"Well, you know. If we're going to live there eventually, we might as well check it out and see where we want to live."

"*What*?" Molly scooted back in her chair. "What are you talking about, Jared?"

"Okay, okay, Moll, you don't have to get so upset about it. We could go somewhere else for our honeymoon. We can check out Brazil later."

Mouth gaping, Molly cried, "What are you saying, Jared? Are you still planning on moving us to Brazil? I thought we'd talked about this. I gave you an ultimatum when we last talked on the phone: it was Brazil or me. I thought you chose *me* when you came marching into the bakery unannounced with this engagement ring in your hand." Her voice had begun to rise in pitch. The audience tried not to stare as she rose from her seat.

"Molly, please! You know how much this medical missionary work means to me. I thought you understood. I thought having the ring would make you happy. We can work this out. Come on, Moll. We can do this together. You know I love you. This could be such an adventure. I want to share it with you. Don't you love me?"

"How dare you march into my town and make me think you'd agreed to live here! That's the problem, Jared: you don't really listen to me. You want what you want—your way, your timing. You never once asked if this 'adventure' is what I want. There's no compromise with you. All I've done all these years is compromise. I've delayed all my future for you, given up precious years of my life waiting for you to follow through on your promises. 'Just let me get through undergrad, just let me get through med school, internship, residency, the myofacial surgery training thing.' That's another five years. When is it going to end, Jared? When's it my turn, huh?"

He stood up.

She poked her finger in his chest, harder with each word. "All I do is wait on you, and now you have this wild idea about moving to Brazil, to some jungle." She threw her hands up in the air. "Well, I didn't sign on for that! This is not what I have been waiting for my whole adult life. I thought when you walked into the bakery this afternoon that you finally understood what I've been saying. I thought you had finally begun to think about me and what I want for a change. Well, I was sadly mistaken." Molly fidgeted nervously with her ring, finally pulling it off and slamming it down on the table. "Oh, and you can keep the ring! I'm done with waiting!" she yelled. Molly stormed out the door with a roar of applause following her.

Jared stared at the door in shock, as Clyde walked over and handed him the bill. "Do you want that lobster to go?"

Another moonlit night wasted, Phil thought to himself. *Maybe the night breeze will clear my head. If I could only erase my thoughts with a delete button*, he mused. This time Phil played a more haunting strain, "The Bells of New York City" by Josh Groban. Hadn't Molly told him that Groban was one of her favorite musical artists? Little did she know that Phil knew almost every Groban song by heart. If only she were here now....

The applause from the customers in the restaurant still ringing in her ears, Molly rounded the corner and headed for home. Fearing that Jared might follow, she took a different route. She could enter from the back of the house so that he wouldn't know she was there. Molly never wanted to see him again. She increased her speed to get off the main street before he would have the chance to see her. Walking briskly in her stiletto heels, she looked back over her shoulder. At that same moment, her heel caught in the poplar tree root that had cracked the sidewalk so many years ago. She flew forward, sprawling, leaving the heel of her shoe behind. With her knees and hands scraped, Molly sat down on the uneven sidewalk and sobbed. For a few minutes she just sat there, trying to regain her composure. When she had calmed down a bit, Molly stood up unsteadily, picked up what was left of her shoes and her dignity, and hobbled on. Now off her regular route, she heard the sound of the lonesome piano, but this time not as distant as it had always been on her way home. Sniffling, she followed the sound and found herself in front of a large, blue Victorian. All lights were off, but the front window was open. Molly thought it odd that someone was playing a piano in the dark, but then again, the tune was rather melancholy.

Maybe it is time for me to move on, Phil thought. He loved this old Victorian that his uncle had left him, but was there really any other reason for him to stay? With his programming skills, he could live just about anywhere. Maybe he should move someplace far away like New York, or maybe even somewhere in Europe. "That's it," he said aloud. "Italy. I guess I'd have to learn to speak a bit more Italian first." The song almost at an end, he heard something out near the front porch. *What the heck is that*? he wondered. Curious, he stopped playing and walked over to the front window.

Her breath suddenly caught in her throat. Wait, was that "The Bells of New York City" she heard? Who would be playing that song at a time like this? She ventured to the walkway leading to the front door, shoes in hand. Almost to the porch, she strained to see who the shadowy figure was at the piano. Abruptly the song stopped, and a face appeared at the window. A familiar voice called softly, "Molly?"

She dropped her shoes. "Phil? Is that you? Don't stop playing."

Phil came running out of the house and grabbed her hand. "What happened to your knees? You'd better come inside." He stooped down to pick up her shoes and saw the missing heel. "Your shoes! What did he do to you?"

Molly limped inside, sat down on the soft, overstuffed couch, and said, "Just play."

Laying aside his own broken heart, he played each note for her. At the end of the song, he turned on the piano lamp and looked at Molly. "What happened?"

"You know what happened. He thought a diamond would satisfy me, when what I really wanted all this time was him. He still plans to do even more years of training and then have us wind up living in Brazil. Eleven years I've waited for him. Eleven years! Well, no more! I can see what our life would be like together. He's never going to care about what I want. Even if he walked in here right now and told me Brazil was out, that he'd give it all up for me, I would tell him we are through. Let him go follow his dream. I've wasted my life waiting for him to follow through."

"What do *you* want, Molly? Don't you love him anymore?"

"I'm not sure that I do. He hurt me so badly tonight that I think it finally snapped the fishing line."

After turning on the light, Phil doctored her scraped knees and hands. The two of them found themselves at a loss for words. "Maybe I'd better drive you home."

"Wait. Do you take requests?"

"What?"

"On the piano."

"Sure, I guess."

"Do you know 'Gone' by Jim Chappell? Because that's just how I feel right now."

"Yep, I was actually playing it earlier today. I was moping about Ronnie. I guess I could do an encore." He sat on the piano bench and patted the spot next to him, offering her a seat. His hands flowed effortlessly over the keys. At the crescendo, he felt his sadness give way to peace. She sighed and leaned her head on his shoulder for a few moments, and he wondered if this could be the key he'd been looking for.

Molly surveyed her surroundings. The walls were painted in a soft, warm butter hue. An armoire stood against the wall opposite the couch. There was a plant stand by the window housing a shaggy Boston fern. Although most of the furnishings were antique, they were well maintained, and the room was surprisingly orderly for a bachelor. Phil led her through the kitchen where a partially eaten sandwich sat reproachfully on the table next to his laptop. Beadboard covered the walls. She noticed the large country kitchen sink with envy, but noted that his ancient lace curtains were dingy with age.

Phil opened the garage door and turned on the light, revealing a shiny antique automobile. "You—you've got a Bentley?" Molly exclaimed.

"Yeah, it was my uncle's. He left it to me; it was his pride and joy. I hardly ever drive it. Usually, I take my Prius. I'm too afraid of dinging up the Bentley. Come on. I'll take you for a ride in it." He opened her door for her, and she slid into the richly upholstered seat. He took his place behind the wheel. "Where to, Madame?"

"How about a loop around the lake?" She ventured a smile. As they drove off, she commented, "You're just full of surprises. First, I find out that you're the mysterious piano man I've been hearing for so long. Next, I discover you own a Bentley. What other secrets are you keeping?"

"Wouldn't you like to know?" He chuckled. "Let's make this fair. It's your turn to divulge a couple of your secrets."

"Well, I do have a secret addiction. I'm uh—a milkaholic. Can't get enough of it. Go through about two gallons a week. And we're talking the hard stuff—two percent. None of that fat-free, watered-down dishwater. I'm a regular dairy food junky."

"Is that so?"

"Oh, and I'm a registered Democrat living in this Republican town. I registered at eighteen as a Democrat just to rattle my parents' cage. Never bothered changing it. Don't really care—hate politics. Is that good enough for you?"

"Your secrets are safe with me." He turned his head to smile at her.

"How come you never told me what a virtuoso you are?"

"You never asked. Besides, I'm way too humble," he replied with a grin.

"Where'd you learn to play?"

"My dad taught me, but he mostly played classical. He taught me everything he knew, and then I took lessons for years. I wanted to go to music school. I actually got accepted, but decided to go into computers instead. Figured I'd have a better chance of getting a steady job and making a decent living. Sometimes I wonder what might've happened if I had gone down that road. I still play every day, though."

"Yeah, I hear you when I'm walking home from work. I've been wondering who the piano man was."

"Well, now you know. So how long have you had this milk addiction? Have you thought about buying your own cow?"

"I must admit the thought has occurred to me."

"Does this involve all dairy products? Did one lead you to another, like from low fat to cream cheese? Do you find yourself craving gouda or havarti in the middle of the night?"

"Yes! Yes, you do understand!"

"When did this all start?"

"My earliest school memory was in kindergarten at nap time, when they made us all lie down on the floor on towels and rest for a few minutes while the teacher tried to take a break. I remember this one day in particular. I nodded off and dreamt that I was in a room with floor to ceiling refrigeration units, and stacked as far as the eye could see were cartons and cartons of icy cold milk. I was never the same after that."

"That's just sick, Molly. I'm not going to lie to you: that's quite an addiction you have."

"Are you addicted to anything?"

"Your apple fritters."

"Aw …"

Their talk continued, and before they knew it, they arrived at Molly's house. "What's that on your porch swing?" he asked.

"Oh no. It's Jared. I don't ever want to ever see him again."

"I'd like to give that guy a piece of my fist. Do you want me to take care of this?"

"No, I'd better take care of it myself." She left Phil in the car. "Thanks for the ride."

Jared stood up from the porch swing and marched up to Molly. "Now I've got it. *He's* the reason you gave my ring back."

"What?"

"Who is this guy? You've been two-timing me. If you knew all the women I've turned down to be faithful to you, and here you are with this nerdy-looking geek …"

"Jared, what are you talking about? Phil has nothing to do with this. I don't love you anymore because you don't love me enough to stick to the promises you made me. I've waited faithfully all these years, Jared, even though you've totally ignored me for months at a time. I counted on you staying true to your promises too."

Jared grabbed her by the shoulders. "You've been seeing him, haven't you?"

"Phil and I are just friends. But did you ever intend on moving here and starting a life with me? Or was that just to string me along? Did you? Answer me, Jared!"

"Of course I did … at first. But things have changed."

"They sure have! I don't want this sham of a relationship anymore! Go to Brazil. Be a hero to everyone but me!" Jared's grip on Molly's shoulders tightened. "Ow, you're hurting me," Molly cried.

That was all it took. Phil was out of his car and on the porch in an instant. "Get your hands off her," he yelled.

"So you're the reason behind all this, Nerd Boy," Jared spoke in an even lower tone.

"Jared, don't," Molly pleaded.

"Stay out of this, Molly," Jared warned, releasing his grip.

"Jared, stop it!" Molly yelled with all her might, rousing curious neighbors from their television screens.

Without warning, Jared's fist connected with Phil's nose, knocking him to the ground. Blood flowed from his nostrils.

Phil stood, faced Jared, and said, "If Molly were my girlfriend, I sure wouldn't leave her waiting around for eleven years. I'm amazed someone hasn't come along and swept her off her feet while you play doctor in another state. You haven't even thought about what she's been going through, waiting on you while you took your sweet time. You're too selfish to care about anyone else. You could've married Molly long ago while you were doing all your med school crap. You could've gone to med school in California and been with Molly this whole time. Instead, you chose to live in some academic ivory tower where no one else's feelings can reach you. She's had enough, and frankly so have I." With that, Phil sprang forward with ready fists and surprised everyone with a right hook to Jared's jaw.

Jared stumbled back, landed halfway on the porch swing, and then fell down on the porch. The swing, set in motion from his fall, smacked him another good one on the back of the head.

"Maybe you can get one of your ivory tower cohorts to fix that glass jaw of yours," Phil growled. "Now get out of here and don't come back."

Molly's mouth had long since dropped open. She had no words left.

Completely embarrassed and shocked, Jared got up and shoved Phil out of his way as he barged past him and left the porch. He turned back and caught her eye. "Molly, is this really what you want?"

"Yes, Jared. Please, just go."

On his way down the driveway, Jared gave a testosterone-driven kick to the side of the helpless Bentley, leaving a huge dent. He stormed off to find his rental car back by the bakery where he had left it.

Stunned, Molly watched him—and her dreams—walk away. "I'm so sorry about your car Phil, and the nose. Thank you for coming to my aid."

"Never mind that; check out my hand. His teeth took out a chunk of my knuckles. Can you get him to come back here? I think I need stitches."

Molly put her hand to her mouth, stifling a chuckle.

"It's okay. You can laugh now—I'm just messing with you. I haven't been in a fist fight since I was twelve years old. This is the first time I actually won. I'm really pumped."

"I've never seen him like that before."

"Well, he's never been about to lose someone as precious as you."

"I can't believe he hit you. He really thinks there's something going on between us. I mean, more than just friendship."

"Yeah, whatever gave him that idea?" He hoped she wouldn't hear the sarcasm in his voice. "Would it be too much to ask for some tissues? I seem to be bleeding all over your porch."

"Come on, Phil. Let's get you cleaned up. It's the least I can do after you took care of my knees."

The next morning Lyra noticed Molly kneading bread dough more intently that usual, slamming the dough down on the table with uncharacteristic ferocity. Lyra ventured, "Do you want to talk about it? News travels fast in a small town. Heard you got a standing ovation at Clyde's last night."

"Oh, that's not the half of it, Lyra." She proceeded to recap the events that led to the applause.

"Why would he bother coming to town with a ring if he didn't intend on living here like you'd planned?"

"Because he thought I'd cave, just like every other time.

Never again, Lyra. Never again." Molly went on to describe the impromptu boxing match on her front porch.

"I guess chivalry isn't dead after all. Is Phil okay?"

"He'll be fine. He's actually really proud of himself. What's killing me is that Jared thought I'd been cheating on him—with Phil."

"Is that so far-fetched? There's nothing wrong with Phil," Lyra said in his defense.

"No, not at all. It's just that I'd never cheat on anyone." At this point the memory of her weekend with Phil at Ronnie's wedding filled her mind with doubt. Hadn't she enjoyed kissing him? It started out as a ruse, but was it really? Hadn't she found dancing with him a little too exciting? Pangs of guilt forced their way into her heart. She slammed down the next batch of dough even harder and dismissed them.

Uncharacteristically late, Phil swaggered into the bakery.

"Where have you been all morning?" Molly scolded.

"Just out doing the usual hero stuff."

"Really. Well, I have to tell you just how sorry I am that you got caught in the crossfire with Jared."

"I'm not. He had it coming. Jerkizoid." He triumphantly made his way to his usual table. "Thinking about auditioning for some ninja warrior show. I don't even have to throw more than a single punch with these lethal weapons." He struck a bodybuilder pose.

"Don't quit your day job just yet," Molly counseled.

Lyra walked out from the back room. "Hi, Phil, where've you been? And what are you doing? Are we playing charades? I get it—you're the Hulk, right?"

"World-class boxer, that's my secret identity." He threw some unconvincing punches into the air.

Molly laughed. "Phil, you twit." She looked over at Lyra and explained again, this time for Phil's benefit, "Phil and Jared had a little … disagreement last night. As you might have ascertained from his victorious attitude, Fearsome Phillip here prevailed."

"Yep, sure did." His Adam's apple bobbed with pride in a way that said, "I am macho—fear me."

Lyra shook her head, sighed, and headed back to glaze some doughnuts.

"Really, Sweetie Pie, what am I going to do with you?" Molly said with a toss of her head, sending her curls dancing.

"Bring me an apple fritter. No, wait!" he said with an air of urgency. "Make that a bear claw!" he thundered.

CHAPTER 8

A Cup of Joe

Molly needed time to think, and there was nowhere better to think than the old, abandoned dock on the lake. Ever since she was a teenager, when she needed to be alone, make decisions, or contemplate life, she would find her way to the dock a quarter of a mile around the lake. No one was ever there, and so she claimed it as her own.

There was so much to consider today. Her world had been turned upside down. Molly longed to talk to her mom, who could make sense of the madness. Why did she have to die so young? She missed her. Later this afternoon, Molly would talk with Pastor Joe. Maybe he could shed some light. What she really needed was to talk with another woman. She sat down at the end of the dock and took off her shoes. Dipping her toes into the lake, she kicked her foot and sent a hundred silver coins dancing across the calm surface. She watched the concentric circles converge into one another.

For many years, Molly didn't understand what was wrong with her. She simply knew that from the time she was in second grade, she had this horrible feeling sweep over her frequently, a feeling of dread and darkness, a different kind of sadness that came often with no apparent reason. It was accompanied by fear and anxiety. Frequently, she couldn't even eat. As she got older, there were times she felt she was suddenly plugged into a socket at night and would receive a jolt of electricity, awakening her with a terrible dose of apprehension. Molly was grateful that the horrible, all-consuming depression that she had experienced for so many years no longer plagued her. She was extremely sad at the moment, but wasn't slipping beneath that old, dark, suffocating blanket that she used to live under. How had she withstood it all those years? She had to force herself out of bed so many mornings back then, not wanting to face each day with her constant companion, depression. She had always acted like everything was fine on the outside, and very few people ever knew her secret.

Denise knew. Molly remembered talking to Denise one summer afternoon when she was just seventeen. Molly had been on the verge of suicide and had even begun to plot her way out of this life. Thank God that Denise had talked her out of it and invited her to the youth group at her church. She had refused the invitation to join Denise's group—that was, until Denise showed Molly some photos of the latest youth group outing. Molly wasn't very keen on the idea of going until she spotted a young man in one of the pictures. *God works in mysterious ways sometimes*, she reasoned. Molly agreed to go to the meeting just to see the intriguing set of dimples in real life. She liked what she saw and kept coming back to the youth group week after week in response not only to the dimples, but to the truth she heard from God's Word. Within weeks she had given her heart and life to Jesus, and from that time on she had what she needed most: hope. Her depression had not gone away, but she now knew that God would help her through. She could depend on Him. Though the hopelessness had vanished, it wasn't until years later that she was completely healed from her depression. What a day that was. She had so much to be thankful for.

Jesus, she prayed silently, *thank You for freeing me from depression and all that it brings with it. Right now, Lord, I need a friend.*

Someone my age I can talk to. Someone wise who will listen and give me her perspective. Since Denise moved away after high school, I've never had another really close girlfriend. Maybe I should call and invite her to come for a visit. Lord, I don't know what to do. I'm so confused.

Molly picked up the Bible she'd brought with her and opened to the page she'd left off reading a couple days ago, Romans chapter 8. As she read, verses 26–28 and 38–39 leapt from the page.

> And in the same way the Spirit also helps our weakness; for we do not know how to pray as we should, but the Spirit Himself intercedes for us with groanings too deep for words; and He who searches the hearts knows what the mind of the Spirit is, because He intercedes for the saints according to the will of God. And we know that God causes all things to work together for good to those who love God, to those who are called according to His purpose … For I am convinced that neither death, nor life, nor angels, nor principalities, nor things present, nor things to come, nor powers, nor height, nor depth, nor any other created thing, shall be able to separate us from the love of God, which is in Christ Jesus our Lord.

Pray for me, Holy Spirit. I don't even know how to pray about this. I just want Your will for my life.

Wind and sun had weathered the dock, but she didn't care. Molly lay on her back and looked up at the sky. "Whatever you want, God," she sighed. A lazy white cloud meandered by, casting a shadow on the dock below. The staunch cottonwood that guarded the boat launch surrendered its leaves of gold to a new breeze that stirred Molly's hair to life. A lone dove winged its way overhead.

"You have all this figured out, God, so I guess I don't have to." She lingered in silence for a while and felt a growing sense of comfort—the kind that doesn't require answers or even understanding. Peace.

Molly dumped the whole story of Jared's proposal into Pastor Joe's lap. "What was he thinking, Joe? He knew what my conditions were for marrying him."

Joe sat back in his chair, took a sip of his coffee, and was silent for a minute. "Nobody's really right or wrong here, Molly. You two fell in love years ago, before you really knew God's plans for your lives. You both assumed that you were on the same path, and you were for a while. Looks like God has taken you in different directions now. There's nothing wrong with that. If Jared's convinced that missionary medicine is where God's leading him, then you need to let him go. If you've searched your heart and prayed God would change your mind about being a missionary, and you still don't feel led that way, then you need to set Jared free and see what God has planned. Don't expect Jared to give up his calling from God just to appease you. It's no one's fault. Jared's trying to please both you and God, but he can't. You can't blame the guy for trying. He's just hoping you'll love him enough to change your mind."

"But what do I do with all these emotions? Especially the anger?"

"Surrender it up as a sacrifice to the Lord. Whenever you think about how unfair it seems, how angry you are, how much it hurts, or how much you love Jared, put it on the altar of your heart and sacrifice it up to God. Ask the Lord to help you. Accept His will, even when it hurts. Tell Him you want His plans for you more than your own. Slowly, over time it will hurt less. Down the road, you'll see the new path He has for you. You can trust Him. He knows what He's doing. He's been doing this job for years. But you know, Molly, you can't just change who you are. You have a unique personality. Your interests, your experiences, your abilities—all those things come together to define your calling and make you who you are. Somehow it doesn't seem to add up to you swinging a machete in the jungle, but that's just me. Now, if God were to truly call you to the life of a missionary, would you be willing?"

"Yes," she replied.

"Well, there you go."

"But I'm not called."

"There you go. Besides, what would this town do without your croissants and pumpkin pie cheesecake?"

"So, what am I supposed to do, Joe?" Molly asked.

He stood up and gestured toward the door with a big grin on his face. "Go bake something, and next time how about bringing me a coconut cream pie?"

"Men," she huffed, half smiling as she exited his doorway.

Molly started her walk back to the bakery. Joe was right; he always was. Darn it! She could see it was going be to a battle to surrender. *No wallowing*, she told herself. *I need to get over Jared and get on with my life. God help me.*

"I connected, and he fell backward on the porch swing and hit the ground. Then the swing hit him in the head. I couldn't have planned it any better," Phil finished as he retold the story to Joe.

"I wish I could've seen it, Phil."

"He really had it coming, Joe. He's messed with Molly's heart for way too long. If I were him, I'd have married her years ago."

"But that's just it: you're not him. He has a calling to help the less fortunate in Third World countries. You don't."

"Yeah, well, he should have broken up with her then."

"Maybe so, but he didn't know for sure she wasn't going to

go along with it. He might have thought God would eventually call her too. You can't blame the guy for wanting to hold on to someone like Molly."

"You're right on that one."

There was an awkward silence. Joe had learned over his years of counseling to let the silence happen. It was in those uncomfortable moments when people were trying to get up the courage to say what they really needed to. Joe waited patiently, looking at the painting of a salmon jumping out of a stream on his wall. *I've got to get in some fishing this week*, he told himself.

"Okay, Joe … I'm in love with her."

"I knew that. Just wanted you to admit it out loud." Joe took a big gulp of the last of his second cup of coffee, which had gotten cold by this time. He knew he'd be on his third one soon, the way things were going. "So what do you plan on doing about it?" he inquired.

"I haven't decided what to do … yet. I figured I was on the rebound, you know, after Ronnie got married. And Molly's been unreachable, being engaged and all."

"She was safe," Joe interjected.

"I think that's why I haven't been afraid to get to know her and let her know me, because she was unavailable. I didn't have to worry about what she thought of me since we could only be friends—until now. I'm not sure what to do next."

"Can I give you some advice?"

"That's what I'm here for," Phil said.

"Be there for her. She really needs a friend right now, someone she can talk to, someone she trusts. Give her time to heal. Pray for her. Encourage her. And don't wait too long to make your move. Girls like Molly are hard to find these days. Don't let her get snatched up by someone else. Word's out that she's not engaged anymore, you know."

"What do you mean, make my move?"

"You know, take her out."

"You mean on a date?"

"No, I mean to the trash. Good grief, Phil, what have you been doing your whole life? Of course I mean on a date!"

"Like to where?"

"I don't know. What does she like to do for fun? You really need to get out more."

"She likes music—we both do."

"Maybe a concert, then. A movie, picnic, hiking, skating, dinner. Think about what she likes and then plan something."

"How long should I wait before I ask her out?"

"I don't know. A few weeks, maybe. In the meantime, talk with her, listen, let her know you care about what she's going through. Be there for her, and then make your move. It's time you had a life, Phil. Molly too."

As Phil walked home, he reminded himself not to wait too long to make his move. *Joe's right*, he thought, *it's time I had a life.*

Instead of going home, he turned around and strolled to the bakery to see what Molly was up to. During his walk, he took out his iPhone and started looking for concerts she might like in their neck of the woods. *Dash Fortran! I know she likes his music*, he thought. *We both do. I'll buy the tickets now, well in advance. That way, I'll have a deadline to get the courage up to ask her. I always work better with a deadline.*

He purchased the tickets on his cell phone and, with a bit of a bounce in his step, headed straight to Molly's Sunshine Bakery, humming a Fortran song.

Phil was feeling pretty good about himself, having confronted Jared and sent him packing. Joe had counseled him to ask Molly out in the future, which meant that Joe thought Phil might actually have a chance with her. And now he had tickets reserved for the two of them, which he knew she couldn't resist. *When to tell her about the tickets? Better wait a week or two*, he guessed. But what if, in the meantime, she planned something else for that date? He'd better ask her soon—but not today. Then again, he could tell her he'd gotten the tickets just to cheer them both up, make it sound like another "friend thing." That was safer. No rejection involved, no real spilling out of his feelings for her. Yes, that was what he would do.

Smiling, Phil rounded the corner and almost collided with Lyra, who was headed out on her afternoon break.

"Still basking in your triumph, I see. Good thing you didn't die of a broken nose or something during the night. How's it doing?"

"Never been better." Phil smiled. Lyra reached up to touch his nose. He winced. "Ow, be careful, Lyra."

"That's what I thought," Lyra remarked. "I'll never understand you guys settling things with fists."

"It worked. Jared left, didn't he?"

"And is that really a good thing?"

"Well, I think it is!" he came dangerously near to shouting.

"Hmm," Lyra concluded. Just as she'd suspected, Phil had fallen for Molly.

Phil sauntered into the bakery. Molly was mopping up a spill a four-year-old had left on the black-and-white checkered floor. "Hey, Phil," she said. "Back so soon?"

Phil made himself comfortable at his table. Molly sat down in a convenient chair next to his. "So how are you doing, Molly?"

"I've been better. I had a good chat with Joe this afternoon though, and I think he set me straight on some things."

"Like what?" Phil probed.

"Like it's not Jared's fault that God called him to do this missionary doctor thing. I need to get over being mad and just accept it and move on with my life. But how do I do that?"

"Day by day." The virtual tickets on his cell phone were starting to burn a hole in his pocket. When he could stand it no longer, he blurted, "I got us some tickets to see Dash Fortran in concert."

"What?" Molly looked at him quizzically.

"Yep. I figured we both needed something to cheer us up, and I knew you liked his music as much as I do." He cleared his throat. "I thought it would give us something fun to look forward to." Phil raised his eyebrows, questioning, hoping that she'd say she wanted to go.

"Oh, Phil, that was so sweet of you, but I don't think I'm up for that right now."

"It's months away. Don't worry; you'll feel better by then. Come on. Say you'll go with me." He turned on an extra helping of boyish charm, which seemed to do the trick.

Molly smirked. "Of course I'll go, if you'll stop that basset hound look."

"Actually, it's my boyish charm face." Inside, Phil was high-fiving himself and letting out a big *Woo-hoo!* "Great," was all he said on the outside. It was a date … sort of. At least it was a start.

Later that evening, Molly called Denise and recounted the recent events. It had been a few months since they'd last talked, and it felt good to hear her voice.

"I can't believe all this has happened with you and you haven't even called me! And what's wrong with that Jared? He should've married you years ago when he had the chance. I've got a three-day weekend coming up, and I could use a break from my classroom. How about I fly up Friday night? I miss you, Molly."

"I miss you too, Denise. A lot. Come on up. Just let me know when your flight gets in, and I'll pick you up."

"Frankly, I could use your advice too. Sean and I are going nowhere. What is it with these guys nowadays? They're so afraid to commit. I'll tell you all about it when I see you Friday."

"Love ya."

"Love ya more."

Molly hung up the phone. She felt better already.

Denise's plane landed on time, and Molly was waiting at the baggage claim as Denise came down the escalator and made a beeline for her. They hugged each other, emitting high-pitched squeals.

"Why did we wait so long to see each other?" Molly wondered.

"Well, between you and your 'carb shop,' and me and my thirty-two second graders, we've both been crazy busy. We'll just have to make up for lost time this weekend. Hey, I'm starved!"

"Me too! Let's go to Clyde's for dinner."

"I haven't been to Clyde's in years," Denise reminisced.

"It's as good as ever."

A short while later, the girls were sitting at a table at Clyde's overlooking the lake. Lights from Canterbury Heights reflected on the undisturbed water.

Clyde made his way over to the table. "Denise? Denise McDuff? Is that you?"

"Clyde! Long time no see."

"What have you been up to?"

"Well, I have thirty-two kids now."

"What?!"

"Yep, I'm a teacher in San Diego. I'm here visiting Molly for the weekend."

Looking at Denise, Clyde was reminded of her flowing auburn hair and striking green eyes, which had captivated him back in high school. He was happy to know she hadn't changed a bit. Here she was, back in town, at his restaurant. He'd blown his chances years ago. Maybe God was giving him another shot. "Well, it's good to see you back home, Denise."

"Yeah, it still feels like home." She looked around. "I love what you've done with the place."

"When I took over the restaurant for Dad, I figured it needed some updating. Can I get you ladies started with some drinks?"

"Iced tea for me," said Denise.

"Would you like to try my new tropical blend mango ice tea?"

"Did you say mango?"

"That's the stuff."

"Sure," Denise warbled.

"Make that two," Molly said. "Since when have you had mango ice tea?"

"Uh, it's brand-new. I'll go get your drinks started." Clyde walked away, wondering how he was going to make tropical tea. Good thing he had bought plenty of mangoes this week. They were, he remembered, always a favorite of Denise's.

While serving Denise's coconut shrimp and Molly's petite filet mignon, Clyde couldn't help overhearing Denise talking about some guy named Sean. It sounded to Clyde like she was about ready for a breakup. He found himself smiling as he brought another fresh but unnecessary basket of warm french bread and butter to the table.

Molly thanked him and turned to Denise. "Sounds like you're stuck in the same situation with Sean that I was with Jared: going nowhere."

"Yeah, at least Jared knows where he's going. Sean has no idea. He can't even commit himself to a brand of toothpaste. I'm sick and tired of waiting around for him to decide about us. My biological clock is about to detonate."

"Mine too. What is it with these guys?"

"Oh, no need to explode, ladies. Have some dessert instead," Clyde offered.

It was amazing what a weekend with a lifelong friend could do. Molly and Denise spent the whole time laughing, crying, and reconnecting. Why had Molly waited so long to reach out? It was refreshing to have someone reach back. The weekend ended with hugs at the airport and promises to stay in touch.

Molly walked back to her car feeling freer than she'd felt in a long, long time.

CHAPTER 9

Burgundy Tuxes and Other Humiliations

Unable to wait until the Fortran concert, Phil decided a miniature-golf challenge would suit them to a tee, especially since he considered himself an above-par contender.

"The idea is to keep your eye on the ball," Phil instructed Molly. "Swing lightly, bend your knees—that's right, like that. Now give it a good tap."

Molly's bright red golf ball went straight down the middle of the miniature-golf course green, through the windmill, and knocked Phil's blue one out of the way and stopped three inches from the hole.

Disgusted, Phil remarked, "Yes, just like that, except you were supposed to leave my ball where it was."

"Oops, was I? I guess you should have mentioned that before. I'm just learning, you know." She glanced past him at the orange sunset, which mimicked an expanse of ocean punctuated with lavender islands.

"Something tells me you've played the game before." Phil looked at her with narrowed eyes as his mouth turned downward into a skeptical frown.

"Maybe a time or two." Molly barely nudged her ball into the hole, stooped to pick it up, and blew the pretend dust off it as the mini-golf course bedecked itself in garish lights for the evening. "Care to make a little wager on our game?" Molly suggested slyly.

"You're on! What'll we play for?"

"How about loser buys dinner and dessert?" Molly challenged.

"Okay, but let's make the stakes a bit higher, shall we? Loser also has to tell the most embarrassing thing that's ever happened to her."

"You mean him," she corrected.

"Yeah, whatever. Deal?"

"Deal," said Molly, and they solemnly shook on it. Molly's hand was even softer than he remembered. Phil had to force himself to relinquish it.

At the next few holes, Molly didn't do as well, lulling Phil into a false sense of security. Along about the sixth, Phil caught a little sparkle in Molly's eyes as she teed off. The ball went through the middle of the castle door just as it opened. They could both hear that delightful clunking sound as the ball ran through a pipe and onto the green below, ending its journey as a hole in one.

"Yes! Yes!" Molly jumped in the air and cheered, her golf club raised above her head.

Phil looked down and let out a mock "Yippee," unenthusiastically twirling his index finger around in the air. "You're a shark. You know that, Molly?"

"Yes," was all she said, holding her club like a dancer would hold a cane, shuffling her feet sideways.

"Well, what I neglected to tell you was that I was the captain of our golfing team in high school."

"Phil, they didn't have golf teams in high school back then."

"Okay, we didn't, but if they had one, I would have been the captain. Now stand back, and look out."

Phil held his own throughout the rest of the game. On the last hole they were tied.

Molly's ball made it up and into the reluctant volcano after three tries, triggering a dramatic mechanized volcanic belch. Phil took four strokes, forfeiting his "captain of the golfing team" title by one shot.

"I'm feeling extra hungry now for some reason," Molly proclaimed.

"Yeah, yeah, yeah." Phil replied. "Whatever. Where would you like to go for dinner?"

"Someplace with fish on the menu," she said, her nose haughtily tilted upward, her putter pointing the way to the exit.

"Shark, maybe?"

"Very funny, Phil. How about Clyde's?"

"Sounds good to me, Captain. Clyde's it shall be."

At Phil's car, he stopped to take something out of the trunk. Phil handed her a gift, its fluffy pink tissue climbing out of the bag.

"What's this?" Molly asked.

"Well ..." he started to answer, but there was already tissue paper flying through the air.

Molly found a little stuffed bunny tucked inside, feather soft and oh so fluffy. Its floppy ears pleaded for her to cuddle it close. She took it from the bag and hugged it tight. "Aw, it's so adorable. What's this for?"

"Just a little something to cheer you up, something you can hold on to at night when things get tough. I don't know. I was walking by the toy store the other day, and he was thumping at me through the window, asking me to take him home to you. I couldn't refuse those eyes. He looks happier now, really. He was much sadder the other day."

"Aw, he's so sweet! Thank you, Phil. What should I name him?"

"How about Trigger?"

Molly frowned.

"Pickles? Hopalong? Jeeves? Welsh Rarebit? Thyroid? Poopsie? Icon? Fletcher? Fauntleroy? Bacon?"

Each suggestion was met with one progressively raised

eyebrow and a shake of her head. "Where do you come up with these things? You can't name a stuffed bunny Bacon or Thyroid or any of those. I shall have to think of a proper name for him later. Now let's get to Clyde's—I'm absolutely famished. Victory will do that to you, you know."

Phil opened the Bentley's door, and Molly slid onto the seat. The cobalt-blue interior matched Molly's shoes; she couldn't help but notice. "Is this the original interior on this beast?" she asked. "I just love that old car smell."

"Old car smell? I'll have you know my uncle had the seats, carpet, and headliner redone. It was all pretty worn out when he got it. He had the interior done in cobalt blue because it was my aunt's favorite color."

"What happened to your aunt?"

"She passed about ten years before he did. They never had any children. She died of cancer of some sort; I can't remember which kind. Uncle Ben really loved Aunt Alice. Up until the very end, he was right there by her side. I always looked up to them as my example of what a really good marriage would be like. They weren't materialistic. Didn't need a lot to make them happy, just each other.

"She had this intense gardening streak and was always out back with her hands in the dirt. Flowers, vegetables, and fruits galore. Weeds trembled at the sound of her voice, or at least it seemed that way by the looks of it. And she could make dinner out of almost nothing and make it so good you'd be back for thirds and fourths.

"Uncle Ben was a gentle soul, never in a hurry, but always quick with an encouraging word. He had such a love for baseball. I remember him listening to the game with his earphone on his transistor radio while Aunt Alice and I were watching TV. Every once in a while he'd give a whoop or holler when his team would score a run. It'd scare Aunt Alice and me to death." He paused, smiling. "He always had a tank full of tetra fish on the fireplace mantel. I used to love to watch them swim together in unison, like some kind of line dancing with fins. Ben and Alice were great people. I always enjoyed visiting them every summer. I miss them a lot these days. Uncle Ben always gave me the best advice."

"Kind of like Joe," Molly added.

"Kind of like Joe," Phil agreed. "Now let's head to Clyde's and see if he has any *shark* for you."

"You're just jealous because you had to resign as captain!"

"Yes, yes, I am." Phil nodded. "You know, this golf tournament really should have been the best two out of three."

"I'll take you on anytime," Molly said, asserting her championship prerogative.

At Clyde's, Phil watched Molly as she sampled her honey-glazed grilled salmon and rice pilaf. She closed her eyes. "Mmm …" Phil took advantage of the distraction and studied her face. So sweet, so innocent, so …

Molly opened her eyes and caught him staring. "Something wrong?"

"No, something right." Phil turned his attention to the halibut and twice-baked potato with bacon and cheese oozing out the top.

Betsy and Bob Peterson were seated at their usual Friday night table, across from them. "Now that is the kind of man Molly should be dating, if you ask me," Betsy observed.

"I don't remember asking you," Bob said casually, looking over the specials of the day.

"Well, you should have. I have a way of knowing these sorts of things."

"Oh, really. And you acquired this skill how?" Bob teased.

"Doesn't matter. I knew you were the one for me when we first met, didn't I?"

"All right, I'll give you that much."

"It's a match. Just look at the way he looks at her when she's speaking. Come on, Bob. Look."

"Betsy, let them have their privacy."

"And look at the way she throws her head back when he makes her laugh. She never did that with that other guy. Remember?"

"How could I forget? That's all I've been hearing you and Maggie McCreary yak about ever since."

"Well, not a lot happens in this small town. We women have to have something to talk about, you know."

"Yeah, yeah …" Bob replied. "Like how about the halibut on his plate?"

"Now who's being snoopy, hmm, Bob?"

Just then Molly and Phil burst into laughter.

"Ah, shoot! I missed something," whispered Betsy.

"Good thing, or you'd be laughing along with them, and then the jig would be up."

"You're right. I'd better be careful, or they'll know I'm listening."

"So, what do you think about Scott? He seems to be doing so much better these days." Bob tried to divert Betsy's attention with talk of their son, who had recently returned from the war with post-traumatic stress disorder.

"Yes, he is, and he and Violet are growing much closer. It does my heart good to see him taking an interest in his daughter for a change. Violet is beside herself with joy. Don't you think Violet's teacher, Dori, and Scott would make a great couple?"

"Oh, here we go again, Betsy. Do you always have to be matchmaking?"

"Yes, as a matter of fact I do. People used to pay good money for matchmaking services back in the day, you know. I could've made us filthy rich!"

"You could've made us something, but I'm not sure it would be rich."

"Oh, look! They're getting up. You made me miss their whole conversation."

Just then, Phil looked over and gave Betsy a wink.

"I think he found you out, Betsy," Bob chuckled.

"Oh, phooey," muttered Betsy.

Molly climbed into the front seat as Phil prepared to shut her door. He saw her reach over and grab the stuffed bunny and set it on her lap. He smiled widely as he walked around the back of the car to his side.

"Something?" Molly asked as she noticed his smile.

"Nothing."

"Come on, now. What is it?"

"Nothing. It's just that you look so cute with that rabbit on your lap."

"Well, I couldn't very well just let him sit there on the seat alone, and maybe risk him sliding off and getting hurt, now could I?"

Phil smirked, and she slapped him on the arm.

"He's a stuffed toy, Molly."

"Yeah, but stuffies have feelings, too. He was thumping at you through the window at the toy store. You know as well as I do that they come alive at night when we're sleeping and have a life of their own, don't you?"

"Huh?"

"You know it's true—you just don't want to admit it."

"Okay, when I was a kid, I used to think something like that too. I had this stuffed bookworm toy named Ted. He liked to hang with me whenever my brother Matt and I would read our comic books. Ted had little red reading glasses and at least a dozen legs. He liked to perch on my shoulder and would occasionally jump off and dive bomb my brother, making him lose his page. That Ted was a mischievous little rascal."

"Then you *do* understand. See, so that's why he has to ride on my lap. End of story."

"Okay, then," Phil murmured.

"Now for dessert, mister," Molly enthused.

"What do you feel like having?"

"Ice cream, maybe. Frankly, I'm tired of pastries."

"I wonder why." Phil savored the irony.

"I want something I don't usually make myself."

"How about gelato? There's a new gelato place that just opened on the east side of the lake," Phil suggested.

"Oh yeah, that's the stuff!"

As they arrived at the shop, A Lot o' Gelato, Molly reminded him that because he had lost the bet, he would now have to tell her the most embarrassing event of his life. He had been hoping she would forget about *that* part of the bet. They ordered extra big servings; Molly had pistachio and Phil ordered toasted almond. They sampled each others' flavors but settled down to their own.

"Okay, spill it, Phil. Let me hear about your greatest disaster."

"Do I have to?" he whined.

"Yes, it's part of the deal."

"Okay, Captain, but there are just so many to choose from."

"Pick the worst one," she insisted ruthlessly.

"Well, there was this girl in high school who was really nice. She was into the drama club, and yet she was just nerdy enough to be friendly to me."

"Yeah?" Molly encouraged as she leaned forward in her chair so as not to miss one syllable of the story.

"Well, after Ronnie stood me up for the senior ball, I got the bright idea of making her jealous. I decided to get tickets to the theatre in San Francisco to see *Les Misérables* and take Jan—that was the drama girl's name—with me. I knew it was a production she would want to see because they would be doing that play at the end of the school year. She was really excited to go, but her parents said she could only go to San Francisco if it was a double date, so she asked her best friend Donna, and I asked Mitch if they would tag along with us if I picked up the ticket costs. Donna and Mitch agreed, and thus began the night of infamy.

"I picked up Jan, and her bratty little six-year-old brother, Jason, jumped into my car and demanded to go with us. He had a penny in his hand and kept telling me he'd pay me if he could come along. He was messing around for quite a while in my car before Jan finally had to pick him up and drag him back to the house.

"Everything was going fine. We picked up Donna and Mitch. It was the first time I'd seen Mitch really dressed up. I don't know if he was going for the effect, but he had that Napoleon Dynamite look about him. We headed off to the city. It almost made up for not going to the senior ball with Ronnie. I was actually having a good time, and Donna and Mitch started cracking jokes in the backseat. Jan and I started laughing so hard that I started to miss our exit for the theatre. Jan noticed, and yelled, 'That's our turnoff!' With my usual lightning speed, I reacted and turned the car, but just a little too late. I hit the cement ridge at the edge of the ramp and we were airborne for a few seconds. When we finally touched down, it blew out both front tires on my dad's old Thunderbird. We all screamed and thought we were going to die. Luckily, there was no one in the lane next to us at that point. We came to rest on the side of the freeway exit. After checking to see if everyone was okay, I decided to find a service station that would have two tires, since there was only one in the trunk, and it was flat too. I scaled a cyclone fence and took off running to find some tires. I didn't know I was in the middle of the red light district. Here I was in a tux and bow tie—burgundy, no less—and all these ladies of the evening were yelling at me to come on back. I passed a few gas stations, and they were either closed or didn't have my tires. This was, of course, all before cell phones, so I did the only thing I could do at this point: find a pay phone, call my dad, and ask him to bring me the tires. He laughed so hard that I thought he'd bust a gut. I told him where the car was, and he said he'd meet me there. I ran rather briskly back to the car, surrounded by the cat calls and whistles from the street walkers.

"Jan and Donna had jumped ship, hailed a taxi, and taken their two tickets from the dashboard. When my dad got there, he was still laughing. The three of us guys changed the tires. By the time Mitch and I got to the play, it was in its last few minutes. Didn't make a lot of points with Jan—that's for sure. On the way home we stopped at a Chinese restaurant, where I promptly choked on a long, black mushroom—basically a strangler fungus—and Mitch had to give me the Heimlich maneuver to get it out. Let's just say it wasn't a pretty sight when the fungus came up and deposited itself on Jan's plate."

Molly's mouth got wider and wider as Phil told his story, until she finally burst out in a guffaw. "Are you serious?" she snorted, causing Phil to crack up and suddenly spit a burst of gelato across the table, spraying Molly in the face.

"And so the humiliation continues," Phil spluttered. This made them laugh even harder until finally he got a grip on himself, apologized, and used his napkin to clean up Molly's face.

"If this gelato wasn't so darn good, you'd be wearing some of mine about now," warned Molly.

Their eyes met, and for a few seconds they held each other's gaze. Molly could feel a quiver starting in her stomach that she hadn't felt in years. She dismissed it as the effect of really good gelato. After all, they were just friends, and she was getting over Jared. She realized that she hadn't thought of Jared all evening until now.

Phil felt it too, that awkward but oh-so-sweet feeling when two people's eyes meet and neither wants to look away.

Molly cleared her throat. "So how did the end of the date go?"

"I dumped Donna and Mitch off first, and then we pulled up in front of Jan's house. I was getting ready to walk her up to the front door—you know, to make sure she got in okay. I was resigned to the fact there was no way on earth I was getting a good-night kiss. Her seat belt got stuck, and we couldn't get it off. I leaned across, trying to unlock it, but it just wouldn't budge. Then I saw it: the penny her brother left as a token of his appreciation, stuck inside the seat belt's locking mechanism. I had to go up to the door and ask her mother for a pair of scissors to cut the belt off. Her little brother followed me back out to the car and kept asking, 'Did you kiss her? Did you kiss her yet?' I gave him a quarter to go back in the house and quit saying it. I sawed my way through the belt with the dull scissors. It took quite awhile. In the process I managed to accidentally snip a small hole in her dress. When she was finally free, I showed Jan her little brother's penny, still stuck in the locking mechanism, so that she wouldn't think I somehow trapped her on purpose.

"She was not amused and swiftly set off for the front door, thanking me for the 'interesting evening.' She never spoke to me again. I lucked out because it was such a mortifying date that she and Donna never mentioned it to anyone else at school. Saved my bacon. Once I saw them walking home in the pouring rain as I drove past. She and Donna were sloshing miserably from puddle to puddle. I pulled over and offered them a ride. Jan turned, looked at me, raised an eyebrow, and just went right on trudging along in the rain. So there you have it. One of my innumerable most embarrassing moments. Now it's your turn, Molly."

"Oh no, no, no! I'm not the one who lost the bet. I must say, though, that your experience with Jan was truly humiliating. I'd like to hear more of these stories."

"Yeah, well, I'd better be getting you home soon. You have to get up 'many earlies' tomorrow."

"The work of a baker is never done, I'm afraid."

They walked to the car, and Phil held open Molly's door.

"Hey, what happened to your dad's Thunderbird anyway?"

"That's a whole 'nother story. Some guy stole it, and the steering went out on it while he was making his getaway. He got in an accident and tried to sue my dad for having faulty steering in the car. I'm pretty lucky the steering didn't go out on me on that fateful night. I dodged that one, at least."

"What? He tried to sue?"

"Yep. Pretty crazy world we're living in. I figured it was poetic justice for stealing the car. The judge luckily agreed with me on that one. My dad junked the car and bought a Land Cruiser. Loved that one! What kind of car did you drive as a kid?"

"I saved up and bought a very used Volkswagen Thing. It was so weird that it was cool, you know? I had so much fun with it. Speaking of cars, you've gotta let me pay for the repairs on the Bentley that Jared caused when he kicked it."

"Don't worry about it. It's just a car. Now I don't have to be upset when it gets its first dent. Jared took care of that for me. I'm actually using it a lot more now that it has battle scars. I'm kinda grateful that he dented it."

"But, Phil, it's a collector's item, an antique. Please let me pay to have it fixed."

"No, I kind of think of it as a reminder of my first successful fight. I'm thinking of getting another one on the other side to match."

"You're a complete nut! You know that, don't you?"

"Yep, and I wouldn't have it any other way."

They pulled into Molly's driveway. "I haven't had this much fun in awhile—well, since Ronnie's wedding reception, I guess. Thanks, Phil, for dinner, dessert, and for cheering me up." She held the plush rabbit up to her face. "And for my little friend here." Molly reached out and gave Phil another one of those lasts-a-little-longer-than-necessary hugs like he'd received outside their hotel rooms after Ronnie's wedding. He'd never forget that hug.

As Molly went inside and closed the door behind her, she leaned against it and held her honey-colored bunny up by its front paws, and said, "I think I'll call you Philabuster. Then I can call you Phil or Buster for short."

CHAPTER 10

Saved by a Personal Casio Keyboard

Molly's weathered boat dock was about a quarter of the way around the lake from the bakery. Until today, Molly had never been there with anyone but family. Phil and she had been gliding across the lake in his uncle's old green canoe, cutting silently through the stained glass surface.

"Not a breeze to be seen today," observed Molly. "Doesn't it remind you of ice skating across a freshly frozen pond after the first big freeze?"

"Uh, not really, since I've never ice skated in my life."

"What? Never ice skated? We'll just have to fix that next winter," Molly threatened.

"I knew I shouldn't have said anything," Phil said under his breath. "Hey, there's that old dock. We can have our picnic there."

"Well, I don't know. That *is* my special spot. I only share it with family. Jared hasn't even been there."

"Oh come on, Molly. It's just a dock."

"Just a dock? Just a dock! It's my most intimate thinking place. I've always gone there to nurse my wounds, make decisions, and weigh things out."

"Did you go there when you broke up with Jared?" Phil asked.

"Yes, as a matter of fact I did, but I didn't really have to."

"Why not?"

"I guess because I had you to talk to, and I really didn't have to make any decision. He made it for me when he made his final choice." Molly looked down at her left hand, devoid of the short-lived engagement ring, and sighed. "Hey, wait a minute. You're heading toward *my* dock!"

"Yep, I sure am. I can be honorary family for the day."

"Well, I'll share it with you this once, but just for today, and you can't go telling anyone else about it, okay?"

Phil agreed, and they made their way to the dock. He hopped out and dragged the canoe onto the shore.

Molly took his hand as he helped her and the picnic basket out of the watercraft.

"Let's have our lunch on the dock," Phil suggested. What do you think?"

"Sounds good to me," Molly replied. "I'll set out the blanket."

A few ducks paddled by hopefully, trolling for leftovers.

"Just as I suspected: we have company. Good thing I brought some day-old bread from the bakery in case we had guests." Molly put her hand into the bag and flung what she thought of as stale bread to the ducks, who bobbed about, greedy for the larger pieces. "Hang on, guys, there's plenty for everyone."

"I can't believe you're feeding them perfectly good bread. Heck, your bread would be good for a week, I bet. It never has the chance to go stale, I eat it so fast. In fact, I think it's better the second day."

"Do you, now? Well, let's see." Molly tossed a piece of bread at Phil, who caught the edge of it in his mouth.

He took a big bite. "There you go, throwing food again. Really, Molly, such manners," he chided.

"I guess I should have said 'duck' first, huh?"

"Very funny. Now what's in that pick-a-nick basket?"

"Careful, Yogi, don't spill the strawberry pie."

"Strawberry pie? Let me at it!"

"Not so fast. There's the lunch part first. We're having Chinese chicken salad, my ancient family recipe. I'd tell you what's in it, but then I'd have to kill you."

"Hey, but I thought I was honorary family today."

"Not that honorary. Now sit." Molly served up the chicken salad from her favorite bowl, a hand-painted ceramic with two happy bunny faces gazing up from the bottom. The fluted edges always made her think of the endless ruffles her mother would sew on special dresses she made for her as a little girl. "And there's homemade strawberry lemonade. Can you get the lock-lid bottle out of the basket for me, and the glasses?"

"Whoa, you really know how to pack a picnic, woman! And how'd you know I like strawberries?"

"I seem to recall you really enjoying some chocolate ones." They shared a smile, each remembering the fateful strawberries they'd shared. "Would you pour, please?"

As they munched on their salad, Phil asked, "So, tell me your life story, Molly."

"What? No one's ever asked me that before. What brought this up?"

"Well, since we're honorary family today, I just thought we should get to know each other a little better. Come on, Molly. Everybody's got a story."

"Hmm, where do you want me to start?"

"How about when you were a kid, or a teenager? Wherever you want."

Molly knew she could trust Phil, but she wasn't used to sharing her life this way with anyone. "Phil, I'm kind of afraid to share. You may not like what you hear. I don't know how to begin."

"Okay, that's easy enough. I'll just start asking some questions, and you'll get the hang of it. Start by telling me how you became a Christian."

"Hmm, that's an interesting story. Okay, here goes. Let's see ... when I was about seven years old, I started realizing that there was something different about me. I was a shy little thing and quite full of fears of all kinds. Before school every day, I'd get stomachaches. I had no idea why or just what I was afraid of. I often felt like a stifling wet blanket of oppression and doom hung over my head and wrapped around my shoulders. It was frightening. I had no idea that I was depressed and full of anxiety. Heck, I didn't even know what those things were. I just knew there was something wrong with me. Then the panic attacks came, and I was really terrified and thought I was dying. My parents didn't know what to do. I didn't tell them much and tried to pretend everything was all right. Then the throwing up happened, most days before school."

"Oh, Molly, I had no idea you had those kinds of things going on. What did you do?"

"There wasn't much I *could* do at that point. I just lived through it. My parents took me to all kinds of doctors, and they ran a ton of tests and never could find anything wrong, which made me feel even more horrible. This must be something that had no cure, I thought. I would just have to live with it. Thankfully, my parents talked to me about God from the time I can remember. I had a good Christian background to lean on. I prayed so hard for so many years for God to take this burden away from me. I lost weight and eventually had malnutrition. I really thought I was going to die of this thing that didn't even have a name.

"Years went by, and the throwing up stopped. I would have occasional relief from the depression, but it always ended up coming back. Then the summer before my senior year in high school, I was so depressed that I finally started planning to take my own life."

"What? Oh, Molly, I wish I had known you then. I would've talked you out of it." He laid his hand on hers. "So what happened? You obviously didn't kill yourself."

"Thank God that my best friend, Denise, was there for me. She knew I was depressed but didn't know that I was planning to overdose on sleeping pills as soon as I could get my hands on some. We were talking, and she showed me some pictures from her church's latest youth group activity. God can use anything when we're at the end of our rope to make us want to climb back up. One picture was of this adorable guy with dimples beyond all reasoning. I think I told you about him on the plane while we were going to Ronnie's wedding."

Phil smiled, not only at her description but also because he himself possessed exceptional dimples, and he knew it.

"I saw his smile, and for some reason I wanted to keep on living to see it in person. I started going to Denise's youth group, and I eventually left my parents' very formal church and went to her church full time. I met Rob, the dimple guy, and I was really head over heels for him. It was the weirdest thing: I could go just about anywhere and there he would be—the record store, the Autorama, you name it. Then he was in a play at church, and I literally couldn't take my eyes off of him the entire time. He was not only handsome but was one of the funniest guys I'd ever met. I can't resist funny."

The spark in her eye gave Phil a surge of hope.

"I really loved who Rob was and what he stood for. Between Denise, the kids in our youth group, our youth pastor, and Rob's influence, it wasn't long before I committed my life to Jesus and never looked back."

"So your depression and anxiety stopped when you became a Christian?"

"Heck no. I just knew then that I could never take my own life. That wasn't up to me anymore. I was God's now, and He'd just have to get me through it. I started reading my Bible every day, and I still do. I memorized scripture like somebody was going to take the book away, and I prayed long and hard daily. The depression let up a bit at this time. Rob asked me out, and I was walking on air. We went out a few times and had so much fun together, and then, like I told you on the plane, he told that girl that he never went out with me. I was so devastated that someone I loved so much would be ashamed to admit that he'd been dating me. I wore that wound for years. When I met Jared, it healed up some, but it's still a very painful scar to this day. Rob will never know how much he hurt me. I never had the guts to confront him, which is what I should have done. Instead, I crept back under that familiar old, smothering blanket that I was so accustomed to.

"Years went by, and nobody but the few people closest to me knew what I was going through with my deep depression. But they didn't really understand, wanting me to 'just snap out of it.' Even though I tried, I just couldn't—I couldn't overcome it. I hid it very well and acted happy even when I was in the pits of despair. But there was God, ready to handle it one day at a time. I felt like Job. I wore my Bible out so much that I had to have it rebound twice over the years. I can now say I'm grateful for all that agonizing because I have at my disposal a scriptural arsenal of weapons to fight with.[1] Little did I know how strong He was making me, and how I'd be able to empathize with lots of people going through the same thing."

"Do you still struggle with it now? Are you just putting on a happy face? Because if you are, you've got us all fooled at the bakery."

"I thank God every day that I'm past that time in my life. God really used Jared to help me realize that I needed help. He finally asked me one day in college, 'Why are you putting yourself through this when there's a way out?' I thought he meant I was crazy and needed a shrink, but he explained something to me, and it finally sunk in. He said, 'If you had a migraine headache, wouldn't you take some medication to make it go away?' I said sure. He went on to say, 'Well, what's the difference? What you have is clinical depression. It's chemical. You've had it for years, not just when you had something tragic happen. You've suffered under this weight all your life. It's time to do something about it

[1] See the appendix for a collection of verses.

now. You have many more years ahead of you. Why suffer your way through life when you don't have to? Let's get you in to see your doctor. Today.'

"I don't know why, but I went for it. I hadn't gotten help before because I was afraid that I wouldn't be trusting God, that my faith just wasn't strong enough to make this go away, and I'd be copping out getting medication. My doctor immediately put me on an antidepressant and anti-anxiety medication. I went in for some counseling, and within a few weeks I felt free! It's the way most people feel every day of their life, but to me it was the greatest freedom I'd ever experienced. To be 'normal' wasn't normal to me. It was inexpressible joy. I could finally, for the first time in my life, *choose* not to worry about something. Worry and depression no longer had control over me! I will *never* take this freedom for granted. I may have to be on this medication for the rest of my life, but diabetics and heart patients take medications daily. What's the difference? I'm so grateful to feel normal."

"Man, that is some story, Molly. I had no idea. I'm really glad you got help. I guess Jared wasn't such a bad guy after all. God really used him to get you the help you needed."

"Yes, He did. I can't believe how I've gone on for so long. I'm sorry, Phil. But now you know the truth about me."

"Don't worry, Molly, your secret's safe with me. I won't ever tell anyone about your depression or having to be on medication."

"I know I can trust you, Phil, but I don't care if everyone knows that I take meds for depression. It doesn't matter what people think. Those who would object don't understand what it's like to face that kind of battle every single day and night. It's nothing to be ashamed of, and it's everything to be grateful to God for. I've told quite a few other women I know about getting on antidepressants, and it's very freeing. I don't know why we feel like spiritual wimps when we have to get help. I think it's just another tactic the enemy uses to keep us from being free." Molly paused. "Now, my dear Phil, it's your turn. Tell me your story."

"Well, I wasn't always the handsome, dapper young man you see before you today. I was once … a geek," he whispered. "No, really, it's the truth!"

Molly fell backward on the blanket in hysterics. "You, of all people! I would never have suspected."

"Ah, 'tis strange but true. My idea of a good time was drinking Mountain Dew and playing Atari with my best bud Mitch. I was both gawky and awkward, so I coined the term 'gawkward.' I'm rather proud of it really, being socially inept and all. Thankfully, Mitch was almost as gifted in the art of nerdery. You can imagine how we were always a real hit with the ladies. We never went to senior ball. I was supposed to go with Ronnie, but she changed her mind at the last minute when Linebacker Boy called and asked her out. With him being the captain of the football team and all, it would further elevate her status, so she obviously had to break our date. I had the tux and the corsage, and I'd even rented a limo. I'd used my paper route money I'd been saving up. She gave me only a few hours notice, and so I couldn't cancel the limo. Mitch and I rode around town in it, me in my tux and him in his marching band uniform. Too bad we didn't know your friend with the saxophone; he could've made our big night out even more entertaining. We drank every soft drink in the limo. The driver felt sorry for us and pulled over to get us another six pack of Mountain Dew. We got out to stretch our legs, but mainly to be seen getting out of a limo by some sophomore girls who were hanging out in front of the convenience store. Just then, when I was strutting over to them, I was hit in the chest by an angry frog. For real."

Molly wiped the tears from her eyes. It had been a long time since she had laughed so hard.

"No, I'm serious! Never did know where he came from—some nearby pond, I guess. It startled me so much that I screamed like a girl and threw my hands up in the air, yelling, 'Get it off! Get it off!' The girls laughed their heads off, and so I played it up that I did it all on purpose, just to make them laugh. Word spread fast, and the next week at school, the kids started calling me Frogman. I never did live that down. Humiliation: I live for it. To this day, frogs just freak me out."

"You are a total nut, you know," Molly squeaked. "So how did you start your spiritual journey?"

"Well, it all started with my personal Casio keyboard and Mitch's ukulele."

"What? Were you playing gospel songs?"

"No, mostly Michael Jackson music. We thought we'd be real chick magnets, but it turns out we were more like chick maggots for all the attention we got from the ladies. We kept it up anyway, and one day some of the 'nice kids' heard us playing and came up to hang out with us. They were so different that Mitch and I thought there was something wrong with them. They were just so nice, it seemed too good to be real, or so we thought. Turns out they were part of a Christian group, Young Life, and they just happened to need a Casio and ukulele player to lead their music. Coincidence? I think not. We went to their youth group and liked the people so much that we kept coming back. They talked about Jesus loving everybody, and I took that to mean even nerds. It finally clicked, and I realized that God accepted me for who I was. I remember kneeling down beside my bed one night and telling God I really needed Him. I knew I'd been sinning in my thoughts, since no one actually wanted to sin *with* me, but I knew I needed to clean up my act in so many ways, and I knew I would never be good enough on my own. I think that was what held me back for so long, thinking I'd come to Him when I got myself together. I felt so unworthy to be loved, especially by the one who made me and knew my faults and failures all too well. But I had it all backward. Instead of me cleaning up my act to be acceptable to Him, Jesus took me just as I was and helped me to make those changes I couldn't make on my own."

"Profound, Phil. So that's how you got so handsome and dapper?"

"Precisely."

"Tell me about your family," Molly urged.

"Not much to tell, really. My parents loved me. I knew that from the time I was little. Mom took my brothers and me to church as kids, until we rebelled in junior high. She tried bribing us with comic books and Slurpees if we'd go to church without complaining. It was a formal church—like a sedative, really, not much life or joy demonstrated there. We did get some of the basics but missed the point. I don't ever remember them talking about salvation or how you actually make it to heaven. It all pointed toward following rules and somehow being good enough. I knew I never could be so I just gave up, until I got the rest of the story about Jesus being good enough in my place and taking the punishment that I deserved. I tried getting this across to my dad, but he got really defensive.

"Dad had a drinking problem. It wasn't every day, but it snuck up on you, and just when you thought he wasn't drinking anymore, *wham!* He'd come home late after drinking with the guys. He and Mom would start arguing. She'd always manage to incite his wrath with the phrase, 'Oh, Harry, you've been drinking again!' He'd accuse her of being holier-than-thou along with a lot of other choice words, and there we were, off to the races again. After all the words they never should've said, when Dad had sobered up, everyone pretended that nothing ever happened, so nothing ever got solved. At least not until Mom had finally had enough. She told him he had to choose between our family and his booze. Mom actually had us kids packed up before he knew she really meant business. Dad finally got help through AA, and they've spent the last fifteen years rebuilding their relationship. I decided at a young age that I'd never drink anything stronger than Mountain Dew. I don't want to end up like that. I vowed my children would never have to grow up with an alcoholic father. If I never start, I never have to stop."

A brief silence ensued until Phil queried, "Hey, whatever happened to that strawberry pie?"

Chapter 11

Go Fly a Kite

Molly walked to the bakery window. "The wind's just not letting up the last few days. It's going to blow all the pretty leaves off my liquid amber tree before I've even had a chance to enjoy them," she complained.

"Yes, it's wreaked havoc on Mrs. McCreary's cosmos patch; all their long stems have been bent in half by the wind," Lyra commiserated.

"Oh, come on now, ladies. It's not that bad. It's perfect kite-flying weather," Phil said, expounding on the proverbial silver lining.

"I haven't done that since I was a kid," Molly said.

"Then we should do it this afternoon," Phil suggested.

"Like I have time," said Molly.

"I can handle the bakery while you two crazy kids run off. Go fly a kite!" Lyra shooed them to the door.

"Are you sure, Lyra?" asked Molly.

"I've got you covered," Lyra replied with a wink.

"Don't you have to work, Phil?"

"I told you I set my own work schedule," Phil said.

"I'll make sure Pastor Vicente's wife, Estrella, gets her order of pan dulce for church tomorrow. Now scoot!" Lyra said as she opened the door.

They walked to Phil's house to get the kites. In the garage they found the skeletons of two forlorn kites well past their expiration date. "These are ancient," Molly noted.

"As a matter of fact, they are. These were uncovered in an Egyptian tomb and were part of King Tut's private kite collection, once lost in a major sandstorm."

"Yeah, right, Phil; I've read about them in *National Geographic*." Molly rolled her eyes.

"But really, Dad and I used to make kites all the time when I was a kid. I saved the best two. They're kinda falling apart, but nothing that a little glue and paper can't fix."

They took the dilapidated kites and supplies into the kitchen for repair.

"I want mine to look like a flying pie with a latticework crust on it." She took the paper and started sketching a steaming apple pie.

"Fine for you," Phil said. "Mine's gonna be Mario with an appetite for pastry." Phil drew the much-loved video game character holding a knife and fork.

"Yeah, we'll see about that." Molly grabbed the felt pens Phil had taken out of his drawer and began shading in the elaborate crisscrossed crust. She finished it with steam rising from the top.

Phil was not to be outdone. His rendition of Mario was surprisingly accurate right down to the "M" on his red cap—no doubt the result of many hours at the control pad. Mario had a lean and hungry look.

They rummaged through Phil's rag bag in the garage for suitable kite tails. "Oh, what is this?" Molly held up a pair of old boxer shorts.

Phil snatched it from her hand. "Uh, you didn't see that." He gave it a backward toss over his head and willed his face not to turn red.

Molly snickered, "What else do you have in there, Phil?"

"Never mind. Here's an old sheet. This'll work just fine." He tore it into thin strips and tied them to the kites. "Now for my secret weapon." Phil found his old kite reelers hanging on pegboard hooks. "My dad made these. They're designed to feed out string as you crank the handles. You can reel it in by reversing direction. It keeps your string from getting tangled too, with this metal feed loop made from an old coat hanger. My dad could make anything out of next to nothing."

"Cool! And I see you have two of them. You must be willing to share your secret weapon, then."

"Well, I have to make it fair. Let's head off to Rambling Oaks Park. I'll show you how to really fly a kite."

"You're on," Molly accepted the challenge.

They meandered down Main Street, kites in hand, oblivious to stifled chuckles brought on by the sight of their rather unusual-looking kites and the conspicuous absence of children in tow. By the lake, Pastor Joe, who had been fishing unsuccessfully all morning, caught sight of them jostling and smiled. "Attaboy, Phil," he said quietly to himself. "Looks like you're making your move. Leave it to Phil to come up with kite flying." He felt a sudden tug on his line. "Well, how about that? Looks like I caught one too."

As they approached the park on Cherry Street, Mrs. McCreary looked out of her bent glass picture window and smiled as Phil and Molly passed by, kites fluttering like eager birds awaiting their freedom.

An old oak tree beckoned. Its two swings with weathered wooden seats swung gently in the wind, as if manned by children of years gone by. Phil glanced at Molly. "Ya wanna?"

Molly needed no encouragement and had already started scampering over to the highest of the two swings. "Whee! I haven't done this in years. Come on, Phil." She watched her cute red loafers pointing skyward as she swung forward.

Not to be outdone, Phil sat on the lower swing and backed up to launch himself forward like a slingshot.

Molly threw her head back, laughing. "I feel like a kid again."

"Me too," Phil replied.

Their swings very quickly got in sync. They shared a glance, and neither could look away. Phil reached out his hand to Molly, and she grabbed it. She felt more alive than she had in years. There was a delicious tickle rising from her heart that expressed itself in her laughter. Just as suddenly, Phil's swing got out of rhythm, and he nearly jerked her out of her seat. They didn't let go, collided, and wound up face-to-face.

"Promise me you'll never grow up," Molly said softly.

"Only if you never do."

At that moment, Molly realized that she was falling in love with Phil. His youthful exuberance awakened the little girl in her that had long since fallen asleep. She would never forget riding those swings together.

She giggled as they jumped from their swings and headed back to the path.

"This is a good spot," Phil decreed.

"Actually, I think over there would be a better spot." She pointed a few yards away.

"Fine then; you have your spot, and I have mine. Let's see whose kite takes off first."

"Care to make a little wager on that?" Molly asked with a smug expression.

"I'm not much of a gambling man, but since this is a sure thing, name your wager, Muffin."

"Well, since I'm going to win, I say you have to learn to ice skate," Molly taunted.

"Since you're going to lose, you have to wash and wax my Bentley."

"Great, humiliation for the loser—which we both know will be you." Molly folded her arms in defiance. She kicked off her shoes and dug her toes into the lush grass.

"You're stalling, probably out of fear would be my guess. Can't say I blame you." Phil searched the sky for menacing branches. His kite caught an unexpected gust of wind and launched itself before Molly could even ready hers. Mario was up and darting back and forth, looking down on Molly's kite in disdain. "Personally, I prefer Turtle Wax, and watch the windows. There's nothing worse than that waxy buildup, ya know."

"Harrumph," was her reply.

After many failed attempts at launching, Molly was getting winded. Just when she thought it was a go, the kite would suddenly take a nosedive straight into the grass. Finally she succumbed to Phil's offer to help her. He held her kite up high while keeping his own line taut. "Just one more try, Muffin. Run like the wind." The kite immediately caught air and snapped right out of his hand, resonating like a paper drum. "There you go. I knew you could do it—with my expert help, of course."

They flew their kites parallel to each other for a few minutes until an unexpected gust caught Molly's and snapped the string. Her apple pie sailed away from Mario's awaiting utensils.

"Aw, Phil, my kite is flying away!"

"I'll see if I can catch it." He handed her his kite reeler and ran after the errant kite, which seemed to be destined for foreign lands.

Molly watched him disappear over the rise of a hill. A few minutes later he returned empty-handed and crestfallen. "I tried, Molly, but she got away." He couldn't help but fear that this was a foreshadowing of things to come. He forced away the premonition.

"I'm so sorry, Phil. I know that kite was special to you."

"Wind happens, Molly. Not much we can do about it. Looks like Mario will have to fly solo. But fear not, I have a special kite-flying technique that for many years has been kept top secret—along with the reelers. Only the most elite kite pilots would dare to attempt such a feat. In fact, it's all about feet."

"There you go again. So show me already."

"Okay, so first I'll take my shoes off." He stepped out of his Topsiders, sat down on the ground, and patted the grass next to him. Molly joined him. "Observe!" He lay down on his back, bent his left knee, and placed his right ankle sideways on top of his bent knee.

"What are you doing?"

"Trust me, King Tut did this all the time."

"You are certifiable!"

"You dare to mock the Ancient Egyptian Kite Rite?"

"Uh, yes I do."

"Silence! You have spoken enough foolishness. Now, do as I do," Phil ordered.

Molly reclined and assumed his position, snickering.

"Here comes the tricky part. You must fly the kite between your toes."

"What?"

"Yes, like thus. Observe." He put the kite string between his first and second toes of his right foot and straightened out his right arm to provide an impromptu pillow for Molly's neck to rest upon.

She moved in closer to his side. "Ah, this is the life," she murmured. The kite circled a bit downward, and Phil had to tug it in a bit until it caught an updraft.

"Looks like this is the lazy man's way to fly a kite." She poked him in the side with her elbow.

"Nah, it takes years and years of intensive training to perfect. I assure you it's a very difficult and dangerous art."

"Let me try it!"

"Are you sure you're ready for this?"

"I live for danger," Molly assured him. "Who else do you know that spends most of her time with her head in an oven?"

"Good point, Molly. Okay, careful now … slowly …" He moved the kite string cautiously over to her magenta-painted toes with his foot.

Her eager toes grasped the string. "This is fun," she squealed. "It's a cinch!"

"Oh, really, now? We'll see about that."

"What could possibly go wrong?" she asked as the kite took a dip downward and started to spiral out of control. "Oh, no, what do I do? What do I do?"

"Watch and learn, Grasshopper." Phil took the string back and mysteriously righted the kite.

"How'd you do that?" Molly gasped, thoroughly impressed.

"Ancient Egyptian secret."

The two of them lay back and enjoyed the breezy afternoon light filtering through tree branches in the gnarled oak trees nearby. A comfortable silence ensued as Mario scouted in the distance for a runaway pie.

"I could stay like this all day," Molly said softly, snuggling a bit closer to Phil's side. "When was the last time I had a chance to just relax and enjoy the sky and the breeze? I really needed this, Phil. Thanks."

"You work way too hard, Molly. Have you ever thought of hiring another person so you'd have more free time?"

"Well, I have been wondering lately what it would be like to take time off now and then. How do you manage having free time, Phil?"

"That's the beauty of working from home. I can plan my work schedule around what I want to do. Sometimes I work really early in the morning, sometimes I stay up late. I love having the flexibility. I can work super long hours for a couple days and then take time off. As long as I'm meeting my deadlines, no one cares."

A little blond-headed boy with a face full of freckles who often frequented the bakery with his parents walked up to Phil and Molly, who were still lying on the ground. "Whatcha doing, Miss Molly?" he asked.

"We're flying an ancient Egyptian kite in the traditional way King Tut used to fly his kite, Toby. It's called Tomokitee," she replied.

"Really? Can I try it?"

"Sure," Phil offered. He and Molly stood up and Toby took

their place in the grass. "Here you go, Toby. Let me help you get started."

"Thanks," Toby said. "This is so cool. Wait till I tell my friends." Toby must have had the knack for the ancient art of Tomokitee because the kite danced happily in the air all the while.

"I've got more planned for us this evening. How about we head over to the theater?" Phil said.

"Sounds wonderful, but what about your kite and your dad's kite reeler?"

"I think Toby could really get some use out of them. What do you think, Toby?"

"Really? I'll take good care of them."

"I know you will. Have fun!"

Molly looked at Phil in wonder as they walked away. "That was your dad's special kite and reeler. Why did you do that, Phil?" she questioned.

"Seemed the right thing to do. Every kid should have a kite, ya know. We can always build new ones, right?"

"I guess we can," replied Molly as she picked up the second kite reeler and then reached over and took Phil's hand.

CHAPTER 12

Wax On, Wax Off

Molly arrived early the following morning, eager to get the whole ordeal over with. Phil was pleasantly surprised to see her decked out in her almost Daisy Duke cutoffs and red button-down shirt tied in the front. Mouth agape, he gestured for her to come in, almost tripping on his tongue as he tried to speak.

"Good morning," she practically sang.

"It is now," Phil crowed.

"Well, I'd better get right to work washing and waxing old Matilda."

"Is that what you call her? Her name is actually Floretta. I thought I'd introduced her earlier."

"No, actually you haven't. Floretta it is then. Now let's get this done."

"*Let's*? Who said anything about 'let's'?"

"I figured since you're taller, you could at least help me reach the top of the roof."

"Oh, all right, if I must."

Molly grabbed her bucket, soap, and sponge from the front porch and headed around the side of the house. Unable to take his eyes off her, Phil unwittingly tripped over the hose he had neglected to roll up a few days ago. He landed on all fours.

Molly heard him fall. She turned to find him pretending to search for something on the lawn.

"Oh, here it is—my lucky leaf." He held up an insignificant bit of foliage.

"Yeah, right." She strolled to the side yard and waited for Phil and his lucky leaf to bring out the car. He'd need more than his lucky leaf.

Molly started to fill her bucket with water and was just getting ready to pour in the soap when Phil held up his hands in mock horror. "No, not the ordinary dish soap on Floretta! You've got to be kidding! I use only the finest automotive wash on her. She's delicate, you know. A princess among vehicles."

"Come on, Phil. She's just a car."

"Oh! Just a car?" he repeated. "What you said!" Phil bellowed. "Uncle Ben will be turning over in his grave. Just a car? And I suppose your stuffed rabbit is *just* a stuffed animal?"

"Now you've gone too far, Phil! Give me the precious soap and let me get on with this."

"Use only a quarter cup to a bucket of water," he instructed. "Anything more will scald her delicate complexion."

Molly put her hands on her hips and leaned forward. "Really?" she challenged.

Phil smiled smugly. "And she prefers to be sponged counterclockwise because she's British, and you know how they like to drive on the opposite side of the road," he said, pleased with his logic.

"Whatever." She sighed in exasperation. "You're going to make this as torturous as possible, aren't you?"

"Who, me?" he asked innocently. "Would I do something like that? I wouldn't think of asking you to do anything more than I would do for the lovely Floretta. Oh, you missed a spot," he teased.

"You mean this spot, right here?" She threw a loaded sponge into his unsuspecting face.

"That's it! This means war!" He grabbed the hose as she scrambled for the lost sponge and reloaded. "I mean it, Molly. Put...the... sponge...down, and no one gets hurt."

The neighbors on the west side of the fence were peering over the pickets, wondering what was going on. When she saw Molly in those shorts, Mrs. Forsythe grabbed Mr. Forsythe by the collar and dragged him away to the side door of the garage and into the house. "That's enough for you, George," she hissed.

"Ah, and just when things were getting good," he complained as he headed up the stairs, hoping to watch from the spare bedroom window.

"George, come away from there!" Martha scolded.

"Can't a man do his crossword puzzle in peace?"

"That's not a crossword puzzle you're looking at."

"He must mean business. He just took off his shirt!" George exclaimed.

"What? Let me see!" Martha pushed him aside.

"Now who's the busybody?"

"Oh, my," said Martha, her hand to her throat.

They both watched, riveted to the window pane.

"You wash, I'll rinse," Phil suggested.

"Yeah, right. Not on your life, Phil. Put the hose down and let me get my job done. Just set it down and walk away...slowly."

It looked like Phil was going to comply. He reluctantly bent over, seemingly to put down the hose, when all of a sudden he took aim and fired full blast on Molly. She shrieked and threw the sponge with all her might. The sudsy sponge hit Phil square in the face again. "That should be good for your complexion too," she said, shaking the water out of her hair.

George and Martha were howling with laughter by this time. Phil and Molly could hear them right through the window. Phil looked over at them and gave a good-natured squirt in their general direction, daring them to come out and join the war effort.

Martha pulled down the shade as George went to the next window to continue watching the battle.

The water fight raged on as Phil took hold of not only the hose, but Molly's favorite oversized sponge. "Whatcha gonna do now, huh?" he taunted, very proud of himself.

"This!" Molly shouted as she flung the entire bucket of water and soap at Phil, covering every square inch of him with suds. Phil's mouth dropped open in shock as she flung the bucket again, causing the remaining dregs of soapy water to land in his gaping mouth. Molly put down her bucket and ran toward the front of the house for cover, laughing hysterically.

"Can you believe that?" Martha gasped, looking over George's shoulder. "That girl has spunk!"

"That girl's got a lot more than spunk," George noted.

Phil muttered and spat out the fancy-pants soap. "Bleah! That stuff is nasty!" He raised the hose to rinse out his mouth just as it was jerked out of his hands from the front yard.

He headed out front to assault Molly as the Forsyths ran to yet another window for a view of the front yard. "Truce! Truce!" Phil feigned.

"No truce, Sweetie Pie, until you quit telling me how to wash your car."

"Okay, okay! I'll stop, Muffin," he said as he walked over and hugged her tightly, getting as much soap as possible all over her without neglecting her face. She tried to get away but wriggled in vain.

"Ugh! That stuff tastes disgusting. Poor Floretta!" Molly sputtered.

"Try having a whole mouth full of that soap flying at you. Give me that hose. I've gotta wash it out of my mouth."

"Poor Phil. I'm sorry, Sweetie Pie." She repented and handed him the hose.

He rinsed and spat a few times, and got the soap out of his hair and eyes.

"Ah, our first fight," she said sweetly.

"Well, it certainly won't be our last," he said as he turned the hose on her.

Eventually the Bentley did get washed and dried, and now it was time for waxing.

"Now here's how you do it," Phil directed while Molly folded her arms and glared menacingly.

"So you're at it again, I see," she said.

"What?"

"Telling me how to wax a car. I *know* how to wax a car, Phil."

"Just let me give you a few tips." He picked up the waxing cloth. "Unlike the soap, you apply the wax in a clockwise manner, like so." He demonstrated. "You do a small area, rubbing the wax in with a clockwise motion, and then you let it dry and move to a second area, doing the same. When the first area is dry, you go back with a polishing cloth and wipe the area off in a counterclockwise circular motion. You see? Wax on, wax off."

"I still have a bucket, Phil, and I know how to use it."

"Okay, okay." He put his arms up to shield his face. "I'll back off. Just remember, wax on, wax off." He pulled up a lawn chair and made himself comfortable. "Lemonade?"

"No thanks, not until I'm done here."

"Suit yourself." Phil dripped his way into the house.

He was greeted by Dorian, who asked, "What was all the commotion about?"

"Just washing the car."

"How come you're all wet and soapy?"

"Well, Molly has a special technique for washing cars; it includes washing the driver. She's very thorough."

"What? Molly's washing your car? How'd you get that to work? I need to know for future reference."

"As you might have guessed, it's all a matter of superior kite-piloting skills," answered Phil as he picked up the pitcher of lemonade and two glasses and headed back out the door.

"Huh?" Dorian wondered in his wake.

"Mmm, sure is good lemonade," he gloated to Molly. "Sure you won't have some?"

Sweat joined the water dripping down Molly's forehead. "Not till I'm done here. I've just got the center of the roof to go." She jumped repeatedly, trying to reach her goal. "Could you give me a hand here? I can't quite get it."

He swooped up on her from behind and lifted her by the waist so she could access the uppermost regions of the fair Floretta.

"How gentlemanly of you, Phil."

"Oh, it's nothing."

"A stepladder would have worked just fine. I hate for you to actually have to exert yourself."

"Yeah, but a stepladder wouldn't have been as much fun."

"Careful. I'll bet I could polish your teeth too, while I'm at it. Wax on, wax off. There. I'm done; you can put me down now."

"Chivalry is not dead," he informed her as he set her back down on her feet.

They both stood back to admire Floretta's luster as a well-fed pigeon flew overhead, releasing its liquid stamp of approval.

"Well, my job is done here. Not my problem," Molly said as she sauntered over for her lemonade.

CHAPTER 13

Till the Cows Come Home

Molly and Phil had gone out several times. Not really *date* dates, just as friends. At least, that was how it appeared; it was safer that way. But now their good-night hugs were telling them they were more than just friends. Phil had decided to take her exploring in the foothills to a lake he knew of. His Uncle Ben used to take him there years ago; they'd camped, fished, and explored the whole area when he was a kid.

Phil had packed a lunch for them, calling his mom for directions on making Cornish game hens and her world-class potato salad. Given that Molly was a professional pastry chef, he knew he had to try his best to impress her. Fortunately, he had stopped in yesterday to get a baguette of Molly's best sourdough. The salad and game hens done, he cut up melon, peaches, and strawberries and put them in a container in his ice chest. He had to pack some cold drinks, and then he'd be ready.

He picked her up, and they headed for the hills. They eventually stopped near a small lake surrounded by a golden meadow. Phil parked the car by a splintery fence and carried the picnic basket and badminton set about a half a mile in. Tucked into the grass bloomed a profusion of black-eyed Susans, white clouds of yarrow, and a diehard patch of California poppies.

Molly took out her iPhone and started snapping pictures right and left. She even took some of the two of them, their heads together while sitting in a carpet of brilliant orange leaves. There was a slight breeze up, and it moved Molly's tresses in the most alluring way. "Perfect kite weather," observed Molly.

"Yeah. Too bad we don't have them anymore." Phil set out the blanket and basket of edibles while Molly chased a few butterflies from flower to flower with her camera.

She came waltzing back to him asking, "What did you make for us, Phil? Hmm? What's in the basket?"

"Nothing much, just a few things I had lying around in my fridge."

Molly squealed when he uncovered the Cornish game hens stuffed with rice and seasoned with garlic, onions, and orange peel. "I just love, love, love Cornish game hens! What else?" She flipped the lid off the potato salad and nearly salivated over the contents. "Phil, how did you know that I adore potato salad even more than macaroni salad?"

"Ancient Egyptian mind-reading technique," he beamed. "I've also got a loaf of your sourdough, which I magically turned into garlic cheesy bread."

"Scrumptious! When do we eat?"

"Not so fast, Muffin. Gotta bless it first."

Phil started praying, and after a sentence or two, Molly interrupted. "Say amen! Say amen!"

He paused for a second. "All right. Amen."

"Let's eat," cried Molly, and she was filling her plate. In between bites she said, "I haven't had anyone cook for me since my mom died, unless you count Clyde."

"Didn't Jared ever cook for you?" Phil asked.

"Nope. Can hardly boil water and lives mostly off of pizza. I used to cook for him all the time in college. Those days are long gone. This is so delicious, Phil. What kind of onions are in this potato salad? They're so sweet."

"Vidalia onions; they're the pride of the underground vegetable world."

After a meal that far exceeded Molly's expectations, along with a few rounds of badminton (which the shuttlecock finally won by perching itself high atop a pine tree), the two set off on a little hike. There was a very special place that he wanted to show her, something from his childhood. He hoped that the same phenomenon still occurred these days. The sun was now low in the sky as they found the spot he hoped would still be there. He spied the old, smooth-stoned house that stood among the black-eyed Susans and a rambling rosebush, long since abandoned. "Come on, Molly. Sit here with me. I have to share this with you." They sat down in the field, their backs leaning against the sturdy old rock wall he remembered so well. "Now close your eyes and listen."

Molly wondered who had once lived behind these walls. What was their story? She closed her eyes. They both sat in silence for a few minutes. Molly was taking in all the sounds of the falling dark. Red-winged blackbirds were squabbling, vying for the choicest accommodations for the night in the nearby cottonwood trees. An occasional splash of a hungry bass and the slow chirping of fall crickets tuning up for the evening serenade awakened her ears. How rare it was to be still and quiet long enough to attend to the symphony unchanged since Eden.

While Molly sat in reverie, Phil was utterly distracted by the scent of her hair. He let his hand touch hers. Then all at once it started. It was faint at first, but the sound built as, one by one, a herd of cows came from over the hill from a far-off pasture, finding their way back home for the night. The resonant sound of their cowbells, like so many cathedral bells ringing their different tones, transformed the pasture into a place both ancient and holy.

Molly grabbed Phil's hand. It was the most enrapturing sound she had ever heard, transporting her to another time when things were simple, pure, and honest. "I will never forget this moment," she whispered, opening her eyes.

Phil had been staring at her, and somehow it seemed just right. "Neither will I," Phil whispered back. He could hear Joe's advice in his head: *Don't wait too long to make your move.* Phil leaned over to Molly, and her lips were waiting for his. It was a tender, soft kiss. As they pulled apart, their eyes opened and focused on each other. There was no awkwardness to their silence, just a deep understanding of how much they cared for each other. "I love you, Molly," he heard himself saying before he could stop.

"I love you too," Molly said softly before pulling him close to her for another kiss, this one more passionate than the first, followed by many others.

The sun was done setting now, and the cowbells were silent. Phil took Molly's hand and helped her to her feet. "Now for the encore: crickets," Phil said. The chirping had already begun in earnest. Hand in hand they walked unhurriedly through the field and found their way back to their picnic spot. They gathered their things and walked back to the car by a full moon's light.

This was the most overwhelming love Molly had ever experienced. What she had felt for Jared paled in comparison. She sent a silent prayer of thanks heavenward.

They made their way back to her house and sat on the front porch swing for an hour or two, talking and kissing, kissing and talking. Molly finally said good night for the final time as Phil's car drove away. She knew she'd never fall asleep tonight. She felt that little quiver of joy welling up in her heart again. She went inside, flopped down on her bed, and hugged her little Philabuster bunny tightly. Surprisingly she dozed off for a few hours, only to be wakened by her alarm clock at eight thirty. At first she thought she'd overslept, but soon realized it was Sunday morning.

As she lay there, Molly thanked God that Lyra would be able to take on more of the bakery duties. If things kept going the way they were with Phil, maybe Molly would have to hire another assistant so that she could have more free time. Her feet barely touched the floor as she made her way to the shower.

CHAPTER 14

For the Love of Cat Food

It had been such a wonderful date with Molly last night. A beautiful woman he was madly in love with actually felt the same way about him. She had to be the most gorgeous, intelligent, witty woman he had ever met. Man, was he lucky. "Thank you, Lord," he enthused as he rolled out of bed. He'd go fix some coffee and get it brewing before he took a shower and got ready for church. On his way downstairs he thought about writing Molly a song on the piano, until he saw something strange moving below and froze in his tracks. A skunk in his living room! *What? How'd that thing get in here?* he wondered. He slowly retraced his steps back upstairs as the skunk turned and looked his way. "Nice skunky, pretty skunky," he muttered softly. Once back upstairs, he woke up Dorian to warn him about their unwelcome visitor.

"What'll we do?" Dorian shouted.

"Shh, we don't want to upset it. I have a plan. You just stay put and close all the doors up here, then call Animal Control. That thing must be after your cat's food that we store in the garage."

"I was wondering why Catalina was eating so much lately, when she was always meowing that she was hungry. Now we know why."

"We're going to have to get rid of that cat door from the

backyard into the garage. That's probably how it got in, and then it got curious or hungry and came in through the kitchen cat door, looking for more food." With a clenched fist, ready to charge, Phil announced, "Okay, I'm going in! Call Animal Control Now!

Phil headed for the window at the end of the upstairs hallway and opened it.

"What are you doing, Uncle Phil?"

"Just trust me. I've got a plan."

"You're not going out on the roof?" Dorian asked, incredulous.

"Yes, I am. Now close the doors up here and call for help!"

Phil climbed out the window and noticed at that point that he had neglected to put on slippers or shoes of any kind. No time for that now. He shimmied down the latticework and held onto the drainpipe, and then made a gallant leap to the ground below, landing in the very wet lawn. *Ha ha!* he thought as he reached the garage door, and then realized that he had left his keys upstairs in his room. "Oh, man," he grumbled and began his ascent up the latticework to the roof. It was much harder going up than down, he decided, and thought longingly of his ten-foot ladder safely tucked away in his garage. Bummer. He eventually made his way back through the window and grabbed his keys from the dresser top. Heading back to the window, he saw Dorian sticking his head out of his doorway.

Dorian asked, "What are you doing?"

"Never mind. Have you gotten hold of Animal Control yet?"

"Well, sort of. I left a message on their machine and gave them our number to call us back. It's Sunday; I don't know if they're even open today."

"Call back and leave a message that it's an emergency. Call the police. I don't know. Call somebody." Phil was in a panic as he headed back out the window, hopefully for the last time. *Darn*. He'd forgotten his shoes once again, he realized, as his bare feet met the shingles on the roof. He descended the makeshift ladder and got about halfway down the latticework when it gave way, and Phil found himself sprawled in his pajamas on his back in the sopping wet grass. That was it—he was going to install an escape ladder upstairs for emergencies like this.

Alerted by the sound of his descent, his neighbor, Martha Forsyth, looked out her side window. *I wonder what he's up to this time*, she pondered.

When Phil caught his breath, which had pretty much been knocked out of him, he got up and headed for the garage door, unlocked it, got Catalina's bowl, and filled it with a can of her best cat food. He ran around to the front porch on now-muddy feet, almost slipping once on the way. He put the heaping bowl of cat food on the porch, unlocked the front door, and opened it slowly, so as not to upset his guest. He moved to the side of the house and peeked around the corner, watching hopefully for the skunk's appearance. Phil realized he couldn't get past the skunk to close the front door if it ventured outside. He ran back to the side of the house and whisper-yelled to Dorian upstairs. He quickly gave up the attempt at whispering and full-out yelled up to the window until Dorian eventually came and stuck his head out, obviously nervous.

"Okay, Dorian, I have cat food as bait out on the front porch. It's the good stuff. There's no way he can resist it. The front door's open, and now we just have to wait for him to take the bait. I'll keep an eye on the front, and when he comes out, I'll run around here and let you know it's time to go downstairs and shut the front door. Got it?"

"Me? Shut the front door? What if it runs back inside before I get to the door?"

"That's a chance we've got to take. Now stay by the window, and I'll let you know when it's time. Ready?"

"No!" was Dorian's reply.

"Too bad. Now be ready." Phil crept up to the front of the house and peered around the corner again. No sign of Pepé, as Phil had named him. He stood in the azalea bushes a good twenty minutes, mud oozing between his toes, before he caught sight of it on the threshold. "Yes!" he whispered to himself. "Here we go." It took another few minutes before Pepé actually made his way over to the bowl and started munching. Phil tiptoed away from his hiding spot and then ran to the window. "Now!" he yelled up at Dorian. "Hurry up."

"Okay, okay," he muttered, quite unnerved at the thought of possibly encountering the skunk face to face. He stealth-walked downstairs, got close to the front door, and slammed it shut.

Phil had hidden himself back in the azaleas to watch. At the slamming of the door, Pepé was so startled that he raised his white-striped tail, stamped his paws, and let loose a steady stream of stink onto the porch and front door. Then he waddled away, retreating through a nearby hedge and into the neighbor's yard.

Phil, now unable to enter through the front door, ran back to the garage, nailed the cat door shut, and barreled in through the kitchen door, breathless. Needless to say, with a full day of de-odorizing ahead of him, he didn't make it to church that morning.

After a quick shower, Phil headed over to the grocery store in his Prius. Twenty tomato juice cans later, the door and front porch still smelled of eau de phew.

"Let me try," Dorian said. "I've heard that vinegar works." Five jugs of vinegar later, the smell had changed from purely skunk to a vigorous blend of vinegar and skunk—a skunk salad, as it were. "I've heard baking soda absorbs just about any odor. Mom used to keep some in her fridge." Dorian tossed the contents onto the porch where puddles of vinegar were still standing. The foaming would've done a rabid dog proud.

Phil scolded, "What? You didn't wash off the vinegar first? Honestly ..."

"I think it's kinda cool."

Phil said, "Scratch that one. Where's the hose?"

"What do we do now?"

Just then, his neighbor on the east side, Greg Jacobs, strode up to them. "I can smell you have a problem here, Phil. That varmint's been hanging round my garden and digging up my vegetables. I don't know how to get rid of him, but I do know how to get rid of the stink."

Phil would have gotten down on his muddy knees and begged. Instead, he pleaded, "Please. We've tried everything and then some."

"I know—I've been watching you. What you need is PU's Instant Skunk Eraser. Removes skunk odors in three and a half seconds. As a custodian at the school, I've had to use it on more than one occasion to deskunk things. Works like a charm. Within moments you're breathing easy again. You can't buy it, though. They only sell it wholesale to professionals."

Phil's face dropped.

"But I just happen to have a bottle of it in my garage. Now rinse off that other stuff you've been trying, and let's do this right."

A few minutes later, Phil and Dorian were singing Greg's praises. "Amazing stuff," Phil said. "How can I ever thank you?"

"Just being neighborly," Greg replied. "But I also did it out of self-defense. It was stinking up the whole neighborhood." He gave a chuckle. "But come to think of it, I sure would fancy one of your girlfriend's pumpkin pies."

"Consider it done," Phil said, shaking Greg's hand.

CHAPTER 15

If You Give a Cowboy a Cookie . . .

"Steph, are you okay?" Lyra put her hand on her new friend's drooping shoulder after church service had ended and the congregation had cleared out.

"Uh, I'm okay," Stephanie muttered.

"Don't lie to me, girl. I recognize all the signs. Spill it."

"It's my mom. She lost her job again. All she does is sleep, if she's not staring out the window waiting for Dad to come back. Like that's going to happen—ever. I've gotta find a job and forget about college. We've gone through all our savings since Dad left, and we're behind on our house payments. We're gonna lose our house and be out on the streets soon if I don't do something."

"It shouldn't be up to you to save your family. Can't your mom get another job?"

"She could, if she wasn't so depressed. Some days she doesn't get out of bed. Even little Stevie can't make her smile anymore. I don't know what to do, but I need a job, and I need it now."

Lyra had an idea in her head, but decided not to say anything just yet. Instead, she said, "Let's pray about this. God knows what to do."

Stephanie's prayers revealed the depth of her anguish. Until now, Lyra had no idea what a weight this seventeen-year-old carried on her shoulders. Her long, honey-colored hair was now damp with tears. Lyra swept it back in a motherly gesture.

"I was in a similar place less than a year ago. I was homeless and scared to death. God helped me find a job, and look at me now: independent with a home and a job doing what I enjoy. He can do the same for you."

"What am I going to do with my sister Stacy and little Stevie?" Stephanie wondered. "I can't just leave them and go out on my own. I don't even like to leave Stevie at home alone with Mom. She's always sleeping and doesn't keep an eye on him. Just yesterday I caught him standing on a box on top of a chair, trying to reach the cereal on the shelf. He could've killed himself.

"My mom keeps waiting for my dad to come back, but he's not going to. He ran off with the hot young office manager from his construction company. We'll never see his unsorry face again. How could he do that to Stevie? He's only four and he idolizes Dad. He doesn't understand where Dad is or why he left. Stacy's fourteen, and she's so mad at Dad that she'd like to kill him. Sometimes she talks to me about how she'd like to finish him off. And the sad part is, I'd like to help her. I don't think Mom will ever be the same. He just came home one day and said he didn't love her anymore, doubted if he ever really did. He took his things and walked out of our lives just like that, like we didn't even matter." Stephanie's jaw tightened as she twisted her flimsy copy of the church bulletin. "It's just not fair! We loved him so much, but we obviously meant nothing to him!" She hung her head and started sobbing.

Pastor Vicente saw the girls up front when he was getting ready to lock up. He silently prayed as he heard Lyra comforting Stephanie and decided to come back a little later. It did his heart good to see Lyra, who was so lost herself not long ago, now reaching out to help someone in similar circumstances.

Lyra and Molly were working together early Monday morning. "Did you and Phil have fun on your picnic Saturday?" Lyra asked.

Molly turned brighter than the cinnamon candies on the heart-shaped cookies she had just frosted.

"Aw, Molly's got a boyfriend," Lyra teased.

"Well, maybe I do. Heck, I don't know. We had a wonderful time Saturday."

"What did Phil make for you two to eat?"

"Cornish game hens with all the fixings."

"Sounds good. Then what did you do?"

"We played badminton."

"Yeah, and then what?"

"Oh, Lyra, never mind … okay, he kissed me, all right?"

"What? I want details!"

Molly sighed. "It was so right—the cows, their music, the dusk." She closed her eyes and could almost hear the sound of the lowing cows and their bells as they slowly made their way over the hill in the gathering gloam.

"Cows? Making music? Where on earth were you anyway? A livestock circus?"

"We were up in the foothills, and the cows were headed home for the night. Their bells were chiming like music—hundreds of bells like an outdoor cathedral. I was transported to another world. It was the most ethereal experience I've ever had. And then … he kissed me."

"Wow! I'm really happy for you, Molly." Lyra swallowed her disappointment that Phil was now taken and she wrapped her arm around Molly and gave her a sideways squeeze. "Phil's such a great guy. You two deserve each other."

They worked in silence for a while. Molly asked Lyra to remove the day-old bread and box it up for the homeless shelter.

"Oh, I've been meaning to ask you," Lyra broached the question. "I have this friend at church, and her family could really use some food. Do you think we could let her have a loaf or two of your day-old? She's got a fourteen-year-old sister and a four-year-old brother that aren't getting enough to eat. Her mom … well, the dad left them, and her mom, Sylvia, is too depressed to take care of them. Stephanie's trying to find a job so they won't lose their house and starve."

"Sylvia? You mean Sylvia Platt—I mean, Harrison?"

"Yeah. Do you know her?"

"Yes. She's a few years older than I am, but I remember her coming into the bakery with her boyfriend, Pete Harrison, when I was in junior high. I always looked up to her because she was so beautiful and seemed to have it all together. Pete was a football star at the high school. They were quite the item back in those days. I remember my mom doing their wedding cake right after they graduated from high school."

"Well, her daughter Stephanie is a friend of mine from church. Do you mind if I send a couple loaves over to them?"

"By all means. Take them a dozen cookies too, while you're at it. Sounds like Sylvia is depressed to the point of uselessness. Maybe I'll pay her a visit sometime. She may need help with more than food."

Molly got to thinking. Business had really picked up lately due to the wedding cakes she had been making for the people on the other side of the lake. The wealthy customers had finally begun to realize the treasure that Molly's Sunshine Bakery was, and consequently she was having a hard time keeping up with demand. Maybe it was time she thought about hiring another assistant. Since Lyra already knew Stephanie, maybe she'd be a good fit for the bakery. It was worth a try.

"Hey, Lyra," Molly called from the back room of the bakery.

"Yes?" replied Lyra, sticking her head around the doorway.

"What do you think about possibly hiring Stephanie to help out here in the bakery? We've been swamped lately."

"She'd love to work here, and I know they could really use the money. That's a great idea, Molly!"

"Maybe I'll pay her a visit and take over the day-old bread and cookies. What do you think? Do you want to come with me after work?"

"Totally—I'm right behind you." Lyra beamed. When she went back around the doorway, she gave a little, "Yes!" and thought, *Lord, You really did hear our prayers. Thank You, Lord*! Her dark green eyes twinkled as she waited on customers for the rest of the afternoon.

The stairs creaked a weary welcome as Molly and Lyra stepped onto the porch that surrounded the front of Stephanie's house. They each held a bag of baked goods for the family. Lyra knocked on the screen door.

Little Stevie opened it. "Hi, Lyra!" he said, jumping up and down in his oversized cowboy boots.

"Howdy, partner!" Lyra said.

Stephanie came running downstairs saying, "Stevie, you know you're not supposed to open the door, honey. Oh, Lyra! Hi! What are you doing here?" Stephanie smiled at her new friend and looked over at Molly, wondering what was going on.

"Steph, this is Molly, the owner of the bakery."

Stephanie held out her hand to shake Molly's. "So nice to meet you, Miss Molly. Lyra has told me a lot about you—all good things, of course."

"Hi, Stephanie. I've heard a lot of great things about you too. Oh, we brought you some things from the bakery." Molly and Lyra handed her the bags.

"What is it? What is it?" asked Stevie, his black cowboy hat falling behind him as he looked up at his sister. Molly instantly fell in love with the little red-haired boy.

"Cookies and bread for you, Stevie," Molly said, choking back a lump in her throat.

"Cookies?" By this time Stevie had dropped his trusty stick horse and begun prancing around in his old, worn-out jeans with holes in the knees. "Can I have one, please?"

"Of course you can. They're for your family to share," Molly replied.

"Whippee! Cookies!"

Stephanie reached into the bag and pulled out a big butter cookie dripping with sprinkles.

"Yummy!" Stevie exclaimed. "Thank you, Cookie Lady," he said, dancing into the kitchen to get a glass of milk to go with it.

"He's adorable," Molly sighed, wishing she had one just like him.

"Isn't he, though? That boy keeps me going. I don't know what I'd do without him," Stephanie replied.

"We came by for another reason too," Molly said.

"Would you like to come in?" Stephanie asked.

"Sure." Molly and Lyra entered the very tidy living room and sat down on the couch together as Stephanie sat in a chair facing them.

"Lyra told me that you've just graduated from high school at seventeen."

"Yes. I worked really hard and graduated a year early. I've been home-schooled all my life."

"That's wonderful," Molly commented.

"I was hoping to go to college this year, but money's tight. I need to get a job and save enough to make it happen sometime in the future. I guess you've heard about my dad leaving us."

"I'm so sorry, Stephanie. Maybe he'll come back." Molly tried to sound hopeful.

"Not much chance of that. So what can I do for you two?" Stephanie asked.

"Well, we could really use your help. The bakery has become way too busy for Lyra and me to handle on our own, and we were wondering if maybe you would be interested in working at the bakery part-time with us," Molly offered.

"What? Would I? Yes! Yes! Oh, thank you, Miss Molly!" Stephanie stood up to hug her.

"Just call me Molly," she said as she rose to return the hug.

Not one to miss a hugging opportunity, Lyra joined in.

"When can you start?" Molly asked.

"When do you want me?" Stephanie inquired, a huge burst of hope rising through her entire being.

"How's tomorrow morning sound—say, around five?"

"I'll be there! Oh, thank you so much, Miss—I mean, Molly!" Stephanie practically yelled.

"What's all the racket?" said Sylvia, coming downstairs dressed in her yellow fleece bathrobe. "Oh, sorry, I didn't know we had company." She cinched up the tie on her robe.

Molly walked over to shake hands with her. "Hi, Sylvia. I'm sorry to have disturbed you. I'm Molly, from the bakery."

"I remember you. What can I help you with?" she asked skeptically.

"Oh, Lyra and I just came by to offer Stephanie a job at the bakery. We could really use her help—we're swamped with business."

Sylvia, obviously embarrassed to be caught in her robe so late in the afternoon, tucked the collar a bit tighter around her neck. "Well, that would be much appreciated. Things have been a little tough around here lately. Thank you, Molly."

"Look, Mama!" Stevie ran in from the kitchen, another cookie in hand, and gave it to his mother. "They brought cookies!" He did his little happy dance, hopping from one foot to another in a circle.

Sylvia bent down to Stevie's level and said softly, "That cookie is for you, my sweet potato boy." She gave him a weary smile along with the cookie.

"Whippee!" he cried, dancing off to the kitchen again to finish his milk with his second cookie.

Molly noticed how thin Sylvia had become. She recognized the symptoms of depression that used to define her own life. There had to be a way to instill hope back into Sylvia, to help her realize she could begin to live without her cheating husband and start over. *Lord,* Molly prayed, *how can I help this woman? Please give her hope. She needs You.* Molly decided to make an effort to get to know Sylvia and do what she could to help her. That Stevie had stolen Molly's heart, and she couldn't stand the thought of him having a mommy who merely took up space. Molly resolved to go talk to Pastor Joe about her this week and get some ideas from him on how to handle this.

Fourteen-year-old Stacy walked to the door of her bedroom, listening to what was going on downstairs. She rested her head full of wavy brown hair against the door jamb, and she wondered who this Molly woman was. This was the first time in days she had seen her mom actually go downstairs. What was it about this Molly that had raised her mom from her deathbed? Was it possible that her mom could actually come back to real life? All Stacy knew was that whatever this Molly woman had that made her mom leave her self-imposed tomb, Stacy wanted some of it too. She heard Molly and Lyra leave and saw her mom actually sit on the couch, talk to Stephanie, and cuddle Stevie on her lap. As she started down the stairs, Stacy saw an inkling of life coming back into her mother's eyes—the first time she had seen this since her father had run out on them.

Chapter 16

A Day to Pie For

A late-November maple leaf was stuck in the windshield wiper of Phil's Bentley, causing a repetitive squeaking rhythm as the wiper swept slowly over the windshield. Almost hypnotized, Molly shook her head and spoke up. "It was so nice of you to invite me to your parents' house for Thanksgiving. I don't think I could've stood another Thanksgiving alone."

"You spend Thanksgiving alone?" Phil was shocked.

"Yeah, ever since my parents died, it's just been me. Last year I had a frozen turkey dinner and went to bed early."

"Well, not this year, Muffin."

"Do you think your mom will like the strawberry rhubarb pie?"

"It *is* her favorite. No one else in the family can stomach rhubarb, so she would never make it for herself. But your caramel apple, pumpkin, and banana cream pies will be a big hit for the rest of us."

She looked out the window and couldn't help but notice the newborn carpet of green spreading across the coastal hills, coming back to life, tender and awakening—just as her heart was. "So your parents live in Danville, huh?"

"Yeah, that's where I grew up. They still live in the same house. Just added on a bit."

As they exited the freeway, she commented, "This is a beautiful area."

"Yeah, my dad's done pretty well for himself."

"What does he do for a living?"

"He's a financial advisor."

"Must've taken his own advice," she observed, taking stock of the very upscale neighborhoods they passed through. "How about your mom? Does she work outside the home?"

"Nah. She was a librarian, but she quit working when she had my older brother."

"Librarian? Did she categorize your books by the Dewey Decimal System?"

"Well, actually, she tried that once. No one could find a thing."

"You're joking, right?"

"No. That's my mom."

As they pulled into the cobbled circular drive complete with a stone fountain, Molly's eyes traveled upward. "Oh, my gosh, Phil, this is your house? You grew up here? This place is a mansion!"

"No, not really. It's just home. Come on; leave your suitcase. I want you to meet my folks."

Molly had to glance in both directions just to take it all in. Topiary shrubs embellished the extensive flowerbeds. Stands of redwoods shaded each side of the house, and camellias, which had long since ceased being bushes, towered over the ferns below.

The arched doorway featured an intricate scroll pattern sculpted into the stonework. The doors themselves were arched with floral stained-glass embellishments consisting of water lilies and dragonflies.

Phil turned the engraved brass doorknob and announced, "Mom! I'm home!"

"Harry! Phil's here!" His mother scurried from the kitchen, her hands sporting oven mitts. With arms wide open, she ran to greet him.

Phil picked her up and spun her around.

"Phillip James, you stop that!" she scolded through her laughter. "You always were such a scamp."

He put his mother down and introduced Molly. "Molly, this is my mother, Charleen. Mom, this is my girlfriend, Molly."

His dad came in from the dining room. "Girlfriend, eh?"

"Yep, that's what I said. Molly, this is my dad, Harry. Dad, this is my Molly."

"Pleased to meet you both." Molly shook Harry's hand. When she turned to Charleen, she was welcomed with a hug.

"Well, come on in, kids. I've got some snacks."

They followed her into the kitchen. Molly had a hard time keeping her mouth shut. Here was her dream kitchen realized. Gleaming pink granite countertops seemed to go on forever. The appliances disappeared into the cherrywood cabinetry. The island in the middle looked like it was big enough to launch a boat. A double-wide, country-style sink with fancy gooseneck faucet suggested that perhaps doing dishes wouldn't be so bad, but of course there were twin dishwashers standing by.

The expansive kitchen window showcased a meticulously groomed herb garden encircling a gazing ball. Molly sighed.

"So, Molly, I hear you own a bakery."

"Yes, I sure do. It was my parents' and my grandparents' before them." She turned around, taking it all in. "Oh, what I could do in a kitchen like this! It's beautiful, Charleen!"

"And well used," Charleen added. "Thank you."

The sage-scented aroma of roasting turkey escaped from one of three ovens and … was it coconut? Sitting on a large silver platter was an assortment of inch-and-a-half-tall macaroons, some frosted in chocolate and others in butterscotch. "Please, help yourself." Charleen gestured to the mini quiches, crackers, cheeses, crab puffs, and fruit. In the center of it all were three oversized margarita glasses with iced prawns draped about the edges and an assortment of cocktail sauces for dipping.

Molly wasn't shy. She knew a good spread when she saw it.

After taking a bone china hors d'oeuvres plate, she began to sample the "snacks," as Phil's mom called them. The prawns were begging her to take them first, and so she obliged, dipping each into the seafood sauces. "These are wonderful, Charleen," Molly complimented wholeheartedly.

"Try the crab puffs next. They're Phil's favorite," Charleen offered.

"Gimme one of those!" Phil said, grabbing half a dozen.

"Oh my! These are fabulous!" Molly said through a mouthful, embarrassed by her lapse of manners. These "snacks" could make a person forget their own name. They were that good.

"Phil, why don't you bring in your suitcases?" his mother suggested, hoping to spare some crab puffs for the time being.

"I brought some pies," Molly informed her, resisting the call of the dwindling crab snuggled in its puff pastry.

"What kind of pies?" Harry asked with lifted eyebrows.

"Well, there's strawberry rhubarb, caramel apple, pumpkin, and banana cream."

"Let me carry them in. I insist," Phil's dad offered.

"And no sampling the merchandise until after dinner," Charleen warned.

Molly snickered as the guys headed out to the car.

"So, Molly, how did you and Phil meet?"

"Actually, we met in the bakery. He's my most loyal customer. Every morning, like clockwork."

"Sounds like he was interested in more than just the pastries," Charleen said with a smile.

"I don't think so, at least not at first. Maybe I just grew on him. And going with him to Ronnie's wedding sort of brought us together."

"Quite the fiasco, I hear. I never did understand what he saw in her anyway."

"Well, she *is* beautiful," Molly suggested.

"Not any prettier than you."

"I don't know about that," Molly said. Embarrassed, she tucked a coil of her springy hair behind her ear. She changed the subject quickly and asked, "So what can I do to help?"

Charleen was pleased. "Not a thing at this point, but I may take you up on your offer when we get closer to dinner." *Looks like Phil has chosen much more wisely this time*, she thought. Charleen looked Molly over a bit as they munched on hors d' oeuvres. A *little less than average height, tiny waist, great figure—and those big brown eyes! Low-heeled red shoes with bows, darling pleated navy skirt, and red sweater, and such an interesting, large locket around her neck.* Nothing escaped Charleen's attention. "I love your locket, Molly. Where did you find it?"

"Oh, this is my most prized piece of jewelry." Molly fondled the large, oval locket with grapes embossed on the front and carved scrollwork on the back. "It was my Great Aunt Hettie's. She left it to me when she passed away in her nineties."

"It looks intriguing," Charleen commented as she bent over to take a closer look. Molly handed it to her. "This is quite an antique."

"Yes, it is. It has an interesting story to it too. Go ahead, open it and look inside."

Charleen opened the locket and saw a yellowed picture of a very dignified, handsome young man. "Is this your great uncle?"

"No, actually, this is the man who was in love with my aunt. He pursued her for many years evidently, and wanted to marry her."

"Why didn't she marry him?" Charleen wondered. "Didn't she love him?"

"She must've loved him. She wore this locket often and always had his photograph in it. Hettie was one of four sisters. One sister married and moved away from the others after their parents passed. Hettie and her other two sisters were elementary school teachers, and all lived together in the family home in San Jose. In those days, teachers weren't allowed to marry and keep teaching. She chose teaching, and he eventually gave up trying to convince her to marry him. He married another woman some years later. Hettie taught until she was quite old. Years after she retired, she fell, and broke her hip, and wound up bedridden in a nursing home. The man in the locket came to her bedside in the hospital. Long widowed, he proposed to her one last time."

"You're kidding! So they finally got married."

"She said no again!" Molly stamped her foot on the tile floor. "Can you believe it? It just breaks my heart for that poor guy. I've always wondered who he was. I was too young to ask questions about him when I was a kid, but I sure wish I had."

"Wouldn't it be fascinating to find out his story? I wish we could somehow."

"Me too. I wouldn't know where to start, though. All I have is this picture and the locket."

The men entered the kitchen, suitcases and pies in hand.

"Looks like I know what I'll be eating for dessert tonight," Harry exclaimed. "This caramel apple pie is calling my name."

"I can't believe you brought strawberry rhubarb pie. It's my favorite, and nobody else in the family will eat it."

"I know," smiled Molly. "Phil told me, so I thought I'd make this pie just for you."

"How thoughtful!" Charleen beamed, winking at Phil. "It sure smells delicious, and the crust looks so flaky."

"Put it down, Char. If I can't have any before dinner, neither can you," warned Harry.

Charleen frowned at him. "Phil, why don't you show Molly to her room? She's staying in your old bedroom, and you're sleeping in the guest room with Matt. His room is reserved for Melissa." She turned to Molly. "Melissa is Matt's girlfriend. We're going to have a full house tonight. Phil's older brother, Tim, and Tim's wife, Bette Anne, are staying in his old room, and their son, Dorian, is sleeping in the den."

"Gotcha," Phil said. "Come on, Molly. I'll show you to your room."

"I'll be back soon," Molly said. "I can't stay away from all the goodies for long." They exited the kitchen and headed toward the stairs.

Charleen said to her husband, "Oh, Harry, I like her! She's really sweet and polite and so sincere. She even asked if she could help with dinner. Do you realize how long it's been since anyone has offered to help me with anything? He'd better hold on to this one."

"And boy, can she bake!" Harry had reached his hand under the apple pie's box lid and broken off a tiny piece of crust.

Charleen slapped his hand. "Now you just wait, mister!"

On their way to the stairs, Molly stopped to admire the grand piano in the formal living room. "That piano is amazing. It's huge, and just look how it shines. Is this where you practiced piano when you were a kid?"

"Yep. I spent more hours with this piano than I'd like to admit, I'm afraid."

"Well, it paid off. I fell in love with your music before I even knew it was you playing it. I heard it almost every day as I walked home from work, and I always wondered who the mysterious piano man was."

"Aw, shucks, and I had no idea I had an audience." He gave her a hug and a quick kiss.

Molly looked around the room at the grand style in which Phil had been raised. How could she possibly fit in with all these wealthy people when she was from such humble beginnings? And yet, they seemed very down to earth so far. *Hmm*, she wondered, *would this work*? She'd have to wait and see. Heck, the material for the drapes in the piano room alone would gobble up more than a month's income for her. How many pies would that be? This was not the cozy house like the one she'd grown up in, the one she still lived in. She reminded herself not to judge Phil's family by outward appearances, just as she hoped they would not judge her. After all, they had produced Phil, who was about as down-to-earth as one could get: no phoniness, no pretension.

Their feet hardly made a sound as they climbed the richly carpeted stairs. After reaching the top, Phil walked her to the end of the long hallway where his old bedroom waited. It was large for a child's room. Molly was drawn to an inviting window seat with thick, comfy cushions atop it. A queen-sized bed with a gold down comforter and an ornately carved walnut headboard stood between matching night stands and chest-of-drawers. The closet door sported a crystal-faceted antique door knob that led to a large, walk-in closet. *Good grief*, she thought, *do people really live like this*? An antique walnut armoire faced the bed. Walnut shelving covered one whole wall, interrupted by a window in the middle, looking down through a redwood tree and into the side garden.

"Wow, Phil, you never told me your family was so well off."

"Sorry, Muffin, I guess I should've mentioned it. I didn't think it would matter much to you."

"It doesn't—I mean it shouldn't. I'm just in shock, I guess. I expected a smaller home. Your family is … rich."

"You say that like it's a bad thing."

"No, it's not bad. I just wasn't expecting this. What if your parents don't like me because I'm not … you know … from money?"

"They're not like that, Molly. They're real people who worked hard and now just happen to be wealthy. Mom and Dad don't judge people by how much they have. Really. I know they'll like you—they already do. I can tell."

"Really?"

"Really." He walked over to hug her, and just as they began to kiss, they heard a stern male voice.

"What do you two think you're doing in there?"

"Hey, Matt," Phil addressed the voice before looking up. He grinned. "How are you doing, man?"

"I'm fine. Looks like you're doing pretty well yourself, dude!" Matt said, holding out his hand to greet Molly.

"Matt, this is my girlfriend, Molly. Molly, this is my little brother, Matt."

Molly's heart did a flip flop at the sound of the word, "girlfriend."

"'Little' brother." Matt sighed. "I'll never live that one down. Nice to meet you, Molly." He met her hand with a firm grip and an easy smile.

"Nice to meet you too, Matt. I've heard a lot about you and your love for DC Comics."

"Ah, my reputation precedes me, I see."

"Yep, she's heard all the dirt on you, all right," Phil said.

"Only nice things," corrected Molly, slapping Phil playfully on the arm and giving him a frowny face.

"Where is everybody?" came a female voice from the hall. In a cloud of Moi Toujours Moi "Victorious" perfume, strode a tall, slender woman in a timeless yet style-conscious ensemble with dangerously high heels and perfectly dyed blonde hair.

Molly could see that the newcomer spent an inordinate amount time in front of a mirror. Every hair was secured in place by an invisible web of hair spray. In a way, she looked a bit mannequinish to Molly. She reminded herself not to judge by appearances.

"Melissa, this is Phil's girlfriend, Molly. Molly, this is Melissa."

Molly reached out her hand and took Melissa's, which was hesitantly offered without so much as a squeeze to acknowledge Molly's presence. She was tempted to check for a pulse on the cool, limp hand. Instead, she said, "Nice to meet you, Melissa," forcing a smile.

"Yes, it is," Melissa uttered.

"So this is the lady who's got Phil's attention. We've heard about what a great cook you are, Molly," said Matt.

Melissa's narrowed eyes were obscured by a dark forest of false eyelashes.

"I'm just a baker, really. It's been a family-owned business for generations. My parents left it to me when they passed away." Molly could feel Melissa sizing her up. She could tell that she hadn't passed inspection. "So, Melissa, what do you do for a living?"

"I'd be bored out of my mind in a kitchen." Melissa shrugged her disdain. "Cooking is a waste of a woman's energy; that's what personal chefs are for. And since I'm a buyer for Angstrom, I travel constantly, you know. I'm always on the go. No time to be enslaved by a kitchen." She gave a glittering smile.

"That must be interesting, looking at clothing lines all over the country," Molly observed.

"All over the world, really," corrected Melissa without looking up from her perfectly square-tipped nails.

"Wow," was all Molly could conjure up.

"To each her own," Phil said. "Now, why don't we go downstairs and hit Mom's crab puffs? I'm starving."

"Great idea. I'm right there with you," Molly agreed, eager to escape this awkward encounter.

Phil took Molly's hand, and they headed back to the stairs.

"We'll be down in a minute," Matt called after them.

Melissa whispered a bit too loudly to Matt, "Really, what does your brother see in that girl? She's just a cook, for goodness' sake."

"Shh! Not so loud; they'll hear you," Matt warned. "I like her. She seems nice, and Phil is evidently crazy about her. I think it's good that he has somebody, now that Ronnie's married. He was stuck on her for so many years. She was all wrong for him anyway."

"I think he could've *had* Ronnie if he had just played his cards right. He needed to man up."

"Looks like he's doing fine for himself now."

"That's your opinion." Melissa looked him in the face and then turned deliberately away.

"Yes, of course, it is my opinion—that is, if I'm allowed one." He sighed. "Ready to join everybody downstairs?"

"I suppose." Melissa followed him down the hallway.

In the kitchen, things were starting to get more lively. Dorian had arrived, much to Molly's delight; a familiar face was always comforting in unfamiliar company. He came over and gave Molly a hug. "I just talked to my folks on my cell. They'll be here any minute now."

"With egg rolls?" asked Harry with an edge of urgency.

"With egg rolls," assured Dorian. He turned to Molly and advised, "My mom makes the best egg rolls ever. She makes them for every holiday. Grab one as soon as they come in—they disappear fast. You'll love her, Molly, and her cooking."

"I can't wait to meet her … and her egg rolls," Molly said, smiling. "If there's one thing Phil and I have in common, it's our love of food."

"Obviously," Melissa said under her breath as she swept into the room.

Phil cleared his throat. "I think I hear a car pulling up out front. Come on, Molly—let's go see if it's Tim and Bette Anne. We can help them carry stuff in, especially those egg rolls."

"Hey, don't eat them all," called Dorian.

While heading for the front door, Phil murmured to Molly, "Sorry, Molly. That Melissa is a real piece of work. How Matt got stuck with her, I'll never understand. She's so opposite of him. He's so laid back. They've been dating for a while now, but I don't think it'll last much longer. I give them another six months, max."

"She certainly doesn't approve of me—that's for sure."

"Maybe that's a good thing. Don't worry about her. She doesn't approve of anyone, including my brother. My parents don't like her much. Mom thinks she's just after Matt's money. He'll catch on eventually, I'm sure." Phil didn't sound convinced, but Molly chose not to point that out to him.

"I hope so," was all she had to say as Phil opened the front door.

"We're here!" came a sweet southern drawl out of the rolled-down window of the black Lexis in the driveway. "Hey, Sugar, who's that pretty little gal by your side?"

"Hi, Bette Anne. Hey, Tim. This is my girlfriend, Molly."

There went Molly's heart again, skipping a beat.

Despite her solid figure, Bette Anne easily sprang out of the car. "Girlfriend? Nobody said anything to me about a girlfriend! Well, hey there, Miss Molly," she said, hugging her generously before Molly could even extend her hand. "So good to meet ya, honey."

"It's great to meet you too." Molly returned the hug, liking her immediately.

Tim was out of the car by this time and came around to shake Molly's hand. "Wow, Phil, better not let this one get away."

Molly looked away, avoiding everyone's gaze, a little unsettled by all the attention.

Phil changed the subject for Molly's sake. "We came out to help you carry your stuff in."

"Sure, but I'm not trusting you with the egg rolls this year," was his sister-in-law's reply. "Remember what happened last year?"

"What?" inquired Molly, her eyebrows raised.

"Well, Sugar, he took to hiding his own private stash, and by the time they made it into the kitchen, they were half gone. We never did find the missing egg rolls," Bette Anne declared, giving Phil a pointed glance.

"I'll never tell," Phil announced, unashamed.

"Molly, would you do the honors of carrying in my egg rolls? They're in the backseat."

"Sure, I'd be glad to, and I'll guard them with my life, at least until they're in the kitchen."

"That's all I ask," Bette Anne said solemnly.

The men grabbed the baggage and a large pan of yams, which smelled of heavenly butter, sweet cream, cinnamon, and brown sugar. "These are going to disappear fast too, Molly. Be sure to grab some before Dorian gets his hands on them," Tim warned. "She's won prizes for her yam recipes back in Georgia. Sweet yam pie, yam bread, yam butter, yam just about anything you can name."

"I can't wait to try it," Molly said, almost drooling by this time.

Walking toward the door, Phil attempted to sample the egg rolls and was met with a smart slap of Molly's hand.

"Ouch!" Phil whined.

"You heard the lady," Molly reprimanded. "Wait till they're in the kitchen, Sweetie Pie."

"I'm seeing a whole 'nother side of you, Muffin. I'm intimidated."

"Go for another egg roll, and you'll be more than that," she threatened. "We cooks have to stick together, you know."

"I'm just quaking in my loafers."

"I like you, Molly. You've got spunk," said Bette Anne.

"Thanks, Bette Anne. I know we're going to get along just fine."

"You betcha," Bette Anne replied.

Once in the kitchen, Molly was deluged by hungry family members, all greedily vying for the first egg roll. Molly set the platter down and stepped back so as not to be trampled. When the lid was off, the egg rolls began to magically disappear. Phil got the first few and managed to keep them from prying hands until he reached Molly's side.

Melissa looked on in disgust from the corner of the kitchen, shaking her head and wondering what all the to-do was about an egg roll, anyway. She'd never tasted one since it was not on her fat-defying diet.

She's no fun at all, thought Molly as she sunk her teeth into the warm, fried, flaky crust. It was love at first bite. The chicken and veggies seemed to melt in her mouth—cabbage, carrots, bean sprouts, onion, and garlic, all chopped up and spiced to perfection. She grabbed another one out of Phil's hand.

"Hey, Muffin, what do you think you're doing?"

"It's every man …" she coughed, "woman for themselves at this point." She took a huge bite of the second roll. "Mine now." She smiled a simply evil smile as she polished off the second egg roll and headed back to the frenzy to acquire more.

As dinnertime approached, Molly assisted Charleen with the last-minute preparations. There were potatoes to mash, gravy to prepare, salad to dress, and sundry other details to attend to. Molly could almost read Charleen's mind, completing tasks before she was even asked.

"We work quite well together, don't we?" Charleen observed.

"We sure do. It reminds me of when my mom and I used to work together in the kitchen," Molly said with a hint of sadness.

"Your mother …?"

"Yes, she passed away a few years ago, after my dad died. I miss them both so much, especially around the holidays."

"I'm so sorry, Molly." She was quiet for a minute. "Well, I always wished I had a daughter to cook with, and you miss your mom, so maybe we can fill in for each other."

"I'd like that," Molly said softly.

"Let's get Harry to carve the turkey, and we'll be ready to feed the thundering herd," Charleen said.

"I don't know. That could be quite dangerous after the egg roll incident." Molly shook her head dubiously.

Charleen patted Molly's shoulder, and a smile passed between them as Molly received a sideways hug. "Let's do this," Charleen commanded. "We're going in."

When everyone was seated for dinner, Charleen asked Phil to say grace.

"Father, we want to thank You for all of us, friends and family, sitting here at this table. You've been so good to us this year, and we want to say thank You for all those blessings. Help us to give back to You all the resources You've entrusted to us. We love you, God. In Jesus's Name. Amen."

He opened his eyes to see Melissa looking off to the side with a raised eyebrow.

After the passing of the yams, dinner progressed at a more leisurely pace. Sighs of delight and contentment punctuated their conversation. Toward the end of dinner, Matt stood up and got everyone's attention. He clinked his knife against his crystal goblet. "I have an announcement to make."

Everyone was silent, a creeping sense of dread coming over them.

Oh no, Phil said to himself. *Lord, please don't let it be ...*

"Melissa and I are engaged," Matt announced.

Melissa looked like a cat that had just lapped up the baby's milk.

Harry and Phil simultaneously choked on their final bites of food while Molly bit the inside of her cheek.

"Congratulations," said Bette Anne, though she was not at all pleased with the proposed addition to the family.

"Have you set a date yet?" asked Charleen with feigned enthusiasm.

"Not yet, but the sooner the better," Matt answered.

Polite congratulations were offered from around the table.

"Matthew and I plan to use the country club for the reception," Melissa informed them.

"We'll have to check on openings in their schedule," Charleen suggested. "Any idea what month you're looking at?"

"We were thinking February, near Valentine's Day. That would make it easier for Matthew to remember our anniversary. You know how forgetful he is."

Here we go with the constant insults, thought Charleen. "Oh my, that is soon. Are you sure you can pull together a wedding in that short a time?"

"We were hoping you could help us put it all together, Mom, since you are so good at that kind of thing," Matt pleaded.

"No, darling, we won't be needing your mother's help after all. I've already acquired a wedding planner from San Francisco. He'll be taking care of all the details. Your mom won't have to do a thing but show up, tastefully dressed."

How much is all this going to cost us? wondered Harry and Charleen. Melissa's mother, Shirley, was a would-be socialite with no money of her own to pay for the big wedding Melissa would demand. According to Matt, her father had long since run off with another woman and completely divorced his family years ago.

"How do you two propose to pay for a San Francisco wedding planner? Those people in the city charge a fortune," Harry commented.

"We can talk about this later," Matt suggested. "Aren't you happy for us?"

"Yes, dear, it's really something," Charleen stretched the truth beyond the breaking point. "This calls for a celebration. Break out the pies!"

Molly and Charleen got up and hastened to the kitchen to procure the pies, dessert plates, and coffee.

"Celebrating with pies?" Melissa complained. "What happened to champagne?"

"You know my dad doesn't drink anymore," Matt reminded her.

"Not even on a special occasion like his own son getting married?" she whispered loudly to Matt.

Phil cleared his throat. "I'll go see if they need any help in the kitchen."

When he ducked through the kitchen door, his mom was on the verge of tears. "I can't believe he doesn't see through all of Melissa's phoniness." She shook her head.

"He's blinded by his love for her, Mom," Phil said quietly. "I was the same way with Ronnie for years."

"We can't let him make this mistake, Phil. What can we do? She's going to ruin his life."

"We can pray, Mom. He has to make his own choices, but we can pray that God opens his eyes to what she's really like."

"You're right, honey, you're right. I'm sorry you have to hear all this, Molly."

"It's okay, Charleen. Every mother wants her child to marry the right person. I don't blame you at all."

"Let's all put on a smile and serve these delicious pies. I could sure use a piece right now. Phil, would you bring the pot of coffee?"

"Got it, Mom."

The pies didn't disappoint. Everyone raved at the flavors and tempting crusts. Charleen was enraptured by the strawberry rhubarb, and even Melissa had a small piece of banana cream pie and enjoyed it thoroughly, secretly wishing for another slice, though she would never admit it. But no one was more pleased than Molly, now that she knew her pies were such a hit.

After dessert, Molly and Phil insisted on cleaning everything up. Charleen protested profusely at first, but she was outnumbered and eventually gave up.

"I know my way around this kitchen," boasted Phil. "As kids, Matt and I were on dish duty every night. I still think Tim faked too much homework to get out of doing dishes most of the time. If you need to know where anything goes, just ask."

Molly smiled and readied the huge sink full of hot, sudsy

water, and they commenced pre-rinsing everything for the dishwashers. "Two dishwashers," Molly marveled. "This is kitchen heaven. Look at all this room for dishes! It'll all fit, every last utensil and plate." She started scrubbing the roasting pan while Phil loaded the second dishwasher, cleaned off countertops, and put leftovers into the double-wide fridge.

"We're quite a team, Muffin! The winning team."

"We sure are! I really like your parents, Phil. They make me feel so welcome."

"That's 'cause you are." He came up behind her, put his arms around her waist, and kissed her neck. She turned around and put a dollop of soap suds on his nose. "Big mistake, Muffin!" He grabbed a fistful of bubbles and plopped it on her cheek.

The bubble fight would have escalated further had Charleen not entered at this point, laughing in spite of herself. She stopped the potential free-for-all. "You two are having way too much fun in here. Wow, just look at my kitchen. It's as good as new! Thanks, kids. You've done enough work. Come take a break and visit with the rest of us."

"It was nothing compared to all the work that you did, making this delicious dinner. Thanks so much for inviting me," Molly said with heartfelt sincerity.

"It was my pleasure. Now you two get in there and visit."

The visiting lasted a couple of hours, interrupted by a pretty competitive game of penny poker, a yearly tradition. Molly was betting on some pretty good hands of her own, but she was outshone by Tim, the family card shark.

As the evening came to a close and everyone headed off to bed, Phil asked Molly to stay up for a while to talk and listen to some piano music he had written. One piece in particular stood out above the rest. Molly clapped at the end of the song. "That was stunning, Phil. I didn't know you wrote music too."

"I'm glad you liked it. I wrote it for you."

"For me? No one has ever written anything for me before. I love it!"

"And I love you, Molly."

"I love you too, Phil." They sat side by side on the piano bench. Molly snuggled up to his shoulder and rested her head on it.

He kissed her. They were interrupted by Harry, who had gotten out of bed to sneak another piece of caramel apple pie. "Don't let me interrupt you two," he said, embarrassed.

"I was just getting ready to go upstairs for the night anyway," said Molly.

"You two kids stay up as late as you want. Just don't tell Char I stopped in for more pie," was Harry's response.

"Good night to both of you," Molly said. She gave Phil a peck on the cheek and headed for the stairs. Phil followed his dad into the kitchen for a secret slice of caramel apple pie himself.

"I really like her," Harry commented, brushing a bit of wayward crust from his cheek. "So does your mother. Molly's so helpful and sweet. Pretty too. I think you lucked out, Phil. Don't let her get away."

"Why does everyone keep saying that to me?"

"Because girls like her don't come along every day, son. I can tell she's that one in a million. I wish your brother could find someone more like her."

"I can tell you're as thrilled about Matt and Melissa as Mom is. I must admit I'm really unhappy about them getting married too, but it's his choice. I don't want to interfere."

"Someone has to warn him. He's gonna be sorry for the rest of his life."

"Well, don't look at me. I don't want to be the one."

"I think you'd be the best one for the job, son. You've had that situation with Ronnie, and, besides, you're his big brother. He's always looked up to you, even if you couldn't agree on comic-book heroes."

"Dad, I shouldn't get in the middle of this. It's his life."

"Think about it, Phil. He needs your advice right now. You heard them: they want to get married right away."

"In February," interrupted Charleen, who had quietly entered the kitchen, seeking her own slice of pie. Harry lamely attempted to hide his pie under a kitchen towel. "Forget hiding it, Harry. We all know what we're here for. Hand me the strawberry rhubarb." She cut a substantial slice, brought a forkful to her lips then set it back on the plate, untouched. "Honey, we have to work fast. We can't let your brother walk right into her trap. She's only interested in him for his money. She's so shallow, and she's always putting him—and everyone else—down. Please try and talk some sense into him."

"Mom, it's none of my business. He has to make this choice for himself."

"It *is* your business, Phil. Don't you wish someone would have broken Ronnie's spell over you years ago? Look at all the time you wasted. And you would have married that … woman if she had plotted it like Melissa is doing to Matt right now. She doesn't love him, and you know it. Please, honey, just try to wake him up. You've seen how she's belittled him the past couple years. Do you want him to be stuck with her for life?"

"Mom, he won't listen to me any more than I would've listened to him warning me about Ronnie. He'll marry her anyway and hate me for trying to break them up. Honestly, I don't think it'll do any good."

"It's a risk worth taking," Harry said. "She's already been trying to drive a wedge between him and the rest of us over the past year."

"Okay, okay. If the opportunity arises, I'll try to talk to him this weekend. I've gotta pray about this first."

"Thanks, honey. That's all we ask," said a relieved Charleen.

Phil finished off his banana cream pie. He was going to need it.

Upstairs, Molly slipped into her cotton nightie and looked over Phil's old bedroom. On the top of his dresser was Ted, the stuffed bookworm she had heard about. She picked him up, gave him a hug, straightened his glasses, and tapped his little nose with her finger. She tucked him under her arm and wandered about the room. On his wall of shelves were a number of old photo albums. She picked up a few and walked over to the window seat on the other side of the room. After nestling in amongst the overstuffed pillows and throw blanket, she opened up an album. Pictures of Phil as a kid made her smile at what a cutie he was. She surely would have had a crush on him when she was a girl. Here was a picture of Phil and Matt reading comic books on the floor together. Matt still had that same innocent smile. She wondered how much longer that smile would last.

Family pictures followed. Here was one of Phil and his dad flying their legendary kites with those special kite reelers. The stories she'd heard seemed to come alive now that she had seen actual pictures of them. The next album revealed images of junior high- and high school-aged Phil and his buddy Mitch. There were a few shots of what she guessed was Ronnie. She looked so much sweeter in junior high. Molly could see a progression downward as Ronnie grew up: a smug, selfish look began to emerge in her photos. More pictures of her in her cheerleader uniform followed. The girl next door image was erased by puberty and a sudden need for social power and status. *How sad*, Molly thought. *Poor Phil had fallen in love with her when she was actually nice, and he could never let her go—until recently, that is.*

The next album held more high school images. Here was the big night with Phil in his burgundy tux, getting into his dad's Thunderbird with the ever-present Mitch. They must've been heading off to pick up their dates. *Poor Phil was doomed that night*, she remembered. *Too bad we didn't know each other then.* Here were Phil and Mitch all dressed up and getting into a limo. That was the night Ronnie had cancelled their senior prom date for a "better offer." He sure had bad luck with the ladies, but not anymore.

She smiled. Molly loved him so; she knew she had never loved even Jared as deeply. His sense of humor, his giving heart, and his love for God made him all the more dear to her. He was much more the romantic than she had imagined. Molly adored him and wanted to spend every minute in his company. She believed he felt the same about her. She prayed that they would be married someday if God wanted it to be. Molly couldn't imagine loving any man more. Time ... that was Phil's biggest gift to her. He planned dates, dropped by the bakery every morning, and seemed to want to spend all his free time with her. *He's nothing like Jared,* she thought. Molly hugged Ted tightly.

When she was finished with the albums, she returned them to the shelf. She saw an old scrapbook, she picked it up, and walked over to the bed with it. He had won numerous awards for his musical talents, recognition he'd never mentioned, as well as scholastic awards in English and the sciences. She was so proud of him. On one of the final pages, she found an acceptance letter to Julliard, along with another paper promising a full ride scholarship to the prestigious school. *Hmm ... he never told me about that.*

She slipped out of bed, slid the scrapbook back into its spot on the shelf, and climbed back into bed. After switching the light off, she lay awake in the darkness for an hour or so, turning the day's events over in her mind, marveling at being introduced as Phil's girlfriend, and wondering why he didn't pursue an education in music. Finally she drifted off to sleep.

While she slept, Phil and Matt were in the guest room polishing off a secret stash of egg rolls.

CHAPTER 17

The Travesty of Uneven Egg Rolls

The egg rolls were dwindling. It was tragic. Phil and Matt could both see there was an uneven number of them left. That could only mean one thing.

"You know what this is going to come to, don't you?" Matt warned.

"Yep. I'm ready to take you on, little brother. Best seven out of twelve?"

"You're on. Spock, paper, scissors."

The tournament began.

"Ha ha, scissors cut Spock's pointy ears off!" Matt cried.

"Keep playing, chump." Phil didn't like losing to his baby brother—ever.

"Yes!" Phil hissed. "Paper dulls scissors!"

Play continued until the score was six to six.

"This is it …! Paper! Spock makes origami starship out of paper. I win! Gimme that egg roll, brotha!" Phil loved to gloat.

"All right, all right. But I think you cheated. You know I always go for Spock's help when I'm in trouble."

"Whatever. Hand it over."

"So what do you think, Phil?"

"I think we need more egg rolls," Phil stated the obvious while stuffing his mouth full.

"No, be serious for a minute. What do you think about Melissa and me getting married?"

Oh no, Phil thought, *now I've gotta tell him what we all think. How to do this, Lord? Help!* He sent a prayer balloon skyward while chewing a little longer than usual, stalling. "Congratulations, bro." More stalling.

"Thanks, but what do you think about us? A good match, huh? Like Mom and Dad?"

"Well, not exactly like Mom and Dad, but you know Melissa better than I do."

"What's that supposed to mean? You don't like her?"

"I never said I don't like her."

"Come on, then. Tell me what you think. I can take it. We're brothers, right? You can tell me anything."

"No, I can't."

"Yes, you can."

"It's none of my business, okay? You get to make your own choices. I'm sure you've thought this through before you proposed."

"Now you've *got* to tell me. So why don't you like her? Come on. Spit it out."

"What? That last egg roll?"

"No, you chump."

"Look, Matt, she doesn't like any of us in the family."

"What? She likes all of you. I know she does. She just doesn't feel like she fits in."

"Yeah, well, she constantly makes snide remarks to all of us. She's always rolling her eyes and making rude comments under her breath, but just loud enough for us to hear. No one calls her on it because we're trying to avoid confrontation, and mostly because we know you're in love with her."

Matt crossed his arms. "What? You know she's just kidding.

You just don't get her sense of humor yet. Give her a chance. You need to get to know her better is all. Geez, and I thought you had a good sense of humor all these years."

"She's not kidding, Matt. All those things she mutters under her breath are her true feelings. I just can't believe you'd let her get away with treating everyone the way she does—especially you! She runs you down all the time, every chance she gets."

"She does not! She's joking. And she's always building up my confidence. She's always saying how much she appreciates how hard I work, and how well my business is doing."

"Doesn't that give you a clue about what she really cares about?" Phil leaned forward. "Think about it. She builds you up when it comes to money. What does that tell you?"

"That she's proud of me and wants us to have stable finances. You know, for us and our future kids."

"She wants kids?"

"Sure! Well, we haven't ever really talked about it, but I'm sure she wants them like I do. Remember how much fun we had as kids growing up together? Of course she must want that kind of family."

"Matt, I think you guys should go to premarital counseling."

"We already took care of that with our lawyers." Matt's face flushed red. "Besides, Mom and Dad never went to anything like that, and they've gotten along just fine. They're still married, aren't they?"

"Mom and Dad sure could have used counseling. They got through Dad's drinking by the skin of their teeth. Premarital counseling and marriage counseling would've done them a world of good. But we're talking about you and Melissa here. I don't think you are seeing her the way everyone else does. I really want to like her, Matt, I really do. But she's just so mean to you, and remember, she's at her best right now, before you get married. Remember Ronnie?"

"Of course. I never did understand what you saw in her, once you got past the looks anyway. She used you and did nothing but hurt you all the time."

"Bingo! I didn't see it because I was too much in love with her. I didn't get it. I didn't *want* to get it. I was too deep into it to care how she treated me. I saw what I wanted to see. I'm afraid the same thing is happening with you and Melissa. I think she's using you."

"Using me? No way, man. She loves me. I know she does."

"Really? Well, what do you think would happen if suddenly your business went under, and you were broke?"

"She'd love me anyway. I'm sure of it."

"If I were you, I'd find out before making any hasty wedding plans. Look, I don't want to be a downer. I want to be happy for you, I really do, but I also don't want you to get hurt like I did over and over with Ronnie. I've been there, remember?"

"What do Mom and Dad think about Melissa?"

"I won't speak for them, but I definitely think you should talk to them this weekend. I also think you should call Melissa on all her rude comments and put-downs. She's gotta know that's not acceptable. Would you want your kids to grow up with that attitude? If she treats you and all the people you love like that, how do you think she'll treat your kids? She's nothing like Mom. Do you want Melissa to be the mother of your children?"

They were silent for a few minutes, then Phil spoke up. "I wouldn't have said anything if you hadn't asked. Sorry, Matt. If you decide to marry her, I'll do my best to support that decision. I just don't want you walking into it blinded by your feelings."

"Well, you certainly hit the jackpot with Molly. She's nothing like Ronnie." He paused. "Y'know, you're right; Melissa wasn't friendly to Molly when she met her today."

"I know, and we were all too polite to stand up to Melissa. We were taught that it's good manners to overlook bad manners, but I promise you, I *will* say something the next time she puts Molly down."

"I understand, Phil. I'll stand up to her put-downs—if that's what they really are. I still think it's really just her sarcastic, cynical sense of humor, though."

"Well, whatever the reason, she's got to stop it. She's hurt Mom's feelings a lot, but Mom's too nice to say anything, and she never will. She'll put up with it like she did Dad's drinking all those years. Do you want to just put up with Melissa's attitude for the rest of your life?"

"I think you just take her too seriously. She's just joking, really!"

"What would she do if you started treating her the way she treats you?"

"She'd be fine. She'd get it. She'd think it was funny."

"Whatever, man. You believe what you want to believe." Phil shrugged. "Forget it! Let's go steal some more egg rolls. I saw a few hiding in the back of the vegetable drawer under the cauliflower, wrapped in foil. Such an obvious hiding spot. They deserve to be stolen."

"I thought we ate the last of them," Matt said, conflicts forgotten for the moment.

"Think again. Are you in this or not?"

"I'm right behind you."

At breakfast the next morning, Charleen chopped up the ingredients for omelets and fried crispy bacon while Molly worked on tantalizing, fluffy waffles. The scrumptious smells wound their merry way up the stairs and into the waiting nostrils of the rest of the household, nudging them gently, promising that waking would be worth their while, really it would.

"The secrets for my dad's famous waffles are using malt in the batter and extra whipped egg whites folded gently in just before they go into the waffle iron," Molly explained.

Charleen's mouth was watering at this point. "I love a good waffle. They beat pancakes all to pieces, as far as I'm concerned."

"I agree. My dad used to make them with precooked bacon crisscrossing in the middle of the waffle. Ah …"

"Molly," Charleen said with a smile, "I'm so glad you came to join us this Thanksgiving. It's a real joy cooking with you."

"I'm so happy to be here, Charleen. You've raised the most wonderful son. It's so nice to finally get to meet the woman responsible for the person he's become. You did a great job."

"Well, I tried my best, but he still doesn't put his socks in the dirty laundry hamper. I hope you realize that," she warned in mock earnestness.

Molly laughed as the sleepy-headed family members strolled in one at a time. The waffles and bacon had definitely done their job.

In the afternoon, Phil and Molly found themselves sitting in the library, Phil's favorite room of the house. There were welcoming, overstuffed chairs and a double recliner love seat in the middle. Shelves were built into the walls and lined the entire room, except for the fireplace and a set of french doors.

Water cascaded musically down the three-tiered stone fountain just outside the double doors, inviting readers to inhabit the white wicker chairs situated just outside of splashing distance. Camellias turned upward, catching the filtered light through the branches of the redwood trees. Japanese anemones stood knee high, bravely pink, surrounded by the blossoms of the dwindling daylilies which refused to succumb to autumn's summons.

"How does your mom have time to keep up all the gardens she has?"

"She loves gardening as much as cooking. It wasn't until recently that she's had someone help her with weeding and trimming. Her garden is important to her, as you can see by the massive amount of gardening books that dominate her section of the library. We all have our own shelves. Mom's books are all over here to the right." He motioned with his hand.

"You can tell a lot about a person by looking at their bookshelves," Molly reflected, reaching for her mug of hot chocolate.

"Yeah, you're right. Mom's section is all gardening and cooking, historical fiction, classics, crafts, knitting, sewing, world travel, music, and the art of decluttering.

"Dad's books are behind us, and they're mostly business and investment stuff. He's also into biographies and astronomy. No fiction for him—it's all very black-and-white, serious stuff."

"And whose are these to the left of the fireplace?"

"Those are some of Matt's. He took a lot of his books to his place but still leaves quite a few here that he doesn't use as often but can't part with. Tim, who's ten years older than me, took all of his books when he married Bette Anne a long time ago. He has a pretty large library. They're all law books, though—as exciting as a day at the snail races."

Molly rose to look at Matt's titles. "Seems to be business-type titles like your dad's books."

"Yeah, but there's fiction too. And, of course, there's a section between the two of ours that houses our infamous comic book collections. You'll note the ones on the right are *his* DC comics."

Molly smiled a knowing smile.

"And, of course, the leftmost ones are *my* Marvel comics."

"I gathered that much." Molly looked at Phil's numerous shelves of books. They ranged from *Hitchhiker's Guide to the Galaxy* to *The Screwtape Letters.* His literary choices ran the gamut.

"What kinds of books are on your shelves, Miss Molly?"

"I've saved all my old kids' books, like *Winnie the Pooh, Charlotte's Web, Wind in the Willows,* and *Anne of Green Gables.* I don't have much time to read these days, but I do love fiction—good fiction like Steinbeck and Dickens. I'm not much for historical stuff—too many wars. I like a book that can lift me out of my everyday life. Wish I had more time to open a book."

"Maybe it's time you had more free time. Have you thought about giving Lyra and Steph more hours?"

"Y'know, that's something to think about. I could sure use more time … to spend with you, Sweetie Pie." She tweaked his nose. "I'll bet you did a lot of thinking in this library."

"Yep, this is the place where I wrote my bucket list, among other extremely relevant writings. I've done some of my best cogitating here in this hallowed room."

"Have you, now? You have a bucket list? I want to see this required reading."

Ceremoniously, Phil produced his list, hidden behind his Marvel comics collection, third shelf down. "Ah, here it is: my masterpiece, written at the wise old age of seventeen. Let's see what still applies today and which items I can now check off."

"Lemme see!" Molly grabbed the list out of Phil's grasp.

"Ah, ah, ah!" Phil snapped, snatching it back. "Maybe there are things I might not wish to divulge at this point."

"Yeah, right! Gimme that thing!" She snagged the list and got up on the sliding library ladder to fend off Phil's paws. "Let me see now …"

1. Make Ronnie fall in love with me
2. Win first prize for best costume at the Star Trek convention
3. Learn to speak Klingon
4. Visit Nintendo Headquarters
5. Learn to speak fluent Japanese
6. Learn how to fence (not the stolen property kind)
7. Visit ancient Egypt
8. Learn to speak ancient Egyptian
9. Explore Italy

10. Learn to speak Italian
11. Own a purple harpsichord
12. Have a family of my own someday

Molly waved the page in front of him.

"Give that back," Phil threatened, "or else."

"Whatcha gonna do to me, huh?"

"This!" Phil grabbed the ladder, which was attached to rollers on a rail that made a complete 360-degree circuit of the room. He set the ladder in motion as Molly squealed, half terrified and half thrilled at Phil's rendition of an amusement park ride.

"You're going to have to give that back and beg for mercy, Muffin."

"Never!" Molly cried defiantly.

Phil sped the ride up a bit.

"Okay, okay, here's your old bucket list. I've already read it all anyway. It's now of no use to me since its secrets have been divulged."

Phil held out a hand to help her down from what he called the Ladder of Doom.

"That actually was pretty fun," Molly admitted. "Bet you guys played on that thing all the time as kids."

"Heck no—my mom would have killed us. We only did it when my folks weren't home. In fact, she probably wanted to kill us that last time when Matt was riding a little too fast, and it started to derail. He jumped off just in time as we watched the ladder crash through the french doors. He hit the ground and got the wind knocked out of him, and the police showed up on our doorstep because a neighbor heard the noise and thought someone was breaking in. We were so busted. It took forever to clean up the mess and pay for those doors. Mom's still not over it completely. But enough about my list. I want to know what's on *your* bucket list."

"Well, I don't have a formalized list like yours. Mine's in my head. I wish I had written one at seventeen. It would be fun to see how much it had changed over the years like yours has."

"No, only one thing has changed really. Only the first thing on the list."

"Well, that's a relief to me. But you still want to learn Klingon?"

"Not nearly as badly as I used to. So what's on your list?"

"I've always wanted to learn to paint in watercolor, for one. I want to publish a cookbook, visit Italy, Switzerland, and Scotland, and I'd love to learn to ballroom dance. I never went to my junior prom or senior ball, but I really love dancing."

"Why didn't you go to your dances?"

"No one ever asked me."

"I find that hard to believe."

"It's true. I was really shy and dorky in those days. No guys wanted to go near me."

"Not if I had known you."

"Aw, you're so sweet, Phil … Anyway, back to the list. I've always wanted to knit a whole sweater; I never end up finishing them when I start one. I've always wanted to have a big pie fight my whole life, just like the ones in the Three Stooges shows: tons of pies, lots of participants. Ronnie's wedding reception came close with the cake, but it would be so much more satisfying with real, honest-to-goodness pies."

"That seems sacrilegious somehow, but I guess you get pretty sick of pies," he said, suddenly longing for a piece of that caramel apple pie. "Anything else?" he asked, salivating.

"Well, most of all I would love to get married and have a family."

Grinning, Phil picked up their not-so-steamy mugs. He handed Molly hers and raised his in a toast. "Here's to our bucket lists. May God fulfill each one—except for my first item. That one's getting crossed out right now. And I think I might want to add a little something to mine because of you."

They clinked mugs as Molly smiled from her toes up.

CHAPTER 18

I AM *the Bride!*

"Nothing like a run through the park to really wake a person up," Matt said as he breathed in the cool morning air. "Check out that squirrel, Melissa. He's gotten himself onto that thin little branch. What's he going to do?"

"What squirrel? You know you are too much of a morning person. Could you tone it down a few notches until I get some coffee?" Melissa hated running. Hated mornings. Hated a whole lot of things. But in order to keep her pencil-thin figure, she had to force herself to run … with Matt.

"Well, look at that!" Matt watched the energetic squirrel spring from the very thin branch to a more-sturdy limb of another tree. "He made it! Just took a leap of faith, and he's free."

"Would you stop with this endless morning chatter? You're like a squirrel yourself." Melissa halted.

Matt stopped in his tracks.

"Honestly, do you always have to go on and on with meaningless nature updates and insignificant observations? Really, Matthew, I don't care about a stupid squirrel and what he's doing. Big deal, so he jumped to another tree. Next you'll be telling me what kind of nut he's chewing on."

"Well, actually, it's an acorn."

"See what I mean? What is this thing you have with nature and play-by-play comments about whatever you see? Who cares?"

Matt took off running, leaving Melissa in the dust.

Matt and Melissa had a lunch date at the country club where their wedding was to take place. They were meeting with the wedding coordinator, James Penbrooke. Matt was very cool toward his intended after receiving her morning tongue lashing. They were seated at a table for two, waiting. Matt wasn't entirely sure what for.

"You seem tense, Matthew," she observed.

"Tense? Well, maybe it has something to do with how you treated me this morning."

"Oh, that. You know how I am before I have my morning coffee."

"Right. I think an apology is in order," Matt stated flatly, standing up for himself and feeling rather good about it.

Melissa pushed herself back in her chair, sat bolt upright, and folded her hands condescendingly. "Well, I'm sorry you felt hurt about the stupid squirrel. Is that what you felt? Hurt?"

"Yeah, I felt hurt and put down, and disrespected. Can't I even comment on what's going on around us?"

"I'm sorry you felt that way."

"You can't even apologize for what you said. It's always, 'I'm sorry *you felt* ...' You never admit your part in any of our arguments. You could just say, 'I'm sorry I hurt you.' Like the time I talked to you about how you constantly put down my folks. You said, 'I'm sorry *you feel* that way.' It's never, 'Gee, Matt, I'm sorry I put your folks down. I'll try not to do that anymore.' You never accept any of the blame."

"First of all, why do you insist on saying 'folks?' That's so ...

folksy. They are your *parents*, Matthew. And another thing: I'm just stating facts, so why should I apologize?"

"Because they're my *parents*, and I love them. You never hear me trash-talk your mother, do you?"

"Oh, look, here comes the wedding coordinator," Melissa glibly changed the subject.

"This discussion isn't over, Melissa."

"Let's just put it on hold for now, Matthew. Here he comes!"

A very well-groomed man in an Armani suit strolled up to their table. "You must be the happy couple," he said cheerily. "My name is James Penbrooke, and I will be assisting you in your wedding planning here at the Willow Glen Country Club. You must be the lovely Melissa." He took her hand in a courtly manner. "And this must be Matthew McGuire, computer mogul extraordinaire," he flattered, giving Matt's hand a limp-rag handshake.

"Nice to meet you, Mr. Penbrooke. I actually go by Matt."

"Sure you do. You may call me James Penbrooke." He gave a stage laugh. "Now let's get started, shall we? Today you will be sampling some of the finest selections for your wedding banquet. We will follow that up with cake samples. The chef here comes to us straight from Paris, France. Wait until you taste his Parisian Passion Fruit Perfection Cake—my personal favorite."

"Oh, Melissa, I mentioned to you that I wanted Molly to do our cake."

"Why trouble the poor thing, Matthew? Really, the cakes here are the talk of the town. I don't want some old, dried-out cake served at *my* wedding."

"That's *our* wedding, and her cakes are outstanding; Phil tells me they are perfection. I think we should sample her cakes before we decide."

"And what would your brother know about haute cake? He's just infatuated with his small town girl anyway." She smiled at James Penbrooke, who returned a knowing nod.

James Penbrooke took his cue. "Now, about the ceremony. How many attendants are there going to be?"

"I have ten bridesmaids to attend me."

"Ten? I thought we were having a smaller wedding party. I don't have ten guys. It was just going to be Phil, John, and Steve, remember?"

"Well, you'll just have to find more groomsmen. I can't have my girls walking down the aisle unescorted. Oh, and nix Jonathan. He's much too tall and gawky to walk with any of my bridesmaids."

"His name is John, not Jonathan. No one calls him Jonathan, not even his own mother. Why does it always have to be a formal name with you?"

"It's his given name, and this is a formal occasion, Matthew."

"It's Matt, Melissa. Matt!"

Penbrooke interrupted. "Now, now, it sounds like our groom has some prewedding jitters. Let's sample some meals, shall we? Here comes the veal. Observe how white the meat is under its demi-glace."

Matt suffered through the array of snooty dishes, wishing for something more recognizable. Then came the cake samples. Several flavors of cake sat on a crystal sampling plate.

"Oh, the Parisian passion fruit is to die for! Try, it, Matthew."

"Which one is it?"

"The one right here." She pointed to a yellowish orange cake sample. "We'll take the passion fruit!" Melissa gushed. "It's simply divine."

Matt took a small bite. "I'm sorry, Melissa, but this tastes like I'm eating a flower."

"Yes, isn't it exquisite?"

"No. I really think we should sample some of Molly's cakes before we make the final decision."

"But I *have* decided, Matthew. It's the passion fruit, and I am not going to sample some doughnut-slinger's sad excuse for a wedding cake. Your brother is dating someone that is so beneath him. What's wrong with him anyway? Is he blind? Now, this is *my* wedding, and it's going to be just how I've always imagined because, after all, *I am* the bride."

"And how do you think we will pay for all this? Are your mother and her current rich boyfriend paying? Or how about your deadbeat daddy? Sorry, I mean your deadbeat father."

"How dare you talk about my parents that way! Your parents are paying, remember?"

"Oh, my *folks* that you constantly put down and make snide comments about under your breath. They can hear you, you know, and so can I. You've said your last rude remarks about Phil and Molly too."

"You don't get it, Matthew! *I am the bride*!"

"Then find yourself another groom!" yelled Matt as he threw down the linen napkin on the cake samples and stormed out.

"Oh, my," gasped James Penbrooke, raising two fingers to his lips.

CHAPTER 19

I'll Be Home for Christmas

"Geez, Molly, you look tired. Were you up all night again?" Lyra asked as she worked alongside her.

"Yeah. The holiday season is wiping me out this year."

"You have so many orders. Is it always like this around Christmas?"

"Not usually this busy. Business has really picked up since we've started getting so many customers from the other side of the lake."

"Let me take some of the load, and you get some rest tonight."

"I think I'll take you up on that," Molly said, rubbing her lower back. "I don't feel so snazzy."

"Hope you're not getting what our pastor had recently. It knocked him out for over a week."

"Nah, I'm just tired," she hoped aloud. "I can't be getting sick now; we're way too busy. Maybe Stephanie would be interested in working more hours this week."

"I'm sure she would. I'll give her a call. You just go home and get some sleep for a change. If you're feeling rotten tomorrow, don't even bother coming in on Christmas Eve. Steph and I can handle it."

Molly sighed and put her hand to her forehead. Maybe it was

just the heat from the ovens she felt. "I just can't be getting sick." She could feel the fever coming on. "I'm supposed to go with Phil to his parents' house tomorrow night, with their pies."

"Don't worry about it. Just go home and get well before you get us all sick," Lyra coaxed her out the door.

Molly trudged home, barely making it to her front door.

The bell jingled enthusiastically as Phil burst into the bakery.

Lyra stepped out of the back room, dusted with flour.

"Hey, Lyra, where's that beautiful boss of yours?"

"I sent her home."

"What? Yeah, right. Was she behaving badly? Maybe she started a Christmas cookie fight?"

"No, she was trying to infect the whole town with her flu germs."

"Huh? What are you talking about?"

"Molly's sick, Phil. I think she has the flu. It's no wonder, considering how many hours she's put in lately. She's run herself down."

"She can't be sick. Tomorrow's Christmas Eve."

"Oh yes, she can. Germs take no holidays. Maybe you should drop by and check on her—if you're willing to risk it."

"I have a fantastic immune system, I'll have you know. Germs fear me," Phil bragged.

"Good. Then scare them away from Molly. Off you go." She scooted him out the door and checked her watch. "Closing time," she said as she flipped the Open sign to Closed and locked the door. Without delay, she called Stephanie to come help and then got back to work. Even with the two of them, it would be a long night, and an insanely busy day to come tomorrow.

Phil knocked urgently until Molly finally came to the door, looking like she had been through the spin cycle too many times, corkscrew curls frizzing in every direction.

"Hey, Molly, wanna go dancing?" he teased.

She gave him The Look normally reserved for obstinate children, turned an appalling shade of green, and darted off for the bathroom, leaving him standing in the golden porch light.

"I guess I'll take that as a no." Hoping that germs did indeed fear him, he took his chances and stepped inside. "Molly? I'm coming in."

"No, Phil! Go home. I don't want you to catch this."

"Germs tremble at the sound of my name. I eat them for breakfast. Now what can I do for you, my poor Muffin? Some ginger ale, chicken soup, chorizo?"

There was The Look again. It made him shiver. "I'll be fine, Phil. Just let me get some sleep. I feel disgusting."

"Let me take care of you. I bought some ginger ale on the way over. You go back to bed, and I'll bring a cold cloth for your forehead."

"No, Phil. Honestly, you have to be at your parents' tomorrow. You don't want to make them sick. Go home. I'll be fine. I just need to sleep ..." She quickly covered her mouth and ran back into the bathroom. It was going to be a long night here on Periwinkle Way.

Phil read the thermometer: 103 degrees. It had climbed two degrees since he had arrived two hours ago. He got a cold wash cloth and replaced the steamy one on her forehead. Remembering how his mom would take care of him, he crushed some ice and attempted to feed her ice chips with a spoon. At first she refused them, but with some encouragement she finally agreed to try some. It seemed to cool her down a bit.

He kept the night shift going from the wooden rocking chair

he'd dragged next to her bed. She fell asleep in the wee hours, and Phil dozed in the rocker. She awoke to find Phil sleeping in the chair beside her. Molly tried to creep quietly to the bathroom so as not to wake him, but on her way back, Phil opened one eye and then the other.

"Where do you think you're going?" he asked, yawning.

"Going? I'm going crazy," Molly replied. "I've got to get well right now. I've got too much to do to be sick."

"I don't think so, Muffin. You've got the flu—face it. Lyra and Stephanie will take care of things." He helped her back to bed and pulled her blue and yellow flowered quilt under her chin to stave off the shivers as her fever gave way to chills.

Phil spent the rest of his day fixing chicken noodle soup and attending to his flu-ridden patient. Late in the afternoon Molly urged him to head off to his parents' house for Christmas Eve, but he refused to leave her. Her fever waxed and waned throughout the day and began to climb again as evening fell. He quietly called his folks to let them know he wouldn't be coming.

"I'm so sorry you're missing Christmas Eve, Phil," Molly mumbled through her lingering fever.

"I'm not missing Christmas Eve, Sweetie. I'm right where I want to be: with you. Now try to get some sleep."

Molly soon nodded off.

Phil went out to his car, brought in the Christmas gifts he'd wrapped up for Molly, and slipped them under the small Christmas tree they had decorated together earlier in the month with ornaments of different varieties of birds and silk magnolia blossoms. He hung two stockings on her mantel and filled hers up with little presents. Then he returned to the rocker to keep vigil over his sweet angel. He dozed off somewhere in the night to the sound of her steady breathing.

Phil awoke to a small dusting of snow on the ground. Not much snow dared to stick in River Oaks, so he knew the kids in town would be delighted to have a little snow for Christmas. He tried to unkink his neck as he tiptoed into the kitchen to make a little light breakfast for Molly when she woke up. Maybe she could handle some oatmeal this morning, since the soup had gone down well last night. He looked around to find all the necessities for making oatmeal with brown sugar and golden raisins. Along about the time he'd finished the culinary masterpiece, Molly shuffled into the kitchen with her fuzzy pink slippers.

"Merry Christmas," Phil said cheerily, giving her a hug.

"Careful, I've got germs."

"I snack on them, remember?" gloated Phil.

"Uh-huh?" Molly raised one eyebrow.

"Yes, I do—wheat germ, to be specific."

"That doesn't count, Phil."

"That's what you think. Now how about some oatmeal?"

"No one has made me oatmeal since I was a kid." Molly smiled. "How sweet of you!"

"I figured it might be bland enough to a sensitive stomach. Did you see there's snow this morning?" he asked as he spooned the oatmeal into a red and white bowl.

Molly walked over to the kitchen window. "Oh my, it hasn't snowed on Christmas in forever. I remember my dad and I playing in the snow on Christmas Day once when I was about ten. I secretly stuck a snowball in his pocket, but it didn't stay secret for long."

"Looks like Santa came last night when we were sleeping. He left you something under the tree. Let's go check it out after you eat breakfast."

Molly was beginning to get her appetite back, and the fever seemed to have vanished during the night. She still felt pretty weak, though.

Treeside after breakfast, Phil carried a tall, narrow box to her. "I think you'll like this. At least, I hope you will," he said.

Molly ripped off the silver wrapping paper and bow. She could hardly wait to see what was inside. "Oh my gosh, Phil." She fanned her face, trying to fend off tears. "It's that painting of the little girl dancing with her daddy—the one we saw at the Gallery Restaurant after the concert. You remembered! But it was so expensive. You shouldn't have spent so much!"

"I knew you loved it. So where do you want me to hang it?"

"I think it'd be perfect in the dining room. But let's hang it later. You have to open your present from me now." She stood unsteadily to retrieve it from the back of the tree. "It's that purple harpsichord you've always wanted," Molly joked.

"Hardly big enough," Phil reasoned as he tore the side seam of the red polka-dotted wrapping paper. "What is this?" he wondered aloud as he pulled away the wrapping. "A Rosetta Stone Italian language course!"

"Complete with live online lessons, interactive software, and cell phone and tablet apps. You'll be ready for Italy in no time, Phil."

"Learning Italian was on my bucket list. Wow! And games too! I'm going to love this."

"Speaking of bucket lists, I got you a little something else." She pulled a small package from under the couch. "Here you go."

"Two presents?" He wasted no time opening it. "A Klingon dictionary? You crack me up, woman. I love it!" He pointed to the mantel. "Why, look at your Christmas stocking—it's bursting with surprises."

"What? I didn't put up any stockings. I haven't done that since my parents died. Phil, how did these get here?"

"Must've been Santa." Phil snatched them both from the mantel. "Look, Molly, I got a rock!" He pulled an old granite rock out of his stocking, pretending to admire it. "What's in yours?"

Molly was secretly hoping for a rock of a smaller, sparklier nature. There were three boxes. She saved the smallest one for last. The largest box contained an assortment of fine chocolates, the work of an artistic chocolatier. The second box held boxes nested in boxes until she reached one containing a gift card to Robins's Nest, the local yarn store.

"Now you can knit that sweater from your bucket list," Phil said with a chuckle.

"I just might, now that I have two assistants at the bakery." Molly smiled. "Thank you, Phil." She took a deep breath as she cradled the remaining tiny box. She opened the lid and saw a black velvet box inside. Stifling a gasp, she slowly opened the box revealing … a lovely pair of half carat diamond earrings. Not the kind of ring she'd had in mind, but lovely nonetheless. "Oh, they're gorgeous, Phil," she said, admiring them and tucking the idea of a ring away. "Look at how they sparkle, even in this dim light."

"Just like you, my love," Phil crooned. "Now, you need your rest. It's off to bed for you. I'll be back later on this afternoon to check on you." He gave her a big hug and tucked her back into bed.

Chapter 20

When Love Is Over the Top ... of a Casket

"Are you sure I'm dressed okay, Phil?" Molly spun slowly before him in her living room. She modeled her brand-new, deep-forest-green version of a little black dress and matching low vamp heels.

"Uh, yeah. Spin around again." Molly obliged. "I'll be the envy of every man there."

"Oh, Phil, go on." There was a pause as he admired her. "Ahem. I said, 'go on.'"

"Uh, yeah, sorry, I just got a bit mesmerized. You look amazing, stunning, gorgeous, breathtaking ... well, buoyant."

"What? I float?"

"You float my boat!"

"You're a crazy man, you know that?"

"Crazy about you."

"At this rate, we'll never get to your class reunion."

"You say that like it's a bad thing."

"Come on, Phil." She pulled him by the tie. "You've missed all your other reunions; you're going to this one. By the way, why didn't you go to the five- or ten-year ones?"

"Didn't have you to go with—or to force me to go."

After arriving in the Bentley, Phil opened Molly's door and admired her grace as she stepped out of the vehicle. Suddenly, someone grabbed his right shoulder and ordered in an authoritative voice, "Step away from the car, and no one gets hurt."

"What?" Phil spun around, ready to defend, when he realized who it was. "Mitch, you Death Legion Drone, you scared me to death. I lost two whole lives. Now my stats are all down."

"Hey, Frogman, just getting revenge for all the times you clobbered my Dronemaster."

"How the heck are you, man?"

"I'm doing good, but obviously not as good as you're doing! This must be Molly."

"Who's Molly, Phil?" Molly asked jokingly.

Phil played along, enjoying Mitchell's discomfort. "Uh, this is … Milly."

"I thought you said her name was Molly in all of your e-mails."

"We'll talk about this 'Molly' person later, Phil," she threatened, giving him a believable stink eye.

"Sorry about getting your name wrong, Milly." Mitch cleared his throat. "So, uh, how long have you two been dating?" he asked cautiously this time, wondering what had happened to the Molly he had heard so much about.

"Not long," Molly answered, "and maybe not much longer, now that I'm hearing about this Molly woman. Tell me, Mitch, how long has he been talking about this other woman?"

"Uh, I don't know. I'm not that good with time," he said lamely, looking at Phil and pleading for some help. Phil raised his eyebrows, clearly in need himself. "It was … a while ago."

"So Mitch," Phil appeared to be very nervous and attempted to change the subject. "How's business going?"

Greatly relieved at the change in direction of the conversation, Mitch replied, "Business has never been better. My games have been picked up by a major gaming corporation. A new one is set to be released here in America in six months. It's already been breaking records in Japan and Europe. Who would've thought all those hours playing Death Legion could have led me into a career designing my own games? I'm loving life, and they're loving me in Japan. You should come with me sometime."

"That would be so cool," Phil said. "I've never been to Japan … or much of anywhere, for that matter."

They reached the door of the Art Nouveau Hotel, where the reunion was being held, and were guided to the ballroom where their classmates were talking and laughing in small groups. The jocks and cheerleaders were together on one side of the room, busy impressing each other, while the remainder of the groups were scattered around the rest of the room.

Kind of like the two sides of the lake at home, Molly thought to herself. The haves and the have-nots often seemed to separate themselves out. Life was strange that way. But somehow Phil had crossed over and found himself on her side of the lake. She was sure glad he had.

She wondered how much longer she should carry on the charade of being Milly with Mitch. It was fun, but sooner or later they'd have to tell him the truth and let him off the hook.

Phil was thinking the same thing, but he hoped to carry off the deception a little longer for vengeance's sake. After the scare in the parking lot, Phil owed him one.

A former cheerleader, Margie, was making her rounds with husband and former football captain Ken in tow. She walked up to Phil, Mitch, and Molly; said hello; and, trying not to be conspicuous, glanced at Phil and Mitch's name tags. She clearly had no idea who they were. The name tags weren't much help—she had not much noticed either of them fifteen years ago either. After looking to Molly, who was not wearing a name tag, Margie wondered who this perky brunette was. She concluded the newcomer must be a date. Margie certainly would have remembered such a rival in the good old days when she was queen of the campus.

Margie had obviously taken good care of herself and might have already had work done to enhance things. *Not a smile wrinkle to her name*, Molly observed.

"Hi, I'm Margie, and you are …?" she addressed Molly.

"This is my girlfriend … Milly." Phil hesitated, not knowing whether to say Milly or Molly with Mitch standing there.

Molly continued to play along, not caring who this Margie chick thought she was anyway.

"Hello, Margie," Molly said, shaking her hand. Molly could sense the cheerleaderness oozing from each pore of her new acquaintance.

"This is my husband, Ken," she announced a bit too loudly, making sure everyone knew that she had landed the captain of the football team.

Molly smiled. "Nice to meet you both."

"So what are you all doing with yourselves these days?" queried Margie.

"Selling lots of video games," Mitch piped up, having always had a secret crush on Margie and happy for some attention from her—already more than he'd ever gotten in high school.

"Still working at some video game store, huh?" Ken asked.

"No, I'm designing games for Mind Benders now. Had a few strokes of luck, producing Megakill and Doomvaders. My latest game is coming out in a few months."

"Are you joking?" Ken was in shock. "Megakill is like my all-time favorite game, man. You're a genius!"

"Wait till you see my latest one, Zombie Nations Two. It leaves my other games in the dust."

"Hey, wait. I remember you now: you're the little short kid we used to pick on in PE all the time. Sorry about that. I was pretty stupid back then. I never knew you'd turn out to be such a cool dude."

"That's all water under the bridge now." Mitch pretended it didn't matter anymore, though if he listened hard enough, he could still hear the insults that never seemed to go away. "So what are you doing now, Ken?"

"Tore my ACL in college football, never healed right, couldn't play ball anymore. I sell insurance now. Worked my way up in the business." He sniffed proudly, puffed out his chest, and reached into his shirt pocket for some business cards. After handing them out, he continued. "Working mostly with big corporations now, providing life insurance to their employees. But I could work out something for old friends like you." He cleared his throat, drawing everyone's straying attention back to him. "I hardly have to work anymore, got so many people working under me. You know how it is." He rocked back on his heels and looked over at Phil's name tag for some help. "And you … what are you doing these days?" Ken's eyes wandered. He winked at Molly, who was not in the slightest impressed by the former football hero.

How strange, she thought, *that some people have fallen right back into those old high school roles. Poor Ken, holding onto his glory days. High school was obviously the pinnacle of his life, with nowhere to go but down. He must have lived for this reunion, even if it was only a night to remember how highly he had once been regarded.*

"Still programming. Still playing piano. Not a very glamorous life, I'm afraid. I leave all the glamour to Milly here."

Molly held on tight to Phil's arm and looked up at him adoringly. "Phil is the best thing that's ever happened to me," she fawned.

"So, you two married?" Ken quizzed, a bit too interested, as Margie, squeezing his arm much tighter, began leading him away toward the next group of potential admirers.

"Not yet," Phil answered the retreating insurance salesman.

Interesting answer, Molly thought to herself. *He made it sound inevitable.* She couldn't help but smile in spite of herself.

"Those two were a royal pain in the buttocks," Phil said when they were long out of earshot. "Everyone was beneath them."

"I was literally beneath them," Mitch said. "More than once Ken knocked me down and sat on me in phys ed. He made me the laughingstock of the gym and had no mercy. I wish I'd been taller in high school. I didn't get tall until I was nineteen." Mitch was at least six foot three now in stocking feet, Molly guessed. "I'll bet I could take him at basketball these days."

"Shame on him for being so mean in high school," Molly said. "There must've been some nice kids at your school."

"As a matter of fact, there were. Let's go find our friends from Young Life," Phil suggested.

While looking about the room, Mitch spotted a group of their old friends standing over by the punch bowl. The three of them walked over to join the group.

"Hey, guys, look! It's Frogman and Mitch!" announced one of their former youth group friends.

Introductions of Molly/Milly were made all around. Everyone caught up on what they'd all been doing for the last fifteen years.

A rather shy-looking girl made her way over to Mitch's side. "Hi, Mitch, remember me?"

"Of course I do, Cindy." He bent down and gave her a long, warm hug. "How are you doing?"

"I'm doing great. How about you?" She pushed past her shyness successfully.

"I'm good too." An awkward silence came upon them. "So, what are you doing with yourself these days?" Mitch ventured.

"Still working for my dad's construction company, keeping the books and office managing. Nothing very exciting, really." She looked up at him, having a hard time keeping eye contact. "What about you?" she asked.

"I'm still into video games, except now I'm designing them."

"I know. I've been following you online. I really love your games, especially Stargrinder's Revenge. I like the sci-fi theme. The graphics are awesome; when I play that game, I feel like I'm really there, in another world."

Mitch remembered Cindy. She was always painfully shy. He had wanted to get to know her better, but she had always turned red and panicked whenever he approached her in their youth group. *Looks like she's a bit more outgoing nowadays*, he decided.

Dinner was announced, and Mitch took a chance and invited her to sit with him at his table.

Their group found two large, unoccupied tables and filled all the chairs. Mitch glanced to see if Cindy was wearing a wedding ring. He'd hit pay dirt: there was none. *This might turn out to be an interesting evening after all*, he thought. Now here she was, sitting next to him and actually conversing.

Cindy mustered up all her courage just to say hello to Mitch. She had been waiting for the class reunion for months now, and she'd even lost twenty pounds, hoping he'd show up this time. She had come to previous reunions only to leave early, disappointed at not finding him there. Cindy had told herself that if he was here this time, she would force herself to go up and talk to him, to find some way to connect. She had been fearing the worst: that he would be married. That would be the end of her two-decade-long crush on him. Luckily, he bore no sign of a wedding ring, and not even a tan line where one might have been. She told herself this was her one big chance to make an impression on him. Her heart was beating wildly as she found herself actually sitting beside him.

Mitch remembered how smart Cindy had been in math and science classes. They had always been seated next to each other because their last names started with the same letter. He had been grateful for that. They had been lab partners a few times. Mitch had attempted to joke with her, and she would invariably look down and blush. He had found this very endearing. She was a bit of an enigma, and he still wondered who she was, hiding behind that veil of shyness and thick glasses. She was, however, wearing makeup these days and had beautiful, long lashes. Her skin was now smooth where acne used to encroach, and he couldn't help but notice her curves.

Cindy stole a quick glance at his profile when he turned to talk with Phil. There was that larger-than-life nose that she loved so much, but man, had he grown taller. She could hardly believe it was him at first. He'd barely been taller than she was at only five foot six back in school. Now he was almost a foot taller with that wild mane of wavy brown hair. And he seemed so confident. Here he was, a big-time video game designer. What could he possibly see in her? Still, she would enjoy and treasure this evening the rest of her life, just to be asked to sit next to him at dinner. Enthralled with his smile, she grew dazed until he turned to look at her. She found herself blushing as she looked down to study her salad plate, which her fork had hardly touched due to her nervous stomach.

Molly felt Cindy's uneasiness and made conversation with her as they excused themselves to use the ladies' room. "So, Cindy, which construction company do you work for?"

"Cornerstone Construction. I've been working there since I was sixteen."

"Keeping books and office managing must be a pretty challenging job." Molly kept the conversation going.

"Not really," Cindy said. "I've been doing it for so long that I could do it in my sleep. How about you? What do you do, Milly?"

"I'll let you in on a little secret. My name's really Molly. Phil and I are just playing a little joke on Mitch. It's an ages-long story of revenge, I'm told. I guess they've been playing tricks on each other all their lives. This just happens to be another one. I'm playing along for now."

"What did you say you do for a living?" Cindy inquired.

"I'm a baker. I run the family business in River Oaks. It's a small town north of here."

"I love baking," Cindy said. "I just lost twenty pounds for this reunion, so I haven't been baking much lately. The guys at the shop are disappointed in me on account of it. I usually bake for them on Thursdays."

"Well, you look great," Molly complimented. "Congrats!"

"Thanks. I had to lose weight just in case.…" She caught herself.

"Just in case what?"

Cindy sighed. "In case Mitch showed up at this reunion." Her cheeks bloomed a bright pink. "I probably shouldn't tell you that. Please don't say anything to Mitch." She regretted divulging her secret, especially to someone she had just met.

"Don't worry, Cindy, I wouldn't dream of telling him. Is this a crush since high school days?"

"Yes." She studied the soap bubbles on her hands. Without looking up, she confessed, "I fell for him at thirteen when he and I were lab partners in physical science. He was just so funny. He and I competed for the highest scores in science classes all through high school. I've been praying for him ever since then. I remember how excited I was when Mitch and Phil starting coming to Young Life. I was with the group of kids who invited them one day on the quad when they were playing the Casio keyboard and ukulele. My prayers were answered a few weeks later, when Mitch decided to become a Christian."

"And he has no idea that you were praying for him all this time?"

"No. I've always been too scared to talk to him … until tonight."

"Well, let's not waste any more time. Let's get you back out there. Maybe he'll ask you to dance."

"Oh, I couldn't possibly! I don't know how to dance."

"It's easy. Just have fun and follow his lead. I'll be praying for you."

"Thanks, Molly. I appreciate it."

"No problem. Now let's go."

When Molly and Cindy returned to the table, they found the group reminiscing. "I remember all the practical jokes they used to play on each other in Young Life," said former cheerleader Debbie. "Like when Mitch put his sister's panties in Phil's gym locker and stole his underwear. It was the talk of the school. It even made it into the yearbook. They were always making us laugh."

"Thanks a lot. I'll never live that down," Phil muttered.

"And the legend continues," gloated Mitch.

By this time Phil thought he should tell Mitch Molly's real name. As the girls came back to the table, the main course was served: prime rib, au gratin potatoes, and grilled asparagus. Phil figured he'd wait until after dinner to tell him.

"So, how did you two meet?" Mitch asked Phil.

"Tell them, Muffin." Phil stuck Molly with coming up with a good story. Molly stepped on his foot under the table, but he nodded, urging her on.

"Well." She wiped the sides of her lips with her linen napkin to stall for time. "We met at a funeral, actually. Didn't we, Sweetie Pie?" She nudged him with her knee.

"Ah, yes, yes we did. We were both up front viewing the deceased at the same time. You know how you all take turns? She commented on how nice the dead guy looked and said that she didn't know that Mr. Wimple ever owned a suit, and how much weight he'd lost since she last saw him. And I said something about using the same fake body for all their funerals and just switching heads. She burst out laughing right there in the funeral parlor, and the rest is history, isn't it, Muffin?"

Molly could hardly believe he would make up such a story, and couldn't help bursting into laughter. She decided it was time to tell Mitchell the truth, but Phil continued.

"Our first date was in a parking lot in the rain. She didn't know me very well, so we agreed to meet in the parking lot at a nearby Mr. Pancakehead restaurant for breakfast. It was just pouring, and I couldn't see through the windows of my car, so I had to stand out under the awning, waiting. The wind was howling, and I was soaked to the skin. But what I didn't realize was that she had already gone inside and found us a table. An hour passed, and I thought she had stood me up. I finally went inside to dry off and get a cup of coffee just as she was getting ready to leave, thinking I was a no-show. I slipped and fell as she was walking toward the door. She stepped over me, looked down, and said, 'What'd you do, swim? You'll need to swim faster if you're gonna catch me.' She walked out the door. I knew at that very moment that she was the one. 'Milly!' I yelled, "Milly, come back! You're the one!' The rain drenched our lonely bodies, but it couldn't cool the passion we felt for each other. At that moment I touched her cheek, which warmed under the heat of my caress. 'Yes,' she said, 'you are my one true love. I knew it from the moment I set eyes on you from across the casket.' We embraced the sweet surrender of our hearts and knew it would be a forever love."

Phil was having a hard time not laughing at his own version of a romance novel. Here, he paused to compose himself.

His pause was met with a chorus of sighs from all the women at the table. All the men's mouths were gaping in disbelief that this once-nerdy guy could live such a life of unbridled passion.

"Phillip! So glad you could make it," gushed Ronnie, who had just paraded up to their table. "Oh, I see you've brought *her* with you. Hello, Milly, I see you've taken off your flour-covered blue collar and decided to join the white-collar class. Now nicely you clean up."

"Hello, Ronnie," Molly said smoothly. "So nice to see you again. I almost didn't recognize you without cake on your face."

"Fried any greasy doughnuts lately? It must be nice to do such mindless work. Manual labor has never been my strong suit. Seems to fit you nicely, though."

The men at the table closed their mouths and prepared for the cat fight.

"Ronnie, that's enough!" Phil stood up to face her.

"I don't know what you see in this little nobody. Why would you want to cross over to her side of the tracks? For this … Molly?"

"She's Milly," everyone at the table said in unison.

"Stand down, Veronica," warned Mark, their former classmate who happened to be a lieutenant in the Marin County Police Force. "You're getting out of hand, and nobody wants you at this table."

His wife, Sherrie, spoke up with a quote from *The Wizard of Oz,* "Begone before someone drops a house on you too."

Both tables of former nerds and friends laughed out loud.

Ronnie, unable to devise a comeback, turned on her very high heels and joined Michael at the bar.

"You were telling us about your first date with Milly before we were so rudely interrupted," prompted Sherrie.

"I have a confession to make. We were playing a joke on Mitch here. Milly's name is really Molly, and we actually met at her bakery."

His audience responded with a chorus of disappointed sighs and groans.

"We don't care if you made it up. Just finish the story already!" Sherrie pleaded. "This is better than one of those cheap romance novels."

"You got me again," Mitchell said as he face-palmed himself. "You Saturnian Whelp, you! I'll get even if it's the last thing I do."

"You should know better than to mess with the Sultan of Prank," Phil crowed.

"Hey, what's with Ronnie anyway?" Mark questioned.

"I think it has to do with her wearing her own wedding cake," Molly answered.

"What?" everyone asked.

"Yeah, she's been in a bad mood ever since. Never mind her—I want to hear what you've all been doing," Phil said.

Dinner ensued as Margie got up to the podium to give her spiel, talking about the "good old days" in high school. She gave away gift certificates to the longest married couple, the one who had the most children, the one who had been married the most times (a dubious distinction), and the one who had traveled the farthest to attend the reunion. Then she and her former cheerleader friends got up and did some of their old cheers. Everyone was happy when she was done and the dance floor was pronounced open.

The band began playing old favorite songs from their high school days. They got down to "Funky Town," grooved to "Beat It," and chilled to "Ghostbusters."

As "The Eye of the Tiger" wound down, Phil recognized the first few notes of the next song. He grabbed Molly and said, "Listen, they're playing our song!"

"'Walk Like an Egyptian'? When did that become our song?"

"Okay, *my* song. Let's dance."

Mitch and Cindy found themselves alone at the table. "So, do you come here often?" Mitch asked in his smoothest voice.

Cindy giggled a reply. "No one's ever asked me that before."

"Me neither." He smirked. "Want to dance?"

"Uh, I don't know how to," Cindy struggled with her reply.

"Neither do I, but we've got to be better dancers than Phil when he gets going."

"Oh, I don't know …"

"Come on. I'll show you how. Here's a slow dance. Just follow my lead." They stepped out to join the other dancers. "Here, hold my hand like this. You put your other hand on my shoulder. That's right. And I'll put my hand on your waist. Now just step when I step, and I'll guide you forward or backward with my hand. That's the way. You've got it. We just move to the music."

Cindy watched the other couples cozy up to each other so comfortably. She couldn't believe she was here in Mitch's arms. It felt amazing, even better than she had imagined it would. She dared to look up at Mitch, and he was smiling down at her.

He spoke softly. "You know, I always wondered what it would be like to dance with you. In high school I always had a kind of crush on you. You were always so smart and cute, and you always twirled you hair around your finger when I talked to you. I hoped you were just shy, and you weren't just being polite and actually wanting me to go away."

"Oh, I would never want you to go away—I mean, I'm just, you know, shy." She paused, gathering her courage. "This is nice, dancing with you."

"It *is* nice, and you look lovely."

Cindy wasn't used to compliments and didn't know what to say. She looked down. "You know, I always had a secret crush on you back then, too." She couldn't believe she had admitted it, but there it was.

"Well, then, we've wasted an awful lot of time, haven't we?"

She put her head on his chest, supremely happy. They danced.

The group sat back at the table and started talking about some of their classmates who hadn't attended the reunion. "What ever happened to Vincent?" Phil asked.

"Oh yeah, that kid who always got bullied. The one you taught piano to," said Alan, the stockbroker.

"I thought you knew, Phil," Mitch replied. "He's in Europe doing concerts on tour. Didn't you read that online?"

"Wow, I knew that he was good, but I had no idea how good."

"Well, he never would have learned to play if it wasn't for you," said Mitch.

"All I did was teach him the basics; the rest was up to him."

"He's just being modest, Milly—I mean Molly," Mitch told her. "Vincent didn't fit in anywhere. Phil took it upon himself to befriend him and give him somewhere to belong. Once Phil brought him into our group, we all did our best to encourage him. We found out later that he'd been planning to commit suicide. Sure glad you jumped into his life, buddy." Mitch patted Phil on the back.

Molly looked up, admiring Phil. What a heart he had. Her parents would have been so happy that she had found someone so caring. Wasn't she the luckiest woman alive? She reached over and grabbed his hand, so proud of the person he was.

The evening wore on, and it was well past midnight. Phil and Molly had a drive ahead of them. They said their good-byes with a promise to have Mitch and Cindy over for dinner at Molly's soon.

"I wish this night would never end," Cindy breathed.

"Why should it? Let's go over to Mr. Pancakehead's," Mitch suggested. "Maybe if we're lucky, it'll start raining."

Chapter 21

When You Give a Dope a Rope

Molly decided to put together a mystery date for Phil. Once she decided what they were going to do, she cleverly left a trail of misinformation behind for him to follow.

"Lyra, I'm going to need your help," Molly said, dusting flour from her hands.

"You know, 'kneading' is my specialty. Just what do you 'knead?'" Lyra teased.

"You're starting to sound just like Phil," Molly scolded. "I'm going to trick Phil into thinking that we're going cave exploring. I'll be 'inadvertently' dropping clues for him here and there, and I'll need you to play along with me and maybe drop a few hints of your own over the next couple days. Are you game?"

"Sounds fun. Of course I'll help."

"So here's the plan …"

Phil had no idea what he was walking into that morning as he came in for his usual apple fritter. As he sauntered in, Molly and Lyra hurriedly attempted to refold a large map they had been pretending to study together.

Molly whispered just loud enough for him to hear, "Lyra, take this in the back room, quickly."

Lyra disappeared, fumbling with the map.

"What are you two girls doing with a map?" Phil could never resist a mystery.

"Oh, nothing, Phil. How are you doing this morning? Your usual?" she asked a bit too quickly.

"Yeah. So, what are you girls up to anyway?"

"I told you, it's nothing. How is that apocalyptic work project going? I haven't seen much of you these past couple weeks."

"It's all going to end soon, with a big bang. Looks like I'll be done with it by Wednesday. Gotta take a trip into Sacramento on Thursday for a meeting to make sure everything's running smoothly. I just love being ahead of schedule on a project."

"I'm so glad it's almost done. I've been really missing you. As a matter of fact, I'm planning a little date for us on Friday, if you're up for it, after you wrap up this thing you've been slaving over."

"Great! It'll give me something to look forward to, a reward at the end of the tunnel. This job has been a real bear. So where are we going?"

"Oh, that's a secret."

"What? How intriguing! Are we leaving town? I saw you and Lyra looking at a map. So where to?"

"I'm telling you nothing. All I'm saying is wear old clothes that you won't mind getting dirty. And there are a few things you'll need to bring. Here's a list." She brought forth a paper from under the counter. The list contained the following items: heavy duty flashlight, extra batteries, thirty feet of rope, and shoes with good traction.

"What? And just what have you got up your sleeve, little missy?"

"Only my arm. We'll be leaving at the crack of noon, if that's not too early for you."

"I think I can manage that. Sure you don't want to tell me where it is we're going?"

"That's for me to know and for you to find out."

"Bring it on! I love a challenge!"

"Oh, and bring something nice to change into for … afterward. We'll probably want to go to dinner after our adventure. Oh, excuse me a minute; I need to run over to the store. I'm almost out of butter; my dairy delivery didn't show up today. And don't you go getting into any trouble while I'm gone. I'll be back in a flash."

"Right," Phil mumbled through a mouthful of fritter. As soon as she was out of sight, Phil made a dash for the back room and threw apart the curtains hanging in the doorway. He grabbed the map before Lyra, who had her hands full of dough, could stop him. "Ha! A map of Calaveras County!" He threw the map open and saw the yellow highlighter marks circling the words, "Cave City."

"No! Give that back!" Lyra yelled convincingly. "You can't look at that! You'll ruin Molly's surprise!"

"Spelunking! So that's what she's up to, huh? Just as I suspected."

"Yeah, right, Phil." With doughy fingers, Lyra wrestled the map from him and put it behind her back.

"It's okay, Lyra. I don't need to see it anymore; I know where we're going now."

"Phil! You totally messed up her surprise. She's going to be so sad. She's worked so hard, planning something special for you. Now you've gone and spoiled it. Shame on you! Well, there's only one solution; you've got to pretend that you don't know where you're going and act surprised when you get there." Lyra shook her finger at Phil. "Got it, mister?" She left flour dust hanging in the air.

"You're right. I don't want to disappoint Molly. Okay, I'll pretend I don't know where we're going."

"Now get out there. She'll be back any minute. And eat a lot of your fritter so it looks like you've been just sitting there, eating. Hurry! I'll cover for you."

"Thanks, Lyra. You're a pal." Leaving her wincing at the all too frequent title she had come to resent, he ran back out to his table and wolfed down half of his fritter in one huge bite. He managed to swallow the last bit of it as he saw Molly rounding the corner. He grabbed his cup of black coffee and gulped a few swallows to clear the last glob from his throat. Phil crossed his left ankle over the top of his right knee, trying his best to look nonchalant as Molly walked in the door, jingling the silver bell that hung over it.

"Wow, that was quick," Phil commented.

"Yep. Didn't need much." Molly took the five pounds of butter to the back room and handed it to Lyra. They gave each other a wink before Molly headed back into the dining area and sat at Phil's table. They chatted awhile until Phil excused himself to get back to his all-consuming project. As he left, Molly walked into the kitchen and gave her partner in crime a high-five.

"Hook, line, and sinker," Lyra cried.

"More like hook, line, and stinker," Molly laughed. "How dare he try to discover my secret plan! He'd have to get up pretty early in the morning to outsmart me." Molly and Lyra joined in a maniacal laugh and gave each other a double high-five.

With his deadline satisfied, the poor, unsuspecting Phil stumbled right into Molly's trap. At precisely noon, he rang her doorbell, the requested supplies in a box at his feet and the thirty feet of rope slung, *Raiders of the Lost Ark* style, over his shoulder. Phil waited in an ancient pair of 501s and an old flannel button-down shirt.

Molly let him in. With unspeakable finesse, he tossed the rope onto the couch and hurried over to give her a debonair kiss.

"I'm almost ready," she said. "Just gotta get my shoes. I'll be right back."

Phil sat on the couch and looked over at Molly's coffee table. Under a stack of magazines he spied a *Spelunking for Idiots* book. *Oh, yeah, just one more piece of evidence. Molly clearly isn't very skilled in the art of deception. That's okay with me.* He would act surprised when the time came. Phil knew he could pull this off, being the excellent actor that he fancied himself to be.

"Okay, I'm ready," she said, finishing a knot in the red bandana around her neck. Molly was in a pair of old denim overalls, an equally old long-sleeved red shirt, and hiking boots. He had to admit that girl looked hot in anything. Was he the luckiest man in the world, or what? "I'll grab our snacks and drinks, and we can be off. You did bring a change of clothes with you for dinner, right?" Molly said, disappearing into the kitchen for the basket of goodies.

"Oh, yeah. I thought of everything," he bragged. Phil rummaged through the box and produced a lantern and some waterproof matches." Here're a few things that weren't on your list. I looked for bat repellent online. Funny, I couldn't seem to find any."

"Bat repellent? Why would we need that?"

"You never know. So where are we going to eat?"

"Oh, I don't know. We'll figure something out. There're lots of places to eat down there."

"Down there? So we're heading south, are we?"

"Oh, shoot! No more hints! I must be more careful about what I say," she reminded herself.

Phil grabbed the basket, and Molly handed him the rope. She picked up her change of clothes and shoes, turned the key in her front door, and smiled a sly smile. "Bat repellent. Hmph. Off we go, then," she commanded. "We're taking my car this time. I'm driving, since I'm the only one who knows where we're going. Hop in."

Phil smiled to himself knowingly. "So you like adventure, then?"

"Oh, yes. My dad and I used to go on treks together. Mom wasn't much for the out-of-doors. Dad and I went where we're going today and did some exploring. I'll bet you've never been where we're going."

"You'd be surprised, Molly. I'm a man of mystery, intrigue, and keen adventure."

"Let's just see how good your sleuthing abilities really are then."

They drove, chatting and joking for a while. "Have you figured it out yet, Phil?"

He had a big grin on his face, feeling rather smug. "Yes, I believe I have, in fact."

"Very good. I need to stop for gas and use the facilities," Molly said. "I need a little help with my map too." She pulled into a gas station with a convenience store. Phil pumped her gas while she went inside, presumably to ask for directions.

He watched through the window as Molly spoke with the guy behind the counter. "She's so lost already," he chuckled. Then he saw the attendant start laughing. Molly joined in. *Hmm, I wonder what that's all about.*

When she returned, Phil spoke up. "You really didn't need to ask for directions. I think I could easily get us there from here."

"Oh, really? Well, I do know how to navigate, and you don't know where we're going anyway." Molly pulled out of the gas station and turned the car in the opposite direction.

"Hey, Muffin, you're going the wrong way," Phil corrected.

"Oh, am I now? Who's the one who planned this trip, anyway?" Molly replied, trying hard to conceal her glee.

"I'm not kidding, Molly. We're going to get lost. This is the wrong way."

"Just trust me, Phil. Sit back, relax, and let me handle it."

At least we have a tankful of gas now, Phil consoled himself. *Who knows how lost we're going to get*? "Really, Molly, we're headed north now. You do realize that, don't you?"

"Don't be silly, Phil. I know which way I'm going. Relax, chill out, and enjoy the view."

This will be a wonderful story to joke about in years to come, thought Phil. *The time Molly got us so lost we ended up in Canada.* He chuckled to himself.

"What are you laughing about, mister? I know where I'm going."

"Nothing. Just don't blame me when you discover we're hopelessly lost."

"Harrumph," Molly pouted. "Now tell me all about this big assignment you just finished for work."

Before Phil knew it, they were way up north, far off course from Cave City, and up in the Sierra Nevada Mountains. Every once in a while she would pretend she was lost, but determined to reach their destination going the wrong way.

"Where the heck are we?" Phil finally asked.

"Right on course," Molly proudly announced as they pulled into a parking lot at another gas station. "Time to change clothes!"

"What? What are you talking about? What happened to cave exploring? We don't want our good clothes to get all messed up in the cave."

"What cave? Who said anything about caves? What are you talking about, Phil? Now where are your good clothes?"

"My good clothes?" groaned the dumbfounded Phil. "They're in the trunk of my car, back at your place! I thought we would be taking my car."

"You forgot to switch them to my car? Oh, that's bad, very bad for you," Molly snickered. "Now what'll we do?"

"What do you mean, what'll we do? Where are we, and what are we doing here? You tricked me, Muffin. You led me to believe we were going spelunking."

"See, that's what you get for trying to uncover my secret plans. Serves you right."

"You are much craftier than I suspected. But I will get even if it's the last thing I do. You do realize this means war?"

"I'm just shaking in my hiking boots. Now where are we going to get you some decent clothes around here?"

"What, these old jeans aren't good enough for you? Where are we going, anyway?"

"Wouldn't you like to know?" Molly got out her smart phone and checked for a clothing store. Finding one nearby, off they drove to get Phil something decent to wear. Molly picked out a pair of dark blue slacks, a light blue dress shirt, and a cobalt-colored tie for Phil to try on and model for her. "Ooh la la! You look so sharp, Phil! Let's take you over to the check out and pay for these. We'll just have time for them to cut off the tags for you."

"I've got to find shoes and socks first. I'm guessing you won't let these boots slip past your inspection."

"Yeah, you're right. Let me pick them out for you, okay? I'll be really fast."

"All right, all right, but I'm starting to feel like your personal Ken doll."

"Ooh, how fun!"

"Okay, now, let's just get what we need and get out of here," Phil pleaded.

A half hour later, they were walking out of the store with a whole new look for Phil and a very satisfied personal shopper. "Okay then, now I need to find a place to change," she said. "Let's stop at that park back there, and I'll use the restroom. You might want to eat a light snack from the basket I brought while I change."

They pulled into the park, and Phil greedily devoured the slice of lemon meringue pie Molly had packed for him. A few minutes later she appeared from the restroom in a stunning, teal-colored, figure-hugging dress, with matching heels. She had a black velvet wrap around her shoulders. Upon her ears glimmered the diamond earrings Phil had bought her for Christmas. So simple, yet truly stunning.

Phil had to loosen his tie as she approached, and he stood up to greet her. She walked straight into his waiting arms. "Where have you been my entire life?" Phil whispered, then stood back to admire her.

"I didn't take that long, did I?"

"No, I mean … you know what I mean."

Molly smiled a bewitching smile and gave him a kiss as he once more took her in his arms.

"We're going to be late if we don't hurry now."

"The reservations can wait, I'm sure," Phil said, still enraptured.

"No, I'm afraid they can't," said Molly, grabbing him by the hand and yanking him to the car.

They got there just in time. The *Tahoe Queen* was poised to leave the dock for her Emerald Bay cruise. Molly pulled the tickets from her purse, and they charged up the gangway not a minute too soon.

"What? A cruise? Molly, I'm totally surprised!"

"Of course you are, silly! I really had you going there, didn't I? You're quite gullible, I'm afraid."

"But you and Lyra and that map … It said we were going to some cavern in Cave City."

"Your point?"

"You little deceiver," Phil said, aghast.

"Yep."

"Then you drove the wrong way toward Cave City on purpose just to throw me off. I thought … Oh, you little sneak. I'm going to have to watch you like a hawk!"

"Go right ahead. You'll have all evening. This is a dinner cruise, after all."

"You little stinker."

"Yep, that's me."

Lake Tahoe embodied the word blue, with its multihued

striations surrounded by evergreen guardians. The air was mountain-fresh and brisk.

Current seemed to surge between their fingertips as they walked around the deck holding hands, watching the blue give way to pristine turquoise approaching Emerald Bay. The captain occasionally pointed out items of interest, but they didn't hear much of it as they stood and gazed at the sun settling on the water. They changed decks when approaching Fannette Island to get a better look at the famous Vikingsholm Castle. An older couple saw them taking pictures of the castle and asked if they would like their picture taken with the castle in the background, an offer they readily accepted. Phil slipped his arm around Molly's waist and drew her in close to him as the older gentleman snapped their picture—one they would never forget. Phil and Molly thanked them and returned the favor.

"I wonder what it would be like, living on your own island like that?" said Molly.

"Heavenly, if I were with you," he said quietly into Molly's ear, sending a delicious tingling sensation down her spine.

A magnetic force was at work between them. They both felt it as a peaceful silence descended with the twilight. There was something so powerful about that silence in each other's arms, a comfortable quiet where no one felt the need to speak. Molly's plentiful curls brushed gently on Phil's cheek.

The captain announced dinner. To the aroma of roasted chicken and rosemary, they made their way inside and found their table for two. Dinner was scrumptious. They dined on stuffed mushrooms, Caesar salad, chicken cordon bleu, sautéed rosemary baby red potatoes, and grilled zucchini. There was cheesecake with fresh berries and drizzled chocolate on top for dessert. After dessert and a leisurely coffee, they wandered out onto the deck again and watched the moon dazzle across the water. While holding each other close, they danced to soft orchestral music under the star-studded black cloak of sky. It couldn't have been a more perfect evening.

"This is the best day of my life," Phil confessed as he dipped Molly at the end of their dance.

As he lifted her back upright, she sensed his strength and knew he'd never let her fall. "Me too. I wish this night would go on forever."

Phil gave her a very long kiss that ended as the music began again with a faster-paced song. Molly had to admit Phil was a great slow dancer and kisser, but when it came to fast dances, she just had to smile at the sheer abandon in his moves. He was having the time of his life and didn't care what anyone thought but Molly. That was one of the things she liked most about him. She threw her head back, laughed, and joined in on his unconventional moves. Oh, how she had grown to love that man! He was so much more fun than she'd ever dreamed, so funny, so down to earth, and so in love with her. She just knew it.

It was a long drive home. Phil drove Molly's car; he knew she kept bakers' hours and would have to be at work soon. He carried Molly to her door, since she had fallen asleep in the car on the way home. Phil unlocked her door, pushed it open with his new shoe, and carried her inside. She awakened long enough to give him a kiss and a hug good night.

"Sleep well, my sweet," he whispered. He lingered there on the front porch long after she had locked the door for the night. It was so difficult saying good night to Molly and having to wait until the next day to see her again.

Phil resolved that night to take their relationship to a more permanent level. It was time to start looking for a ring and thinking up a unique way to pop the question. He walked to his car with a spring in his step he'd never had before. While tossing his keys up in the air and actually catching them, he began to concoct his plan.

CHAPTER 22

Kismet, or One Too Many Kebabs

Jared left the exam room with a big smile. Little Alex's life would never be the same. By the time he was old enough for school, people would hardly notice that he'd been born with a cleft palate. The look on the boy's mother's face made all those years of studying and sacrifice worth it. He thought of Rosa, his first appointment of the day. Someday she would go to her prom with a confident smile, never to hear the epithet harelip. She would have a normal life. He felt joy at changing someone's future for the better. Now if he could only change his own …

His smile faded. *Living without Molly is no life at all. I've been so busy preparing for our future that I've lost sight of the present. Maybe Phil was right: I've been living in an ivory tower where the real world can't touch me. But now it's time to climb down.*

Traffic was like a slow drain on the freeway as he drove home. Passing the park, he caught sight of a young couple holding hands and laughing together. *When was the last time Molly and I were happy like that? It's been longer than I care to admit.* "I'm sorry,

Molly," he said to his rearview mirror. "What can I do to make this up to you? How can I get you back?"

It was raining as he trudged up the stairs to his spartan apartment and unlocked the door. No need to buy much furniture since he practically lived at the hospital. Still wearing his damp scrubs, he headed down the hall to the kitchen table and paused to look at the wall's sole occupant--a framed eleven by fourteen of him carrying Molly with her arms wrapped around his neck. He remembered that day well. They had just finished ice skating, and it was the day he first told her that he loved her.

His laptop stared at him expectantly, waiting for more than an hour for him to finish up his electronic charts. He finally closed the lid and watched the light fade from the wooden kitchen table. It had gotten dark outside since he sat down. No lights were on. He felt even more lost and lonely than he was before. "What am I working so hard for?" he asked himself out loud. He went to the fridge. Cold leftover pizza was his only choice. He hadn't felt like eating much lately. He microwaved a piece of sausage and mushroom pizza and sat down with a glass of slightly expired milk. *Might as well drink it from the jug,* he thought. *No one else is going to be here to mind.*

It had been a while since Molly had given him back the engagement ring. Many times he had tried to call her, but she never picked up the phone or returned his messages. She never answered his e-mails or texts either. Molly believed it was over, but he knew it wasn't. How could she throw away all those years? He realized his missionary doctor dream was the straw that broke the camel's back; nevertheless, his calling was undeniable.

Suddenly it dawned on him. *Why haven't I thought of this before? This is what I need to do to win her back.* He called his attending physician and managed to get three consecutive days off. He got on the Internet, booked a flight, and threw a few things in his old brown college suitcase. He grabbed the engagement ring and put it in his pocket before he found his keys and hurried out the door, leaving his laptop snoozing quietly behind him.

The door to Daryla's Flower Shop opened as her service dog, a corgi named Foxy, ran to greet a friend. "Hi, Phil," Daryla said. "What brings you here?"

"Hey, Daryla, I need some advice."

"Sure, what's up?" She turned her wheelchair to face him.

"Well," Phil paused uncertainly, "I'm looking for some flowers. Really special flowers."

"Uh-huh." Daryla was rather enjoying Phil's discomfort. *What a cute guy,* she thought. *He must be making his move with Molly—at last.*

"For an important night out," he continued.

"Yes?"

"I want to give her flowers before we go to the Dash Fortran concert tonight. Can you help me pick something out? I'm not very good at this kind of thing."

Daryla chuckled. "Of course I will, Phil. Would these be for Molly?"

"Yes." He looked down at his feet and found Foxy there looking up at him. He reached down to pet her behind the ears, and her bottom wagged even more than usual.

"Okay, then they should be her favorite. Do you know what that is?"

"Daisies, I think."

"Yep, good observation, Phil. You get ten points for knowing such vital information. So what's her favorite color?"

"Yellow—no, red. She doesn't wear yellow. And she looks great in red."

"Excellent! Ten points more. You're better than you thought at this."

"Really? Cool. Okay, will you help me pick them out?"

"Sure. Come on over to the display case. I'll show you what I've got. Now, I don't have any gerbera daisies tonight. Molly loves the red and pink ones."

"Aw …" Phil was clearly disappointed.

"Do not fear, my friend. I happen to know that she also loves pink roses."

"Really?"

"Yes, and I have these extremely long-stemmed beauties imported from Ecuador. The blooms are the largest I've ever seen. I ordered them for a wedding on the other side of the lake and wound up with too many. How about these? Check out the red veins running through the pink petals. I've never seen anything quite like them."

"Perfect! I'll take them!"

"All two dozen?"

"Yep."

"Does she have a vase big enough for these stems?"

"Oh, yeah, a vase. I don't know. Maybe I'd better get one of those too."

"Here are a few long-stem vases. Pick whichever one you like. They're all the same price."

Phil picked the translucent gold one and brought it to the counter. Daryla spent a couple of minutes explaining the care and trimming of the stems to Phil before he exited with his surprise for Molly.

Foxy pranced excitedly as Phil left, as if she understood what was going on. Perhaps she did.

"Molly's in for a nice surprise tonight," Daryla said to Foxy. "Up," she beckoned her little dog onto her waiting lap. "Good girl," she crooned to Foxy as she loved on her furry companion.

Not an hour later, the flower shop door opened again with a tall, lean, handsome man coming into her shop. Foxy ran to greet the customer. Right off the bat, he seemed very determined, knowing exactly what he wanted. "Your finest red roses, please."

This guy didn't beat around the bush like poor Phil. What a contrast. Must be for some girlfriend on the other side of the lake, she thought. *Never seen him before.* "Sure, let's take a look at what's in my display over there." She wheeled to the refrigerated glass doors. Foxy followed behind, sniffing the stranger's pant leg, hoping for a pat or kind word.

"Those. Right there," he said. "The red ones. I'll take all you've got."

"That's thirty roses, sir. Are you sure you want that many?" *This must be some occasion!* she thought.

"Yes, that's fine."

"Do you need a vase for them?" Daryla felt a bit of déjà vu coming on.

"No."

"Okay, let me tell you how to trim them so they'll last longer."

"That won't be necessary. I'm kind of in a hurry."

"All righty then." Daryla wheeled back to the register and rang up his purchase. As he paid with his credit card, Daryla couldn't help comparing Phil to this man from the other side of the lake. *Such a difference,* she mused. *I'm sure glad I live on this side. It seemed those other people are always in a hurry, know just what they want, and never take time to slow down and pet my dog. Hmm, I sure sold a lot of roses tonight. Those two cleaned me out.*" She wondered about the girl receiving the thirty long-stemmed roses. *Is she used to that sort of thing, being from the wealthy side of the lake*? Daryla couldn't imagine the woman reacting like she knew Molly would when Phil gave her the stunning pink roses tonight. She could hardly wait to talk to Molly tomorrow morning at the bakery. "Come on,

Foxy. It's closing time," she said as she started closing up for the night.

Molly stepped into the blush pink, slinky dress she had found the week before; it was half off, and with that additional 30 percent coupon she had been saving, they nearly had to pay her to take it out of the store. *Now where are those perfectly pink suede pumps I bought a few years ago? Ah, there they are. A match made in heaven. It sure is fun dressing up again—and having someone to dress up for.*

She thought of Phil and his breathtaking dimples. He would be here soon in his Bentley to pick her up for the concert. She stepped into her pink shoes and clicked her way on the hardwood floor to the bathroom. She'd never felt very adept with makeup. A little blush, shadow, mascara, and lipstick, and she was done. *Never could draw a straight line with eyeliner,* she thought as she put the liner back in the drawer with the rest of the "spooky-eye stuff," as her dad had called it. She touched up her curls with her hair pick, and at the sound of the doorbell, she grabbed her black purse and flew to the door.

Phil was standing on her porch with his hands behind his back. She threw the door open, ready to embrace him when two dozen pink roses magically appeared from behind Phil. "For me? Oh, they're lovely, Phil!"

"But obviously not as lovely as you. And look at that, they're color coordinated too." *Yes,* Phil thought. *He shoots, he scores!*

"How'd you know I was going to wear pink tonight?"

"Ancient Egyptian secret, my love," he said, stepping inside.

At the sound of "my love," Molly's heart did a little quiver. *Glee—that's what it was.* "There's so many! I don't think I have a vase big enough for all these," Molly said.

"Wait, I figured this might be a problem." Phil stepped back onto the porch and brought in a lovely hand-blown glass vase in shades of gold. "Voilà, a flower holder." He smirked.

"Oh, my!" was all Molly could say.

"Let's put them in water." Phil escorted the vase into the kitchen and started filling the container with water. "We should cut the stems underwater at an angle before we put them in the vase." He filled the sink up partway and began trimming. Molly stood next to him, watching him work on the roses like it was something he did every day.

"Phil, this is so sweet of you. Do you know when the last time a man bought me flowers was?"

"When?"

"Never! This means so much to me. And the gorgeous vase too …" Her eyes filled up with tears, which she quickly willed away so as not to ruin her eye makeup. Secretly she hated makeup, but there was a time and place for it, and she wanted to look extra special for Phil—not to mention for Dash, should he happen to look her way tonight. She still had a bit of a schoolgirl crush on the captivating singer.

"Well, your flowers are prepared, and your carriage awaits, my dear." Phil sat the vase of roses on Molly's coffee table in her living room and held the door open for her as she grabbed her purse and keys and locked the front door.

She stopped Phil in his tracks and gave him a long hug and kiss, promising more later. They held hands as Phil drove them to Sacramento. Eager concertgoers were already filing in past the security guards and the scanners, tickets in hand.

As Phil and Molly drew nearer and nearer to the stage, Molly began to squeak, "Look how close we are! I've never had such good seats in my life. How'd you find them?"

"Just lucky, I guess," replied Phil, knowing full well the small fortune he had spent to get the best possible seats. He excused himself for a minute and came back with a Fortran hoodie in

Molly's size slung over his forearm, looking like an old-fashioned waiter. "For you, madam," he announced.

"Oh, Phil, you spoil me so!"

"Just doing my job, ma'am. Must keep you warm on our little expeditions."

The lights dimmed, and the concert was about to start. Molly held onto Phil's arm with both hands in excitement until he slipped his arm away and put it around her shoulders. It stayed there most of the evening, long after the blood had retreated from it and it had gone seriously numb. He finally had to move it as the prickly pain became too distracting. From that point on, they held hands instead.

The concert was far better than any performance Molly had ever attended. Dash truly gave his all. He started with his latest songs from his newest CD, which were a hit with the audience, then did some old favorites. When he sang "Autumn's Song," Molly squeezed Phil's arm so tight that he felt like it was in a tourniquet. "I take it you like this song," Phil whispered into Molly's ear.

"One of my top ten all-time favorite songs," she whispered.

The two sat back and drank in the music and the liquid tones of Dash's voice. At the end of the song, he decided to do a bit of talking. He explained that this Sacramento arena was the first place in which he had ever actually been paid to sing. It held a special place for him, so he wanted to get to know some people from the area. "You two there," he said as the spotlight hit Molly and Phil in the face. "Yes, you in the pink dress there, and the guy sitting next to you. Come on up here on stage with me."

"What?" Phil exclaimed. "No way, Molly, you go up there. I'm staying here."

Molly pulled Phil's arm to tug him out of his chair. "Come on, Phil. This is the chance of a lifetime! He chose us! Let's go!"

"No, he chose you and your pink dress. You go. No way am I going up there."

Molly looked straight into Phil's eyes and begged, "Please, Phil, for me?"

"Oh, okay. What'd you have to wear *that* dress for anyway?"

The crowd clapped wildly, and young women throughout the auditorium seethed in jealousy as Molly made her way to the stairs with Phil in tow—literally. She had him by the tie. As the laughter and cheers died down, Dash asked their names and what they did for a living. Molly was beside herself with excitement. Phil, unused to any kind of limelight, looked for someplace to hide. After a short interview, Dash announced that he was going to attempt to give them a quick piano lesson on stage.

Molly clapped her hands in anticipation.

Phil, having his own little secret of knowing his way around a piano, began to relax and enjoy himself. If only he could stop that infernal shaking at the thought of being on stage. Luckily, the stage lights were bright enough that he couldn't see most of the people past the first few rows. Phil was lost in thought as Dash began teaching Molly her part of the song. Fortunately, Molly had a good ear and picked her part up quickly.

Now it was Phil's turn. Dash had Phil sit down on the piano bench next to Molly. Phil decided to play dumb and pretend he knew nothing about the piano. Molly sensed what he was doing and kept his secret with an air of expectancy. As planned, he acted as if he couldn't find the notes and purposefully hit wrong keys as the audience laughed. After a few minutes of Phil's humiliation, Dash started up the accompanying musicians and began to sing.

Molly and Phil awaited their cue for their solos. The audience, expecting cacophony, were stunned by the piano solo delivered by Phil's ready hands.

Dash's mouth dropped open along with most of the listeners. Phil finished out the rest of the song with his impromptu concerto and arose with Molly to take a bow at the end. Molly hit the highest note on her end of the keyboard as her contribution to the finale.

As the audience settled down, Dash asked Phil, "Why didn't you tell me you knew how to play the piano?"

"You never asked," was all Phil said.

"So, Molly and Phil, are you two married?" Dash quizzed.

"No," they said in unison, Molly giggling.

"Dating?" Dash inquired.

"Yes," was their one-word reply.

"Well, how about if I send you two virtuosos out to dinner tonight on me?" Dash handed Phil a sealed envelope and put an arm around each of their shoulders. "How about another hand for Molly and Phil?"

As they exited the stage, Dash whispered to Phil, "Great job, man. If you ever decide to go pro, I know people. Just let me know. And don't wait too long with Molly. Someone's liable to snag her, if you know what I mean." He slapped Phil on the back and winked at Molly.

"Well, how can you top that? I've never had so much fun in my whole life! Phil, thank you, thank you, thank you for taking me to the concert. Can you believe he picked us to go on stage?" Molly's words tumbled out of her mouth as the two of them made their way out of the arena doors, amidst compliments from people they'd never met.

"What a night! I couldn't have planned it better. It's all because of you, Molly. You look so amazing, how could he not have noticed you?"

"Phil, you crack me up," was all she could say, unaccustomed to compliments.

"No, really, Molly." He stopped right there in the parking lot and turned to face her. "You don't realize just how beautiful you are. It's part of your charm. You don't need makeup or expensive dresses to make you beautiful—you just are." He looked deep into her soft brown eyes, deeper than any man had looked before. It was as if he had looked into her and seen her soul, and was in love with it too.

When she could stand it no longer, she whispered, "It's the shoes. They're my little secret. Take off the shoes, and I'm just plain old me again." She winked slowly.

They had reached the Bentley now, and Phil took her in his arms. Their kiss was interrupted by a group of concert goers watching and clapping from a distance. "They won't be single long," an older woman yelled from her sports car. She honked as she drove past for good measure.

"Come on. Let's go," Molly said, tugging him toward the Bentley. "I'm starving."

They climbed into the car. Molly could hardly wait to see what was in the envelope Dash had given them. "So where are we going to eat?" she wondered out loud.

"Let's see here." Phil tore into the envelope. "It's for The Gallery. Ever heard of it?"

"Yes! It's an upscale restaurant housed in a local art gallery. Everything from blown glass to etchings. I hear the ambience is charming."

"Let's go!" Phil started the engine and attempted unsuccessfully to peel out.

They found their way to the restaurant but had to park a few blocks away. While they waited to be seated, they meandered through the gallery, admiring the wide range of art pieces. Phil was taken with a particular painting of a couple sitting together on a piano bench at a grand piano. "Molly, look! Just like us tonight."

"Yeah, but look at the price tag. You could buy a piano for that."

"Okay, then. Next ..."

Molly had her eye on a small but poignant vignette of a young girl dancing with her father, her feet atop his shoes. "Now there's a real slice of life. I remember dancing like that with my dad when I was a kid."

"You know, you've never talked much about your dad."

"My dad ... He was one of a kind. Everybody loved him, but he didn't have a lot of close friends. His precious spare time was spent with family, though he never turned down anyone in need of his help. His talents weren't limited to baking; he could make or fix anything. I miss him." Molly looked at the price tag next to the painting. She sighed and walked away just as their restaurant pager began to blink. "They're ready," she announced.

Their entrees arrived on elaborate plates, each one a piece of artwork in itself. Molly's had an Italian look about it, a Tuscan sunset over a rolling vineyard. Phil's plate depicted an abstract look at pyramids done up in metallic glaze which was not revealed until his kebabs and rice were consumed. "Look! Look, Molly, it's a sign."

"What? What are you talking about?"

"My plate—it's a picture of Egypt. Just look at the pyramids."

"Phil, those are just gold triangles, some abstract artist's idea of geometry."

"No, look at the depth of meaning. It is clearly this artist's attempt to capture an ancient civilization in a span of a mere twelve inches. Can't you see what this means?"

"No, Phil, what *does* this mean?"

"I don't know. I was hoping you would. But it's clearly a sign." He was having a hard time keeping it serious.

"Okay then. My plate must have some hidden meaning in it too."

"Yes, yes, I see it now. An adventure in Italy is clearly in your future."

"Really? I've always wanted to go there for as long as I can remember. Phil, did you somehow plan the plates?"

"Yes, just like I planned that Dash Fortran would give us this free dinner at a restaurant I've never even heard of. Come on, Muffin. Don't you believe in kismet?"

"Kiss who?"

"Kismet. It's Sanskrit for fate or destiny."

"Phil, I think you've had one too many kebabs—and what were they marinated in anyway?"

"Oh, ye of little faith. Go ahead, reject your fate. I'll send you a postcard from Pharaoh's tomb. Then you'll take me seriously." Unable to contain his mirth any longer, he sputtered into a laugh.

Trying to restrain her own laughter, Molly brought her hand to her mouth to prevent spattering him with her last bite of chicken marsala.

All attempts at straight faces were lost at this point. Their unrestrained laughter got the attention of the neighboring tables as well as their waiter, who offered them the dessert menu in an attempt to speed their departure.

Phil ordered Turkish custard while Molly decided on coconut ice cream inundated with an assortment of fresh berries and kiwi. They took their time savoring each bite and punctuating dessert with bursts of laughter, much to the chagrin of their waiter and the snobs at a nearby table.

"Who's parked in front of your house?"

"I don't know. I don't recognize the car," Molly said.

"Looks like someone's sitting on your porch swing."

"Who is that?"

Phil's car swung into the driveway.

"Oh my gosh … it's Jared. Again." She leaned her head back and studied the Bentley's headliner. "What's he doing here?"

Phil jumped out of the vehicle and stationed himself protectively in front of her car door.

Jared got off the swing and walked toward the car.

Molly opened up her door.

"Molly, I need to talk to you," Jared said in a low voice.

"Jared, what are you doing here?"

"I have something to tell you," he said.

"Well then, say it," she responded curtly.

"In private."

"Anything you need to say to me, you can say in front of Phil."

"No, this is between you and me," Jared said.

"I'm not leaving, Molly," Phil asserted.

"It's okay, Phil. I can handle this. I'll see you tomorrow. Thanks for the most lovely evening," Molly told him in a very small voice. "Apparently, Jared and I need closure."

"Good-bye, Molly," Phil said just above a whisper, wondering if this were a final good-bye. Judging from the handsome man bearing her cherished strawberries and a truckload of roses, it very well might be. He took one last look and drove away. It had been such a perfect evening. Had been …

CHAPTER 23

Beige-Colored Flowers in the Chapel of Love

"Please, Moll, can we go inside?"

She dropped her keys. Retrieving them with shaking hands, she opened the door. "Jared, why have you come back? It's over between us. Didn't I make myself clear?"

"Come sit down." He gestured to the couch. "I have something to tell you."

She complied hesitantly, walking past Phil's magnificent Ecuadorian roses.

Jared laid his gifts on the couch and went down on one knee. "I know I've blown it. I'm so sorry, Moll. You were right. It's been about me all along. But I realized I love you more than my work, more than my life, more than everything. I wouldn't even have a life without you. We can settle down here in River Oaks, raise a family, whatever you want. I can just do a two-week missionary trip once a year. You don't have to come with me. We can compromise. Look at me." He gently lifted her face. "Do you hear what I'm saying? I want you to be my wife no matter what I have to give up to make you happy." After an uncomfortable silence, he sat next to her on the couch.

Studying the box of chocolate-covered strawberries, Molly remained silent.

"Do you remember how I gave you my last strawberry when we were in the cafeteria in college? That's how it all began." He brought a photo album from under the roses and placed the enormous bouquet on her lap. "I thought you might need a reminder of how it used to be." Jared opened the album.

Each image hit Molly like a hammer blow to the chest.

"Do you remember how we used to bicycle across that footbridge that led to campus, how we used to stop in the middle and throw my bread crusts down to the ducks? And, yes, I still won't eat the crusts."

"Remember how we used to meet your friend Tina in the coin-op cafe and laugh the whole time because she had just met her latest 'Mister Wonderful?' Or how about when I'd wait around and walk you to your car on Thursdays, when you had night classes? I'd always have an Almond Joy to share. I looked forward to that long hike through the parking lot all week. I don't know about you, but those were the happiest days of my life. It can be that way again, Moll. Don't the promises we made to each other mean anything to you? I'm still in love with you; I always will be."

A suffocating silence ensued as Molly stared at a photo of Jared grinning, sprawled on the ice at the skating rink. Fight it though she did, a warmth crept into her heart at the sight of his sweet smile she had once so treasured.

She saw a photo of the two of them all dressed up for a friend's wedding that they were both in, Jared in his tux and her in a maroon velvet gown, with those suede shoes that she loved so much. That was the night they had danced together for the first time.

"Think back on our first kiss. You laughed until you cried. Do you remember that? We were watching the sunset from the footbridge on campus, and I was so nervous. My timing was off, and it started with an air kiss. We got to laughing so hard; it was even worse than that dance class you talked me into taking. I thought

I'd die when I dipped you—more like tripped you, and we wound up on the floor. The instructor used us as an example of what *not* to do, *ever.* That was our first and last attempt at ballroom dancing. But I counted it all as preparation for our wedding dance someday."

Molly looked up.

"Yes, I knew it, even back then. We were meant to be together. Can't you see, Moll? It's God's will. Why else would you have waited for so long? You knew it too." He waited for a response, but, with none forthcoming, he flipped the page. "Here's one of us at Halloween. You made the perfect Tinkerbell."

"You were a pretty cool Peter Pan yourself," she replied.

"Remember what happened when we were bobbing for apples? The cap on my front tooth came off in the apple."

"Yeah, here's one of you with no front tooth and me smiling next to you with my front tooth blacked out with an eyebrow pencil, so that we could match and you wouldn't feel so bad." Molly smiled in spite of herself.

"And here's you in that red dress at Denise's Christmas party. You never looked prettier … until tonight."

She put her head down and closed her eyes.

"Remember the first time we watched the sun come up together after we talked all night in my car before I left for Washington, DC? We just couldn't say good-bye. Remember how you said you'd never forget that moment as long as you lived? Remember how you promised you'd wait for me?"

She finally turned her head. "Jared, don't!"

He gently guided her head back. "What about this picture right here?" He fingered the edge of a photo of her horseback riding on the beach. "We found a bottle in the sand that day and put our message in that bottle. Do you remember what it said, Moll? Do you?"

"Of course I remember, Jared."

"We made promises to each other and sealed them in that bottle. You promised, Molly. You promised me. I believed you."

"That was before you ignored me for all those years. That was before you decided our whole future without even consulting me." A lone tear splattered the album. Molly sniffled back its waiting companions.

"Say something, Moll. Tell me you don't love me anymore, and I'll leave." His eyes bored into hers with such intensity that she was forced to look away and study the roses sitting forlornly in her lap. "What do you want?" Jared asked. "Tell me. You owe me that much." Molly remained wordless as he continued his scrutiny, looking for the faintest spark of hope. "Molly, please! It's now or never!"

"I need some time, Jared," she said softly, not daring to meet his gaze.

"Haven't you had plenty of time to think? Wasn't that the problem? I'm here now, and I've done everything you wanted me to do. I'm giving up Brazil for you. Isn't that enough? I love you more than anything," Jared pleaded. "What's holding you back? Is it that Phil guy?"

Molly cried softly. "I love you, Jared. I've just waited too long."

"Then why wait any longer? Forget the past, and let's start our future together right now."

"What are you saying?" Molly looked up into his eyes.

"Let's get in the car, drive up to Reno, and get married now," Jared urged. "What's stopping us?" He reached into his pocket and pulled out the dazzling engagement ring. "You made me a promise years ago. Are you going to keep it, or does your promise mean nothing?"

Molly thought back on all the memories they shared and felt the gentle stirrings of love rekindle in her heart. He had fanned the flame—and with it, a firestorm of guilt. *I should never have gone to that wedding with Phil. I was being unfaithful to Jared. What have I done? This is all my fault.*

There wasn't much time to think. Jared needed an answer. Now.

Molly reached out with unsteady hand, took the ring, and

looked at it. She hesitated and then slipped the ring on her finger. "Let's go," she said.

With growing enthusiasm, Jared talked about their future as they crossed the state line into Nevada. Molly looked down at the ring on her finger and watched it sparkle even in the dim light. Here she was. It was finally happening, the day she'd been dreaming of for all these years.

Jared droned on. Molly had long since tuned him out; her heart was torn. *Am I doing the right thing, to stand by my commitment to Jared, when all I can think of is Phil? I should never have let myself fall in love with Phil. There it is. I'm in love with Phil. Dear Lord,* she prayed silently, *what am I going to do? I still love Jared and need to do the right thing, but what about my heart? What about Phil? Help me. I need to know what You want me to do.*

"What do you think, Molly?" Jared's words burst her overly full thought balloon.

"What? I'm sorry, Jared. I was distracted by this … stunning ring," Molly lied.

"I'm so glad you like it, Moll. It looks gorgeous on you. You should've had this years ago." Jared reached out for her hand. "I'm sorry I kept you on hold all those years. Those days are over now."

Molly bit her lip and attempted a smile.

"So, I was asking you where you want to go on our honeymoon. Anywhere you want—except Brazil." He gave an awkward laugh.

"Let's just stay in Tahoe on our way back." Molly began thinking about the moonlit dinner cruise with Phil and felt what was going to become a familiar pain. "No, on second thought, let's just stay here in Reno. Anywhere is fine."

"Not the big, beautiful wedding you always dreamed of, but at least it's finally happening," he said.

Molly nodded.

They pulled into a large, up-to-date casino.

"Well, Moll, here we are. I checked out this place online. It's got two chapels, and they're open twenty-four hours. We can get a deluxe suite, stay here tonight, and then go anywhere you want in the morning."

"Great." Molly tried to sound excited, and so far she was somehow fooling Jared. *What's wrong with me? I've got to let go of Phil. Maybe I should've let him stop Ronnie's wedding.* She forced away her feelings for Phil and stuffed them way down deep. She could never look at them again. She was about to marry the love of her life. Molly grabbed Jared's hand and walked with new resolve as they began their trek from the car to the doors of the casino.

Jared stopped, took her in his arms, and kissed her with more passion than he ever had before. Molly's knees were weak. *Guess that's what love does to you,* she reasoned.

"This is it!" Jared said as they entered the smoky atmosphere where dreams were made and lost. "The chapel is supposed to be on the second floor."

They rode an escalator up and exited to the left. Molly didn't notice the lavish, Tuscan-themed swimming pool behind the expansive windows. All she could see was the door of the wedding chapel.

"You look beautiful, Molly. Let's go make our promises official." Jared wanted to shout his love for Molly to the weary gamblers stumbling back to their rooms.

"We want to get married. Tonight," Jared spoke to the woman straightening brochures in the chapel.

"Yes, we've waited way too long," Molly said with feigned enthusiasm.

"Well," said the young chapel assistant with perfectly manicured nails, "are you going to need to rent a bridal gown or a tux for the occasion? We have a lovely assortment of wedding attire to choose from. All the latest styles."

"No," Molly stated. "I don't think that will be necessary."

"Yeah, we're kind of in a hurry," Jared added.

"Well, then, are we waiting for any family or friends to arrive for the ceremony?"

"No," Jared replied. "It's just the two of us."

"Okay, then, I'll have you two fill out this paperwork while I go get the justice of the peace who will be presiding."

"Aren't you excited, Molly?" Jared said as he looked up from his paperwork.

"It's what we've always wanted."

"I can't wait to get you alone tonight," he whispered into her ear.

For years, marrying Jared had been the greatest longing in her life. She set her mind on forgetting Phil and focusing on her love for Jared. Phil would now have to be a thing of the past.

The attendant reentered the room, took their papers, and asked for their driver's licenses. "So you two are from two different sides of the country."

"Yes, it's been a very long-distance romance," Jared answered.

With resolution Molly took Jared's hand and walked to where the justice of the peace had just entered the room. Molly couldn't help but notice that the justice looked quite sleepy; she wondered if his assistant had just woke him up. A photographer appeared from a side door to capture the "I dos." Molly guessed that this person doubled as the second witness for the signing of the marriage certificate.

The justice introduced himself and made small talk before asking, "Well, are you ready to begin?"

"Yes," they replied in unison. Molly and Jared held hands and faced each other under a metal archway painted off white and decorated with neutral, bland beige silk flowers. This was not at all what she had pictured her wedding, but she knew she had always pictured Jared as her groom.

The justice began, "We are here today to join ..." He looked down at the paperwork to find out the groom's name, "Jared DeLucca and …" He looked down again. "Molly Talbert."

"Um, that's Tauber," Molly interrupted.

"Oh, sorry, Tauber in holy matrimony. If there is anyone present who knows just reason why these two should not be joined together, let them speak now or forever hold their peace."

Molly heard quick footsteps in the hallway outside the chapel door. *It's Phil,* she thought. *He's come for me!"*

The justice heard it too and delayed a few moments. The sound of the footsteps faded. The justice smiled to himself, having seen more than a few such scenes that halted a wedding. He proceeded with the ceremony.

"Do you, Jared, take Molly to be your wedded wife, to have and to hold from this day forward, for better, for worse, for richer, for poorer, in sickness and in health, to love and to cherish until death do you part?"

"I do," Jared asserted with jubilance.

"And, do you, Molly, take Jared to be your wedded husband, to have and to hold from this day forward, for better, for worse, for richer, for poorer, in sickness and in health, to love and to cherish until death do you part?"

Molly hesitated a moment, waiting for Phil to magically appear and stop her. "I … I can't go through with this," she stammered as she began to cry.

"What?" Jared yelled. "Molly, what are you doing?"

"I just can't do this, Jared. This is a mistake. I know I promised, but I'm not even sure how I feel anymore. I'm sorry! I'm just so sorry!" Molly bolted from the room and took refuge in the nearest ladies' restroom.

Two elderly women were washing their hands at the ornate sinks. Molly didn't care who heard her crying at this point and collapsed on a red velvet settee. One of the ladies brought a handful of tissues to Molly and sat down beside her. "What's the matter, my dear?" asked the silver-haired woman.

Her friend walked over and stood in front of them.

"I just ran out on my own wedding ceremony," Molly cried. "No matter what I did, I would've hurt somebody." Molly's story unfolded to their sympathetic ears.

"Sounds to me like you did the right thing," the first lady commiserated. "If you're not sure, you should never make a lifelong commitment."

"People today take their vows too lightly," the second lady concurred. "From what you're saying, you really do love the man back home more than the one you almost married just now. Sounds like you were going to marry him out of obligation or guilt over promises you made. People change, you know. My advice is to let him go, and head on back to the man you love and tell him how you feel."

"I'm kinda stuck here now. I can't go back in Jared's car with him after all this. I wouldn't blame him if he left without me."

"You're being too hard on yourself, young lady," the first woman said. "You did the right thing. Think of the world of hurt you would've both been in the rest of your marriage. Let him go."

"Y'know, we came on a gambling bus from Sacramento."

"I'm from River Oaks," Molly replied.

"Well, how about that? Our bus stopped there on the way up to Reno. There were a few empty seats. Maybe we can get you a spot on our bus. We're leaving in a couple hours. Why don't you go to breakfast with us after you tell the young man good-bye? We'll be eating at the Picasso Cafe on the third floor. We'll save you a seat at our table."

"Thanks, ladies. You've been so kind to listen to me. I don't know what I would've done without you both."

"It was nothing," said the first lady, who then introduced herself as Iris.

Molly introduced herself and learned that the second lady was Martha. Molly wandered off to find Jared, who was nowhere to be found. She returned to the chapel to ask if the wedding assistant knew where he had gone.

"Home, I think. He said something about catching a plane to DC. Can't say I blame him," was her reply. "He stormed out of here and went down the escalator. He's long gone."

Heading up to the third floor to meet Iris and Martha, Molly felt all the more guilty, but she knew she had done the right thing. She felt horrible for devastating Jared, for breaking her promise, and for humiliating him in the chapel, but she knew it would have been worse to actually marry him when she was really in love with Phil. *God,* she prayed silently as she walked off the escalator, *thank You for stopping me from making the biggest mistake of my life. Thank You for the footsteps outside the chapel door that made me realize I wanted Phil to rescue me. I'm sorry, Lord, for leading Jared on. I know I've hurt him. Please forgive me. Please help Jared to heal and find the right woman. I'll never be that woman.*

Molly stepped off the escalator, spotted the Picasso café, and went to meet her new friends for breakfast. The sun had just risen with a peach and lavender sky. She would be home soon to tell Phil how much she loved him.

CHAPTER 24

When You Let Evil In

Tethered to the silent phone, Phil waited. And continued to wait, his heart scarcely daring to beat. As minutes became hours, he was seized with dread and found himself willing the phone never to ring, never to bring him the crushing news that he was no longer loved.

As he waited, Phil searched the Internet for places he could move to, somewhere far from the cheerful bakery and its lovely proprietress. Since his house was paid for, he could sell it and walk away with a comfortable sum. Italy came to mind. *But maybe I'm just jumping to conclusions. Maybe she'll turn Jared down again. Maybe I should just watch something on TV and get my mind off of things*, he thought. *Something funny—that's what I need right now. I'll just have to wait until morning to find out what Molly decided.*

Phil had been thinking about proposing to Molly for weeks now. If she turned Jared down, he'd better not wait too long to ask her. He settled down to watch *Napoleon Dynamite,* one of his favorite movies of all time. He had his feet up on the antique coffee table and a comforting bowl of Cherry Garcia ice cream in his lap. Out of nowhere there was a desperate pounding at the front door. *Molly!* He rushed to the old carved door. The rapid knocking rattled it in its frame before he could open it. He had visions of Molly on the other side, ready to jump into his embrace.

He flung the door open and was shocked as a bruised and disheveled Ronnie threw her arms around his neck and fell forward into his arms.

"Ronnie? What happened to you? What are you doing here? Where's Michael?"

"Oh, Phillip, it's over between me and Michael. He beat me up! Look at my face. He's not the man I thought he was."

Phil was shocked at the large bruise on her cheek bone. "What? Why would he hit you? Have you called the police?"

"It's a long story, Phillip," she said tearfully. "Can I come in? I need you."

"Of course, come in. Here, have a seat on the couch. I'll get you an ice pack for your cheek." Phil returned with the ice, handed it to her, and sat down at a respectable distance. "What happened?"

"Oh, Phillip, it's been just dreadful. Michael has been such a monster to me," she sobbed.

Phil snatched a nearby tissue box and sat it between the two of them. "So what happened?" he coaxed.

"Right after my honeymoon, he started getting so bossy, telling me I couldn't do this or that. Then he took control of my money. He started arguing over the smallest things. It's been a nightmare. He started controlling what I wear, how I spent my money, who I hung out with, and where we went on vacations. He even made us get a dog—a filthy, smelly black Lab. He said it would be good practice for when we had kids. Kids? Who said I wanted kids? I'm not ready for that! The anger has been building up for months now, until finally today I'd had enough. I told him off and said I was through with him controlling me. We yelled at each other until he finally hit me in the face. Oh, Phillip, it was the worst thing that's ever happened to me!" She squished the tissue box barricade as she moved over and threw her arms around him, burying her face into his shoulder and neck. His arms automatically went around her to bring comfort as only a hug can. She sobbed for a good ten minutes as mascara tears stained his shirt. Finally she whimpered, "Help me, Phillip. I don't know what to do. I don't know where to go. I can't go back to him now."

"You can't let him hit you again—that's for sure," Phil consoled. "You've got to get some counseling, and I know just the counselor: my pastor, Joe. Maybe you can talk with him tomorrow. In the meantime, you need to call the police."

"Oh, I did that first thing. They took pictures and everything. They advised against going home right now. So I guess I'll be staying here until things blow over. I knew I could count on you to take care of me. You always have."

Just then, Dorian came in the front door. "Oh, sorry, Uncle Phil. I didn't mean to interrupt anything. I didn't know you had company."

Phil stood up quickly, looking horrified. "It's okay, Dorian; it's just Ronnie."

Dorian walked over to make her acquaintance and noticed her face wasn't the only evidence of a fight. Her knuckles were bruised. Clearly, she was one who could dish it out as well as receive it.

"Ronnie's going to be sleeping upstairs tonight. I'll stay down here on the couch. She's had a rough time lately. She's going to talk to Joe in the morning."

"Gotcha," Dorian said. "Well, it was nice meeting you, Ronnie. I'm going to turn in now. See you both in the morning."

Phil showed her upstairs and went back down to the couch. His melted bowl of Cherry Garcia whimpered to him. *Oh man*, he thought as he slurped down the remains of his beloved ice cream. He made himself as comfortable as he possibly could on the rather small couch, his six foot one inch body not quite fitting. He wrestled with his pillow as well as his thoughts and emotions. *How could Michael hit her? What would drive a man to hit a woman*? He tossed and turned and couldn't quite get to sleep.

Meanwhile, upstairs Ronnie went through Phil's closet and found a white, button-down dress shirt. She slipped off her clothes and put it on. It had that familiar Phillip scent that she adored. She walked around, surveying his room. Ronnie picked up a kazoo from his dresser and gave an exasperated sigh. *I would've thought he'd outgrown this kind of thing by now.* A photo on his dresser caught her eye. *It's that Milly girl. With my Phillip. What's that castle in the background? Where were they*? She moved over to his desk. Next to his laptop sat a large, tarnished cowbell. *What in the world would he be doing with a cowbell? Electronic candles still in the box? What would he need electronic candles for*? She gasped. *I'll bet they're hers! And pink—my color too.* Everywhere she looked there were pictures of "Milly." *Well, I'm going to have to do something about this.* When she finally made it over to the bed, she pulled back the covers and sat down to turn off the lamp on the bedside table. Her eyes fell on a small, black velvet box, and she popped it open. "What? An engagement ring?" She shuddered as she studied the one-carat marquise diamond in its satin bed. *And it's almost the same size as mine—and twice as shiny. Look at that sparkle. What a waste on that little nobody.* She took off her own wedding ring and slipped the ring out of its case and onto her finger. Ronnie viewed the ring from every angle. The marquise cut seemed to lengthen her already elegantly slim fingers. *A perfect fit. This was meant for me.*

She heard footsteps in the hall and wondered if it was Phil coming to see her. It wouldn't do for him to find his ring on her finger—not yet, anyway. Her attempts to remove the ring were unsuccessful. An unfamiliar sense of panic swept over her. She ran to the bathroom to soap her finger, but the ring wouldn't budge.

Ronnie heard the door down the hall close and realized it wasn't Phil at all, but his good-looking nephew. Her numerous attempts to disengage the ring had left her finger swollen. *I guess I'll just have to wait until tomorrow morning when my finger's not so big*, she decided. She sat back down on the bed, resting her head against the tall, carved cherry wood headboard, and spied yet another framed eight-by-ten of that woman she despised, a saucy, curly-headed, petite brunette in a little black dress. "Milly," she muttered. "Why, that little …" She took the frame and slammed it face down on the bedside table. Seething, she hissed, "He's mine," as she turned out the light.

Phil didn't sleep a wink. He finally gave up at around six in the morning, wadded up his bedding, and shoved it in the coat closet. He might as well fix Sunday breakfast for the three of them. As the bacon started to sizzle, he began to realize the dilemma he was in. Ronnie needed to talk to Joe, and she sure could benefit from one of his sermons, but how to get her there without upsetting Molly—if she was still in the equation at all? She must never know that Ronnie had spent the night. He placed the first batch of his famous blueberry pancakes on a plate, wishing that he could get off the griddle just as easily. "What am I going to do?" he asked Dorian's cat, Catalina, who was weaving around his legs, hoping for breakfast. "How can I get rid of her before Molly finds out and jumps to conclusions?"

Just then there was a knock at the door. His heart in his throat, Phil walked the Green Mile to the door and looked through the peep hole. It was Molly. Out of the frying pan and into the fire. Catalina ran for cover. Phil slowly opened the door. "Molly, I've got to talk to you about something … Wait! The bacon's burning!"

He ran to turn off the stove just as Ronnie crowned the top of the staircase wearing Phil's white dress shirt and her lacy pink panties. She began her descent as Molly's jaw dropped open. "Well, hello, Milly. Phillip, why don't you set another place for our uninvited guest? Whoops! Looks like your place has been taken." She slunk down the last step with a swivel of her hips. "Sorry I'm not dressed. It was a *very* late night, and we've worked up quite an appetite, haven't we, Phillip?"

Molly gasped, turned, and ran from the house, her face as red as Ronnie's lips.

Phil charged out of the kitchen, yelling, "Molly, I can explain everything. Wait! Come back, Molly! Please!"

"Oh, let her go, Phillip," Ronnie sighed. "What's for breakfast?"

"What's for breakfast? Don't you see what you've done? Why did you lie to her? You've ruined everything!"

"It doesn't have to be a lie, Phillip. We could head upstairs and make it the truth." Ronnie stepped closer and put her arms around him.

Phil pulled away. "You disgust me! Get out of my house, now! And don't ever come back."

"If that's what you really want." She turned and sashayed up the staircase enticingly. "You'll regret this, Phillip," she warned as she flipped her raven hair over her shoulder.

Dorian, having heard the commotion, was standing at the top of the stairway.

Ronnie brushed past him, raising an eyebrow as she looked him over. He recoiled from her glance as she model-walked past him to Phil's room and slammed the door. The impact rattled the pictures hanging on the wall.

"What is going on here, Uncle Phil?"

"Total disaster. Ronnie's managed to ruin everything. Now Molly thinks there's something going on between Ronnie and me."

"Well, uh, that *is* what it looks like. You'd better go patch things up with Molly. I'll make sure Ronnie leaves, and I'll text you when she's gone. What a cougar. She was checking me out on the stairs. I hate to say this, Uncle Phil, but you're really in deep kimchi."

Phil threw on his shoes and ran out the door in the rumpled shirt and jeans he had attempted to fall asleep in last night. He caught up with Molly as she was fumbling with her keys at her front door.

"Molly, it's not what you think."

"Then what is it, Phil?" she choked between sobs.

"Can we go inside and talk, Please?"

Molly hesitated and then turned the key. Hastily she stepped inside and slammed the door in Phil's face. He stood facing her closed door and heard the dead bolt slide into place with an air of finality.

"Molly, please! Hear me out! Molly!" He sat down on her porch steps, head in hands for a while, trying to get his bearings. *Lord,* he prayed, *help me. Molly's the best thing You've ever brought into my life. I just can't lose her now. Please help her see the truth. She's got to believe me.* He sat there, waiting for Dorian's text. It seemed an eternity before the Star Trek transporter sound announced the text's arrival. "All clear," it read, and so he trudged home.

After bolting the door, Molly ran into her room and threw herself on the bed. She kicked off her shoes and sobbed into her pillow. *I broke Jared's heart for this? At least Jared never cheated on me. How could I have been so stupid to believe Phil was such a perfect guy and someone like that would love someone like me? I must not be woman enough for Phil,* she thought. *And now Phil has an affair with Ronnie? How could I be such a fool? But I guess I was just his second choice since he couldn't have her. I wonder if he went out with me just to make her jealous. Well, I guess that is how it started. And now she's come back for him. I really thought he loved me.* She reached for her box of tissues on her nightstand. *I guess only God can makes something good out of all this mess.* She blew her nose and tossed the tissue over the side of the bed. *Why, God, why?* Molly lay there in silence. A slow realization crept into her mind, thoughts she didn't want to acknowledge. *I've broken Jared's heart and humiliated him. I left him at the altar because I*

thought I loved Phil more. Isn't that what Phil's done to me? He's tossed me aside for Ronnie, the woman he's loved all his life. So who am I to judge?

It was going to be a long day, followed by an even longer night. She walked into the kitchen to make a consoling cup of tea in which to drown her sorrows. Molly set the kettle to boil and brewed a cup of raspberry tea. Seeing the phone, she picked it up and called one of the few phone numbers she knew by heart. Dejected, she slumped on the living room couch, waiting for an answer.

"Hello? Denise?" Molly spoke haltingly.

"Molly, is that you?" Denise asked, not sure of her friend's weak, wobbly voice.

"It's me," she said before bursting into tears again.

Denise put aside the papers she was grading and settled onto her oak sleigh bed, prepared for a long discussion. "What's wrong? Are you sick or something?"

"Sick of men," Molly cried. "And sick of myself."

"What happened? Tell me all about it." Denise was like that, always caring.

Molly retold the story as her friend listened patiently. "I just don't know what to do, Denise."

"Let me get this right. You drove to Reno and almost married Jared, and you're upset at Phil for being unfaithful? Sounds like a double standard going on. It's all right for you to almost marry Jared and break his heart without telling Phil, but Phil's gotta stay faithful to you no matter what? And how do you know for sure that something actually went on between Ronnie and Phil? Okay now, Molly, before you think it's really over with Phil, don't you think you should tell him what you did and hear his side of the story? You've talked about how manipulative Ronnie is; she could've set him up. Maybe he is innocent. You should at least hear him out before you dump him. Were they all alone in the house?"

"I don't know. Dorian, his nephew, lives there, but I didn't see him."

"Well, before you crucify Phil, maybe you should find out exactly what did happen. And if he's found guilty, I'll help you string him up," she said with a snicker.

"I hope you're right, Denise. I'm so glad I talked to you. You are right: I'm a hypocrite. I need to admit what I did and give him a chance to explain himself. I don't know what I'd do without you."

"You just go talk to Phil and let me know how things work out. I'll be praying for you."

As Molly hung up the phone, she thanked God for a lifelong friend like Denise who wasn't afraid to tell her the truth. She decided that once she'd regained her composure, she'd walk over to Phil's, hoping against hope that Ronnie was gone and would stay that way.

Phil plopped down on the couch while Dorian gave a hair-raising account of Ronnie's departure, complete with her unwanted advances. "She's a man-eater. She tried to leave with your white shirt on, and when I told her to put back the shirt, she started to unbutton it right there in front of me. I went and locked myself in my room until I heard her leave and slam the front door. I came out and watched her drive away, so I knew she was gone. That woman should come with a warning label."

"No kidding. Do you think? She's not who she used to be."

"What happened with Molly?"

"She wouldn't even listen to me. She slammed the door in my face. I can't blame her; it looked really bad. But how can I explain when she won't even give me a chance? And I still don't even know what happened with Jared last night. For all I know, she could've been coming over to break up with me."

"Maybe I can talk to her and get her to hear you out," Dorian offered. "I was here all night—I know that nothing happened between you and Ronnie. Maybe she'll listen to me. Let's give her some time to cool off. I know what it's like to be falsely accused. I hope you'll have better luck than I did."

"Thanks, man. That skunk made a better houseguest than Ronnie did."

"Yeah, she really stunk things up around here."

Phil groaned and headed upstairs. He stripped his bed to remove the last traces of Ronnie and her musky perfume. He sat down on the edge of the mattress and noticed that his portrait of Molly had been flipped facedown on his bedside table. He picked it up, looked at her picture, and whispered, "Molly, I'm so sorry." He picked up the black velvet box to look at the engagement ring, the symbol of his future with her. He flipped it open and discovered Ronnie's wedding ring in its place!

"No!" Phil yelled so loudly that Dorian flew upstairs, half suspecting Ronnie had returned through the second-story window.

"Uncle Phil, what's wrong?" Phil handed Dorian the box. "Hey, this isn't the ring you bought Molly. This diamond's round. Where'd this come from?"

"It's Ronnie's! She's taken the ring I bought for Molly and put this one in its place!"

"What are we going to do?" Dorian asked.

"We're going to get it back—fast!"

"Why would she do something like that? I had no idea she was *that* bad. What did you ever see in her anyway?"

"I was young and stupid when I fell for her. It was a long time ago. I guess she started out nice enough. Hey, I don't understand it myself."

"So, what's the plan?"

Phil ran his fingers through his hair. "I have no idea, Dorian, but we've gotta do it fast before she gets too far out of town. Who knows where she's headed next?"

"Do you have Ronnie's cell phone number? I can try and track her down for you while you stay here and patch things up with Molly."

"What makes you think she'll give the ring to you?" He looked up from writing Ronnie's number down and handed it to his nephew.

"I don't know. I'll think of something. Give me her ring. It wouldn't look good for you to be running after Ronnie. If Molly found out, you wouldn't be able to explain it. This whole thing is pretty weird, you know. Besides, this would be the worst way ever for Molly to find out about her engagement ring."

Dorian gingerly received the ring, holding it as if it had recently been dropped into a toilet, which for him wasn't a far stretch of imagination.

"Be careful, man. She's not going to make this easy for you!" Phil advised.

"My reputation's already shot. What more can happen? Besides, I think I can handle her. I'm taking off now before she gets any farther away. Good luck with Molly."

"Thanks, Dorian. I owe you big time."

CHAPTER 25

The Return of the Ring

The first step of Dorian's plan was to stop off at Lyra's and see if she'd go along with him. Going by himself when it involved a woman like Ronnie didn't sound like a good idea. Luckily, Lyra was home playing with her kitten, Catzo, in Mrs. McCreary's garden.

"Hey, you," Lyra spoke up as she saw Dorian walking toward her. "What's up?"

"Hey, yourself. I need your help, Lyra."

"What's wrong?" she wondered out loud at the sight of his blanched face and widened eyes.

"It's Uncle Phil. He's in trouble."

Lyra scooped up her kitten and stood up. "What happened?"

"You know that Ronnie chick that he used to have a thing for?"

"The one who had that wedding disaster that Phil and Molly went to together?"

"That's the one. Well, she came into town last night saying that her husband had beaten her up—she did look pretty convincing—and talked Phil into letting her stay the night so she could counsel with Pastor Joe in the morning. He gave her his room, and he slept on the couch. Then this morning, Molly comes by when Phil was making breakfast, and just then Ronnie comes down the stairs dressed, as far as I could tell, only in one of Phil's white dress shirts, acting like something had gone on between them last night."

"Oh no! Poor Molly!"

"Poor Phil! Molly ran out. He told Ronnie to leave and he ran after Molly. Molly refused to speak with him. Meanwhile, Ronnie took Molly's engagement ring."

"Engagement ring? What do you mean, engagement ring?"

"That's a whole 'nother story. Please don't tell Molly about the ring Phil bought her. He was planning on surprising her with it sometime soon."

"My lips are sealed." She kissed the wriggling kitten's striped little head. "What do you mean, Ronnie took the ring? She just stole it?"

"I guess. She left her wedding ring in its place."

"This gets sicker by the moment. What are you gonna do now?"

"Well, I was, like, hoping that you would go with me and help me get it back from her."

"You're joking, right?"

"No. Come on, Lyra. I can't do this alone. She's … I don't know …"

Lyra chuckled. "You're afraid of her, aren't you?"

"No, not really … well, kinda. Come on, Lyra. You've gotta help me!"

"Oh, all right, but only because you look so frightened."

"You're a pal, Lyra. I owe you one."

A pal. Always a pal! she thought to herself.

"We've gotta get going quick. She's probably out of town by now."

"Okay, I'll put Catzo back in the house. Just a minute." Lyra managed to mask her snicker with a fake sneeze.

Mrs. McCreary saw Lyra get into Dorian's Corolla. She watched them pull away from the curb. "I wonder where Lyra's going with that handsome young fella she's taken a liking to?" she said to her husband. "I think that's Phil's nephew."

"About time that girl had a social life," he replied, as Mrs. McCreary telephoned Betsy Peterson to inform her of the latest goings-on in her neck of the woods.

"We'd better find out where Ronnie's headed first," said Dorian. "Why don't you give her a call?"

"Me?" cried Lyra. "I've never even met this sleazy dirtbag."

"Well, you're a … you know, a girl."

"I'm so glad you noticed, but what does that have to do with it? Why don't you call her? You've at least met her?"

"Oh, man …" Dorian moaned, pulling the car over to the curb and punching in her cell phone number.

Lyra smiled as he squirmed. *She must really be a piece of work to cause such a reaction in Dorian. He's normally so mellow.*

"Hello, Phillip," came the smooth, feminine voice answering the phone.

"Hello, Ronnie. This is Dorian, Phil's nephew."

"Yesss?" she purred.

"Um," he stammered. "You've got the engagement ring, and you left your ring in its place."

"Yes," she said, clearly meaning, *And what's your point*?

"We want it back. Where can I meet you to make the exchange?"

"If he wants it so badly, why doesn't Phillip come get it himself?"

"Look, lady, what's your problem? You've already managed to mess up things for Phil. I just want the ring back, okay?"

"Meet me at the Lavender Luxury Hotel and Spa in Driftwood in two hours."

"Where? Why don't you just stop your car, and I'll catch up to you? Where are you now?"

"Bye bye now," was her reply as she hung up on him.

"Oh, man," Dorian said to Lyra, "She wants to meet at some hotel in Driftwood. We've got two hours to get there. Do you have any idea of where the heck that place is?"

"Nope, but we can get directions on your cell phone. Give me that."

Dorian relinquished his phone. "Hey, how come you don't have a cell phone?"

"I used to. Can't really afford one now; I'm saving for college. Besides, no one ever calls me anyway except for Molly, and she just calls the McCrearys' house phone."

Dorian wondered what in the world he would do without his cell phone, although no one called him much these days either.

"So how are we gonna work this when we get to the hotel?" Lyra asked.

"I don't know. I just figured we'd both go up to her door and ask for the ring back."

"What a plan," she said sarcastically. "I thought I was just here for moral support. You mean you want me to go in there with you? You scared or something?"

"No, it's just if we're both there, she's bound to hand it over."

"You're scared," Lyra smirked.

"No, I'm not. Okay, I'll do it myself, but if I don't come out in less than five minutes, you gotta come in after me."

"All righty then. I'll wait down the hall and rescue you if you don't come out alive."

"Ha, ha, very funny."

"Yeah, I think so," Lyra answered.

They drove on, joking and laughing and singing their heads off.

Surrounded by a pristine beach, disturbed only by the occasional stand of driftwood, the Lavender Luxury Hotel and Spa was extravagant. Dorian had to call Ronnie again to find out what room she was in. Feeling totally out of place, Lyra and he slunk down the hall of the eighth floor until they found the room number.

"I'll go hide around the corner," said Lyra.

"Don't go too far now," Dorian begged.

"Come on. Just do it, Dorian." Lyra walked down the hall to a corner a few yards away.

He knocked very matter-of-factly on the mauve-colored door.

Ronnie came to the door dressed in a negligee and a smile. "Come in, Dorian, come in," she beckoned him forward.

"Uh, I just need the ring, Ronnie," Dorian said brusquely.

"You'll get it, but first you need to do something for me." She touched him under the chin with her fingers.

He shuddered as she grabbed his T-shirt and pulled him forward.

"Look, lady, I want the ring. Give it over, and I'll be on my way."

"Not so fast, mister. What's the rush? I just want to get to know you a little."

"I don't have time for this. Please, Ronnie, just give me the ring. You don't realize all the trouble you've caused. I need that ring."

Ronnie grabbed Dorian by the shirt with both hands and yanked him down on top of her on the king-sized, lavender-scented bed just as the bathroom door flew open and a male voice boomed, "Someone here, babe?"

Dorian scrambled to get off of Ronnie.

"What the …?" Michael stormed over to the bed.

"Michael, this guy just came in and attacked me. Do something, babe!"

Michael was getting ready to punch Dorian's lights out. He had the hapless young man by the scruff of his shirt.

"Hey, man, it's not what it looks like!" Dorian winced sideways, waiting for the first blow.

Michael took a good look at his soon-to-be victim. "Hey, wait a minute. I know you." Michael was searching his moth-ridden brain for a long moment before recognizing him. "Babe, this is the guy I told you about. He played guitar and sang at that church I went to before I met you."

"What church? What are you talking about, Michael? This guy attacked me! Aren't you going to teach him a lesson?"

Just then, Lyra rushed into the room.

"Who's she?" asked Michael and Ronnie together.

"She's my girlfriend," Dorian lied, wiggling out of Michael's grasp. "Why would I be after your wife when I'm here with my girlfriend?"

"This *fat* girl?" Ronnie laughed.

Lyra looked at Dorian, dumbfounded.

"Girlfriend? Aren't you married to that cute, blonde, model-looking chick from the church?" Michael asked.

"Not anymore. And don't call Lyra fat!"

"Look," Lyra cried, "all we want is the ring back!"

"What ring? What are you talking about?" Michael asked, thoroughly puzzled with the situation.

"She's got my ring. My engagement ring," Lyra said, playing along.

"I thought it was Milly's ring." Ronnie looked shocked.

"Who's Milly?" the three of them asked simultaneously.

"What is going on here?" Michael asked, his innate confusion building.

"Here, you and *Fat Girl*, just take the stupid ring." Ronnie lifted her hand over her head and yanked the ring off after a few failed attempts.

Dorian studied Ronnie's face with accusing eyes. "Hey, how come the bruise is gone from your face? Looks like it must've washed right off. So Michael didn't hit you after all. You're pathetic, lady." Dorian shook his head in disgust.

Ronnie postured like a cat about to pounce.

"Bruise? What bruise?" Michael questioned. "What is this all about, anyway?"

Dorian snatched Phil's ring from Ronnie's hand and tossed Ronnie's ring to Michael.

"What are you doing with my woman's ring, dude?" Michael flexed his biceps, and his meaty hands formed fists.

"Maybe you should ask Ronnie why she took my fiancée's engagement ring!" Dorian let outrage overcome his fear.

"Yeah, I'm sure she can explain everything," Lyra said. She grabbed Dorian's arm and yanked him to the door.

"Babe, what's happening here? You've got a lot of explaining to do," Michael threatened.

"Michael, baby, I can explain everything!" Ronnie was concocting a story—and fast.

"Start talking, woman!"

Once outside the hotel room, Lyra and Dorian took off running for the elevator and the safety of the car. They didn't stop until they had jumped in and peeled out of the parking lot. "That was close," Dorian said, relieved. "Thanks for all your help. You came in just in the nick of time and saved my neck." He looked over at Lyra as they stopped at a stop light.

"Why did you lie?" Lyra dared question.

"I don't know. I thought he was gonna kill me, and I figured he might believe I wasn't after his wife if he thought you and I were together. Thanks for going along with it and saying it was your ring. Sorry, Lyra. I didn't mean to make you lie."

"I'm surprised they fell for it when you said I was your fiancée." Lyra looked down at her feet, at the flesh bulging like rising dough between the straps of her sandals.

"Why is that so unbelievable to you?" Dorian asked.

"Someone like you with someone like me? Come on, Dorian. You're so good looking and all."

"What? And what's so wrong with you, Lyra?"

"You heard Ronnie. In case you haven't noticed, I'm *fat*! I know what I am. No one like you would ever be interested in …"

"You're wrong, Lyra. You're a wonderful person. Any guy would be lucky to have you."

"Yeah right."

"I mean it, Lyra," Dorian asserted.

"Really?" she whispered hopefully.

"Really," he replied with a sweet smile.

Phil had been staring into space for hours before he realized he hadn't eaten since last night's bowl of liquid Cherry Garcia. Stomach growling, he poked around the kitchen, looking for some semblance of food that had survived the morning's catastrophe. The pancakes had turned to leather, the bacon was one step from charcoal, and the eggs … well, suffice it to say that there was no sunny side left. He was just putting the frying pan in the sink when there was a tentative knock at the front door. Phil's heart lurched with both hope and dread. *This could be the end,* he told himself. He opened the door and saw a very tear-stained Molly.

"Why, Phil? Why? How could you?"

"You've got to let me explain, Molly. Nothing happened last night."

"Then why was Ronnie dressed in your shirt, coming down your stairs and waiting for breakfast?"

"I know it looks bad. Ronnie came over late last night, saying that Michael had beaten her up."

"Good for him!" Molly growled through clenched teeth. "Wish I could have helped him."

"Don't we all at this point? She said she needed a place to stay for the night and agreed to talk with Pastor Joe in the morning. Dorian was here; you can ask him about the whole thing. I slept on the couch downstairs—or rather, I tried to sleep. I was too uncomfortable to relax with the she-devil under my roof."

"You do look a little rumpled." She straightened her shoulders. "So where's Dorian?"

"He left. I don't know where he is. You can talk to him when he gets back."

"Why did you even let her into your house?"

"She was all bruised up, a total mess. I had to help her. I just couldn't close the door in her face. She couldn't go back home …" He paused. "I don't know what else I could've done."

"You could've found her a hotel room."

"You're right. I'm sorry, Molly. I was so stupid. Please forgive me!"

"You're not off the hook yet, Phil. I need to talk to Dorian. How do I know I can trust you, after what Ronnie said this morning? How do I know you won't ever let Ronnie back into your life again?"

"I may be stupid, but I'm not *that* stupid. Molly, you're the best thing that's ever happened to me. Why would I throw that away for anyone? Ronnie can't even begin to compare with you." Phil rallied. "And what happened between you and Jared last night? You never even bothered to call me to let me know where I stand. I laid there all night, wondering if you'd taken him back. The least you could've done was call. So what *did* happen between you two last night?"

"Well, frankly, Jared and I drove to Reno …"

"Then why are you even here? Go be with Jared if you love him so much."

"Phil, I didn't marry him."

"Then what *did* you do? Go gambling?"

Suddenly, the door burst open as a jubilant Dorian and Lyra

stormed the room. "We got it! We got it!" Dorian proclaimed at the top of his lungs, holding the ring triumphantly overhead.

Seeing Molly, Lyra elbowed Dorian, who quickly concealed the ring in his pocket.

"What have you got?" Molly turned and asked, one eyebrow raised.

"Uh," Dorian's voice guttered.

Lyra filled in. "We found the missing lyrics to a song we've been working on. I thought we'd lost it forever. Come on, Dorian. Let's go upstairs and get your guitar."

"Not so fast," Molly demanded. "I need to talk to Dorian. Privately."

"Yeah, sure. Let's go in the kitchen," Dorian said. He turned to Lyra and promised, "I'll be right back."

"Lyra and I will go wait on the porch and give you some privacy," Phil suggested.

Dorian and Molly headed to the kitchen table. "Spill it, Dorian. What really happened last night? And I want the truth. Don't try and protect your uncle. I can tell if you're lying."

"When I came home last night, Uncle Phil was talking with Ronnie. She was a mess of bruises. He told me that Ronnie had run away, needing protection from Michael, who had beaten her up. She stayed upstairs for the night while he slept on the couch downstairs. She was supposed to talk to Pastor Joe in the morning. If there ever was a person who needed counseling, it's her."

"So, if Phil slept on the couch, where are the pillow and blanket?"

"I don't know. Maybe he already put them away in the coat closet."

Molly marched from the kitchen and opened the closet. She saw a blanket and pillow forcefully crammed onto the upper shelf. The pillow fell to the floor, landing on her feet. "Hmm. I don't know what to believe. How do you know that nothing went on during the night? He's been in love with Ronnie his whole life."

"Because I know Uncle Phil. If there's one thing he has, it's integrity. He would never cheat on you. He's crazy in love with you. You think he's lying?"

"Well, he lied to Ronnie at her wedding about us being a couple before we ever were, to make her jealous. How do I know he's not lying to me?"

"And whose idea was it to play that game in the first place, Molly?"

"Oh yeah, I guess it was mine." She paused. "Maybe I should go home and think about all this. Thanks for talking with me, Dorian." She walked across the living room and paused at the front door. Molly took a deep breath and opened it. "I need time, Phil," she said as she walked slowly down the porch steps.

"So do I," Phil said, indignant. "I can't believe you even thought about eloping with the man who's put you last for all these years. What assurance do I have that the next time Jared blows into town, you're not going to take off with him—permanently?" He walked inside and slammed the door.

While Dorian and Molly had been talking in the house, Phil and Lyra were having a conversation of their own. She filled him in on all the gory details of recovering the ring, her passionate rendition Tolkeinesque as she related the details of their search for the "one true ring."

Phil was amazed and humbled by all they had endured to help him. "Thank you so much, Lyra. It sounds like Dorian couldn't have gotten it back without you."

"You know, it was actually kind of fun. I felt like a jewel thief."

After Molly left, Lyra and Dorian joined Phil in the living room. Dorian told Phil about his conversation with Molly. "She's not sure whether to believe you," he warned.

"Let me talk to her in the morning at work," Lyra offered. "I'll talk some sense into her."

"Thanks, Lyra. Thanks both of you for all you've done. But I may not be needing the ring, after all. Turns out Molly went to Reno with Jared last night."

Lyra was aghast. "She *what?*"

"Yeah, I guess she almost married him. Don't know what stopped her. I don't think she's ever going to be over him."

Dorian took the ring out of his pocket and handed it to Phil. "Don't lose this again. You still might need it!"

Lyra handed Molly the rolling pin the following morning. "He really loves you, you know."

"Then why did he let in that … that …"

"Let me help you here: that putrefying wad of soulless skin in Angstrom stilettos?"

"You took the words right out of my mouth." Molly blew the bangs off of her perspiring forehead, as she bludgeoned the innocent pie crust dough with her rolling pin.

"How could Phil refuse someone in need? You know how kindhearted he is. He wasn't trying to start something up with Ronnie; he was just giving her a safe place to stay until she could get help the next morning. You know he'd do the same thing for anybody. What this comes down to is, what do you want to believe about Phil? Do you really think he would compromise his morality, his relationship with God, and his relationship with you … for *her*? Come on, Molly. What are you thinking? You know him better than that. And what if Jared showed up all bruised and bloody at your doorstep? Wouldn't you help him?"

"But he's always loved her. Always. How can that kind of love just go away?" Molly rolled harder and harder on the dough.

"Well, what about you and Jared? You two ran off to elope last night. What's Phil supposed to think?"

"Who told you about Reno?"

"Did you expect Phil to just roll over and take it? You can't have it both ways, Molly. You've hurt him, and you're going to have to work to get him back."

She paused. "Yes. Okay, I see your point," Molly conceded as she tossed the overworked pie crust in the trash and started over on a fresh ball of dough.

Phil could hardly concentrate all morning. He closed his laptop and rested his elbows on the table, head in hands. He was all prayed out. He needed fresh air and a change of scenery to clear his head. He stepped out onto the front porch and sat at the table. The empty chair opposite his mocked him. Seeking distraction, he noticed a rustling sound from under the porch again. *The cat must be prowling around down there.* He closed his eyes for a few minutes and remembered back to that magical chorus of cowbells and the first tender kiss in the gloaming. He was startled back to the present by a soft hand on his shoulder.

"Molly," he said, hope lighting his face.

"I think you forgot something this morning," she said quietly. She handed him a small pink box. Her hands smelled of cinnamon.

He opened the box to reveal two apple fritters, one for each of them.

"Mind if I join you?" She sat down on the white wrought iron chair and slid it next to his. "I'm sorry I doubted you, love. I'm so sorry I hurt you. I thought I was doing the right thing, keeping my promise to Jared, but I couldn't stop thinking about you. I heard footsteps in the hallway at the chapel and hoped it was you coming to rescue me. That's when I knew I couldn't go through with it. I was going to marry him out of guilt, but I really don't love him anymore. It's you and you alone that I love."

Phil said, "I thought I'd lost you forever last night. And then when I heard you say you went to Reno ... How could you do that to me? You can't just hand me a pink box and expect everything to be okay, 'cause it's not okay."

"I made Jared a promise. I thought keeping it was the right thing to do. It was almost too late before I realized that promise had become a lie. I'm so sorry. This is all my fault. I know I brought this on myself. I wasn't exactly innocent when I suggested we make Ronnie jealous in the first place. I guess it's only fair that she turned the tables on me. And believe me, I was jealous. Still am! I love you, Phil. Only you. I want to be the one to wear your white shirt someday. If we still have a someday."

"Not *that* white shirt. I threw it in the garbage." He grinned from ear to ear, his cornflower blue eyes dancing. He was about to kiss her when the rustling under the porch resumed.

"What is that? Has Ronnie come back?" she snickered, finally comfortable with the situation.

"I don't know, but I've been hearing it off and on for a few days. Probably just Dorian's cat hunting for mice."

Suddenly, Molly stood up with a gasp. "That's not a cat, Phil. Look!"

Out from under the floorboards of the porch waddled a skunk, resplendent in its black and white formal attire.

"Not again," groaned Phil. He stood at attention, ready to take Molly's hand and run for it. He relaxed as the tuxedoed creature made its exit through the azalea hedge. Phil shrugged. "I guess it can't be much worse than my last house guest."

They both laughed but soon turned stone sober, catching their breath as ten little skunklings pit-padded out in the wake of their well-dressed mother, disappearing into the greenery.

Chapter 26

Twin Dragon at the Bottom of the Cave

Phil started planning a very special mystery date of his own. It had to be something spectacular—nothing else would do. He decided to put a little twist on it.

"We're just going out to eat. Wear something nice, like that blue outfit you wore on the dinner cruise," he told Molly. He left no clues, fake or otherwise, for her to follow. It had taken carefully orchestrated planning to make this all come together, but he was certain it would be worth it.

Molly was surprised when, after a long drive, she found herself standing at the entrance to a large cavern. "What in the world are we doing here?" she exclaimed. "I thought we were going out to dinner."

"There you go, thinking again." Phil smiled.

"I can't go in there dressed like this!" As requested, she was wearing her teal dress and heels that she had worn on their *Tahoe Queen* cruise.

"Yeah, well, I brought you some running shoes, just your size. Here're some socks, too."

"What in the world are you up to?" Wincing at the fashion

nightmare, Molly put on the shoes and socks reluctantly, feeling painfully conspicuous.

"Grab a hard hat. The cave tour is about to start," Phil advised in far too chipper a tone.

"Honestly, what were you thinking?"

"I've been thinking quite a bit, actually." He grabbed her hand and pulled her into the group of would-be spelunkers.

Molly had never set foot in a cave. It didn't take long for her to be enchanted by what felt like an underground cathedral, bedecked in delicate crystalline chandeliers. Its sparkling walls were adorned with dramatic pipe organ–like pillars. She wondered how all this beauty could have been hidden underground for so many years, seen and appreciated only by God's eyes. She felt privileged to partake in such a visual feast. Still, there remained the mystery. Why on earth would Phil have told her to dress up for the occasion? He certainly had diverted her attention away from his plans, whatever they might be. She had to give him credit for that. This must be his idea of revenge for the *Tahoe Queen* incident. Still, she'd been hoping for something, well ... more romantic than looking up at dripping ceilings for a couple hours in her best dress.

Phil took her hand in his. His hand was as cold and clammy as the rock chambers they were cloistered in. *Yeah, real romantic. Phil is all man, make no mistake about* it. This was no sunset cruise, but a total guy-type date. She had to admit it was beautiful, though.

When they reached the bottom of the cave, there was a lovely little lake which the tour group admired for a while before the guide ushered them along. An official-looking park ranger detained Phil and Molly.

"We didn't touch any of the rock formations. Honest," Molly said in their defense.

"Walk this way, ma'am," the ranger said, his face unreadable.

Phil was expending a lot of energy keeping a straight face.

Molly elbowed him. The ranger was sure to pick up his expression and read it as a sheepish mask of guilt.

They rounded a turn and came across a table for two set in linen, with fuchsia gerbera daisies on display in a fluted cut-crystal vase. On closer examination, the plates were of fine bone china, the goblets of pink etched crystal, and the silverware shone in the light provided by dozens of electric candles.

The ranger strode around the corner and returned carrying a lovely silver tray with—could it be?—her teal-colored heels, two sets of chopsticks, and four boxes of Chinese food in their usual white cardboard boxes emblazoned with the twin dragons of her favorite restaurant.

"Wha ...?" was all Molly's could manage, her jaw agape. The amount of work, expense, and creative energy Phil had gone through to pull off this surprise was astronomical. "I ..." She felt that sweet little burst of joy as she hugged him.

Phil was pleased with himself, soaking up the love and appreciation. Once Molly released him from her pythonical embrace, he seated her at the table in a chair which was dolled up in soft pink moire taffeta with a toile bow, the creation of the talented Mrs. McCreary. He took off her socks and running shoes and slipped her shoes onto her waiting feet with a flourish worthy of the original Prince Charming.

"Oh, Phil, gerbera daisies—they're my favorite! Everything looks so beautiful!"

"I know," he said smoothly, "and so do you."

"And Chinese food from Twin Dragon. What'd we get? What'd we get?"

"Open the boxes and see, grasshopper."

"Ooh, fried rice and beef and broccoli—my favorite. Oh, and mu shu pork and cashew chicken! You're the best, Phil!" She picked up the silver serving spoon and loaded her plate.

The park ranger had already retreated a respectful distance around the corner while Phil and Molly dined.

"I can't believe you went to all this work," Molly said.

"You're worth it, Muffin. I love you more than you know."

"No, I love you more."

"Sorry, not possible."

"That's what you think."

Unable to win this argument, they both laughed and busied their chopsticks.

"Have you tried this beef and broccoli yet? Chef Li outdid himself."

"I told him this would be a special night. Hand me the plum sauce, and I'll make you a mu shu delight."

"Oh, Phil, you spoil me so." She looked at him adoringly.

They chatted over their Chinese cuisine until, at the end of the meal, Phil reached under the tablecloth and found his iPhone, which began to softly play Groban's "When You Say You Love Me." He took her hand and pulled her to her feet, and they danced.

By this time, Molly was grinning and laughing.

He kissed her cheek. *Is this romantic or what*? he asked himself. *Now for the score.* As the song finished, he sat her down and rustled under the tablecloth for another Chinese takeout box. "Now, for dessert. Fortune cookies. Here, you pick one." He stepped over to her side of the table and handed her the carton. As she started opening it, he got down on one knee.

Molly looked inside the carton and spied a lush velvet box. She looked down at it, and her heart skipped not one, but two whole beats. She opened the lid. Nestled in black satin was a one-carat marquise-cut diamond ring. Its brilliance made itself known, even in the candlelight. As she admired it, he took her hand and, with words more earnest than he'd ever spoken, said, "Molly Tauber, will you be my wife?"

Molly grabbed his other hand and stood up suddenly, nearly tipping over the table as she drew him to his feet to receive the biggest hug of his life. "That's one heck of a fortune cookie, Phil." She paused ever so slightly and gave him a decisive, "Yes."

Appendix

Molly's Favorite Scriptures for Depression and Anxiety

All scriptures quoted in New American Standard Version, except where noted.

Genesis 18:14—Is anything too difficult for the LORD?

Exodus 14:13–14—But Moses said to the people, "Do not fear. Stand by and see the salvation of the Lord which He will accomplish for you today; for the Egyptians whom you have seen today, you will never see them again forever. The LORD will fight for you while you keep silent."

Exodus 33:14—And He said, "My presence shall go with you, and I will give you rest."

Deuteronomy 28:6–7—Blessed shall you be when you come in, and blessed shall you be when you go out. The LORD will cause your enemies who rise up against you to be defeated before you; they shall come out against you one way and shall flee before you seven ways.

Deuteronomy 33:26–27—There is none like the God of Jeshurun (Israel) Who rides the heavens to your help and through the skies in His majesty. The eternal God is a dwelling place and underneath are the everlasting arms; and He drove out the enemy from before you, and said, "Destroy."

1Samuel 2:9—He keeps the feet of His godly ones, but the wicked ones are silenced in darkness; for not by might shall a man prevail.

Job 2:9–10—Then his wife said to him, "Do you still hold fast your integrity? Curse God and die!" But he said to her, "You speak as one of the foolish women speaks. Shall we indeed accept good from God and not accept adversity?" In all this, Job did not sin with his lips.

Job 8:21—He will yet fill your mouth with laughter, and your lips with shouting.

Job 13:15—Though He may slay me, I will hope in Him. Nevertheless, I will argue my ways before Him.

Job 19:25–27—And as for me, I know that my Redeemer lives, and at the last, He will take His stand on the earth. Even after my skin is destroyed, yet from my flesh I shall see God; Whom I myself shall behold, and Whom my eyes shall see and not another. My heart faints within me.

Job 23:10–13—But He knows the way I take; when He has tried me, I shall come forth as gold. My foot has held fast to His path; I have kept His way and not turned aside. I have not departed from the command of His lips; I have treasured the words of His mouth more than my necessary food, but He is unique and who can turn Him? And what His soul desires, that He does.

Psalm 3:3–6—But Thou, O LORD, art a shield about me, My glory and the One Who lifts my head. I was crying to the LORD with my voice, and He answered me from His holy mountain. [Selah.
I lay down and slept; I awoke, for the LORD sustains me. I will not be afraid of ten thousands of people who have set themselves against me round about.

Psalm 4:3–5—But know that the LORD has set apart the godly man for Himself; the LORD hears when I call to Him. Tremble, and do not sin; meditate in your heart upon your bed, and be still. [Selah.

Offer the sacrifices of righteousness and trust in the LORD.

Psalm 4:8—In peace I will both lie down and sleep, for Thou alone, O LORD, dost make me to dwell in safety.

Psalm 5:1–3—Give ear to my words, O LORD, consider my groanings. Heed the sound of my cry for help, my King and my God, for to Thee do I pray. In the morning, O LORD, Thou wilt hear my voice; in the morning I will order my prayer to Thee and eagerly watch.

Psalm 5:11–12—But let all who take refuge in Thee be glad, let them ever sing for joy; and mayst Thou shelter them, that those who love Thy name may exult in Thee. For it is Thou Who dost bless the righteous man, O LORD, Thou dost surround Him with favor as with a shield.

Psalm 6:8–9—Depart from me, all you who do iniquity, for the LORD has heard the voice of my weeping. The LORD has heard my supplication, the LORD receives my prayer.

Psalm 9:9–10—The LORD also will be a stronghold for the oppressed, a stronghold in times of trouble. And those who know Thy name will put their trust in Thee; for Thou, O LORD, has not forsaken those who seek Thee.

Psalm 9:18—For the needy will not always be forgotten, nor the hope of the afflicted perish forever.

Psalm 13:1–6—How long O LORD? Wilt Thou forget me forever? How long wilt Thou hide Thy face from me? How long will I take counsel in my soul, having sorrow in my heart all the day? How long will my enemy be exalted over me? Consider and answer me, O LORD, my God; Enlighten my eyes, lest I sleep the sleep of death, lest my enemies say, "I have overcome him," lest my adversaries rejoice when I am shaken. But I have trusted in Thy lovingkindness. My heart shall rejoice in Thy salvation. I will sing to the LORD because He has dealt bountifully with me.

Psalm 16:7–11—I will bless the LORD Who has counseled me; indeed my mind instructs me in the night. I have set the LORD continually before me; because He is at my right hand, I will not be shaken. Therefore, my heart is glad, and my glory rejoices; my flesh also will dwell securely. For Thou wilt not abandon my soul to Sheol; neither wilt Thou allow Thy Holy One to undergo decay. Thou wilt make known to me the path of life; in Thy presence is fullness of joy; in Thy right hand there are pleasures forever.

Psalm 17:7–10—Wondrously show Thy lovingkindness, O Savior of those who take refuge at Thy right hand from those who rise up against them. Keep me as the apple of the eye, hide me in the shadow of Thy wings, from the wicked who despoil me, my deadly enemies, who surround me. They have closed their unfeeling heart; with their mouth they speak proudly.

Psalm 18:6—In my distress I called upon the LORD, and cried to my God for help; He heard my voice out of His temple, and my cry for help before Him came into His ears.

Psalm 18:16–19—He sent from on high, He took me; He drew me out of many waters. He delivered me from my strong enemy, and from those who hated me, for they were too mighty for me. They confronted me in the day of my calamity, but the LORD was my stay. He brought me forth also into a broad place; He rescued me, because He delighted in me.

Psalm 18:28–35—For Thou dost light my lamp; the LORD my God illumines my darkness. For by Thee I can run upon a troop; and by my God I can leap over a wall. As for God, His way is blameless; the word of the LORD is tried; He is a shield to all who take refuge in Him. For who is God, but the LORD? And who is a rock, except our God, the God who girds me with strength, and makes my way blameless? He makes my feet like hinds' feet, and sets me upon my high places. He trains my hands for battle, so that my arms can bend a bow of bronze. Thou hast also given me the shield of Thy salvation, and Thy right hand upholds me; and Thy gentleness makes me great.

Psalm 20:1–2–May the LORD answer you in the day of trouble! May the name of the God of Jacob set you securely on high! May He send you help from the sanctuary, and support you from Zion!

Psalm 20:4–7—May He grant you your heart's desire, and fulfill all your counsel! We will sing for joy over your victory, and in the name of our God we will set up our banners. May the LORD fulfill all your petitions. Now I know that the LORD saves His anointed; He will answer him from His holy heaven, with the saving strength of His right hand. Some boast in chariots and some in horses; but we will boast in the name of the Lord our God.

Psalm 23:1–6—The LORD is my shepherd, I shall not want. He makes me lie down in green pastures; He leads me beside quiet waters. He restores my soul; He guides in the paths of righteousness for His name's sake. Even though I walk through the valley of the shadow of death, I fear no evil; for Thou art with me; Thy rod and Thy staff; they comfort me. Thou dost prepare a table before me in the presence of my enemies; Thou hast anointed my head with oil; my cup overflows. Surely goodness and lovingkindness will follow me all the days of my life, and I will dwell in the house of the LORD forever.

Psalm 25:1–6—To Thee, O LORD, I lift up my soul. O my God, in Thee I trust. Do not let me be ashamed; do not let my enemies exult over me. Indeed, none of those who wait for Thee will be ashamed; those who deal treacherously without cause will be ashamed. Make me know Thy ways, O LORD; teach me Thy paths. Lead me in Thy truth and teach me, for Thou art the God of my salvation; for Thee I wait all the day. Remember, O LORD, Thy compassion and Thy lovingkindnesses, for they have been from of old.

Psalm 25:14–22—The secret of the LORD is for those who fear Him, and He will make them know His covenant. My eyes are continually toward the LORD, for He will pluck my feet out of the net. Turn to me and be gracious to me, for I am lonely and afflicted. The troubles of my heart are enlarged; bring me out of my distresses. Look upon my affliction and my trouble, and forgive all my sins. Look upon my enemies, for they are many; and they hate me with a violent hatred. Guard my soul and deliver me;

do not let me be ashamed, for I take refuge in Thee. Let integrity and uprightness preserve me, for I wait for Thee.

Psalm 27:1—The LORD is my light and my salvation; whom shall I fear? The Lord is the defense of my life; whom shall I dread?

Psalm 27:3—Though a host encamp against me, my heart will not fear; though war arise against me, in spite of this I shall be confident.

Psalm 27:4–6—One thing I have asked from the LORD that I shall seek: that I may dwell in the house of the Lord all the days of my life, to behold the beauty of the LORD, and to meditate in His temple. For in the day of trouble He will conceal me in His tabernacle; in the secret place of His tent He will hide me; He will lift me up on a rock. And now my head will be lifted up above my enemies around me; and I will offer in His tent sacrifices with shouts of joy; I will sing, yes, I will sing praises to the LORD.

Psalm 27:7–10—Hear, O LORD, when I cry with my voice, and be gracious to me and answer me. When Thou didst say, "Seek My face," my heart said to Thee, "Thy face, O LORD, I shall seek." Do not hide Thy face from me, do not turn Thy servant away in anger; Thou hast been my help; do not abandon me nor forsake me, O God of my salvation! For my father and my mother have forsaken me, but the LORD will take me up.

Psalm 27:11–14—Teach me Thy way, O LORD, and lead me in a level path, because of my foes. Do not deliver me over to the desire of my adversaries; for false witnesses have risen against me; and such as breath out violence. I would have despaired unless I had believed that I would see the goodness of the LORD in the land of the living. Wait for the LORD; be strong, and let your heart take courage; yes, wait for the LORD.

Psalm 28:1–2—To Thee, O LORD, I call; my rock, do not be deaf to me, lest, if Thou be silent to me, I become like those who go down to the pit. Hear the voice of my supplications when I cry to Thee for help, when I lift up my hands toward Thy holy sanctuary.

Psalm 28:7—The LORD is my strength and my shield; my

heart trusts in him, and I am helped; therefore, my heart exults, and with my song, I shall thank Him.

Psalm 29:11—The LORD will give strength to His people; the LORD will bless His people with peace.

Psalm 30:1–2—I will extol Thee, O LORD, for Thou hast lifted me up, and hast not let my enemies rejoice over me. O LORD, my God, I cried to Thee for help, and Thou didst heal me.

Psalm 30:5—For His anger is but for a moment, His favor is for a lifetime; weeping may last for the night, but a shout of joy comes in the morning.

Psalm 30:10–12—Hear, O LORD, and be gracious to me; O LORD, be Thou my helper. Thou hast turned for me my mourning into dancing; Thou hast loosed my sackcloth and girded me with gladness; that my soul may sing praise to Thee, and not be silent. O LORD, My God, I will give thanks to Thee forever.

Psalm 31:2–5—Incline Thine ear to me, rescue me quickly; be Thou to me a rock of strength, a stronghold to save me. For Thou art my rock and my fortress; for Thy name's sake Thou wilt lead me and guide me. Thou wilt pull me out of the net which they have secretly laid for me; for Thou art my strength. Into Thy hand I commit my spirit; Thou hast ransomed me, O LORD, God of truth.

Psalm 31:7–10—But I trust in the LORD. I will rejoice and be glad in Thy lovingkindness, because Thou hast seen my affliction; Thou hast known the troubles of my soul, and Thou hast not given me over into the hand of the enemy; Thou hast set my feet in a large place. Be gracious to me, O LORD, for I am in distress; my eye is wasted away from grief, my soul and my body also. For my life is spent with sorrow, and my years with sighing; my strength has failed because of my iniquity, and my body has wasted away.

Psalm 31:14–17—But as for me, I trust in Thee, O LORD, I say, "Thou art my God." My times are in Thy hand; deliver me from the hand of my enemies, and from those who persecute me. Make Thy face to shine upon Thy servant; save me in Thy lovingkindness. Let me not be put to shame, O LORD, for I call upon Thee.

Psalm 32:7—Thou art my hiding place; Thou dost preserve me from trouble; Thou dost surround me with songs of deliverance. [Selah.

Psalm 33:18–22–Behold, the eye of the LORD is upon those who fear Him, on those who hope for His lovingkindness, to deliver their soul from death, and to keep them alive in famine. Our soul waits for the LORD; He is our help and our shield. For our heart rejoices in Him, because we trust in His holy name. Let Thy lovingkindness, O LORD, be upon us, according as we have hoped in Thee.

Psalm 34:3–5—O magnify the LORD with me, and let us exalt His name together. I sought the LORD, and He answered me, and delivered me from all my fears. They looked to Him and were radiant, and their faces shall never be ashamed.

Psalm 34:7—The angel of the LORD encamps around those who fear Him, and rescues them.

Psalm 34:17–19—The righteous cry and the LORD hears, and delivers them out of all their troubles. The LORD is near to the brokenhearted, and saves those who are crushed in spirit. Many are the afflictions of the righteous; but the LORD delivers him out of them all.

Psalm 36:5–9—Thy lovingkindness, O LORD, extends to the heavens, Thy faithfulness reaches to the sky. Thy righteousness is like the mountains of God; Thy judgments are like a great deep. O LORD, Thou preservest man and beast. How precious is Thy lovingkindness, O God! And the children of men take refuge in the shadow of Thy wings. Thy drink their fill of the abundance of Thy house; and Thou dost give them to drink of the river of Thy delights, for with Thee is the fountain of life; in Thy light we see light.

Psalm 37:3–5—Trust in the LORD, and do good; dwell in the land and cultivate faithfulness. Delight yourself in the LORD; and

He will give you the desires of your heart. Commit your way to the LORD, trust also in Him, and He will do it.

Psalm 37:7–9—Rest in the LORD and wait patiently for Him; fret not yourself because of him who prospers in his way, because of the man who carries out wicked schemes. Cease from anger and forsake wrath; fret not yourself, it leads only to evildoing. For evildoers will be cut off, but those who wait for the LORD will inherit the land.

Psalm 37:23–24—The steps of a man are established by the LORD; and He delights in his way. When he falls, he shall not be hurled headlong; because the LORD is the One Who holds his hand.

Psalm 37:39–40—But the salvation of the righteous is from the LORD; He is their strength in time of trouble. And the LORD helps them, and delivers them; He delivers them from the wicked, and saves them, because they take refuge in Him.

Psalm 40:1–4—I waited patiently for the LORD; and He inclined to me, and heard my cry. He brought me up out of the pit of destruction, out of the miry clay; and He set my feet upon a rock making my footsteps firm. And He put a new song in my mouth, a song of praise to our God; many will see and fear, and will trust in the LORD. How blessed is the man who has made the LORD his trust, and has not turned to the proud nor to those who lapse into falsehood.

Psalm 42:1–5—As the deer pants for the water brooks, so my soul pants for Thee, O God. My soul thirsts for God, for the living God; when shall I come and appear before God? My tears have been my food day and night, while they say to me all day long, "Where is your God?" These things I remember, and I pour out my soul within me. For I used to go along with the throng and lead them in procession to the house of God, with the voice of joy and thanksgiving, a multitude keeping festival. Why are you in despair, O my soul? And why have you become disturbed within me? Hope in God, for I shall again praise Him for the help of His presence.

Psalm 42:8—The LORD will command His lovingkindness in the daytime; and his song will be with me in the night, a prayer to the God of my life.

Psalm 42:11—Why are you in despair, O my soul? And why have you become disturbed within me? Hope in God, for I shall yet praise Him, the help of my countenance, and my God.

Psalm 44:5–8—Through Thee we will push back our adversaries; through Thy name we will trample down those who rise up against us. For I will not trust in my bow, nor will my sword save me. But Thou hast saved us from our adversaries, and Thou hast put to shame those who hate us. In God we have boasted all day long, and we will give thanks to Thy name forever. [Selah.

Psalm 46:1–4—God is our refuge and strength, a very present help in trouble. Therefore, we will not fear, though the earth should change, and though the mountains slip into the heart of the sea; though its waters roar and foam, though the mountains quake at its swelling pride. [Selah.
There is a river whose streams make glad the city of God, the holy dwelling place of the Most High.

Psalm 46:10—Cease striving and know that I am God; I will be exalted among the nations, I will be exalted in the earth.

Psalm 51:8–13—Make me to hear joy and gladness, let the bones which Thou hast broken rejoice. Hide Thy face from my sins, and blot out all my inequities. Create in me a clean heart, O God, and renew a steadfast spirit within me. Do not cast me away from Thy presence and do not take Thy Holy Spirit from me. Restore to me the joy of Thy salvation, and sustain me with a willing spirit. Then I will teach transgressors Thy ways, and sinners will be converted to Thee.

Psalm 51:15–17—O LORD, open my lips, that my mouth may declare Thy praise. For Thou dost not delight in sacrifice, otherwise I would give it; Thou art not pleased with burnt offering. The sacrifices of God are a broken spirit; a broken and contrite heart, O God, Thou wilt not despise.

Psalm 54:4—Behold, God is my helper; the Lord is the sustainer of my soul.

Psalm 55:1–8—Give ear to my prayer, O God; and do not hide Thyself from my supplication. Give heed to me, and answer me; I am restless in my complaint and am surely distracted, because of the voice of the enemy, because of the pressure of the wicked; for they bring down trouble upon me, and in anger they bear a grudge against me. My heart is in anguish within me, and the terrors of death have fallen upon me. Fear and trembling come upon me; and horror has overwhelmed me. And I said, "O that I had wings like a dove! I would fly away and be at rest. Behold, I would wander far away, I would lodge in the wilderness. [Selah.
I would hasten to my place of refuge from the stormy wind and tempest."

Psalm 55:16–19—As for me, I shall call upon God, and the LORD will save me. Evening and morning and at noon, I will complain and murmur, and He will hear my voice. He will redeem my soul in peace from the battle which is against me, for there are many who strive with me. God will hear and answer them—even the one who sits enthroned from of old—[Selah.
With whom there is no change.

Psalm 55:22—Cast your burden upon the LORD, and He will sustain you; He will never allow the righteous to be shaken.

Psalm 56:3–4—When I am afraid, I will put my trust in Thee. In God, Whose word I praise, in God I have put my trust; I shall not be afraid. What can mere man do to me?

Psalm 56:8–11—Thou hast taken account of my wanderings; put my tears in Thy bottle; are they not in Thy book? Then my enemies will turn back in the day when I call; this I know, that God is for me. In God, Whose word I praise, in the LORD, Whose word I praise, in God I have put my trust. I shall not be afraid.

Psalm 57:1–3—Be gracious to me, O God, be gracious to me, for my soul takes refuge in Thee; and in the shadow of Thy wings I will take refuge, until destruction passes by. I will cry to God

Most High, to God Who accomplishes all things for me. He will send from heaven and save me; He reproaches him who tramples upon me. [Selah.

God will send forth His lovingkindness and His truth.

Psalm 60:11–12—O give us help against the adversary, for deliverance by man is vain. Through God we shall do valiantly, and it is He Who will tread down our adversaries.

Psalm 61:1–4—Hear my cry, O God; give heed to my prayer from the end of the earth I call to Thee, when my heart is faint; lead me to the rock that is higher than I, for Thou hast been a refuge for me, a tower of strength against the enemy. Let me dwell in Thy tent forever; let me take refuge in the shelter of Thy wings. [Selah.

Psalm 62:1–2—My soul waits in silence for God only; from Him is my salvation. He only is my rock and my salvation, my stronghold; I shall not be greatly shaken.

Psalm 62:8—Trust in Him at all times, O people; pour out your hearts before Him; God is a refuge for us. [Selah.

Psalm 68:5–6—A father of the fatherless and a judge for the widows, is God in His holy habitation. God makes a home for the lonely; He leads out the prisoners into prosperity.

Psalm 68:19–20—Blessed be the Lord, Who daily bears our burden, the God Who is our salvation. God is to us a God of deliverances; and to God the Lord belong escapes from death.

Psalm 69:16–19—Answer me, O LORD, for Thy lovingkindness is good; according to the greatness of Thy compassion, turn to me, and do not hide Thy face from Thy servant, for I am in distress; answer me quickly. Oh draw near to my soul and redeem it; ransom me because of my enemies! Thou dost know my reproach and my shame and my dishonor; all my adversaries are before me.

Psalm 73:25–28—Whom have I in heaven but Thee? And besides Thee, I desire nothing on earth. My flesh and my heart may fail; but God is the strength of my heart and my portion forever. For, behold, those who are far from Thee will perish; Thou hast destroyed all those who are unfaithful to Thee. But as for me, the nearness of God is my good; I have made the Lord God my refuge, that I may tell of all Thy works.

Psalm 77:6—I will remember my song in the night; I will meditate with my heart; and my spirit ponders.

Psalm 84:11–12—For the LORD God is a sun and shield; the Lord gives grace and glory; no good thing does He withhold from those who walk uprightly. O LORD of hosts, how blessed is the man who trusts in Thee!

Psalm 86:1–7—Incline Thine ear, O LORD, and answer me; for I am afflicted and needy. Do preserve my soul, for I am a godly man; O Thou my God, save Thy servant who trusts in Thee. Be gracious to me, O LORD, for to Thee I cry all day long. Make glad the soul of Thy servant, for to Thee, O Lord, I lift up my soul. For Thou, Lord, art good, and ready to forgive, and abundant in lovingkindness to all who call upon Thee. Give ear, O LORD, to my prayer; and give heed to the voice of my supplications! In the day of trouble I shall call upon Thee, for Thou wilt answer me.

Psalm 94:17–19—If the LORD had not been my help, my soul would soon have dwelt in the abode of silence. If I should say, "My foot has slipped," Thy lovingkindness, O Lord, will hold me up. When my anxious thoughts multiply within me, Thy consolations delight my soul.

Psalm 105:4—Seek the LORD and His strength; seek His face continually. Remember His wonders which He has done.

Psalm 109:26–27—Help me, O LORD my God; save me according to Thy lovingkindness. And let them know that this is Thy hand; Thou, LORD, has done it.

Psalm 116:1–9—I love the LORD, because He hears my voice and my supplications. Because He has inclined His ear to me, therefore, I shall call upon Him as long as I live. The cords of death encompassed me, and the terrors of Sheol came upon me; I found distress and sorrow. Then I called upon the name of the LORD: "O LORD, I beseech Thee, save my life!" Gracious is the

LORD, and righteous; yes, our God is compassionate. The LORD preserves the simple; I was brought low, and He saved me. Return to your rest, O my soul, for the LORD has dealt bountifully with you. For Thou hast rescued my soul from death, my eyes from tears, my feet from stumbling. I shall walk before the LORD in the land of the living.

Psalm 118:5–6—From my distress I called upon the LORD; the LORD answered me and set me in a large place. The LORD is for me; I will not fear; what can man do to me?

Psalm 119:71–72—It is good for me that I was afflicted, that I may learn Thy statutes. The law of Thy mouth is better to me than thousands of gold and silver pieces.

Psalm 119:147–149—I rise before dawn and cry for help; I wait for Thy words. My eyes anticipate the night watches, that I may meditate on Thy word. Hear my voice according to Thy lovingkindness. Revive me according to Thine ordinances.

Psalm 121:1–3—I will lift up my eyes to the mountains; from whence shall my help come? My help comes from the LORD, Who made heaven and earth. He will not allow your foot to slip; He Who keeps you will not slumber.

Psalm 121:7–8—The LORD will protect you from all evil; He will keep your soul. The LORD will guard you going out and your coming in from this time forth and forever.

Psalm 124:7–8—Our soul has escaped as a bird out of the snare of the trapper; the snare is broken and we have escaped. Our health is in the name of the LORD, Who made heaven and earth.

Psalm 127:1–2—Unless the LORD build the house, they labor in vain who build it; unless the LORD guards the city, the watchman keeps awake in vain. It is vain for you to rise up early, to retire late, to eat the bread of painful labors; for He gives to his beloved even in his sleep.

Psalm 139:23–24—Search me, O God, and know my heart; try me and know my anxious thoughts; and see if there be any hurtful way in me, and lead me in the everlasting way.

Psalm 140:12—I know that the LORD will maintain the cause of the afflicted, and justice for the poor.

Psalm 142:5–7—I cried out to Thee, O LORD; I said, "Thou art my refuge, my portion in the land of the living. Give heed to my cry, for I am brought very low; deliver me from my persecutors, for they are too strong for me. Bring my soul out of prison, so that I may give thanks to Thy name; the righteous will surround me, for Thou wilt deal bountifully with me."

Psalm 143:7–9—Answer me quickly, O LORD, my spirit fails; do not hide Thy face from me, lest I become like those who go down to the pit. Let me hear Thy loving kindness in the morning; for I trust in Thee; teach me the way in which I should walk; for to Thee do I lift up my soul. Deliver me, O LORD, from my enemies; I take refuge in Thee.

Psalm 143:11—For the sake of Thy name, O LORD, revive me. In Thy righteousness bring my soul out of trouble.

Psalm 145:14–21—The LORD sustains all who fall, and raises up all who are bowed down. The eyes of all look to Thee, and Thou dost give them their food in due time. Thou dost open Thy hand, and dost satisfy the desire of every living thing. The LORD is righteous in all His ways, and kind in all His deeds. The LORD is near to all who call upon Him, to all who call upon Him in truth. He will fulfill the desire of those who fear Him; He will also hear their cry and save them. The LORD keeps all who love Him; but all the wicked he will destroy. My mouth will speak the praise of the LORD; and all flesh will bless His holy name for ever and ever.

Psalm 147:3—He heals the brokenhearted and binds up their wounds.

Psalm 147:5–6—Great is our Lord and abundant in strength; His understanding is infinite. The LORD supports the afflicted; and brings down the wicked to the ground.

Psalm 147:10–11—He does not delight in the strength of the horse; He does not take pleasure in the legs of a man. The LORD favors those who fear Him, those who wait for His lovingkindness.

Proverbs 3:5–8—Trust in the LORD with all your heart, and do not lean on your own understanding. In all your ways acknowledge him, and He will make your paths straight. Do not be wise in your own eyes; fear the LORD and turn away from evil. It will be healing to your body, and refreshment to your bones.

Proverbs 3:11–12—My son, do not reject the discipline of the LORD, or loathe His reproof, for whom the LORD loves, He reproves, even as a father, the son in whom he delights.

Proverbs 3:19–26—The LORD by wisdom founded the earth; by understanding He established the heavens. By His knowledge the deeps were broken up, and the skies drip with dew. My son, let them not depart from your sight; keep sound wisdom and discretion, so they will be life to your soul, and adornment to your neck. Then you will walk in your way securely, and your foot will not stumble. When you lie down, you will not be afraid; when you lie down, your sleep will be sweet. Do not be afraid of sudden fear, nor of the onslaught of the wicked when it comes; for the LORD will be your confidence, and will keep your foot from being caught.

Isaiah 12:1–5—Then you will say on that day, "I will give thanks to Thee, O LORD; for although Thou wast angry with me, Thine anger is turned away, and Thou dost comfort me. Behold, God is my salvation, I will trust and not be afraid; for the LORD God is my strength and song, and He has become my salvation." Therefore, you will joyously draw water from the springs of salvation. And in that day you will say, "Give thanks to the LORD, call on His name. Make known His deeds among the people; make them remember that His name is exalted." Praise the LORD in song, for He has does excellent things; let this be known throughout the earth.

Isaiah 26:3–4—The steadfast of mind Thou wilt keep in perfect peace, because he trusts in Thee. Trust in the LORD forever, for in God the LORD, we have an everlasting Rock.

Isaiah 30:15—For thus the Lord God, the Holy One of Israel

has said, "In repentance and rest you shall be saved, in quietness and trust is your strength."

Isaiah 40:29–31—He gives strength to the weary, and to him who lacks might He increases power. Though youths grow weary and tired, and vigorous young men stumble badly, yet those who wait for the LORD will gain new strength; they will mount up with wings like eagles. They will run and not get tired, they will walk and not become weary.

Isaiah 41:9–10—You whom I have taken from the ends of the earth, and called from its remotest parts, and said to you, "You are my servant, I have chosen you and not rejected you. Do not fear, for I am with you; do not anxiously look about you, for I am your God. I will strengthen you, surely, I will help you, surely I will uphold you with My righteous right hand."

Isaiah 43:1—But now, thus says the LORD, your creator, O Jacob, and He who formed you, O Israel, "Do not fear, for I have redeemed you; I have called you by name; you are mine!"

Isaiah 43:18–19—"Do not call to mind the former things, or ponder things of the past, behold, I will do something new, now it will spring forth; will you not be aware of it? I will even make a roadway in the wilderness, rivers in the desert."

Isaiah 43:25—"I, even I, am the one who wipes out your transgressions for My own sake; and I will not remember your sins."

Isaiah 45:2–3—"I will go before you and make the rough places smooth; I will shatter the doors of bronze, and cut through their iron bars. I will give you the treasures of darkness, and hidden wealth of secret places, in order that you may know that it is I, the LORD, the God of Israel, who calls you by your name."

Isaiah 46:4—"Even to your old age, I shall be the same, and even to your graying years, I shall bear you! I have done it, and I shall carry you; and I shall bear you, and I shall deliver you."

Isaiah 49:23—"Those who hopefully wait for Me will not be put to shame."

Isaiah 54:1—"Shout for joy, O barren one, you who have born

no child; break forth into joyful shouting and cry aloud, you who have not travailed; for the sons of the desolate one will be more numerous than the sons of the married woman," says the LORD.

Isaiah 54:4–8—"Fear not, for you will not be put to shame; neither feel humiliated, for you will not be disgraced; but you will forget the shame of your youth, and the reproach of your widowhood you will remember no more. For your husband is your Maker, whose name is the LORD of hosts; and your Redeemer is the Holy One of Israel, who is called the God of all the earth. For the LORD has called you, like a wife forsaken and grieved in spirit, even like a wife of one's youth when she is rejected," says your God. "For a brief moment I forsook you, but with great compassion I will gather you. In an outburst of anger I hid My face from you for a moment; but with everlasting lovingkindness I will have compassion on you," says the LORD your Redeemer.

Isaiah 54:10—"For the mountains may be removed and the hills may shake, but My lovingkindness will not be removed from you, and My covenant of peace will not be shaken," says the LORD who has compassion on you.

Isaiah 55:8–9—"For My thoughts are not your thoughts, neither are your ways My ways," declares the LORD. "For as the heavens are higher than the earth, so are My ways higher than your ways, and My thoughts than your thoughts."

Isaiah 55:10–12—"For as the rain and the snow come down from heaven, and do not return there without watering the earth, and making it bear and sprout, and furnish seed to the sower and bread to the eater; so shall My word be which goes forth from My mouth; it shall not return to Me empty, without accomplishing what I desire, and without succeeding in the matter for which I sent it. For you will go out with joy, and be led forth with peace; the mountains and the hills will break forth into shouts of joy before you, and all the trees of the field will clap their hands."

Jeremiah 17:7–8—"Blessed is the man who trusts in the LORD and whose trust is the LORD. For he will be like a tree planted by the water, that extends its roots by a stream and will not fear when the heat comes; but its leaves will be green, and it will not be anxious in a year of drought nor cease to yield fruit."

Jeremiah 24:6–7—"'For I will set my eyes on them for good, and I will bring them again to this land; and I will build them up and not overthrow them, and I will plant them and not pluck them up. And I will give them a heart to know Me, for I am the LORD; and they will by My people, and I will be their God, for they will return to Me with their whole heart.'"

Jeremiah 29:11–14—"'For I know the plans that I have for you,' declares the LORD, plans for welfare and not for calamity to give you a future and a hope. Then you will call upon Me and come and pray to Me, and I will listen to you. And you will seek Me and find Me, when you search for Me with all your heart. And I will be found by you,' declares the LORD, 'and I will restore your fortunes and will gather you from all the nations and from all the places where I have driven you,' declares the LORD, 'and I will bring you back to the place from where I sent you into exile.'"

Jeremiah 31:3—The LORD appeared to him from afar, saying, "I have loved you with an everlasting love; therefore I have drawn you with lovingkindness."

Micah 7:7–8—But as for me, I will watch expectantly for the LORD; I will wait for the God of my salvation. My God will hear me. Do not rejoice over me, O my enemy. Though I fall, I will rise; though I dwell in darkness, the LORD is a light for me.

Micah 7:18–19—Who is a God like Thee, who pardons iniquity and passes over the rebellious act of the remnant of His possession? He does not retain His anger forever, because He delights in unchanging love. He will again have compassion on us; He will tread our iniquities underfoot. Yes, Thou wilt cast all their sins into the depths of the sea.

Habakkuk 3:17–19—Though the fig tree should not blossom, and there be no fruit on the vines, though the yield of the olive should fail, and the fields produce no food, though the flock should be cut off from the fold, and there be no cattle in the stalls, yet I will exult in the LORD, I will rejoice in the God of my salvation. The Lord God is my strength, and He has made my feet like hinds' feet, and makes me walk on my high places."

Malachi 4:2—"But for you who fear My name the sun of righteousness will rise with healing in its wings; and you will go forth and skip about like calves from the stall."

Matthew 6:25–34—"For this reason I say to you, do not be anxious for your life, as to what you shall eat, or what you shall drink; nor for your body, as to what you shall put on. Is not life more than food, and the body than clothing? Look at the birds of the air, they do not sow, neither do they reap, nor gather into barns, and yet your heavenly Father feeds them. Are you not worth much more than they? And which of you by being anxious can add a single cubit to his lifespan? And why are you anxious about clothing? Observe how the lilies of the field grow; they do not toil nor do they spin, yet I say to you that even Solomon in all his glory did not clothe himself like one of these. But if God so arrays the grass of the field which is alive today and tomorrow is thrown into the furnace, will He not much more do so for you, O men of little faith? Do not be anxious then, saying, 'What shall we eat?' or 'What shall we drink?' or 'With what shall we clothe ourselves?' for all these things the Gentiles eagerly seek; for your heavenly Father knows that you need all these things. But seek first His kingdom and His righteousness; and all these things shall be added to you. Therefore do not be anxious for tomorrow; for tomorrow will care for itself. Each day has enough trouble of its own."

Matthew 10:29–33—"Are not two sparrows sold for a cent? And yet not one of them will fall to the ground apart from your Father. But the very hairs of your head are all numbered. Therefore do not fear; you are of more value than many sparrows."

Matthew 11:28–30—"Come to me, all who are weary and heavy-laden, and I will give you rest. Take my yoke upon you, and learn from me, for I am gentle and humble in heart; and you shall find rest for your souls. For my yoke is easy, and my load is light."

John 3:16–17—"For God so loved the world, that He gave His only begotten Son, that whoever believes in Him should not perish, but have eternal life. For God did not send the Son into the world to judge the world; but that the world should be saved through Him."

John 16:33—"These things I have spoken to you, that in Me you may have peace. In the world you have tribulation, but take courage; I have overcome the world."

Romans 5:3–5—And not only this, but we also exult in our tribulations, knowing that tribulation brings about perseverance; and perseverance, proven character; and proven character, hope; and hope does not disappoint, because the love of God has been poured out within our hearts through the Holy Spirit who was given to us.

Romans 8:1–4—There is therefore now no condemnation for those who are in Christ Jesus. For the law of the Spirit of life in Christ Jesus has set you free from the law of sin and of death. For what the law could not do, weak as it was through the flesh, God did: sending His own Son in the likeness of sinful flesh and as an offering for sin, He condemned sin in the flesh, in order that the requirement of the Law might be fulfilled in us, who do not walk according to the flesh, but according to the Spirit.

Romans 8:15—For you have not received a spirit of slavery leading to fear again, but you have received a spirit of adoption as sons by which we cry out, "Abba! Father!"

Romans 8:26–27—And in the same way the Spirit also helps our weaknesses; for we do not know how to pray as we should, but the Spirit Himself intercedes for us with groaning too deep for words; and He who searches the hearts knows what the mind of the Spirit is, because He intercedes for the saints according to the will of God.

Romans 8:28—And we know that God causes all things to

work together for good to those who love God, to those who are called according to His purpose.

Romans 8:31–32—What then shall we say to these things? If God is for us, who is against us? He who did not spare His own Son, but delivered Him up for us all, how will He not also with Him freely give us all things?

Romans 8:35–39—Who shall separate us from the love of Christ? Shall tribulation, or distress, or persecution, or famine, or nakedness, or peril, or sword? Just as it is written, "For Thy sake we are being put to death all day long; we are considered as sheep to be slaughtered." But in all these things we overwhelmingly conquer through Him who loved us. For I am convinced that neither death, nor life, nor angels, nor principalities, nor things present, nor things to come, nor powers, nor height, nor depth, nor any other created thing, shall be able to separate us from the love of God, which is in Christ Jesus our Lord.

Romans 12:2—And do not be conformed to this world, but be transformed by the renewing of your mind, that you may prove what the will of God is, that which is good and acceptable and perfect.

Romans 12:12—Rejoicing in hope, persevering in tribulation, devoted to prayer.

Romans 15:13—Now may the God of hope fill you with all joy and peace in believing, that you may abound in hope by the power of the Holy Spirit.

Corinthians 10:13—No temptation has overtaken you but such as is common to man; and God is faithful, who will not allow you to be tempted beyond what you are able, but with the temptation will provide the way of escape also, that you may be able to endure it.

2 Corinthians 1:2–5—Blessed be the God and Father of our Lord Jesus Christ, the Father of mercies and God of all comfort; who comforts us in all our affliction so that we may be able to comfort those who are in any affliction with the comfort with

which we ourselves are comforted by God. For just as the sufferings of Christ are ours in abundance, so also our comfort is abundant through Christ.

2 Corinthians 1:8–11—For we do not want you to be unaware, brethren, of our affliction which came to us in Asia, that we were burdened excessively, beyond our strength, so that we despaired even of life; indeed, we had the sentence of death within ourselves in order that we should not trust in ourselves, but in God who raises the dead; who delivered us from so great a peril of death, and will deliver us, He on whom we have set our hope. And He will yet deliver us, you also joining in helping us through your prayers, that thanks may be given by many persons on our behalf for the favor bestowed upon us through the prayers of many.

2 Corinthians 3:5–6—Not that we are adequate in ourselves to consider anything as coming from ourselves, but our adequacy is from God, who also made us adequate as servants of a new covenant, not of the letter, but of the Spirit; for the letter kills, but the Spirit gives life.

2 Corinthians 3:17–18—Now the Lord is the Spirit; and where the Spirit of the Lord is, there is liberty. But we all, with unveiled face beholding as in a mirror the glory of the Lord, are being transformed into the same image from glory to glory, just as from the Lord, the Spirit.

2 Corinthians 4:7–11—But we have this treasure in earthen vessels, that the surpassing greatness of the power may be of God and not from ourselves; we are afflicted in every way, but not crushed; perplexed, but not despairing; persecuted, but not forsaken; struck down, but not destroyed; always carrying about in the body the dying of Jesus, that the life of Jesus also may be manifested in our body. For we who live are constantly being delivered over to death for Jesus' sake, that the life of Jesus also may be manifested in our mortal flesh.

2 Corinthians 4:16–18—Therefore we do not lose heart, but though our outer man is decaying, yet our inner man is being

renewed day by day. For momentary, light affliction is producing for us an eternal weight of glory far beyond all comparison, while we look not at the things which are seen, but at the things that are not seen; for the things which are seen are temporal, but the things which are not seen are eternal.

2 Corinthians 5:15, 17—And He died for all, that they who live should no longer live for themselves, but for Him who died and rose again on their behalf … Therefore if any man is in Christ, he is a new creature; the old things passed away; behold, new things have come.

2 Corinthians 10:3–5—For though we walk in the flesh, we do not war according to the flesh, for the weapons of our warfare are not of the flesh, but divinely powerful for the destruction of fortresses. We are destroying speculations and every lofty thing raised up against the knowledge of God, and we are taking every thought captive to the obedience of Christ.

2 Corinthians 12:7–10—And because of the surpassing greatness of the revelations, for this reason, to keep me from exalting myself, there was given me a thorn in the flesh, a messenger of Satan to buffet me—to keep me from exalting myself! Concerning this I entreated the Lord three times that it might depart from me. And He has said to me, "My grace is sufficient for you, for power is perfected in weakness." Most gladly, therefore, I will rather boast about my weaknesses, that the power of Christ may dwell in me. Therefore I am well content with weaknesses, with insults, with distresses, with persecutions, with difficulties, for Christ's sake; for when I am weak then I am strong.

Ephesians 2:8–9—For by grace you have been saved through faith; and that not of yourselves, it is the gift of God; not as the result of works, that no one should boast.

Ephesians 3:8–21—To me, the very least of all saints, this grace was given, to preach to the Gentiles the unfathomable riches of Christ, and to bring to light what is the administration of the mystery which for ages has been hidden in God, who created all things; in order that the manifold wisdom of God might now be made known through the church to the rulers and the authorities in the heavenly places. This was in accordance with the eternal purpose which He carried out in Christ Jesus our Lord, in whom we have boldness and confident access through faith in Him. Therefore I ask you not to lose heart at my tribulations on your behalf, for they are your glory. For this reason, I bow my knees before the Father, from whom every family in heaven and on earth derives its name, that He would grant you, according to the riches of His glory, to be strengthened with power through His Spirit in the inner man; so that Christ may dwell in your hearts through faith; and, that you, being rooted and grounded in love, may be able to comprehend with all the saints what is the breadth and length and height, and depth, and to know the love of Christ which surpasses knowledge, that you may be filled up to all the fulness of God. Now to Him who is able to do exceeding abundantly beyond all that we ask or think, according to the power that works within us, to Him be the glory in the church and in Christ Jesus to all generations forever and ever. Amen.

Ephesians 6:10–18—Finally, be strong in the Lord, and in the strength of His might. Put on the full armor of God, that you may be able to stand firm against the schemes of the devil. For our struggle is not against flesh and blood, but against the rulers, against the powers, against the world forces of this darkness, against the spiritual forces of wickedness in the heavenly places. Therefore, take up the full armor of God, that you may be able to resist in the evil day, and having done everything, to stand firm. Stand firm therefore, having girded your loins with truth, and having put on the breastplate of righteousness, and having shod your feet with the preparation of the gospel of peace; in addition to all, taking up the shield of faith with which you will be able to extinguish all the flaming missiles of the evil one. And taking the helmet of salvation, and the sword of the Spirit, which is the word of God. With all prayer and petition pray at all times in the Spirit, and with this in view, be on the alert with all perseverance and petition for all the saints.

Philippians: 1:6—For I am confident of this very thing, that He who began a good work in you will perfect it until the day of Christ Jesus.

Philippians 3:7–14—But whatever things were gain to me, those things I have counted as loss for the sake of Christ. More than that, I count all things to be loss in view of the surpassing value of knowing Christ Jesus my Lord, for whom I have suffered the loss of all things, and count them but rubbish in order that I may gain Christ, and may be found in Him, not having a righteousness of my own derived from the Law, but that which is through faith in Christ, the righteousness which comes from God on the basis of faith, that I may know Him and the power of His resurrection and the fellowship of His sufferings, being conformed to His death; in order that I may attain to the resurrection from the dead. Not that I have already obtained it, or have already become perfect, but I press on in order that I may lay hold of that for which also I was laid hold of by Christ Jesus. Brethren, I do not regard myself as having laid hold of it yet; but one thing I do: forgetting what lies behind and reaching forward to what lies ahead, I press on toward the goal for the prize of the upward call of God in Jesus Christ.

Philippians 4:6–8—Be anxious for nothing, but in everything by prayer and supplication with thanksgiving let your requests be made known to God. And the peace of God, which surpasses all comprehension, shall guard your hearts and your minds in Christ Jesus. Finally, brethren, whatever is true, whatever is honorable, whatever is right, whatever is pure, whatever is lovely, whatever is of good repute, if there is any excellence and if anything worthy of praise, let your mind dwell on these things.

Philippians 4:11–13—Not that I speak from want; for I have learned to be content in whatever circumstances I am. I know how to get along with humble means, and I also know how to live in prosperity; in any and every circumstance I have learned the secret of being filled and going hungry, both of having abundance and suffering need. I can do all things through Him who strengthens me.

Colossians 3:1–2—If then you have been raised up with Christ, keep seeking the things above, where Christ is, seated at the right hand of God. Set your mind on the things above, not on the things that are on earth.

Colossians 4:2—Devote yourselves to prayer, keeping alert in it with an attitude of thanksgiving.

2 Timothy 1:7—For God has not given us a spirit of fear, but of power of love and of a sound mind. [New King James Version]

Hebrews 2:14–15–That through death He might render powerless him who had the power of death, that is, the devil; and might deliver those who through fear of death were subject to slavery all their lives.

Hebrews 4:15–16—For we do not have a high priest who cannot sympathize with our weakness, but one who has been tempted in all things as we are, yet without sin. Let us therefore draw near with confidence to the throne of grace that we may receive mercy and may find grace to help in time of need.

Hebrews 5:8—Although he was a Son, He learned obedience from the things which He suffered.

Hebrews 11:1—Now faith is the assurance of things hoped for, the conviction of things not seen.

Hebrews 12:11—All discipline for the moment seems not to be joyful, but sorrowful; yet to those who have been trained by it, afterwards it yields the peaceful fruit of righteousness.

James 1:2–5—Consider it all joy, my brethren, when you encounter various trials, knowing that the testing of your faith produces endurance. And let endurance have its perfect result, that you may be perfect and complete, lacking in nothing. But if any of you lacks wisdom, let him ask of God, who gives to all men generously and without reproach, and it will be given to him.

James 1:12—Blessed is a man who perseveres under trial; for

once he has been approved, he will receive the crown of life, which the Lord has promised to those who love Him.

James 4:7–8—Submit therefore to God. Resist the devil and he will flee from you. Draw near to God and He will draw near to you.

James 4:10—Humble yourselves in the presence of the Lord, and He will exalt you.

James 5:11—Behold, we count those blessed who endured. You have heard of the endurance of Job and have seen the outcome of the Lord's dealings, that the Lord is full of compassion and is merciful.

1 Peter 1:3–7—Blessed be the God and Father of our Lord Jesus Christ, who according to His great mercy has caused us to be born again to a living hope through the resurrection of Jesus Christ from the dead, to obtain an inheritance which is imperishable and undefiled and will not fade away, reserved in heaven for you, who are protected by the power of God through faith for a salvation ready to be revealed in the last time. In this you greatly rejoice, even though now for a little while, if necessary, you have been distressed by various trials, that the proof of your faith, being more precious than gold which is perishable, even though tested by fire, may be found to result in praise and glory and honor at the revelation of Jesus Christ.

1 Peter 3:17—For it is better, if God should will it so, that you suffer for doing what is right rather than for doing what is wrong.

1 Peter 4:12–14—Beloved, do not be surprised at the fiery ordeal among you, which comes upon you for your testing, as though some strange thing were happening to you; but to the degree that you share the sufferings of Christ, keep on rejoicing; so that also at the revelation of His glory, you may rejoice with exultation. If you are reviled for the name of Christ, you are blessed, because the Spirt of glory and of God rests upon you.

1 Peter 4:19—Therefore, let those also who suffer according to the will of God entrust their souls to a faithful Creator in doing what is right.

1 Peter 5:5–10—For God is opposed to the proud, but gives grace to the humble. Humble yourselves, therefore, under the mighty hand of God, that He may exalt you at the proper time, casting all your anxiety upon Him, because He cares for you. Be of sober spirit, be on the alert. Your adversary, the devil, prowls about like a roaring lion, seeking someone to devour. But resist him, firm in your faith, knowing that the same experiences of suffering are being accomplished by your brethren who are in the world. And after you have suffered for a little while, the God of all grace who called you to His eternal glory in Christ, will Himself perfect, confirm, strengthen and establish you.

2 Peter 2:9—Then the Lord knows how to rescue the godly from temptation.

2 Peter 3:8–9—But do not let this one fact escape your notice, beloved, that with the Lord one day is as a thousand years, and a thousand years as one day. The Lord is not slow about His promise, as some count slowness, but is patient toward you, not wishing for any to perish but for all to come to repentance.

1 John 1:9—If we confess our sins, He is faithful and righteous to forgive us our sins and to cleanse us from all unrighteousness.

1 John 2:25—And this is the promise which He Himself made to us: eternal life.

1 John 4:10–12—In this is love, not that we loved God, but that He loved us and sent His Son to be the propitiation for our sins. Beloved, if God so loved us, we also ought to love one another. No one has beheld God at any time; if we love one another, God abides in us, and His love is perfected in us.

1 John 4:15–19—Whoever confesses that Jesus is the Son of God, God abides in him, and he in God. And we have come to know and have believed the love which God has for us. God is love, and the one who abides in love abides in God, and God abides in him. By this, love is perfected with us, that we may have confidence in the day of judgment; because as He is, so also are we in this world. There is no fear in love; but perfect love casts out

fear because fear involves punishment and the one who fears is not perfected in love. We love, because He first loved us.

1 John 5:4—For whatever is born of God overcomes the world; and this is the victory that has overcome the world—our faith.

Revelations 21:2–7—And I saw the holy city, new Jerusalem, coming down out of heaven from God, made ready as a bride adorned for her husband. And I heard a loud voice from the throne, saying, "Behold, the tabernacle of God is among men, and He shall dwell among them, and they shall be His people, and God Himself shall be among them, and He shall wipe away every tear from their eyes; and there shall no longer be any death; there shall no longer be any mourning, or crying, or pain; the first things have passed away." And He who sits on the throne said, "Behold, I am making all things new." And He said, "Write, for these words are faithful and true." And He said to me, "It is done. I am the Alpha and the Omega, the beginning and the end. I will give to the one who thirsts from the spring of the water of life without cost. He who overcomes shall inherit these things, and I will be his God, and he will My son."

Printed in the United States
By Bookmasters